THE
VEIL
BETWEEN

REALMS OF DESTINY
BOOK I

A ⁕ A N N
S I G A F U S

Publishing Coordinator – Sharon Kizziah-Holmes

BLANK 'N SHIP PRESS
Springfield, MO

ISBN -13: 979-8-218-76752-5

DEDICATION

This work is dedicated to Grandma S., who passed through the veil to the other side several years ago. I hear you, and I am searching. Thank you for the signs.

ACKNOWLEDGMENTS

To my editor, Amanda Kruse. Thank you for your gentle critique, your keen eyes, and your encouragement throughout this project. Your input has been invaluable to completing this project.

To my sister and beta reader, Rebekah. Thank you for dedicating your time to reading through it and for putting up with my "Tell me about the rocket..." calls every night.

To my dear children, Daniel, Daron, Anthony, and Klaira—who sacrificed many precious moments as I dedicated myself to this work, helped create cover graphics, and shared their valuable opinions on various aspects. Especially to Klaira, who often nonchalantly asked, "Are you STILL writing your book?"

Brandi, Mercedes, Mandy, John, Austin, Sydney, and Bekah—my wonderful and supportive book club—you mean the world to me. Thank you for always encouraging my writing, embracing my silly ideas, and graciously accepting my divorce jokes with a smile. I'm so grateful to have you all in my life.

Canva and limited AI resources were utilized in the design of the "The Veil Between" book cover.

The Grammarly program was used for editing and technical purposes in proofreading "The Veil Between".

CHAPTER 1

Déjà Vu

Wrenley hummed with pleasure as she lit a cinnamon spice candle on her desk, the aroma filling the little room. She pulled her cardigan tighter around her, feeling the crisp autumn chill leak through the old windowpanes as she sat in her worn office chair. She then reached for her steaming mug of coffee, hoping it would help warm her chilled fingers. She looked out the window of her trim little office nook, noticing that the trees were at the height of showing off their colors. October was beginning, and the maple tree in front of her parents' bed and breakfast was turning into a gorgeous shade of ebony. Wrenley allowed a feeling of security and satisfaction to wash over her at the sights and smells of autumn.

Wrenley recalled the joyful memories of autumns past; the time in the pumpkin patch with her mother picking the largest one and struggling to carry it back to the stand to pay. She recalls snuggling with her father on the couch as they watched spooky movies and sipped hot apple cider, feeling safer than ever in his presence. Picking apples, dancing around bonfires, and trick-or-treating with the bed and breakfast guests, because mom wouldn't let her go too far from home…Wrenley sighed at the memories. For her entire life, the world revolved around autumn coming and going. It was when she felt the happiest.

It was also when she felt most alive. She could not explain it, but she felt extra in tune with nature and others, especially with herself, when the leaves started to release, and the season started to turn over. There was something spiritual about it when the trees gave up their leaves and embraced the winter season ahead. It was a season of reflection and gathering, harvesting, and celebrating the world around with radical acceptance of the darkness to come. To Wrenley, darkness was not always evil or scary; it could also be a source of magic. Wrenley could identify with that feeling of letting go and embracing the bitter season that was indeed approaching.

Wrenley adjusted her body and pulled herself up, feeling the discomfort in her hips and legs as she stood. She carefully watched her feet to avoid her cat, Nyx, who was always lingering and darting between her legs. Though she adored the cool weather, it was hard on her body. Wrenley suffered from a degenerative disease in her hips and spine ever since she was a child, causing difficulty in even the most basic movements: walking, sitting, twisting…Initially, it was not particularly noticeable, but it became more apparent as she aged. The doctors said she would be in a wheelchair by now, but she was not, and she would do everything in her power to stay that way. Wrenley accepted the prognosis of her illness, and even though she had managed to keep her ass out of a wheelchair for now, she knew it would come eventually. She would live her life nonetheless, with curiosity and acceptance. She was determined to still make her life enchanted despite the struggles.

Due to her physical disability, Wrenley lived with her adoptive parents in their small family-run bed and breakfast that was nestled deep in the southern Ozark Hills in a small, quaint town. Steeped in culture and rocky rolling hills, it became a popular tourist attraction for those seeking to discover its allure. Wrenley's parents had owned this historic building since she was a baby, and she had grown up in it. She loved the people she met from all over the world, who would stay and share their adventures with her. She took great pleasure in making people feel at ease during their visits. Wrenley loved her life here, and she was content despite her chronic pain and difficulty in her body.

Wrenley considered herself average-looking. She was not petite by any means; her waist was not skinny, and she was short. Her mother used the word 'square' to define Wrenley's figure, which made Wrenley painfully aware of how 'average' she was. The disease had made her back and legs appear slightly misaligned, which caused her an insufferable amount of self-consciousness. She eyed the guests as they tried to hide their glances at her deformity. She ignored the stares of sympathy and pity they tossed her way when she struggled to carry a breakfast tray across the room. Some days, it made her angry and resentful; other days, she could ignore the humiliation.

Wrenley felt self-conscious about her midsection, which was not flat, and she believed her face was too round. She was socially awkward and would rather talk to the plants and animals than to another person. She enjoyed reading old fantasy books, curling up in front of the fire in the library, and using the stories to escape from the world. Life was hard enough that she just wanted peace and simplicity for as long as she had left. Wrenley was happy and satisfied, or at least what she told herself. However, she felt a tinge of loss because she had never been able to travel and have adventures beyond her little nook. It was a loss she was willing to allow, because safety was more important than any supposed adventure.

She gently blended into the background, drawing a comparison to her lovely Russian Blue cat, Nyx. Like Nyx, she did her best to stay unnoticed, hoping to avoid those uncomfortable, pitying stares. She rarely found herself the center of attention or in the spotlight, mostly making herself small to navigate the world around her unnoticed. No one would have the chance to make her feel any smaller if she were already insignificant.

Wrenley never went to college after high school. Her limited high school acquaintances begged her to go to community college with her, and Wrenley would shake her head, "Mom and Dad need me," or "I'm too busy to go. I have to run the family business." It was not a complete lie. Her parents were getting older, and she did not trust that they could do it alone. But deep down, Wrenley was afraid to leave and knew that, with her physical limitations, it just was not attainable. She was scared to abandon the safety of her home. She hated new things and new people, and she would rather stay in this place forever.

Wrenley's mother and father adopted her when they were older. Wrenley was thirty-two, and her parents were in their seventies. Wrenley was adopted at the age of two months after her biological parents had died in a car accident, and there was no family for her to go to. Ruth and Jim had been her guardian angels, giving her everything she could have ever dreamed of. When she received her diagnosis at eight years old, they did not miss a beat and pushed her to do all the things 'normal' kids did. They told her not to worry and that she was capable and beautiful. They did not talk about her prognosis, as if they ignored its existence. She appreciated the gesture, but also felt they may be in denial of her disease's forecast. That made it hard to have closure and realistic expectations.

As a reminder, a sharp pain shot up her leg and into her lower back, and she grimaced as she limped to the front desk. She hobbled, her eyes shooting up to take in a couple of guests who moved past her awkwardly…the woman giving her a sad look as they passed. Heat flamed her cheeks, and she gritted her teeth, willing her crooked legs forward. Her back was burning along with her face, but she reached the front desk and stooped over to grab the bundle of fresh chrysanthemums from the water bucket.

Wrenley was deep in thought as she arranged the beautiful chrysanthemums in the vase at the front desk. She knitted her brows together, noticing they were golden yellow, purple, and violet—her favorite. She appreciated the smell of flowers, and their petals and leaves fell over the front of her apron. She was so absorbed in their sweet, spicy aroma that she missed the front doorbell ring, and suddenly, she heard someone clear their throat in front of her.

She startled, losing her balance and reaching out to catch her upper body on the desk. She was not quick enough, her hand slipped, and she knew she would fall. A fast, strong hand grabbed her forearm, and she froze to catch her balance. In her attempt not to fall to her death, she dropped her bundle of flowers on the floor in front of the guest.

"I'm sorry! I didn't hear…" she gasped as the arm took the brunt of her weight and stumbled on her words. "…you come in. Can I help you?" Wrenley twisted painfully, pushing her long, golden hair away from her face again. She winced at the agony that shot through her hips and back again and ground her teeth. She looked up and gulped at the man who had rescued her from plunging to her death. He must have been six feet tall, towering over her, his large hand still gripping her arm firmly. He pulled his large hand away slowly, and her skin tingled where his fingers had been. His eyes seemed to scan her to ensure she was firmly on her feet.

"Yes, I have a reservation…" he finally spoke when it seemed he was confident she would not collapse. Gracefully, he bent down on one knee and scooped up her flowers, gathering them into a bouquet. He raised back up slowly and handed them to her with a grin. "I didn't mean to alarm you."

Her heart fluttered slightly at him: the lazy, magnificent grin of pearly white teeth set in a strong jaw flashed at her. Wrenley tried to identify the accent but could not put her finger on it; his voice was deep and rich, almost rumbling from somewhere in his chest. She rubbed her hands on her apron in front of her, noticing they were dirty from working with the flowers and accepting the bouquet from him. Her cheeks had blushed again at her clumsiness.

"Yes, of course…how many visitors?"

"Just one. I have a reservation under Bronson Aughton."

Wrenley fumbled as she attempted to plop the flowers in the vase and turned to the computer. She felt herself tense up, blaming it on the pain now speeding through her legs and back from her twisting so fast. She could not be sure, but she felt like he was staring at her as she searched for his information, misspelling his name twice and having to ask for it again. She knew that look of pity at the poor, disfigured girl that he must be giving her. Wrenley felt self-conscious and acutely aware of her limp and the difficulty she had maneuvering. Wrenley assisted him with his booking reservations and slid a large key across the desk towards him, almost flinching at the scratch of the metal on the wood under her fingertips. He raised a perfectly groomed eyebrow at her when he reached for it.

Wrenley shrugged, "It's an ancient building. We still have the original locks. Part of its charm…."

"Ancient building?" He grinned at her, palming the heavy key and weighing it in his hand. "I hope I don't see any ghosts."

Wrenley felt a chill travel over her skin, causing goose bumps on her arms. His voice was as gorgeous as ever. She swallowed, resting her elbow on the desk and a hand on her hip.

"You never know. I've lived here my whole life, and I wonder sometimes."

Sometimes was an understatement. Wrenley knew this house

was haunted, as she had heard footsteps in the halls at night. She had seen the flickers of light, items out of place, and felt the whispers in the shadows. She had sensed the graze of another against her arm while alone in a room, the tug at her hair, the brush of breath. Wrenley believed in the spiritual world, that some ghosts and spirits shared space with them if one cared to stop and listen.

The man chuckled, and Wrenley felt her gut tighten at the sound. He was surely taller than her, and she could spy his finely built frame, broad chest, and muscular arms, even under his layers of clothes. He wore a wool coat and leather gloves, with a scarf around his neck, and an expensive black suit underneath. She noticed the smile he flashed at her as it touched those dark chestnut eyes…His face was almost familiar, but she could not recall why. He seemed very old-fashioned, not from around here, she mused. He grinned at her one last time and turned to leave.

"Number 201, up the stairs, first room on the left!" Wrenley called out to him as he retreated, and he did not even turn to acknowledge her guidelines. He waved his hand over his shoulder, picked up his bag, and trudged up the stairs, taking two at a time. Wrenley sat there momentarily, watching where he had been standing, trying to untangle the weird feeling suddenly coming over her. It felt almost like Déjà vu, a familiar sense that she could not identify but was very recognizable. It was as if she had dreamed this moment sometime in the past; the masculine smell that rolled off him piqued something in her memory like an itch she could not quite scratch in her brain.

A dizziness settled over her, and she felt the urge to shake her head to dispel it. She noticed a slight tingling in her hands and frowned at them, hoping it was not a complication from her illness. She toyed with the necklace around her neck and felt a sensation in her gut that traveled up to her chest, not pain but warmth. Shrugging, she continued her duties, her mind occasionally drifting back to the mysterious stranger.

CHAPTER 2

Ghosts

I've lived here my whole life and wonder sometimes. Wrenley's words echoed in her brain as she wandered around the downstairs portion of the old bed and breakfast later that evening, ensuring everything was in its place before she headed to bed. She enjoyed this quiet time alone to take in the energy that engulfed the home. Ever since childhood, she had sensed the presence of other beings in this house. From weird items found that could not be explained, to voices in the night, to footsteps in the hall that did not belong to anyone, Wrenley was convinced some ghosts lived with them. However, she was never afraid. Somehow, the presence of whoever they were made her feel safe.

Tonight, she heard some gentle footsteps trailing her, and she did not even turn to double-check. She walked with the spirit for several moments, sensing it traveling beside her, and even a tap on her shoulder tonight. It was not alarming, but rather soothing to her, and she smiled at the intrusion of her personal space. She sometimes talked to the spirits and ghosts, humbled that they felt safe enough to reveal themselves to her. Still, she was restless and wandered to the library after completing her to-do list for the night.

When all else failed, Wrenley poured herself a glass of port wine and quietly walked through the house to the library on the ground floor. It was her favorite place, and it usually was not popular with the guests, ensuring she would be alone. She wrapped a blanket around her and sat in her favorite chair, groaning slightly at the pain of sitting. She opened the fantasy novel she had plucked off the shelf before sitting, one she had read a million times. She downed one glass of port wine and poured herself another, hoping it would help with the pain enough for her to go to sleep.

Wrenley felt the essence of the house differently tonight; she sensed spiritual energies surrounding her, caressing her like a soft spring wind or a gentle current in a stream. She did not feel them as dangerous or evil, but rather as friendly. The complicated feelings and emotions confused her, as she noted the paradox of restlessness and comfort with the room's energy. Wrenley believed in the world of the unseen, that there were things one could not explain. The veil between worlds, whatever those worlds were, seemed thin in October. Nyx felt it too, as the cat weaved in and out of her legs and meowed at her relentlessly. The feline was vocal now, sitting in front of Wrenley, looking at her inquisitively.

Wrenley shrugged at the cat, "What? You've eaten already."

She swore the cat raised a brow at her and meowed again, her eyes darting back and forth. Wrenley could not help but feel like the animal was trying to communicate with her, but she shook her head and put her wineglass down. "Sorry, old girl, you'll have to do better than that."

Wrenley paused as she felt that sensation again —the pricking of her hands and the dizziness she had experienced this morning. She stilled, cocking her head to the side trying to strain to hear even the slightest sound, noticing Nyx darting under her chair. She would not be surprised if it were one of her otherworldly friends coming to sit with her; it happened all the time. As Wrenley listened, she realized the energy was different in some way, and she shivered. Her heart began to thud at a slight movement out of the corner of her eye.

"I thought you were a ghost," a deep voice rumbled behind her, sending a chill through her veins.

Wrenley quivered in her seat, almost spilling her wine as her hand shot out at the sound of a rich voice behind her. She gulped and attempted to push herself up to stand as the stranger moved from the library doorway into her line of sight.

"God, you scared me!" Wrenley yelped and touched her chest, feeling her heart thumping rapidly under her tingling fingertips.

"Sorry, don't get up..." The stranger quickly motioned for Wrenley to stay seated. "I didn't mean to startle you again. I'm Bronson; I think you assisted me earlier?"

Wrenley recognized his tall outline as he stepped into the dim light of Wrenley's reading lamp. Wrenley tried not to gasp again, as he seemed more attractive in the dark.

"I…can't sleep," she stammered, mentally kicking herself for sounding stupid.

"Me either…" his handsome face seemed to survey the room, and he turned back to her, his brows raising slightly, "May I join you?"

Wrenley shrugged her shoulders and motioned to the chair next to her. He sat down, making himself comfortable, crossing an ankle over his knee, and eyed the half-empty glass of wine between them. "You wouldn't happen to have another one of those, would you?"

Wrenley peered at him through narrowed eyes, her heart still thudding in her chest, her hands still burning as she slowly nodded, "I can get one."

Wrenley tried not to groan as she stood and went to retrieve another wine glass. She half expected the stranger to pity her and offer to get the glass himself, but he did not. He neglected to even look up as she struggled to her feet. It was…a relief for him not to make a big deal like everyone else did in her life. She returned to find Bronson flipping through the pages of her book. Wrenley sat again with a 'humph' and poured a glass of port for the man. He grinned as she handed him a glass but still held the book.

"You like this kind of stuff?"

Wrenley nodded, sitting back awkwardly, a blush creeping up her neck at his interest, "It's my favorite series."

"Why do you like it?"

Wrenley contemplated the answer, remaining silent for several seconds. Her gut stirred with suspicion, as no one ever asked for her opinion about her books or anything else, for that matter. Typically, no one spoke to Wrenley; no one noticed her existence, especially not handsome men like the one sitting beside her. She had made it a point not to draw attention to herself. The self-consciousness was overwhelming, and a sadness etched into her subconscious as she pined for something different despite her determination to be invisible. Wrenley wanted to be noticed by someone — by anyone.

She finally responded, "It's like traveling to another world. I can't really do that very well with…well, you know…" She inclined her head downward to her legs. "It's hard to get around."

"I'm an autobiography man myself," he said nonchalantly, holding the book as if weighing it. "Maybe I can borrow one? It may change my mind about the fantasy adventure genre."

"Sure," Wrenley shrugged awkwardly and took another sip of her wine.

Bronson nodded and took a sip, returning the book on the table between them. "Tell me what it's like to live here. Running a bed and breakfast in a small Missouri town out in the sticks must be invigorating."

Wrenley laughed uncomfortably, plucking up the book. "It's more exciting than you think. You should see it around here during the Pumpkin Fest."

Bronson chuckled, and Wrenley dipped her head a little, her cheeks flushing. People often did not think she was funny or charming, if they took the time to listen to her at all. Wrenley heaved herself up again and turned to put the book back on the shelf. She struggled to steady herself as she reached for the books' home on the shelf, where she had to stretch and reach.

"I wasn't making fun of you...I was genuinely asking."

Wrenley froze when she noticed his voice had neared, and he must have gotten up to stand behind her. She sucked in a breath as he gently seized the book from her and looked at the shelf, his height making it a simple task. Usually, she would have been scared to have some stranger so close to her, but not him. There it was again, the tingling in her fingers and that heat in her gut that flooded outward to her arms and legs. She chided herself in her mind for reacting to his simple act of kindness...from a gorgeous man who stood so close to her she could almost feel his breath on the back of her neck. She felt his movement as he reached out, stroking the collection of books with his large, slender fingers. His broad chest barely brushed up against her shoulder as he leaned in to place it.

"This is a marvelous set," he murmured. "May I take one tonight?"

"They are antique copies. Please, help yourself."

"Hmmm...I shall be very careful with it." Bronson tugged Volume Two from the shelf and tucked it under his arm. His voice was masculine and deep, but thoughtful. "Do you believe we have a calling? A deep, sacred purpose like the characters in these books?"

Wrenley shrugged, wrapping her arms around herself. "I hope I do, but I'm happy here even if I don't. Purpose is such a subjective term."

Bronson stood shoulder to shoulder with her now, his arms crossed in front of him over the book, keeping his eyes focused on the shelf. "What's here that makes you so happy?"

"My parents, this house, our business…" She listed them off like she had practiced a million times, but even to her ears, it sounded fake.

"Is that type of adventure enough for you?"

Wrenley frowned and bristled, "I have plenty of adventure in my life, thank you."

Bronson chuckled again and turned to face her. Wrenley had only seen glimpses, but now he fully stood before her, and she had to raise her chin to take him in. She beheld a firm, angled face. His jawline flexed as he looked down at her past his beautifully sloped nose. His eyes reflected the lamplight, but she could see they were a deep shade of brown, like roasted chestnuts. She took in his scent, noticing the aroma of spices, firewood, and cedar. His shoulders were broad, his muscles straining under his black button-up shirt. She guessed he was older than her, maybe in his forties. Despite his age, his clean-shaven face gave a hint of boyish charm. He leaned forward just slightly, his voice now huskier.

"I will leave you to your reading. Thank you for sharing your wine and thoughts with me." He bowed archaically before her. Wrenley was brought back to reality, embarrassed that he may have noticed her staring at him.

"Um, you're welcome. Breakfast starts at seven," she muttered awkwardly. He grinned and was gone, slipping into the house's darkness like a shadow. Wrenley pulled her sweater tighter around her and could not ignore the goosebumps that broke out on her arms for the hundredth time today. She felt uneasy and decided it was time to go to bed. She gathered her glass and book, called to Nyx, and they made their way to her room together.

~ ~ ~ ~ ~

Autumn colors. Oranges and red....
Wrenley felt herself falling; was it out of the sky?
Or into a hole?
She thrashed around, trying to find something to hold onto.
She then saw red...was it blood?
Things spun again, and she felt like she was moving but going nowhere.
She heard a voice, Wrenley? Can you hear me?
A hand reached out...but she could not reach it.
Wrenley... Come find me...

CHAPTER 3

Questions

Wrenley was startled awake by her mother's frightened voice outside her door.

"Wren! We need you!" Her voice was uncharacteristically panicked, making Wrenley catapult out of bed. It took her a moment for her eyes to register the light as her mother barged into the room, wringing her hands.

"What is it?" Wrenley rubbed the sleep from her eyes, trying to fight her annoyance. She reached up blindly to tie her thick mess of curls up in a bun on her head. Her head hurt, her body ached more than usual, and it took every ounce of self-discipline not to scowl at her mother.

"Come quick! The police are here!"

Despite her pain, that was enough to push Wrenley into her clothes and shoes with record speed. Wrenley did her best to keep up with her mother as they made their way through the kitchen to the back of the house and into the courtyard. As Ruth pushed open the heavy, wooden courtyard door, they were greeted by half a dozen police cars, an ambulance, a fire truck, and dazed staff.

"What the hell happened?" Wrenley asked breathlessly and propelled her way through the crowd to where her father stood.

"Dad? What is going on…" Wrenley lost her voice as she looked down at the scene. She grabbed his arm for support and looked at the sight before her. A pool of blood soaked the ground, and what she could only guess was a body draped in a white sheet lay before them. Wrenley felt her gut tighten, and she looked at her father, grabbing his wrinkled hand and squeezing it. *Who is this?* Wrenley's mind jumped to the possibilities, and the stranger from the library popped into her head.

"It's one of our guests...the gentleman from room 205."

Wrenley exhaled, though she did not know why. In the back of her mind, she feared it was the guy from last night. Knowing it was not him made her feel some relief.

"We will need to ask you some questions, ma'am." Wrenley knew Officer Smith's voice; most locals called him Bob. He was usually obnoxious and fulsome but looked unusually rattled at the gruesome view before them. He was one of the five police officers who worked in their small community, so they must have called for backup. Nothing like this happened in her little town, especially outside their bed and breakfast. Wrenley could not remember a time when an unnatural death ever happened, let alone one like this.

"He was stabbed..." Bob and Dad mumbled amongst themselves, casting troubling looks around. "Highway patrol will probably be taking over soon."

Wrenley noticed the officer pull down the sheet to show the wound to her father; she let out an audible breath, seeing his contorted face frozen with horror, and probably his last moments. Wrenley felt cold, but it was different from the October chill that danced around them. She sensed another presence, something shadowy and unsettling.

~ ~ ~ ~ ~

"I didn't feel right last night."

Ruth poured Wrenley and the highway patrol detective a cup of coffee and offered some pastries. Wrenley waved her mother off, but Detective Norway helped himself to the snacks as if he had forgotten to eat breakfast. Norway was a short, pudgy man with a military haircut and a grey suit. He had a thick Southern accent and chatted with Ruth for what seemed like an annoying amount of time. Wrenley just sat there, waiting for them to finish, too preoccupied to hear them. Her mind kept going back to last night in the library, and then the body that had been loaded up into the ambulance. It was a gruesome sight, him lying in a pool of blood, so close to where her family slept. The recollection of the dreadful scene made her sick to her stomach.

"What do you mean, not right?" Norway finally decided to start his questioning, and Wrenley rubbed her face in irritation. "I don't know, I just felt off. I couldn't sleep, so I went to the library to have some wine. Then another guest came in..."

"Your mom shared that you have some mental health issues as well as ..." he eyed her up and down, and Wrenley felt violated as he moved his head slightly to shoot a perverted gaze at her hips, "...and a physical disability."

Wrenley snapped her head up to look at him. "I have anxiety. That's it."

Norway scribbled something in his little notebook, and Wrenley tried not to be visibly annoyed. She felt the urge to slap it out of his hands.

"You have a history of..." he paused smugly, looking at her over his obnoxiously thick glasses, "Hallucinations."

"That hasn't happened in a long time," Wrenley's voice cracked lowly, but she was sick in the pit of her stomach. She did see and hear things — noises, voices, and things in the night. She used to tell her therapist about it when she was younger, but not in years, not after they tried to lock her away for it.

"Which guest did you see last night?"

"Room 201. Brandon, something..." Wrenley massaged her temples, feeling exasperated about the questioning. "I can't remember."

"That must be a mistake, dear. Room 201 wasn't occupied last night," Ruth said, straightening the tray of coffee and pastries on the table. She was acting so nonchalant that Wrenley wanted to scream at her. Why was her mother so calm and collected with all this happening?

"Yes, it was..." Wrenley insisted, "I checked the guest in yesterday afternoon."

Ruth put on her reading glasses and checked her tablet. "Honey, no one has checked in to 201 since last week."

"He took the key.... I remember I slid it across the wooden desk, and it made a scraping noise." Wrenley remembered it as if it were only moments ago.

Norway looked at Ruth with a slightly raised brow. Clearing his throat and leaning forward, he said, "Perhaps it was a different room."

"There is no Brandon in our system, dear. It must be a mistake, but we've been swamped!" Ruth tried to assure Norway, giving him what almost seemed like a fake smile and placing a wrinkled hand on his sleeve.

"Then who was with me in the library last night? He sat right next to me in the chair; he drank some wine with me…"

"Is he in the room now?" Norway made a reasonable effort to keep his face straight, but Wrenley knew he was being a jackass. Wrenley was speechless for a heartbeat, and her mouth swung open, but she could not conjure up a retort. She wanted to hit him in his stupid face.

"No," Wrenley finally said flatly, pushing her coffee cup away and crossing her arms protectively across her chest.

Norway gave her a look, scribbling again in his notebook. "You were drinking then? How much had you had to drink?"

Wrenley's jaw dropped again, and she resisted the urge to slap the smirk off the detective's face. She tried to mask her rage when she said, "Two fucking glasses, not enough to make me visually hallucinate."

"But you do have a…." He flipped through his notes, "A disturbing history of hallucinations? Or seeing things? You've been to therapy a lot…"

"How dare you!" Wrenley slammed her fist on the table, and the detective jumped a little.

"Wrenley, please!" Ruth placed her hands on her daughter's shoulders and shook her head, "This is very upsetting for her, Detective…for all of us. I checked all our rooms this morning, and 201 has not been disturbed since last week. I found the key behind the desk. It must have been knocked on the floor at some point. She squeezed Wrenley's shoulders, as if sending an encoded message to calm down and keep her mouth shut, "Honey, I put it back in the key safe."

Her mother continued, "Wren, I think you need a break. Detective, may I offer you more pastries, and we can talk to other staff?"

Wrenley shoved herself away from the table, scowling in pain, but she was determined not to let it slow her down as she tried to hold back the tears. How dare he! How did he know about her therapy visits? This damn town was so small that confidentiality did not exist here. It did not matter anyway. Wrenley knew what she saw and knew she was not crazy, but still, the shame and guilt crept into her gut.

Or are you crazy? It was a disturbing thought, one she would never mumble out loud. She retreated behind the desk, leaving Ruth and Norway speaking in hushed tones in the kitchen.

~ ~ ~ ~ ~

Wrenley checked for herself, and her mother was right; the key was placed back in the safe. Wrenley hobbled upstairs and found the door to 201 locked. Nothing seemed out of the ordinary or out of place. The towels were folded neatly, and the bed was made to perfection…just like it had been a week ago. Nothing appeared to be disturbed. Wrenley fought the fear festering just under the surface—the fear that maybe she had hallucinated the stranger, or perhaps he had been an apparition.

"This is why we need a damn security system," Wrenley clenched her teeth and muttered, locking 201 behind her and jiggling the handle. Her parents were old-fashioned and refused to install a camera system, even in the lobby. She would have had proof that this mystery guy was there if they had had one. She could not explain why the room was untouched, but knew this was not a hallucination.

Her mind traveled back to a memory of sitting in the therapist's office as a teenager, arms folded stubbornly across her chest. The therapist was an older man with round glasses and a grey goatee. He looked at her with pity as he asked what she would see and hear. She knew better then; a year before this, they had tried to admit her to a children's psychiatric unit for sharing about the ghosts she would see. At that moment, she had been determined to make herself as small as possible. She would be a chameleon, blending in so no one would be able to hurt her. Because as much as she wanted to be seen and heard by others, it was not worth the risk. This is what happens when she dares to open up to others.

The memory activated her, and Wrenley's chest tightened. It was beating too fast, and she knew she was on her way to having a full-fledged panic attack. She retreated to the closest room she could find, which was the library. She ducked in to avoid the highway patrol officers gathering around the front door, terrified they would ask more questions of her. She stumbled in and almost tripped over Nyx, who had been hot on her heels, flying forward and catching herself on the wing-backed chair she usually sat in.

"Dammit Nyx!" Wrenley screeched, the cat darting back and forth nervously in front of her. The cat meowed, still relentlessly rubbing against her ankles. "You could have killed me!"

Nyx gave another yowl, jumped to the chair, and then to the open space on the bookshelf. Jolted, Wrenley raised her head upward to follow the cat. A chill swept down her spine, knowing her lightheadedness must have been all the blood draining from her face. In front of her, her treasured book series was on the bookshelf. One was missing, Volume Two, her favorite of the series—the one she and the mystery man had held the night before—the one he had taken with him to read.

Bronson…that was his name. I'm not crazy; he was real.

It was as if Nyx yowled again with her realization. Wrenley felt a delightful flutter in her heart at the lovely memory of his voice, and she tenderly reached out to brush her fingers over the books just as he had done less than twenty-four hours ago. Bronson was real, and she felt reassured that she was not losing her mind.

CHAPTER 4

Suspicion

Wrenley lay on her bed that night, a cold rain rhythmically hit her window as if beckoning her to sleep. Her dreams were becoming increasingly vivid and colorful, and she kept a notebook on her bedside table to record any details that came to her during sleep. She knew her dreams were related to the old bed and breakfast. She recognized it was haunted, or something was there with them; however, no one would ever talk about it. When she asked her mother about the noises, she would reply, "It's just the wind," or "It's just the wood bending."

Wrenley remembered that the house would become more alive during the fall, and she would look forward to it. She felt safe in the idea that there was more than her existence. With all her anxiety and fears, the things that should have made someone scared did not affect her. She felt comfortable in the presence of the house and its secrets. She felt at home with the ghosts. It gave her hope…maybe there was something more out there than her miserable existence.

Wrenley felt connected to the house, living like a wallflower amongst people in the background and shadows. Time would pass, and it would still be in the same place, unchanged, just like Wrenley. If she inherited it, the house would be her only legacy, as having children was not likely with her disease. That perhaps was the most painful part of her condition; it stole the future right out from under her. She would love to have a child, a family, and a husband, but none of those things were likely. The actuality was that she would not live to be very old. Even if she could (by some miracle) conceive and carry a child to term, she would most likely have significant health issues that would place her in a facility by the age of fifty.

It happened when she was eight years old, sitting in the specialist's office with her mother and father as they diagnosed her with the mystery illness. The doctor's face and tone conveyed that it was not good news. Wrenley did not ask questions as he explained that her condition would continue to get worse. He explained that she would lose the ability to move, to walk, and would probably be in a wheelchair in her early adulthood. He spoke to her parents about 'realistic expectations' for her future, like she already had one damn foot in the grave. The doctor warned that she may not live past her thirties and prepared Wrenley for a limited life.

At the time, Wrenley did not understand exactly what the doctor said. Her parents did not ask a single question. Instead, they nodded their heads, gathered her between them, and shoved her out the door without another word. Afterwards, they took her to lunch, and, again, not a word was spoken about it. The next day, they signed her up for soccer and dance lessons. They continued treating Wrenley like they had not been in the same room with that doctor. As Wrenley grew, she noticed the change in her body, but her mother and father kept pushing her to do things 'normal' kids would do. It was not until her teenage years that Wrenley grasped the reality of her prognosis. She wished she could talk about it with her parents, but they would change the subject when she tried. So, Wrenley held it in, the burden heavy, as she prepared herself for the future.

There was no name for the disease. Wrenley had been to every expert in the state and beyond. No one understood why it happened or what caused it, but her hips and spine were deteriorating. Carrying a biological child would be impossible, and doctors gave her a very short life expectancy with a plethora of complications. Even now, she had difficulties with her bowels and bladder, and continuing to be mobile was a challenge. The thought of putting another person through her pain like that…well, it was out of the question. Putting a husband and a child through this awful disease? No, they did not deserve it. She would remain alone.

Wrenley turned on her bedside lamp, poured a glass of wine, and threw on her robe. She felt drained after the last several days of excitement and stress. The authorities were all over the bed and breakfast, tearing the murdered man's room apart, questioning all the staff and guests, and causing a scene in the community. She then glanced above her bed, the pentagram hanging where she slept, and she could not help but wonder...

Wrenley was not a fool to think there were no biases in this small town. The community had three churches within the same block, and no other religions were prominent for miles until one traveled to the bigger cities. The fact that Wrenley was a practicing pagan, now hidden even from her parents, was a risk. Although her parents had to notice Wrenley's subtle practices, they did not draw attention to them or ask questions. Once again, she was invisible and ignored by everyone around her.

At one point, there had been a rumor and suspicion of Wrenley's 'odd practices' that rumbled through the community, and ever since, people would not look her in the eye. It was silly, but in this rural area, folks were superstitious, if not downright prejudiced. She had a feeling that this might be behind the questioning, the taunting, and the probing by the detective. Who else to blame but the crippled witch spinster? They would not release any information about the dead man except that he was a John Doe. The identification he provided when he checked in was fake, and there was no record of him in the police system. They determined nothing was stolen, but the investigation was still ongoing. Norway specifically reminded Wrenley, "Don't leave town."

She was not a homicidal person, but he was pushing it.

Due to the recent events and the police presence, Wrenley's parents were particularly on edge, with good reason. Not only were they afraid of this violent crime on their property, but how would it affect business. All the guests vacated the house within two days, and cancellations began to pour in. Her father assured everyone it was 'just a season' and would blow over soon, but Wrenley could tell he was worried.

Wrenley breathed the herbs she burned in the small cast-iron caldron on her bedside table. It soothed her, and she grinned as she almost felt the house creak in acknowledgment of her practice of purifying her room. She cracked the window slightly, allowing any evil or negative energy to escape, and the scent of cedar and sage cleansed her space. She had felt an uncomfortable presence lately in the house, and her disturbed dreams kept repeating ever since the murder.

She never could remember concrete details about her dreams, but she knew she was falling through something; time and space moved around her as she toppled through an unexplainable void, with no beginning and no end. Then she felt a presence, a voice, but she could only make out fragments of what it said. There was an image that would appear, but it never came into focus, no matter how she strained to look at it. Then she sensed a hand outstretched to her, and the dream would end with her falling again.

Come find me... the image would say. *Can you see?* But it was always out of reach, no matter how she struggled and strained to see it.

Shaking her head and closing the window, Wrenley climbed into bed and turned off the light, her anxiety lessening. She lay her head down on the soft pillow and felt her eyes growing heavy, and she reached to clutch the necklace around her neck. She felt the small pendant rub against her finger; the pendant of Michael the Archangel, or at least she thought it was Michael. The words had been scratched off with the years of wear, but the image of the mighty angel was bold. Wrenley was not Catholic, but the small piece of metal brought her comfort. It was the only item left from her biological mother after she died; the only piece of her Wrenley had left to hang on to.

Wrenley's eyes shot open, and her body stiffened. A knock? Footsteps? It was probably her father checking every inch of the house before bed. She tossed her covers off, not bothering to turn on the light. She could maneuver the house's second floor with her eyes closed. Wrenley's small room was on the opposite side of the stairs in the east corner, tucked away from the guest rooms. She heard something soft, like footsteps, as she opened her bedroom door. Upstairs was open, like a balcony, where one would walk to their rooms and look down to see the lobby. Wrenley called out for Jim, leaning over the railing.

"Dad?" She called out softly.

There was no response, just the deafening blackness.

Wrenley heard the noise again, identifying it as coming from the west end, near the stairs. Wrenley did not feel frightened; it may just be the house again, a familiar spirit or ghost just having a frolic in the cold darkness. Because of recent events, such as a man murdered on their doorstep, she grabbed a vase sitting on a table nearby, easy enough to swing at someone if needed. She crept along and stopped in front of room 202. She put her ear to the door and listened. She heard her heart pounding in her ears, but no sounds from inside the room. She then moved next door to room 201. Pressing her ear against the door, palm flat to steady herself, she leaned in. Once again, only silence. The door felt ice cold, making her shiver.

Wrenley relaxed a little, deciding that her mother may be right this time. It was probably just the wood of the old house bending. She exhaled and set the vase down on a table in the foyer, turning to return to her room when she heard it again. She froze; the noise was coming from inside 201. Wrenley felt her pulse start to throb, her senses alerting her. She reached down, expecting to find the door locked. She jiggled it slightly, and the door creaked open. It was never unlocked, especially since the murder. A cold chill swept down her spine, flushing into her stomach.

Wrenley held her breath as she pushed the door gently, it groaning as it swung open wide. Despite her better judgment, she felt something beckon her to come, move into the room, and investigate. Wrenley gasped quietly as a soft glow from the fireplace warmed the room. She stood on the threshold for a minute, still feeling as if something on the inside was calling her in.

Wrenley advanced into the softly lit room, goosebumps all over her body. Wrenley scanned around her, knowing that no one should be in there and no one should have lit a fire. She shut the door behind her, trying to limit the noise as much as possible so as not to wake up the rest of the house. She was in the middle of the room, peering around and taking everything in. Things were not bizarrely out of place except…she noticed something on the bed and left the fire's glow to get closer. She bent over and gulped; a book lay on the bed as if waiting for her. Her blood felt like it had turned to ice as a cold wave of fear rippled over her body. Her mind began to shuffle through the pieces and memories of the past few weeks, and her gaze locked onto the cover of Volume Two.

"You were right. It was a fantastic read."

Wrenley screeched and spun around at the familiar voice,

slamming into a prominent figure behind her. She yelped and pushed backward away from it, but her legs and hips had not turned with her, and her knees buckled at a painful angle. She cried out in agony, and a strong arm wrapped around her waist as she almost collapsed in a tangled heap. She felt his warm breath against her ear, then, as she clawed for anything to keep herself from falling, she grabbed the two muscular forearms with both hands, writhing in panic, afraid she would fall and hurt her hips and legs even more. She did not fall, though; he held her tightly as she buckled.

"It's okay, I've got you," he whispered in her ear again as she began to wriggle out of his grasp. His warmth was enveloping, causing her to tremble under his touch.

"Let me go!" She hissed.

"Good lord, calm down…" he uttered. She felt his large arms shift her, gently guiding her around where her back was pressed against him, and he covered her mouth with his palm. She attempted to scream, but his hand had clapped over her mouth tightly. Wrenley felt a sense of panic as he pinned her arms to her side. He bent over and spoke into her ear for a third time. His voice was now a low rumble she felt against her body.

"You're going to wake the entire damn house if you scream; it's unnecessary." His voice was low and quiet, rippling with authority. Wrenley struggled some more, but it did not matter. He overpowered her as she pitifully thrashed. He held her tight as she wiggled, his arms tightening with every move she made. She finally gave up and fell into his arms.

"If I let you go, will you promise to be quiet?"

She nodded, his hand still over her mouth, unsure if she meant it. He gently released her, and she pulled herself away from him, now having her footing.

He looked down at her and sighed, rolling those dark chestnut eyes, "You are being dramatic."

Wrenley looked at the man wide-eyed; he looked exactly like he had the night in the library. It took her a moment to digest his presence in front of her.

"You…. bastard!" The words shot like an arrow, and she pointed a finger at his face, "Where did you go?"

He strolled to a chair near the fire, taking a seat with a relaxed pose. One leg crossed over the other, his arms resting loosely on the chair arms. He gave the impression that he did not have a care in the world. Wrenley was too flabbergasted to be afraid, and she covered the distance between them as best she could, her finger still jutting out towards him.

"You!" She hissed loudly again. "What are you doing here?"

Bronson sighed and shifted, straightening his jacket, "I'm here to return your book."

"You...Y-you were here, and you rented this room, but no one..."

"Yes, I know." Bronson folded his hands and rested them in his lap, looking down momentarily as if to examine his fingernails. "It's complicated."

"Complicated?" Wrenley spat, waving her hands in the air theatrically before she slapped her thighs with them and stomped her foot. "Do you know all the problems we've had since you walked through that door?"

"Tell me?" he said, a grin playing around the edges of his lips. He tilted his handsome face toward her, and her breath caught. She took him in, trying not to be intimidated by the beautiful, powerful man before her. She shook her head to focus again, ignoring his smirk.

"Everyone thinks I'm crazy...there's been a murder...my family's business is in danger..."

"Could you please sit? We can talk this out."

"You know what? No! Who the hell are you? And why are you here? Are you a ghost? Are you a figment of my imagination?" She held her arms out to him. "Am I as crazy as everyone says I am? You tell me!" The words came pouring out, and she was unable to stop them.

Bronson stood abruptly, and Wrenley stepped back, forgetting how tall he was. His short black hair was tussled attractively, and his chestnut eyes seemed to soften as he approached her. He stood before her now, splaying his hands in front of him in a gesture of amity. Wrenley took one more step back and looked at his hands as if they were poisonous.

His face was easy, his voice lenient, "We don't have much time, and there is so much I need to tell you, Wrenley."

He reached one hand towards her now, beckoning her to take it by wriggling his large fingers. Wrenley felt something, a familiar feeling deep in her gut that she could not identify or ignore. She did not know why she was not afraid of him. She reached out and put her hand in his, and he tightened his grip and smiled.

"Touch me, Wrenley…do I feel real to you?"

She eyed his hand, gaze shifting to his face, and swallowed. Slowly, she reached out and touched him, almost gasping as it felt warm under her fingertips.

"I apologize for all the mystery, Wrenley. I had no other choice."

CHAPTER 5

The Veil

Bronson stood and offered Wrenley the wing-backed chair, and she slumped into it with a groan. Rubbing her eyes with the palms of her hands, she grunted and took some deep breaths to calm the peaking anxiety. A cold sweat broke out over her body, her limbs aching with the stress. Her hands shook as she finally lowered them and fisted her nightgown to hide the trembling.

"Choice about what?" She finally asked, eyeing Bronson as he stood before the fireplace. He glanced at her, and his gaze lingered on her as if he were weighing what he should and should not say.

"I have been watching over you, but haven't been able to contact you until now."

Wrenley huffed in frustration, "Why?"

"Haven't you felt out of place your entire life, Wrenley?"

Wrenley shifted uncomfortably in her seat and shrugged. She was not going to spill her guts to this man about her loneliness and pathetic life. She pivoted and crossed her arms, "I'm adopted. Of course, I sometimes feel out of place…"

"Is there any time when you feel more connected and safer? In the Autumn months, maybe?" Bronson shifted to where he was leaning towards her now. "In October? You love the changing of the trees. You love the colors, the smells, and the feeling of it. You sense it, don't you?"

Wrenley did not know what she was supposed to be sensing, but she tried to hear him out. The urge to fold into herself and disappear was so overwhelming that her shoulders curled in. "I'm just…I'm sorry," Wrenley shook her head, "I just want to know why you are here."

Bronson knelt in front of her and held her hands tightly. Surprised by the gesture, she recoiled slightly and tried to tug her hands free, but he did not release her. "Because I have come for you, to bring you home."

Wrenley's mouth fell open. "Home?"

"To Ailios," he said gently.

Wrenley shook her head, "I don't know where that is."

Bronson sighed, still gripping her hands. "Other worlds are the things of stories to those in your world, Wrenley, but not so much in mine. Ours..." Bronson stood, grabbed the book off the bed, and flipped through its pages.

"This realm we are in now is very limited in knowledge about traveling to different worlds beyond the veil, but it appears some humans had an idea or an instinct that there is more out there." Bronson tossed the book back on the bed. He stood before the fire again, arm extended to the mantle, the fire glowing warmly on his handsome face.

"Worlds?"

Bronson smiled, "I think the word you would use is 'dimensions.' Think of it as being in one room, with a wall separating you from the others, but there are many rooms and layers. Some people...like me, have the power to step through the walls to visit other worlds. Some worlds rub against each other...and some with gifts notice it." He looked at her and raised an eyebrow, "Like you."

Wrenley scoffed slightly, "It sounds like nonsense." She leaned back as Nyx appeared at her feet and jumped into Wrenley's lap. Wrenley stroked the feline, finding comfort in her purrs of contentment.

Bronson smiled, "My realm is different from this one. Time moves more slowly, so it was hard to keep up with you when I arrived. You grew very fast, a calculation we missed when your mother decided to send you here."

"My mother?"

A sad but gentle beam crept over Bronson's face, "Not Ruth...when I say your mother, your parents...I mean your birth parents, Wrenley. As you humans say, biological parents would fit. Your born parents are King Dolion and Queen Adinnil of the

Kingdom of Ailios."

Silence stretched between them, a difficult and deafening silence. Wrenley looked up at Bronson and burst out laughing. She laughed so hard she bent over, holding her stomach. Nyx yowled and flew off her lap in a huff.

"You are hilarious!" She hooted and finally composed herself, wiping away tears. "I should be offended, but it's just funny."

Bronson angled his head towards her, eyebrows furrowing as she continued to laugh.

"I'm serious, Wrenley."

"You are being an asshole."

Bronson looked agitated and held out a hand. "Why can't you understand that there is something more than what you can see here?" Bronson's tone was deep. He shrugged his shoulders toward the room around him.

Wrenley stopped giggling and swallowed. "Sorry, I'll be serious."

"Your birth parents were good to their people. They were powerful but generous in their reign and compassionate rulers to Ailios. They had a child very late in life," Bronson turned and leaned on the hearth again. "You were the absolute joy of their existence. The whole kingdom rejoiced when you were born. Flowers lined the streets in celebration. That's why you love flowers so much." Wrenley could see Bronson's face go dim, and suddenly, his expression turned to grief.

"When our enemies came to take the throne, Dolion and Adinnil were ready to fight, but they couldn't take the chance of you falling into enemy hands. So, your mother sent you away when the veil between the dimensions was thinnest. The veil was fragile then; it was this time of year. You probably notice it in October, close to your holiday, Samhain. I traveled across the barriers of worlds into this house, in this room, thirty-two years ago, and we arranged it with Ruth and Jim. They were to watch over you and keep you safe until the time was right for you to return." Bronson looked down at his feet and took a deep breath, his shoulders shaking slightly.

"I was only twenty-five when your mother placed you in my arms that night and commanded me to run and not look back. I did, but it was the last night I saw my closest friend and queen alive.

Your birth parents were murdered after we escaped."

Wrenley felt the stillness in the room and almost forgot to breathe. Was she going mad? Wrenley stood up and began pacing back and forth, which was a chore for her. Bronson watched, seeming empathetic to her inner turmoil. Wrenley scrubbed her face with her hands and shook her head, her hand landing on her lower back because of the pain. "I guess I don't understand. You're not…" She struggles to find the right words. "You don't look that old."

Bronson's lips curled faintly in apparent amusement. "I was twenty-five when I crossed over with you. You were only a few months old. As I said, time travels two times faster here than in Ailios. In this time, you grew thirty-two years older. In mine, I only grew fifteen years, though I feel much older," he mumbled, straightening his back and groaning as if on cue to prove a point.

"So, you're what…. forty-something?"

Bronson's chuckle was like a smoldering fire, "Or something…some days I feel significantly older than that."

Wrenley cocked her head at him. "You saved me?"

Bronson nodded, "I and other seers…loyal to Ailios and our royalty who were chosen to either get you out or fight."

"Seers?"

"You would acknowledge the word 'wizard'…I suppose. We were committed to the service of the kingdom willfully. We have powers and gifts that you would recognize as 'magic'. When the enemy killed your parents, they began hunting us down because they knew one of us had taken you."

Wrenley looked at Bronson in horror as she saw the pain on his face, and he continued, "My brothers and sisters were killed and tortured like animals. A few converted and pledged themselves to the enemy, but they didn't know where you were taken. Only Adinnil, your mother, and I knew what dimension you would go to, and only I knew the location. It was better that way, and the seers all agreed that they would not ask where I would take you. It worked for a while until one of them discovered the rift in dimensions."

"One of them?"

Bronson gave her a sideways glance and murmured, "You found him in the courtyard at the beginning of the week."

Wrenley gasped, covering her hand with her mouth, "That's why you were here?"

"I was here because the time was coming to bring you home. I realized it was just a matter of time before another seer would uncover my secret, but I did not expect it to happen so fast. Now that I know, you are not safe here anymore."

Wrenley sat back into her chair and rubbed her temples with her fingers, a headache forming. "How do I know you are telling the truth?" She stood up again, refusing to groan in pain, and marched past Bronson to the door.

"You can't just reject this, Wrenley. It won't make it go away…"

"I'm leaving."

"Wrenley, wait…"

Before Bronson finished his sentence, Wrenley used the remainder of her strength to throw open the door and inhaled sharply. Her mother and father stood motionless outside the door, ears still positioned to hear every word in the room. They looked guilty, being caught red-handed eavesdropping. Remorsefully, Ruth straightened up and was the first to speak, "Dear, perhaps we all need a cup of tea. We have a lot to talk about."

Jim straightened up as well, shoving his hands in his pockets, and with a hint of a smile said, "We might need something a little stronger than tea."

Wrenley stood in front of them, mouth gaping. She looked at her parents, then at Bronson, and back at them.

"Do you see him?" she asked, motioning towards the seer. Ruth and Jim looked at each other and then at Wrenley, and they nodded their heads in unison.

"Yes, dear, we see him." Mom reached out for Wrenley's hand, but not in time. Wrenley felt a flush of warmth envelop her, hands and feet beginning to tingle as the edges of her vision began to blur. Wrenley stumbled back, not noticing how Nyx was right between her legs again. With her limbs feeling so heavy and pained, she fell backwards and felt the rush of pain in the back of her head. She felt her parents above her, heard Ruth gasp, and felt strong arms lift her as she fell into a deep, magical sleep.

CHAPTER 6

The Crossing

Wrenley stirred at the coolness across her forehead, flinching in surprise. She tried to open her eyes, but her lids felt heavy. Finally, she slit her lids to take in the outline above her. Her mother's worried face swam into view. Wrenley could feel it was daytime, and she stirred again, reaching up to push away the cold washcloth from her face.

"What time is it?"

"You've been asleep for twenty-four hours," Ruth said breathlessly, reaching to tuck a lock of hair behind her daughter's ear. "I was so worried!"

"What?" Wrenley shook herself awake and tried to sit up, but her mother and Bronson grabbed her forearms to steady her and keep her from moving. Ruth sat on one side of her bed, and Bronson on the other, both intently staring at her.

"Your head injury wasn't that bad, and I don't believe you've had a concussion. But your body fell asleep…" Bronson's voice was husky and low. "Did you dream at all?"

Wrenley shook her head, "No, nothing I can remember." It was the usual colors and blurry images she always saw in her dreams, and nothing she could put into words.

"Did you do something to me?" Wrenley murmured groggily. Bronson shook his head, eyeing her warily. "No, I didn't do anything to you."

"Let me guess, you're a magician and a doctor," Wrenley attempted to sit up slowly, allowing Bronson to help her. He chuckled, and Wrenley noticed it was a deep, warm sound that made her stomach flutter.

"I am both, although here in this world, the two are not very friendly to each other. The doctors of your world have no desire to understand the magic in it. There is no difference in mine, which makes us more effective."

Wrenley noticed how Bronson had shed his suit and jacket for jeans and a T-shirt, which made him look less mystical and more 'natural.' She tried not to react to his masculine, spicy scent or his large, muscular arms so close to her. One leg was hanging off the bed where he sat, and the other thigh was on the bed, almost touching her. She closed her eyes, noticing it was a very nice-looking, well-developed thigh. She averted her gaze, cheeks warming at the thought of him so close.

Wrenley tried to make sense of everything, but her head still felt fuzzy from her fall. Her arms and legs were heavy, and her back ached from the strain it endured when she passed out. Then there was…the other matter at hand: the fact that she was a long-lost daughter of someone…somewhere. She shook her head in frustration again, pinching her eyes closed and opening them wide as if that could make things clearer.

She felt anger, that was for sure… Ruth should have told her. How could her parents hide this from her? There was anger there, but then there was curiosity: Bronson had dumped so much on her in moments, leaving her overwhelmed with questions racing through her mind. Finally, self-doubt crept in, making her wonder if she was perhaps inventing all of this. What if she truly was losing her mind?

"Listen, I don't mean to be rude," Wrenley cleared her throat and croaked. "But I need to talk to Mom." She looked up at Bronson and scowled at him. "…Alone."

"Certainly," he said politely and moved away, not seeming bothered by her disgruntled glare. Wrenley observed him as he pulled his sweater over his strong shoulders, his expression neutral, revealing nothing. His muscles flexed with each movement, and the ridges in his back and shoulders were evidence enough that he was physically powerful. She also could not help but notice he was also soft, though, the way he spoke and looked at her. She averted her gaze as he exited the room, closing the door gently behind him. With a soft sigh, she shook her head and tried to refocus on what to say next.

"Mom?" Wrenley did not even know how or what to ask. She

felt tears prick her eyes, her gut knotting up as Ruth shifted beside her on the bed. In one way, Wrenley hoped it was not true, but what if it was? Would that explain so much about her that she could never understand herself?

"Honey, there is so much that I couldn't tell you." Her mother grabbed her hand and held it tight, a tear released and fell down her withered cheek. "When Bronson brought you to us, we lived in this old house and knew it was special. We thought it was a house of old history and a ghost or two. We didn't know that it would bring you into our lives," Ruth was crying now, holding both of Wrenley's hands close to her chest, resting her cheek against them.

"You were the best thing that ever could happen to us, my little Wren. And I know it was tough for you because all along, you sensed there was a world hidden from you. You knew there was something more, and we just couldn't share how right you were; it was all too risky. All this time, you were far too incredible and magnificent for this world; we had to shut you in."

Wrenley felt tears streaming down her face and leaned over to put her head in her mother's lap. Ruth stroked her golden hair, "We knew one day we would have to give you back. My love, these thirty-two years have been the greatest joy of our lifetime. But others need you now; Bronson needs you now."

"Him?" Wrenley sniffed and kept her head buried in her mother's floral skirt.

"He's been watching out for you all these years…he saved your life."

"He did?"

Ruth nodded and lifted Wrenley's chin to look into her eyes, "It's time for you to become what you have always meant to be, and if you ever need us again, Dad and I will be here, waiting. This house will always be here and waiting. There will always be an October for you to travel through. But now, you must go."

Ruth's voice wobbled. Her eyes were still wet with fresh tears.

"But what if I can't?" Wrenley whispered, fear striking her heart and almost knocking the wind out of her. If she had not been lying down, she was sure she would have fainted again from the pain in her heart.

"I am just so…weak." Wrenley felt the words travel through her body.

Ruth smiled and reached over to the nightstand. She grabbed the book and held it to her chest, her wrinkled face amused now, even with the tears flowing down her face. "You think you're the only heroine who has felt inadequate to fulfill her destiny? That's what courage is for...and a little determination and some guts, of which you have all three, by the way."

Wrenley sighed and sat up, plucking the book from Ruth and holding it to her chest as if trying to rally some of her nerve. "I have so many questions I need to ask you."

Ruth smiled, "And one day, I will answer as many as possible."

"But we have to leave, now!"

Wrenley levitated off the bed as Bronson threw open the door and entered the room, his voice dark, his powerful body filling up the space. "Wrenley, I think someone is trying to come through. If we can go first, it will push them back, and once you are away from here, your parents will not be in danger, but we must leave now."

Wrenley looked wide-eyed at her mother and then at her father, who had followed Bronson into the room, and nodded numbly. The next few minutes were a whirlwind of Wrenley gathering essentials and stuffing them into her backpack. She reached for her medications, and Bronson shook his head, "Leave them. You won't need them anyway."

That confused her, but she was too flustered to argue. *So fast, this is all happening so fast*, Wrenley cried on the inside. She tried to stop the events from unfolding and shake herself awake from this dream, but it was all too real, and she could not do anything about it. Minutes later, Bronson and Wrenley stood in the middle of room 201, and her parents stood just outside the door. Wrenley only had a heartbeat to shove a few things in her backpack, and now she stood next to a man she hardly knew, trusting him to take her across dimensions to another world. Even in her head, it sounded so ridiculous!

Wrenley tossed the book to her mother...her favorite one, giving her a knowing look as if to say, *Remember me.* Wrenley trembled and wrapped her arms around Bronson's waist as he instructed. She smiled weakly at her mother and father, and they attempted a very frail grin and wave back, Ruth clutching the book. Wrenley's heart almost exploded from the grief of leaving them with so little time and explanation. There was so much that was unsaid…so much she wished she could say…and there was just no time now to do it. Would she ever have the time?

She felt an arm around her waist, and it pulled her close. She began to feel tingly, and the room started to bend and spin. She began to see colors and hear a roaring sound in her ears like wind.

"We are almost ready," Bronson murmured in her ear, slipping another arm around her. His breath was hot against the shell of her ear, and she shivered as he spoke again. "No matter what, don't let go of me…"

Wrenley raised her arms to link them around his neck, embracing the man she hardly knew with every ounce of strength she could muster. He was huge compared to her, and she had to stand on her tiptoes to hold onto him, her crooked back straining as she reached. She hid her face in his chest and allowed her tears to fall freely, still numb with disbelief. One of his arms came up and grabbed the back of her neck, crushing her face against his chest. She noticed something that sounded like fire. Or was it water? She could not tell, but the sound was deafening.

Blackness surrounded them, and she heard a 'whooshing' sound. She wanted to cover her ears, but Bronson was holding her too tightly for her to move. Suddenly, she felt herself falling, or was she flying? Bronson was still there, and she heard him saying something. He murmured something in a language she did not understand, but the words seemed to penetrate her skin and flush over her. Blackness enfolded Wrenley, and a wave of fear washed over her as she fell into shadow again.

~ ~ ~ ~ ~

Bronson lifted Wrenley into his arms as he felt her go limp. He should have guessed as much; it had been over thirty years since she crossed dimensions. Her system was bound to be overloaded with the pressure of the time and space that raged around them. Bronson tried to ignore the smell of her hair, the feeling of her weak body against his as he heaved her up and carried her along the dark road. His calculations must have been obscured by whoever was attempting to cross over. He had planned for them to arrive near the capital city of Ailios; however, it appeared they were days away from his intended destination. Which, if someone was out looking for her, was probably the safest place for them right now.

The humor hit him. Thirty-two years ago, he had carried Wrenley across the dimensions as she left this realm, and now he carried her as she returned. He would never forget that night, drenched in blood and sweat as he held the screaming infant in his arms. She had been a small baby, desperate for her mother's comfort, but was left in his clumsy hands. He had wrapped her in a wool blanket and enveloped her as they had crashed across the dimensions, his inexperience making the trip choppier than it should have been. He prayed to all the gods he knew to get them somewhere safe...to lead him where they needed. Adinni had given him precise instructions on where to take her, but Bronson had gone blind with his magic. He splayed his magic out into the blackness of the unknown, searching for something...and then felt it. The pull...a tug on his power. It was as if the old house beckoned him, and he crashed into the Earth dimension into the room they had just left.

It felt as though they had been waiting for her. Ruth asked no questions as she opened the door to 201 and saw the young magician holding a crying infant in his arms. Defeated, exhausted, and grieving, Bronson had collapsed onto the floor with Wrenley in his embrace. He could still smell the aroma of spices, the orange glow of the fire in that room. Ruth rushed to him, and without saying a word, she took the bundle from him, murmuring and singing softly to the baby. From that moment on, everything clicked into place.

Bronson had repeatedly replayed that encounter in his mind for the last thirty-two years...or fifteen for him. He spent half of his time in this dimension, visiting Wrenley regularly during her lifespan. In her world, time traveled twice as fast...so he had only physically aged about fifteen years. She, on the other hand, is thirty-two years old. He gazed down at the woman in his embrace and shook his head, muttering quietly about the dramatic irony of the situation. He first needed to find a safe place for them to lay low until he knew exactly what was happening. He should have only been gone maybe a day, but it was hard to estimate until he spoke with his informants.

Quickly, Bronson was able to determine where they were and locate an ally close by. Since the enemy had put a price on Bronson's head, even friends became possible enemies. Could he blame them? The land was wracked with poverty and destitution ever since the war started. He could not fault anyone for turning him in to keep their children fed. Nevertheless, he had to be careful. He looked down at the woman in his arms, and his chest tightened. After watching her grow from the shadows all these years, he realized she was not the child she had once been. She was a woman and one who would hopefully save them all, if he could protect her.

But what if I can't? Bronson took long breaths, being winded from his journey between worlds and carrying her in his arms. His magic helped him, but he had to be careful: too much magic may cause attention in the unseen. Bronson was unsure how many seers had turned to serve the enemy, but he knew someone was attempting to cross into Wrenley's world. He knew it was only a matter of time before the entire realm knew their long-lost royalty had returned.

CHAPTER 7

A King and A Queen

"**I** have questions."

Bronson stirred from his very brief slumber to find Wrenley hovering over him. The cave was nestled underground, the chamber dark. Bronson had regained his bearings in the night and brought Wrenley to a shelter intended to support rebel soldiers who had fled to the mountains. Luckily, they crossed over not too far from the mountain road, and the journey was minimal.

The cave was tucked into the rocks of the small mountain range east of Ailios. It would be almost impossible for anyone to find them, magic or not. Bronson had prepared the cave with supplies for the last few years as troops would move in and out of the mountains to evade enemy forces. Not only was he planning for Wrenley, but he also used it to shelter political enemies, other seers, and friends from the enemy's evil and tight grasp. The economy crashed at the city's fall, and Bronson was able to add 'smuggler' to his already long list of capital offenses. Bronson stocked preserved foods, blankets, medical supplies, and anything else they may need to hunker down for at least two weeks, which was not the case for them. They would be moving on in a day at most.

Bronson had laid Wrenley in the makeshift bed and put together a pallet on the floor for himself. He still had not found deep sleep despite the unlikelihood of anyone finding them. He sat up abruptly, his chest bare, and he could feel the chill in the air. Wrenley jumped back slightly at his sudden movement, noticing his skin. She still sat very near, leaning so close that her hair tickled his shoulder, keeping her eyes on him.

"I have questions," she repeated, her eyes narrowing as she took him in. He knew she would not let anything go until he gave her some answers. Sitting up, he grabbed his shirt and pulled it over his shoulders.

"What do you want to know?" he muttered groggily. *It would be nice if she could hold off until they had ingested breakfast before this conversation*, he thought.

"Everything!" Wrenley looked as if she were fifteen again, a blanket wrapped around her shoulders, leaning forward on the edge of her seat. Bronson tried to ignore her attractiveness and scrubbed his face with his hands.

"That narrows it down..."

Wrenley bit her lip. "I want to know about my birth parents first."

Bronson inhaled sharply, the flood of memories surrounding her parents still stinging. He knew this conversation was coming, and even though he had rehearsed what he would say to her repeatedly through the years, he still struggled to find the words. She deserved to know more, even if he could not share it all yet. He hoisted himself off his pallet and nudged Wrenley with his leg for her to scoot over so he could sit on the cot next to her, and she did. He would not do it sitting on the floor if he had to give her a detailed family history. He dropped onto the bed next to her and groaned.

~ ~ ~ ~ ~

"Dolion and Adinnil were not just my king and queen but also my closest friends. I had grown up serving Adinnil, whose family had been a political force in my homeland for centuries. She had returned to take her place on the throne at twelve, while I was thirteen. She met your father when she was eighteen, and they fell in love."

Wrenley sipped a hot cup of tea she had scrounged up and allowed her body to sink into the mattress, even if their legs were touching. She sat cross-legged on the bed, feeling the warmth of the small fire and inhaling the aroma of the food in the cast-iron pot on the open-sided cookstove. Bronson had insisted on food and changing his clothes before he delved into all the things she had asked of him. She noticed Bronson was tired, looking older than even yesterday. He sat beside her on the bed with his back leaning against the wall, exhaustion overcoming him as he seemed to relax slightly. His muscular shoulders slumped, and his face seemed thoughtful as he accepted the steaming cup of tea she had brewed for him.

"Dolion was the son of a powerful seer and political nobleman in Ailios, and Adinnil was the princess of the royal family." Bronson blew on the hot liquid and took a cautious sip. "There had been some rise and fall of power for the last century. Adinnil's father, your grandfather…was the crowned patriarch then, and she returned to be with him to take her rightful place. Unfortunately, he died of a disease a few years later.

Dolion and Adinnil had known each other socially for several years. The term in your world is 'high school sweethearts,' I think? No one expected it. Dolion wasn't the first choice of Adinnil's father. His family was powerful, but they were also dangerous to the kingdom. If he ever decided he wanted to take control, his family had the power and resources to destroy everything. But…"

"But?" Wrenley scooted closer, and Bronson smiled, looking down into his cup, "You probably can guess the story. They fell in love, were married, and all was well. They tried for years to conceive a child, and when we all thought hope was lost…they had you. I thought that was happy ever after for them. For all of us…" Bronson sighed and set his cup down on the table beside the bed. "The kingdom erupted in celebration. They commemorated for the entire nine months of your mother's pregnancy. Balls, parties, bonfires, food, and drink…it was a festivity like none other. But I fear marriage and happily ever after blinded Dolion from being on guard against the evil threatening us."

"Evil?" Wrenley scrunched her brow with curiosity. "What evil?"

"We weren't sure what it was. It was a fairytale of sorts, or what you would call 'folklore'. There had been stories of a great evil that lived in the West, but it had been generations since anyone had ever seen or heard of it. Generation after generation passed, and I guess we just forgot it existed. I had to search some of our kingdom's oldest and deepest libraries to find the record of it. It had been so long since the evil had been present that it was lost in our history and forgotten until the year you were born."

"Why then?"

Bronson shrugged his shoulders. "I had been appointed to lead an assembly of seers to discover more about the enemy when we first received reports about them. The whispers of its presence first arrived by boat, as fishermen and cargo ships sailing the trade routes reported darkness slithering over the sea. Reports of evil creatures began pouring in across the land; mystical wolves, sea monsters, and other unnatural things…"

Wrenley shuddered, a chill progressing down her spine at the thought.

"I rode west to the coast with our company. We were attacked, and only a few others and I made it back. Our knowledge was limited; however, we discovered that the evil was a powerful oracle who wielded ancient, dark magic. We noticed he had the power to manipulate the elements: the earth, the water, and the weather. He was coming to conquer Ailios."

"Why?"

Bronson shook his head and rubbed the back of his neck, "Well, since it is the law and the way of the magic of our land, the sitting monarchs must be of royal blood and tied in marriage to the magic to receive the full power of the throne. Whoever holds the throne, holds the continent."

"What does that mean?"

"It means that your mother had to marry a seer for her to have the power of the throne. That also means, this seer…oracle…", Bronson's lips curled, and he shook his head, "…was too late in conquering your mother in marriage, so he was coming for you. I pored through our ancient texts and manuscripts and found mention of an ancient dark enchantment that claimed to be a deity. It conquered lands and chose races of people to colonize others in its name. He was only known as Earnesh: the one who battles to the death."

Wrenley heaved a sigh and placed her mug down. She turned herself to Bronson, her legs crossed on the bed, almost touching his thigh. She ignored the tingling she felt just from the proximity. "So, he came to kill my parents, steal an infant, and use me to take control of Ailios?"

"Yes."

"Yuck." Wrenley wrapped her arms around her stomach,

sickness settling in.

Bronson chuckled at her, but his eyes were still sad. "We decided to hide you quickly. It was the hardest day of your mother's life. Adinnil chose me to secretly escort you across because Dolion refused to allow you to leave. He feared you'd never return. So, the queen brought you to me and begged me to help. She didn't even tell him…I betrayed my king that night, but I obeyed my queen."

"What is crossing?" He had briefly mentioned it before, but she still did not understand.

Bronson breathed, "Stepping into another world, or 'dimension', is crossing the veil between our realities. Our worlds are parallel, and sometimes, there are rifts in time and space that we can cross over. Crossing over into these dimensions was something your father and I had been studying together because, one day, we may need this power to survive. We had attempted it many times, but it was only right before you were born that we became confident we could do it successfully, having only attempted it a few times before. Taking you was risky, but your mother felt it was worth the danger."

"Why Ailios? What's so special about it?"

"Your father and I believe Ailios's continent is a geographical area where the veil is thinner…maybe it's the earth and limestone beneath it, or maybe something else. But magic thrives here more than in other places, which is valuable; it could potentially win wars."

"Did you know where you were going when you crossed with me?"

Bronson shook his head and ran his fingers through his thick hair. "Not really. Whether luck, fate, or destiny…there was a rift in the worlds that led me to Ruth and Jim. To my surprise, they were not alarmed. Other beings have been crossing over into their home since moving into that house. I've never encountered these other travelers from different dimensions, but you have."

Wrenley gasped, covering her mouth with one hand, "You mean, those are the ghosts?"

Bronson shrugged, "I can't say one way or the other. Most people in your world will assume they are ghosts, but from my research, I believe it is simply the dimensions rubbing up against each other. One must be trained and use a gift of magic to appear and physically cross over as I did, which is what your father and I were working on. The veil between the worlds is thinner close to the full moons and the solstices. The barriers of the dimensions are the thinnest during the fall equinox and Samhain. That's why there is so much 'paranormal' activity in October."

Wrenley blew air into her cheeks, shaking her head. "You seem to know a lot about this stuff."

"Every time I visited you, I had to learn more about how to cross over and about your world."

"But if I've been gone for fifteen years, who's ruled since my parents died?"

Bronson tensed, "Earnesh has been ruling from the capital, but he hasn't had the totality of the throne's power since he has no royal blood to pair with him. As a result, a civil war has been raging. This conflict has ripped our kingdom to shreds."

Wrenley felt a knot form in her belly at his words.

"It first started with trying to win the people over. Earnesh brought riches, food, and wonders to show the people, and bought some of their love and favor. Most of the kingdom, however, would not be bought after what he did…"

Wrenley's eyes went wide. "What did he do?"

Bronson took a deep breath, sinking his head as if the memories were physically painful. He rubbed his bottom lip with his thumb. "Because your mother commanded me to take you, my power was solely focused on evacuating you. This left your father on his own, fighting Earnesh. Your father was a powerful seer, just wasn't powerful enough…."

Wrenley reached over and placed a hand on Bronson's arm, and he did not pull away. She felt the heat emanating from his skin, the solid muscle beneath his shirt. Her fingers tingled again, and it was as if she could feel the grief through the touch of his skin.

"Earnesh and your father fought long and hard. Your mother didn't leave as directed but stayed to assist in evacuating the castle. After hours of magical warfare, Earnesh created a huge explosion that evaporated your father and his guards. Every trace they had existed vanished instantly; then, Earnesh got to your mother…"

Wrenley did not know if she wanted to hear more. She quickly pulled her hand away from him and clasped it in her lap.

"Because your mother was already married to another man, the king didn't want her blood; he wanted yours. He tortured her for days for information about where I took you. He had his men rape and torture her court, her friends, and even innocent people from the villages. Your mother would not break, and she eventually died after weeks of horror. Her body was…" Bronson's voice cracked slightly, and he cleared his throat…"it was hung on the castle gates as a warning to those who wouldn't submit."

Wrenley felt weakness flush over her, and bile rose in the back of her throat. She thought she might throw up what little contents were in her stomach. Bronson's face was stone cold, a muscle feathering in his tight jaw at the memories, "I was not there to protect your father or mother…"

"But you saved me…" Wrenley whispered, feeling revolted at the thought of the decision he was forced to make.

Bronson nodded, "I followed orders, but I also honored the wishes of my queen, and my friend."

"Were you two ever…"

Bronson snapped his head towards her, "Absolutely not! I was a member of her inner circle and assigned to serve and protect her. She loved your father and was faithful to him."

Wrenley held her hands. "Sorry, just asking."

Bronson seemed offended at the insinuation but continued, "After your mother died, the kingdom erupted into a civil war. The people were not going to accept the death and torture of their beloved royalty without a fight. After entrusting your safety to Jim and Ruth, I resumed organizing the rebellion. I have been going back and forth, checking on you, and returning to fight ever since."

Wrenley felt the tears sting her eyes. This man, sitting next to her, had undergone severe grief and loss for her and her family. How could she ever repay that?

"It's our side against Earnesh now. The rebel forces are dwindling, dying from fighting, starvation, and disease. They are losing the will to keep going because their families are also suffering." Bronson ran a hand through his black hair. "We cannot win without…." Bronson lifted his shoulders slightly and looked at Wrenley, "…you."

"Me?" Wrenley said, surprised, shaking her head and scooting away from him. "I'm not sure I will be able to help…"

"Without you, there is no royal blood; thus, no one can take the throne. But if you return to your throne, you can overthrow Earnesh and his evil and restore Ailios. You can end the suffering of our people, Wrenley."

After that, it was silent between them, the air thick with tension. Eventually, Wrenley laughed nervously and stood up from the bed. She was beginning to feel hot and tossed her blanket off her shoulders. "This does sound like a fairytale," she said.

"If only it were," Bronson said, not even looking at her. He stared at the fire, his voice still cold. He laughed, but it was swollen with sadness. "You know, I loved the times I came to watch over you. It was indeed like a fairytale. You were…so happy. You didn't know what was happening. You were able to be a child and grow. If only your parents could have known you." Bronson's voice trailed off.

She looked at him, taking in his handsome features in the firelight. But he also looked weary. Bronson looked down at his mug and took a reluctant sip, his demeanor solemn. He moved slowly, seeming to focus on the tea and staring off into space. What had he gone through these last fifteen years? What kind of friend was he to her parents, to stay loyal, save her, and watch over her for all these years? She felt the walls he had erected around himself, blocking her ability to read him any more than what she already had.

"Why did you help them?" Wrenley tugged her sweater closer around her, looking down at her feet. "Why did you choose to do all of this for them?"

Bronson looked up, surprised. "They were my friends. I have known your mother since childhood and have served her family my whole life. Your father and I were bonded by magic. We learned how to be seers together. When you were born, it was the happiest day of my life. I was there on their wedding day, the day you were born. I was there when…" He trailed off, sadness returning to his voice.

"That's why she chose you? To…" Wrenley searched for the right words, "…to save me?"

Bronson shrugged, "Your mother chose me to take you to another world because, besides your father, I was the only one who knew how to do it. I chose to stay and watch, protect, and serve you." Bronson stood to his full height, looking down at Wrenley, "And I still do."

She felt her breath catch as she looked up at him. He was picturesque, and she realized that in the last twenty-four hours, she had grown to trust this man she knew absolutely nothing about. Wrenley did not know any other way to move forward but to trust him until he gave her a reason not to. She then noticed something else, and she straightened as she stood. She gasped and took a step. She tested her legs and was surprised to find that she was not in as much pain as before.

She looked back at him in astonishment, and Bronson grinned. "You will find that your body will change here. That disease doesn't exist in our world. Eventually, you should be able to move and walk without discomfort or pain."

CHAPTER 8

Company

The pair left the cave that afternoon, the sunlight making Wrenley wince. Wrenley was provided with appropriate clothing and a horse. Bronson also changed his modern clothing into more suitable clothing with a sword strapped to his back. He wore a dark tunic, black pants, and shiny black boots that came up to his knees. He also wore a long black jacket cut to hug his well-built frame. Wrenley tried not to stare at him, eyeing that massive sword warily and not even asking if he was expecting to have to use it.

Due to her illness, Wrenley had not ridden a horse in her world, but she was able to keep up after getting used to it. Not having the strength to swing her leg over the gigantic beast, Bronson propelled her up into the saddle. She could tell the muscles in her core were weak, and she was having difficulty staying upright without straining when the horse jerked to the side or stopped suddenly. But…it was quite an improvement.

It was rainy and cold. The heavy cloak she had dug out of the cave's chest of extra clothes seemed weatherproof. As Wrenley worked to cover herself with the cloak and reached to bring the hood over her head, Bronson gave Wrenley clear instructions: do not speak, whisper, or even look at anyone else. Bronson would handle all the talking. Wrenley would follow every word Bronson said and keep quiet if trouble arose.

"We are fugitives in this land. You, Wrenley…are the highest commodity of the evil forces. Every malevolent thing is on high alert for you, but they don't know you are here, so we at least have that to our benefit."

"Where are we going?" Wrenley asked above the sound of

heavy rain pelting them on the mountain road as they headed downward into the forest. Wrenley had gotten her horse to move faster, so she was beside him now, trying to keep up. She gritted through the pain in her core as she stayed parallel to Bronson.

"We need to find our company."

Wrenley was unsure who or what a company was, so she stayed quiet. Bronson usually seemed preoccupied with his musing, and she did not want to disturb him. They traveled down the mountain, and even with the rain and fog, Wrenley could not believe the beauty of this place. The forests were green and lush with giant trees that wound in and out amongst themselves. Roaring streams and waterfalls decorated the forest floors, and moss covered almost all the surfaces of the woods. When they entered the forest, the trees seemed to rise and form a canopy, blocking the rain from reaching them.

Wrenley tried to allow herself time to digest everything she had learned in the last few days as they rode. She recalled every single detail, trying to ignore her aching body. Just a week ago, she was a disabled spinster living in a conservative town as a closeted witch who had no intentions of moving out of her parents' house. She had been enjoying her simple life, or at least that is what she told herself. But then, Bronson showed up and turned her reality upside down. Now, she was a fugitive princess on a quest to save a kingdom that belonged to her magical, royal parents. These parents were also slaughtered by an evil deity who wanted to take her so he would have her bloodline powers. Running this scenario in her mind almost made Wrenley laugh out loud.

Once the sun sank, Wrenley was acutely aware of the darkness enveloping her and Bronson as they traveled silently through the forest. Wrenley felt her nervous system prickle as if it detected danger before her eyes or ears could sense it. She turned an ear to listen to the woods, the wind gently rustling the trees. The only sound was of their horses' hooves on the earth beneath them. Wrenley once again rode up to Bronson's side and whispered, "Are we safe traveling at night?"

"It's the safest way to travel," he murmured back, leaning over to her. "We don't want enemy spies to know where we go or what we do. The safest way is in the dark, though the dark has its challenges."

"Challenges?" Wrenley's eyes had grown accustomed to the dark now; her brows shot up in question as she searched Bronson's face. He did not turn his gaze at her but replied, "There are other dangers besides enemy forces, but I'll take that chance."

They rode for several more hours. Wrenley felt her body tiring, but she would not complain. Thanks to her cloak, she was cold but dry from the rain. She had too much adrenaline to be exhausted. Even with her chronic pain dissipating, every muscle in her body was throbbing, but she felt on high alert.

At one point, Bronson stopped in the middle of the road and held up a gloved hand. Wrenley had felt it, too; something was watching them from the forest. The hairs on Wrenley's neck stood up, and she felt gooseflesh break out over her arms. Something was not just watching them but hunting them.

~ ~ ~ ~ ~

Bronson felt tense as they rode deeper into the forest, his senses heightened with every step. He was keenly aware of something watching them from the undergrowth, but could not be sure what it was. It was not surprising, but he wished they could have passed unnoticed. It was just a matter of time before it showed itself, whatever it was out there.

Wrenley was quiet, and he was impressed by her ability to ride so long and hard, considering her inexperience. Seeing her profile in the forest's darkness was difficult, but he knew she was physically changing. Soon, every trace of her 'disease' would be gone, and she would have full function back in her legs and back. Her features also changed, though she would not notice it for a while. Crossing over from dimensions affected one physically, a phenomenon Bronson had handled throughout the years. He had spent much time and energy perfecting this form, so he would not change every time he crossed. Eventually, he would have to explain to her why her body was different here, but now was not the time for that conversation.

Bronson's mind went to the task: to get through the forest, find his company, and somehow move toward Ailios. There was no 'plan' yet, but the hope was to meet up with a large group of rebels who could offer protection as they traveled. Once they knew

Wrenley had returned, it would breathe new life into the exhausted forces of the insurgents. The rebellion was hiding all over the small continent, pockets of them intricately woven in and out of the land to press against Earnesh's forces as they attempted to squeeze the life out of the people. Earnesh could not have total power of the throne, but he could use his treacherous and brutal tactics to scare the population into submission, and he was doing a damn good job of it so far. He spared no life and had no mercy when it came to rebels.

Earnesh had initially recruited an army by bribing them with food, security, and favor, which would account for the human armies that ravaged the land. However, he had created another army from his dark magic, which spread across the countryside like a plague. Because of Earnesh's limited power, these mystical forces were being bred and developed in the capital. Bronson's spies could not get into the city or never returned, giving the rebellion no insight into their numbers.

Since the attempted colonization, a plethora of dark, magical beings had been released into the land, keeping a high alert, including their presence in these woods. Bronson could feel something just beyond his vision, something stalking them. They were being hunted, and Bronson almost missed the glowing red eyes out of his peripheral vision. He felt his stomach drop as his heart began to race.

~ ~ ~ ~ ~

"Go!"

Bronson slapped Wrenley's horse, whose massive frame reared, darting forward. Wrenley shrieked and held on tight, crouching as close to the big animal as possible so she would not fall off. The horse galloped under her, her teeth clacking together as it pounded down the dimly lit path.

"No matter what, don't look back and don't stop!" Bronson bellowed, riding parallel to her.

"What is it?" Wrenley screamed, but Bronson did not reply. They galloped hard for several minutes at an alarming speed before the path broadened, and they came to an opening in the forest. The trees seemed to fold back, allowing the moonlight in. The horses raised back and stopped, shifting and whining, almost screaming.

"Bronson, what…"

"Stay on your horse," Bronson commanded, swinging off his mare gracefully. He reached back in one fluid movement midair and drew the sword sheathed on his back. His legs swung out with unnatural strength, his black coat floating around him as he landed on the ground crouched, and reached out one hand to the ground between his legs to steady himself. Wrenley could not help but stare at him for a moment longer than she should have. Wrenley saw a warrior within the seer: powerful, deadly, and beautiful. He stood to his full height, his dusky eyes flickering up to the blackness surrounding them, his long black coat gently swaying in the breeze. She could see his free hand clench at his side; his face stone cold as he waited…but she was not sure for what.

"Fuck…" Wrenley muttered, attempting to control the horse underneath her. No matter how she maneuvered the reins, it still moved out of control, almost causing her to fall. "Come on now, work with me…" she quietly pleaded with the horse.

She then snapped her gaze up to notice the object of the horse's attention crawling out of the forest. The horses began to screech and whine more intensely, and Wrenley felt the panic flush over her as she saw it. It was a beast, but she was unsure what kind of beast it was. It was nothing like she had ever seen; maybe wolves, but they walked on their hind legs, backs crooked and bent forward, using their forearms for support. They had the head of a wolf but were half-human in appearance. Their black coats shimmered in the moonlight, their unnatural faces seeming to smile wickedly as if they were conscious and aware of the horse's fear. They must have been the size of a bear, an eerie, gut-wrenching sound rumbling out of them. Their eyes glowed red, creeping closer and closer to Bronson and Wrenley.

"They want the horses…" Bronson said slowly, grasping his sword with both hands now. Wrenley could hear the leather creak under his grip. "Wrenley, get off your horse."

Bronson appeared calm and collected, while Wrenley violently shook. She obeyed immediately, sliding down on the side closest to Bronson. She felt her legs wobble, maybe from riding all day or maybe from the fact that some horror story monsters were confronting her. She was not sure, but she wanted to vomit.

"Let the horses go…the creatures may chase after them if we're lucky." Bronson's voice was low and steady, but he did not take his eyes off the beasts before them. The thought of her beautiful horse being eaten by these ugly beasts made Wrenley's stomach turn, but she knew better than to disobey him, and she released her horse.

"There are two more behind us," Bronson positioned himself to fight, his stance wide, sword in front of him, raised parallel to his heart. He reached down and removed a hunting dagger from his boot. One arm held the sword aloft and pointed it at the most significant creature, his face stripped of all emotion; the other hand palmed his dagger, pointing to the left.

Wrenley let go of the reins, and the horses shifted but did not run.

"Shit…" Bronson said under his breath. "Wrenley, I need you to…"

Before he could finish his sentence, one of the beasts crawled towards them with a scream that made Wrenley fall to her knees. She covered her ears as she watched the creature launch at Bronson. Bronson quickly moved forward, sidestepping the animal and plunging his sword into its back near the spine. It yelped, and Bronson leaned in and twisted the blade; the creature squealed in pain and fell to the ground. Blood sprayed, and a metallic-rotting scent assaulted her nostrils. Another came from the side; Bronson kept one hand on the sword but waved his left hand with the dagger, and suddenly, the second beast flew backward as if something had crashed into him. Bronson then used the sword to propel himself up, using his dagger to slice another wolf in the throat.

Wrenley felt numb at the gruesome scene, but she could not tear her gaze away. She was frozen in the moment, fear seeming to have cemented her to the ground. When Bronson moved his body, sparks of light trailed after him. He appeared to twirl and fly, defying any physical laws as his whole body seemed to float in and out, arms moving in a graceful rhythm as he tore through the pack of beasts. It looked like he could move things with his mind, and every inch of exposed skin began to glow.

More wolves appeared, so many that Wrenley could not see Bronson now. They surrounded him; all she could see was his light from the middle of the pack. Wrenley jumped as she heard one of the horses' shrieks. She turned to see a wolf bring down her majestic horse and rip at its neck. The beast killed the horse with one crunch of its powerful jaw, tearing its throat out. The horse was only ten feet away, and Wrenley slowly moved backward, hoping her dark cloak would hide her from being so obvious to the creature, but she did not anticipate her feet getting tangled in her cloak. She fell backward on her ass with a thud, and the beast jerked its ugly head away from the horse and locked eyes with Wrenley. It was as if something was behind the blood-red eyes, an evil that was dark and ancient. Blood covered its face as if it had been drinking the blood from the horse's artery, and it grinned at her.

"Fuck...no," Wrenley mumbled as she scrambled to her feet. She had no idea where she was going, but she ran towards the forest. She was determined that she would not die this way, not to be torn apart by some monster. Limbs heavy and head spinning, she pushed herself to move forward, away from the screams and cries behind her. She heard the wolf getting closer and almost felt its feet stomp the ground behind her. She sensed its breath. She smelled it. The smell reeked of rotting flesh and decay. Wrenley cursed under her breath again and stumbled slightly, her skirt making it hard to run or climb a tree if she could make it to one alive.

Tripping again, she found herself face down in the mud, hitting her chin on a rock and biting through her lip. She cursed and slammed her arms down on the ground, angrier than she was hurt. She flung herself onto her back and froze; it was right there. The ugly wolf-like head was a foot away from her bleeding face, bloody drool falling in thick clumps from its hideous mouth. It stood up on its hind legs now and must have been six feet tall; its massive front legs had claws the size of daggers. It was smiling down at her, probably trying to figure out what she was and how it would start to devour her.

"You are young," he growled, and Wrenley gasped. Was it speaking to her, or was she so scared she was hallucinating?

The beast snickered deeply, a rumbling sound that tightened Wrenley's chest. He eyed her as if eating her was not the worst thing he could do. He growled again and moved closer...

"So young and so fresh," he grinned at her and leaned down to get closer, smelling her with his prominent nose. Wrenley was frozen in place, fear gripping her as she saw the red eyes, smelled the creature's stench, and felt the darkness oozing from it. She could not close her eyes but just stared into it…waiting for it to end her.

Suddenly, the beast arched his back, screamed, and flung himself on the ground. He writhed in pain, gurgling and rolling around frantically. Wrenley shook away the shock long enough to push away from her place on the ground and get back on her feet. She looked back to see the beast thrashing, its cries deafening, the sound turning her blood to ice.

"My lady?"

Wrenley looked up into a stranger's face, and she wanted to weep. She was unsure if he was a friend or foe, but anything was better than that beast. The stranger held out a hand, and Wrenley reached for it. He pulled her up beside him in one flowing motion, ensuring she was steady. He nocked an arrow in his bow and drew back to release it towards the dying beast at their feet. One shot through the top of the skull, and the wolf stilled.

"Stay close. We need to leave now."

"Bronson…" Wrenley yelled, but he reached an arm around her waist and pulled her along.

"…Bronson will be better off without worrying about you."

His tone was firm, his eyes darting back and forth as he pulled her behind him. She followed, not sure what was right or wrong at this point. The stranger led her through the clearing, firing arrows with ease and accuracy as they ran. Arrow after arrow, he pulled from the quiver and launched, every arrow hitting its mark with precision and effectiveness. It was the closest thing to a battle scene Wrenley had ever witnessed, a group of men now yelling and attacking the beasts, but she could not see Bronson. They made it across the clearing and out of the moonlight, where a large horse waited. The stranger quickly heaved Wrenley into the saddle and pulled himself behind her.

They left the clearing and headed deeper into the woods. Wrenley tried to look back for a glimpse of Bronson, but she could not see anything, not even his light. They rode hard until the noise of the battle was inaudible, as if the trees and foliage soaked up the dreadful sounds of yelps, screams, and death. The forest became denser with undergrowth, and soon the stranger motioned for Wrenley to slide off, and he followed behind her. They silently traveled by foot for what seemed like an eternity, with him gently guiding the horse through the thick vegetation. The horse seemed to have to bend down to fit into tight places on the path. Wrenley followed in silence; the moon was now hidden from them. Her surroundings were almost swallowed in pitch blackness. She silently prayed to any god who would listen that she would not get lost out here, sweat beading on her brow despite the cool temperatures. A clearing was in view, and Wrenley nearly fell into it. The stranger grabbed her and kept her from tumbling forward.

"Are you okay?" He asked, draping the bow over one shoulder, gently grabbing her arms, and examining her for injuries as he pulled her along. She was covered in mud mixed with blood from her lips and chin, the copper tang tainted by the mouthful of soil she managed during her stumble.

"You are injured!" The man seemed alarmed, his brow furrowing deeply as he grabbed her chin for a closer examination.

"Where are we?" Wrenley finally choked out, her adrenaline subsiding enough for fear to creep back in. She pulled away from his hold on her chin. "Where is Bronson?"

"He's fine. That pack is child's play for him," He waved his hand to the side, still scrutinizing her as if he was not convinced she was okay, then muttered, "He'll be here soon."

Wrenley noticed that the clearing had turned into a campsite, complete with a large fire and several tents. The stranger guided Wrenley to a log positioned by the fire and sat her down. He let the horse go to fend for itself as he settled Wrenley and gathered supplies. He then kneeled in front of her to clean the gash on her lip.

"Wow, that's a wee cut you have there," he had an accent, but nothing Wrenley had ever heard before. He retrieved a bowl of clean water and linens and gently cleaned the wound. "I'm not a seer or healer, but this doesn't look too bad now."

She studied the man who frowned in concentration, his wavy, grown-out red hair matching his trimmed beard. She would guess he was her age, maybe a few years older. She marveled at his tenderness, not only wiping away the muck from her face, but also his soft words. He was slimmer than Bronson, as if built for stealth and sneaking into places unnoticed.

"Where is Bronson?" Wrenley asked, finally feeling as if she would lose her mind. She had kept her shit together up until now, but her composure was slipping. She stood, shoving away his hands, and pushed the stranger back as he tried to reach out to keep her in her seat.

"Whoa, easy…"

"I need to…to…" She felt the panic, which washed over her like a wave crashing against the shoreline with immense force. Her chest began to ache, and her breath became shallow as she clutched at her throat, "I need to…"

"You need to sit down, my lady."

"Would you stop calling me that!" She screeched now, clenching her fists at her ears and bending over, feeling as if she would pass out. She felt her throat closing in on her. The blackness in the forest was sneaking in around the edges of her vision, and she was terrified it would take her. She finally straightened, the dizziness almost unbearable.

"I want some fucking answers, and I want to know what the goddamn fuck is going on right now!" Wrenley felt like a child, stomping her foot, thrashing her arms, and letting out a string of obscenities that would put a sailor to shame. She could imagine the sight of her; her hair wild, blood oozing from her chin, covered in mud and dirt, and wearing some ridiculous clothing that was nearly the cause of her being eaten by a werewolf beast. She felt the injustice of her predicament seize her, and she allowed her fury to flow freely from her mouth with a continuing string of curse words.

The stranger froze, still holding his hands in front of him in amity. He raised his red eyebrows at her, whether it was shock or concern, but she was unsure and did not care. She noticed as he leaned over to look beyond her shoulder. Wrenley flung around and gasped as Bronson and several other men emerged from the tree line, coming from the thick foliage of the brush. She eyed his blood-spattered face, sweat dripping from his brow, but with a heavy sigh of relief, she determined he was not injured. He looked like shit, but he grinned at her, sliding a cloth along the bloody blade of his sword and sheathing it on his back.

His face fell, replaced with a scowl as he noticed the blood on her chin and what must have been the look of pure terror on her face. She covered her mouth with her hands to stifle a sob as he approached her. Wrenley fell into his arms, her legs feeling like rubber and her shoulders sagging with relief. He scooped her up in his arms and carried her to the privacy of his tent.

~ ~ ~ ~ ~

Bronson examined Wrenley's bruised face, carefully touching it to see where it was damaged. She grimaced but tried to hold still, thankful that she had not lost a tooth during the whole debacle; that would have been the icing on the damn cake. Bronson was gentle and skilled, narrowing his eyes as he grasped her chin and turned her head one way and then the other.

She pulled away from him, swatting his hands away. "I'm fine. I tripped like a dumb ass and hit my face…he cleaned it already." She jerked her head to the man outside the tent by the fire, talking to other rebels. She had felt bad for snapping at him, but what did he expect from her? She pushed down the guilt and shame of her breakdown and tried to scoot away from Bronson's intense scrutiny.

"It's still very swollen," Bronson finally said, refusing to release her chin, and continued to use clean water and a cloth to wipe away the dried blood since it had broken open again. "All you need is a little bacterium for one hell of an infection. Your immune system has not adjusted to this realm yet."

Great. That's all she needed—an infection. Then her lip and jaw would rot off…. She would become septic and die a horrible, long death. Her spiraling thoughts were interrupted as Bronson reached to frame her face with both hands.

"Whoa!" Wrenley yelped and almost fell backwards when Bronson reached out and covered her chin and face with his large hand, a warm, tingling feeling pulsing through her face. A soft light travelled down his arm, through his fingers, and Wrenley could feel it envelop the gash on her chin and lip. She froze, motionless, until the light dimmed. Once his fingers ceased to glimmer, Bronson removed his large, rather handsome hand from her lips.

"What did you just do?" She whispered, and Bronson smirked and leaned back, as if admiring his handiwork. "I told you, I am a healer and a seer. You, my lady, are lucky enough to have an incredibly handsome and talented one."

Wrenley rolled her eyes, but her hand shot up to touch her lip; it was still sore, but not nearly as much, as the crusty scab had almost disappeared. She made an 'oh' with her mouth, and Bronson grinned again, standing to wash his hands in a basin.

"What were they?" Wrenley asked finally after a few moments of silence between them.

Bronson sighed, "Wolves...big wolves."

"Are they fucking werewolves?"

Bronson sniffed in amusement, "I guess you could call them that. They live in the deep forests under the mountains. They are a product of Earnesh's dark power that he unleashed fifteen years ago. I had hoped we would slip by unnoticed. In your world, I suppose you would call them werewolves, but here they don't care about the moon cycle and don't shape-shift like your world's folklore. That's how they are, full moon or not: ugly bastards that like to eat anything that has a pulse."

Wrenley shuddered again but looked past Bronson at the stranger.

"Who's that?" She nodded her now-healed chin in his direction, and Bronson followed her gaze.

"That is Garrick, my closest friend and a captain in the resistance."

"Trustworthy?"

Bronson turned his body to level her with his chestnut eyes and a low voice, "I trust him not only with my life but yours. If you trust anyone else in this miserable war, it will be Garrick."

As if on cue, Garrick came forward, bending to enter the tent, and bowed before Wrenley, which made her uncomfortable. He wore faded pants and boots, a tattered white shirt, and a hat that reminded her of Robin Hood with a white feather sticking out. She looked at him intently, shifting uneasily as he took her hand and gently kissed it.

"My lady, my lads and I are at your service."

"Wrenley, daughter of King Dolion and Queen Adinnil, please meet our company," he opened the tent flaps wider so Wrenley could peer out into the bustling camp. There must have been at least twenty men, some sitting around their fires, some cleaning their weapons, others brushing their horses. Garrick continued, "These people have been faithful to the throne and have surrendered their lives to serve your cause. They will travel with us and defend you with their lives if need be."

"Unfortunately, that is very likely…" Bronson murmured, reaching to rub the back of his neck with one hand, and took a seat on a stool next to Wrenley. "Garrick's company was upwards of a hundred men before the enemy began picking them off in skirmishes over the last year. There are twenty-five of them left now, and I fear we will lose more before the end."

A tightness gripped Wrenley, a shooting sorrow raking through her body at Bronson's words. So many lives lost…so many families devastated…she could not bear to even think about it. How was she to be the one thing to change the tide of this war? She took in the busy camp, the sunken, hollow faces of these men who had been fighting and on the run for who knows how long. A weight like a boulder settled in her gut, and she was unsure that it would not paralyze her.

~ ~ ~ ~ ~

To Wrenley's disdain, it was even colder in the forest than in the mountains. Wrenley lay in the tent, sheltered from the wind and the drizzle, but she was still freezing. She had concluded that the adrenaline had worn off completely by now, and she felt the hostile chill for the first time since leaving the cave. She shook so hard that her teeth chattered, her hands and feet numb.

She missed her warm library and the big bed and breakfast. It could get drafty in the immense house, but it was always cozy. She would sit by the fire, read her favorite book, drink a glass of wine, and snuggle under her blanket with her slippers. Here, there was nothing of home for her to hang onto, and that was probably the worst part for her. She was alone here in this new dimension, with nothing to tie her back to her home.

"It s-seems like ages ago," she whispered into the dark to no one in particular as she struggled to manage her clanking teeth. Her voice shook as she tried to move her frozen lips to form the words.

"It's a difficult adjustment between worlds, but you will adapt."

Wrenley jumped at Bronson's voice, looking to see him leaning over her, holding a mug with steaming liquid. "I brought you some broth. I heard your teeth chattering from out there." He attempted a half grin, but Wrenley thought she detected worry lining his eyes as he looked down at her.

Wrenley took the liquid, whispering a weak "thanks" as Bronson sat beside her.

"Our world is cold," Bronson murmured, groaning as he settled on the ground. "I find that it gets easier to acclimate as I cross from one world to the next, but I'm also getting older."

"You're not that old."

"Maybe not in years, but I suspect traveling has aged me more than I want to admit." Bronson stretched his neck and rounded his shoulders, humming with the effort as if he were aching. Wrenley grunted as she sipped the warm broth, still studying the man next to her. Bronson's taking on a pack of wild wolves hours before contradicted that he was old or out of shape.

"Will you allow me to help?" Bronson looked at her now, and she nodded, though she had no idea how he could. Bronson peeled several layers of clothing off his torso and tossed them aside. He then hoisted off his tunic and undershirt. Stripping down to his pants, he told Wrenley to sit forward as he sat behind her, his legs on either side. He then covered them both with a heavy blanket.

"Lean back against me."

She did, propriety be damned as she almost moaned as she absorbed his warmth. He wrapped his arms around her, and she began to feel limp and sleepy as the cold began to dull. She did not care how awkward it was to lean against his muscular chest; she was freezing, and he was radiating heat. She would steal every ounce of it she could from him.

"Your body will adjust to the cold. Now that you are here, we may see the sun more," he almost mumbled it into her hair, and she shifted in his arms.

"Why?" Wrenley looked over her shoulder at him, confused.

"Because you are the royalty of this land. The elements know you are here…or they will when we draw nearer to the capital city. But until then, you will have to stay warm. If you fall asleep in such cold conditions, you may not wake up. Let me help you if I need to…understand?"

Wrenley nodded, leaning her head against him and feeling how relaxed she became. His voice left no room for questioning. She supposed she should fight it; to refuse to be so comfortable and tranquil in his arms, but she simply did not care.

"It's okay to go to sleep," Bronson whispered in her hair again, but she did not nod or acknowledge him. She felt like she should fight falling asleep, but was too exhausted to succeed. There was nowhere safer than in the arms of this man Wrenley had only known for the last week. She felt like it had been longer than that as she reflected on their journey together so far. Was she a fool to relax momentarily and allow her body to heal? Maybe it was her loneliness or his magic, but she felt her body absorb into his, reacting in a way that was unfamiliar. Her parents had trusted him, she reminded herself, enough for her to drift off into a deep sleep.

CHAPTER 9

The Unseen

Bronson felt her drift off, body slumping against him, and she began to snore quietly. He smiled and felt himself finally relax around her, knowing she would probably not wake up until morning. They were safe deep inside the woods under the mountain, and for the first time since they crossed over, he felt like he could sleep knowing Garrick and his company were watching over them.

Bronson was torn between moving or staying in this position with her, even though he felt every fiber of his being wanting to stay. She was so cold; however, he did not feel right about having her so close. He could not ignore the attraction he had felt sparking in him since he walked into her life a week ago. It had happened before that, if he were honest with himself, maybe even the last year? Maybe two? He had watched her grow up from an infant, and he remembered how difficult it was to see her transition from a child to a teenager, and then suddenly, she was a woman. Within the last five years, Bronson began to see her differently; she was beautiful, funny, and intelligent, not to mention the key to salvation for their people — his people.

And as she grew rapidly, Bronson was frozen in time. She had changed drastically, and he stayed the same, stuck in a nightmare of war and ruin. He may have aged fifteen years, but he remained trapped in grief and pain for her mother and father, mourning a life that he had loved. He traveled back and forth so many times from a dark, war-torn realm to her bright, beautiful world. He remembered that he would be so jealous of her life, as she was unaware of the pain and suffering of her people and her kingdom. His resentment grew to the point where he became angry at her for being ignorant of all the suffering. He would never confess it out loud, but he had been so furious at her in her teenage years that he had stopped coming. She was young, a stupid adolescent full of attitude and drama, and he was fed up with the way he perceived her taking life for granted while his friends were butchered and hung on the gates of villages and cities for the crows to pick at their carcasses.

It was more than that though; every time he looked at Wrenley, he saw Adinnil, and he was angry...so goddamn angry he had to pick between one or the other that day. It was easier to blame Wrenley than to forgive himself for not saving her mother or father. He stayed away for several years. When he returned, the little brat had been gone, and a woman took her place. The years away from her almost killed him...but he made the sorry excuse that the resistance needed him too much to take the time to check on her. It was only when he received intelligence that Earnesh might have had a seer who could cross the veil that he knew she needed to come home—to her land, to her people...to him.

She had experienced the magic, but she did not know it. As she grew, she had sensed him there in the shadows. On the cool nights of October, he often traveled to her when the veil was thin between the worlds, and she would walk the halls of that old house, welcoming the ghosts, shadows, and the unknown. Her spirit was sweet and innocent, without judgment toward the travelers that brushed against her dimension. Just as she welcomed the guests who visited the bed and breakfast, she welcomed other visitors in the unseen with grace and understanding. Her capability for love and acceptance stole his heart.

The magic increased as she physically developed, and the people of her world became less understanding. She had begun to suffer, and the doctors of her world called her 'crazy' or other nonsense. She heard the voices, she sensed the supernatural, and they gave her medicine to try and mask it, but it had peeked in adulthood while he had been away.

Her adoptive parents let it happen, not that they had much of a choice. He had commanded Ruth and Jim to send her away to other family and friends during the months when the veil was thinnest, to ensure no one would find her. He had begun to miss her during those weeks and months that she was away. She eventually refused to leave her home after turning eighteen. She never left to attend college like her friends. She stayed, tied to that place, as if she knew she had to stay close to it; close to him.

There had been times when he toyed with the idea of staying by her side, away from Ailios and the war. He could live in her world away from this misery and pain that was relentlessly sucking the life from him day after day. He could allow the memories of his king, queen, and friends to disappear and be in a world where only Wrenley existed. Yet, his heart throbbed against the promise he made to Adinnil. The memory of his queen's mangled, naked body on display on the city gates—her city—made him return time after time. The oath to destroy Earnesh and see Wrenley back on the throne compelled every step he took. The reminiscence of the pain and suffering of his brothers and sisters…the torture, hunger, and devastation to his people, made him come back again and again.

Instead, Bronson remained suspended in time and space, a nomad in the dimensions, pining for something long lost and almost impossible to regain. At this moment, with his arms wrapped around the woman who snored softly, something seemed different, obtainable, maybe? It was only in the last few years that he had fallen for Wrenley. Bronson knew that his feelings for her were complicated; did he even have a right to feel this way? Her father was his closest friend, and Bronson had promised his queen that he would care for her for the rest of his life, to be her guardian as long as he had breath in him. Was it wrong for him to want more than that? He was determined she must not know of this all right now; she was barely hanging on as it was.

Bronson's breath caught when he looked down and spied the silver pendant hanging around her neck; it had belonged to her mother. Adinnil had given it to him as he held the crying infant in his arms. The sight of the necklace made tears form and fall from his tired eyes, and he wept in Wrenley's hair, holding her just a little bit tighter as the memories flooded him. She felt heavy against him, and he leaned his head back, closing his eyes to attempt to stop the tears. He knew that every bit of this situation was complicated. He was a seer, and his magic was connected to all the seers, whether he liked it or not. He took a risk using his power tonight, but it was either use his power or Wrenley possibly being eaten alive. Luckily, Garrick and his men had come in time.

Wrenley was, by blood, the most powerful person in the kingdom, and she had no idea. It was evident to Bronson that Wrenley did not realize her importance or power. She was considered ordinary and insignificant in her world thanks to the shield of magic he had woven around her. Purposely, he had dulled her beauty and spelled her body to collapse on itself; that way, if someone had gotten through the veil without him knowing, they would not have been able to see her, at least not right away. She probably could not comprehend her worth right now and would never forgive him when she learned what he had done to protect her, but that was a problem for another day.

Anything related to her would be highly noticeable in the unseen, magic, and elements. It was only a matter of time before the enemy would sense she was here. He tightened his grip around her waist, and he heard her sigh. He did not know what the journey would be like, but he knew he had to ensure she would be safe. Bronson knew his feelings for her were risky. He had to be more guarded. He would have to protect her even more now that they were in his world. He would stay away from her as much as he could, avoiding any flare in the unseen…even now his magic stirred under his skin at her closeness to him. He would put distance between them, and she would have to learn to survive, just like they all had. After all the thoughts and memories tumbled through his brain, he allowed himself to sleep then, knowing the days ahead would not be easy.

CHAPTER 10

Finley

It was explained to Wrenley that the journey would be long and hard, and she accepted that this would not be pleasant for anyone, regardless of whether she was royalty. Between the mountains and the gates of the capital city of Ailios, they would face an array of barriers. They would have to ride hard and face both natural and magical elements; they would be riding into areas of conflict and war, and be subjected to angry citizens who knew Bronson had a price on his head. Evil forces would be on high alert for anything unusual, and Wrenley was very much out of the ordinary.

"Have you ever used a weapon before?" Garrick asked slowly, watching her with a hint of dismay as she tripped over her feet and grinned up at the men. She was still adjusting to having full use of her legs and back. The pain had subsided, and her muscles were regaining strength. Bronson and Garrick stood motionless, arms crossed in front of them in consternation. Garrick rubbed a hand over his face, and Bronson inwardly cringed at Wrenley's clumsiness, knowing it could get her killed.

"Okay, well, let's go over some basics," Garrick tried to sound confident, throwing her a miniature sword and clapping his hands together. "I've trained greener men than you."

Wrenley was able to catch the sword but yelped as she grasped it. She flipped it over and eyed it, shrugging, "Mom bought me a taser once. I never had to use it, though."

"What is a taser?"

Bronson waved off Garrick's confusion and moved close to help Wrenley with her grip. "The hope is you will never have to fight hand to hand, but if you do, you must be ready. Garrick will teach you."

"Why can't you teach me?" Wrenley looked up at Bronson with those soft hazel eyes under thick lashes, and he sucked in a breath. Her face was turning yellow and purple as her bruise began to heal. He noticed that her features were still changing, and her lips were filling out; the spell was lifting from her a little more each day. She looked at him curiously and intrigued, and he felt his magic stir. He knew he had to be careful; he could not cause them any distractions or unnecessary attention, but the way she looked up at him...*fuck*. It was every bit a distraction for him.

"Garrick can teach you. I have better things to do," Bronson snapped and walked away from them, feeling her eyes watching him as he forced each leg to move him away from her. He felt a pang of guilt, but he had to put space between them. Not only did he have to think clearly to protect her, but if anything happened between them, it would put both of them at risk. If someone were to investigate the unseen, they could use magic to locate her.

~ ~ ~ ~ ~

Wrenley watched Bronson move away and shook her head in confusion; the hurt stung her just a little. She tried not to read too much into his sharp reply, taut face, and tense body, but it was difficult. Had she done something wrong? She looked at Garrick, his green eyes smiling, and he shrugged, "My lady, let's teach you how to fight."

She practiced all day, fumbling with her newfound freedom to move and twist about like she had not done in years. She could barely remember when it was painless to stand or sit, and though she was still clumsy, she grinned at her new capability. Garrick was a patient teacher; however, she doubted she would be asked to defend the front lines anytime soon, probably never. The sword was too heavy, and her coordination was lacking. She knew Garrick could put her on her ass in a heartbeat, but he took pity on her.

Wrenley did not see Bronson at all during the day, and after the tenth time of catching her looking for him, clearly distracted, Garrick informed her that Bronson was out scouting ahead. Bronson returned late that night, and he did not come to check on her. Not that she needed him to; she was warmer now and no longer needed him to be her heater. Still, she wanted him close, and she realized she felt lonely. He was her only friend in this world, and one day away from him made her uneasy.

Wrenley observed the company of outlaws around her who looked ragged and worn, but she could tell they were passionate about their fight. They had given up their families, livelihoods, and homes to rise against the injustice their people were facing. Many of them were wanted men, and their families were killed or tortured in an attempt to flush them out. Every one of them had seen their comrades mercilessly slaughtered, yet they remained faithful.

The somber reality gripped Wrenley that the men remained loyal to her, to the bloodline, her parents, and the cause. She still struggled to understand why they would risk everything for a royalty who had been missing for over a decade. Perhaps it was the same reason she stayed: the hope of a better future for everyone and the possibility that she could make a difference.

~ ~ ~ ~ ~

The journey officially began the next day. Their party consisted of twenty-five men, all of them 'Forest People' from what Garrick had shared with her earlier that morning. They all talked and looked like him, and when Wrenley asked him about it, he said that Bronson had a different accent because of his 'travels'. Wrenley was unsure if Garrick knew the extent of Bronson's travels, so she did not mention it.

"Where are the forest ladies?" Wrenley asked, unable to avoid the feeling of a deep void of other females in the company. Wrenley never had many friends, but she always had Ruth. Here, she felt like she was an alien to them all.

Garrick sighed, "Hidden. They are scattered in the forest, so Earnesh's forces can't find them, and if they are scattered, they cannot all be killed at once. The men go to their families when they can."

"Do you have a family?"

Wrenley saw something like pain on his face, but he shrugged. "Maybe, but not really."

"No one?"

Garrick nodded curtly, his body visibly stiffening. Her eyebrows raised; she did not know what this reaction was about, but he was not divulging any more information by the way his lips tightened into a thin line.

She quickly dropped it, seeing his discomfort. Garrick was visibly guarded, and guilt washed over her. What did he have to sacrifice for this? Which… had she not done the same? She had to leave her mother, father, and life to come here. She supposed this was the price of this venture they were undertaking, the quest they were on. She knew she could not disappoint them, for their sake and her own. She had to be what they needed her to be, even if she was unsure of what that was. Yet, she was determined to find out and go above and beyond for these people. She would not, could not… let them down.

Garrick was handsome but gruff, more rough around the edges than Bronson. He had a lazy grin and was not easily upset. He was patient and kind to her when she struggled during their travels. Wrenley was under the impression that he was Bronson's right-hand man and held a place of respect with the seer. Garrick's red-trimmed beard gleamed in the sun, his nose was pointed and strong, and his jaw was firmly set. Usually, he had a pleasant smile or grin on his face, which is why his change of demeanor was curious.

They rode hard the first few days, and Wrenley did her best to keep up without complaining. She had felt weaker lately, and she supposed it was due to the long days of riding, the variety of foods, and overall stress. Bronson continued to be distant. When they interacted, he was short and preoccupied. She noticed he avoided eye contact, offered no words of comfort to her, even as her own tired eyes pleaded for him to see how fatigued she was becoming. The kind and considerate Bronson she had known when they crossed over was fading, making her intuition flinch. It was a fight for Wrenley not to give in to the panic that fluttered in her chest at the insecurity it stirred.

As the days passed in a blur, Wrenley felt her strength waning. She noticed herself beginning to turn inward, spending so much of her time daydreaming about home and her bed and breakfast that she would completely forget about the present. She had enough self-awareness to recognize that she was sad most of the time, a dark cloud of depression settling over her that she was unable to share, no matter how hard she tried. She began to eat less, and her sleep was fitful. She would chide and demand herself to 'snap out of it,' but to no avail, despite her constant efforts. She felt as if her head were just above water, and she was drowning.

Wrenley failed to understand the extent of the war's devastation until they passed through village after village affected by the enemy. She covered her face to hide her identity as well as to but stifle the smell of flesh and sewage that occupied most villages and makeshift tent cities. Homes had been burned, and people were living in slums, with no clean water, and hardly any game left to hunt. Wrenley forced herself not to cry as she rode past their hollow, vacant expressions and hungry faces.

Wrenley was instructed not to interact with anyone while they traveled through the countryside. She obeyed, but the guilt she collected with every suffering soul she passed weighed down on her. They were hurrying across a large stretch of open terrain when they came upon the run-down tent city, the worst she had seen. Hundreds of civilians were left to freeze in the harsh winter weather with little more than a sheet covering them for shelter.

Wrenley pulled her horse to an abrupt halt as she gasped, looking down at a child who had wandered into her horse's path. The girl had the same empty eyes as everyone else. Her clothes were filthy, ragged, and not warm enough for the bitter wind that ripped through the village. Her feet were purple and bare, probably frostbitten. The girl appeared to be sixteen, but with the body of a twelve-year-old. Wrenley presumed it was because there was no food. The girl looked up at her with sunken cheekbones and hollow eyes, her hair stringy and clinging to her delicate scalp. The girl did not make a sound but looked up at Wrenley with a blank, despairing expression. A muffled sob exhaled from Wrenley, and she slid off her horse before Garrick could grab her arm. Rummaging through her backpack, she retrieved the cardigan she had brought with her from home.

She trudged through the muck and the mud towards the child, opening the sweater to wrap around the girl, when a strong hand clasped around her arm and flung her around. Bronson pulled her close, his hand squeezing her arm so hard it almost hurt, and leaned down to whisper in her ear.

"What the hell are you doing?" His teeth were clenched, his voice uncharacteristically rough. His tone made her flinch. Bronson had been distant but never cruel or mean. His voice held a hint of heartlessness that made her blood run cold.

"She needs clothes." Wrenley jerked her arm away from him, but he reached for her shoulder with his other hand. "You are drawing too much attention to us. Get back up on the horse, goddammit." He squeezed her shoulder so tightly she almost winced.

"Bronson, this child will die in this cold...let me give this to her." She felt her chin raise in defense. For the first time, she felt anger towards this man.

"I thought we agreed that you would listen to me without question. You listen to me; you stay alive and safe." He was visibly angry now, his face sullen, his nostrils flaring. He was irritated that Wrenley was bucking at his request, but she did not care.

"Bronson..." Wrenley's eyes were pleading now. Her voice quivered as she spoke, looking up at his unmoving chestnut eyes. "She's just a child...let me help her."

"And have her tortured because she has an item that could be traced back to you? Because it could be, you know. The truth is..." Bronson lowered his voice again, grabbed Wrenley's arm, and forcefully pulled her along. "The truth is, Wrenley, the child will most likely die anyway of hunger or disease. I don't want you to get too close and risk being infected. Stop playing hero and let this go."

Wrenley wrenched herself away, looking at him with disbelief and horror. "I didn't think of that..."

"Of course you didn't, because you don't fucking listen to me," his hand was shoving her back towards the horse now, him standing between her and the girl. "You have no idea about our ways, our suffering...our people..." His hand encircled her arm, and he squeezed harder.

And there it was...just a glimpse of the resentment against her he had harbored for all these years. She had assumed that having her so detached from this cruel world was difficult for him, but she saw it clearly now. Was he angry that she had not suffered along with him? What did he want from her? She had not asked for this life; she had not asked to be born at all. Gently, a seed of distrust was planted deep down in the soil of her heart, and she felt a single root take hold in her chest. Wrenley gawked at him, anger suddenly replacing the hurt.

"So, she isn't worth our time? Our compassion?" Wrenley hissed through her teeth; she could hear the ice in her voice, and Bronson stiffened. She stood up just a little straighter and planted her feet firmly in the mud.

"I may not know your ways, but I know the look of death when I see it. I may be the oblivious, sheltered princess who hasn't been able to be here for the last decade…" She ripped her arm away from him one last time and held up one finger to warn him not to reach again when he moved toward her.

"You think I don't see it in your eyes? In the faces of your men?"

Bronson did not reject her words; the only confirmation that he heard her was a single blink.

Wrenley shook her head at him. "I am here now, and I can help to make up for all the time I wasn't even though none of this was my goddamn fault. You can blame me and try to punish me all you want, Bronson, but it isn't going to change a single thing."

Bronson dipped his head, "Wrenley, that's not what I was saying…"

"Oh, I think it is." Wrenley clenched her teeth tightly and looked up to meet his gaze, her voice rough and husky. "Just because she is a poor village girl, should we let fate happen? Only royalty who are good for something are worthy of saving? Maybe you've forgotten, seer, that I was the invisible girl for years, dying of an illness, with no control over my damn life." She leaned forward to him then, her voice dripping with animosity, "If I weren't a princess, you wouldn't have given me a second fucking look, and that's not how I want to be."

Bronson's gaze turned from anger to what may have been guilt, but Wrenley looked away, refusing to meet his stare again. She had no idea what trouble her gesture would cause this innocent child, but she had decided it did not matter. The child would not be invisible, at least not to Wrenley. She trudged past Bronson and Garrick, wrapping the sweater around the child and drawing the girl in for a gentle squeeze.

"What's your name?" Wrenley whispered, taking in the matted hair, the dirty face, and beautiful hazel eyes much like hers. The girl looked at her, taking a ragged breath and drawing the sweater around her bony shoulders as she replied, "Finley."

Her voice was just above a whisper, floating to land on Wrenley's heart as she felt a tear stinging her eyes. "Well, Finley, nice to meet you."

The girl shifted and gave Wrenley a ghost of a smile, her thin lips turning up ever so slightly at the corners of her mouth. Even though she knew Bronson may have a valid point, she hated him for it. How could he walk away from a child in the middle of the road? How could his heart be so cold and calloused that it was just another death? It made her wonder what else he had done in his war…what other atrocities had he seen or even committed in the name of preservation? If things were as bleak as Bronson made them out to be, then this girl would die anyway, and she would do it with a goddamn sweater covering her.

Wrenley gave the girl a reassuring smile and retreated to her horse. She shoved her backpack into Bronson's chest with all her strength as she passed him, but he did not budge. Bronson tried to help her into her saddle with one hand on her elbow, but she used her shoulder to force him away. She lifted herself on her horse and galloped away from where he stood, only slightly ashamed of how she acted towards him. She looked at no one as she galloped past the frail girl now clutching Wrenley's sweater, too overcome with the reality of their world, desperation covering her like a blanket. Wrenley knew she would never forget that face, those eyes, that name for as long as she lived.

CHAPTER 11

The River

The incident caused such a rupture between Wrenley and Bronson that she refused to even look at him, and he did the same to her. Something had changed the moment she saw such coldness in his features, the lack of warmth and empathy she had come to trust when they first crossed over. She could not shake the image of that girl from her mind, with her apparent lack of will to live and a faint hope that something might improve, but accepting it would likely never happen. That look now haunted her in her dreams: Finley's malnourished body standing in the road, clutching the sweater. Truthfully, what did she expect from a man who had been to war for over a decade? That was likely the least terrible thing he had done, and it made Wrenley ache. It was a stark reality that she was in over her head.

The rift was so evident that Garrick and the men avoided each of them, Bronson more than Wrenley. He had not berated her or yelled after, but if looks could kill, she would be dead. She kept away from him and continued spiraling into the bottomless dark pit of her mind. With the way they demanded that she obey every order, she felt more like a prisoner than royalty. Whether it was physical wariness or mental exhaustion, she felt like she was deteriorating. No one seemed to care or notice, and she would be damned before asking any one of them for help. Wrenley leaned on the strength of becoming small, invisible, so no one would have a chance to call her weak.

Two weeks of travel brought them to the thick forest region in the lowlands. This area was more populated, so they stayed off the roads. Wrenley could not believe the physical effort it took to push through the foliage, trees slapping at her face. Cuts and bruises appeared on her cheeks, forearms, and legs as she used her body to press onward. Her muscles screamed in protest, but she kept moving, refusing to let anyone see her slacken or fall behind. Bronson had made some off-handed comment about the company needing to move faster and tossed an annoyed look back at Wrenley. She gritted her teeth and gave him the middle finger as soon as he turned away.

Wrenley replayed the words he had jousted at her days before in the village: *You have no idea about our ways, our suffering...our people...*

The barb hit her where it hurt, and she flinched even now as she replayed the underlying meaning of it. She may have been the long-lost heir, the princess who returned to save them all, but she did not belong. She was a stranger in this land, to these people...they would never accept her kindness, efforts, or sacrifice without the bitter realization that she had not suffered as they had. Somehow, that made her less qualified to be a queen...which, they could add that to the fucking list. She already knew this was a mistake, that she was never meant to be the ruler of a realm and save the dimension from despair and ruin. She knew she was not cut out for this and was merely a commodity. The thought of Bronson thinking that way of her, the one person she thought was her friend, was crushing. She was now impeccably alone in this dimension; he may be her guardian, but he was not her friend.

"I didn't ask for this..." she muttered to herself continually when the thoughts threatened to take over. She forced her mind to think about the bed and breakfast with Nyx sleeping on the bookshelf in the library. Her mind traveled to different realities and scenarios, one where she was valued and understood for who she was. At times, she even considered escaping, but where would she go?

They had to travel slowly and methodically, which took more time. Wrenley began to feel more fatigued, which she would never admit. She was determined not to be the feeble one in their group, and she would never allow Bronson to see her struggle, so he would not have to save her ever again. She would rather die than let him help her, she decided. She and Bronson had not shared a single word since the incident with the child. He would acknowledge her with a nod and then move on, always speaking in low tones with Garrick or wandering off alone. She also did not attempt to talk to him and kept to herself. Garrick endeavored to have a conversation with them separately, but Wrenley did not participate. Garrick was the only one who made her eat, and she barely ate enough to pacify him.

After she noticed her pants and tunic were getting bigger, she realized something was wrong with her. Her mind was in a dark place, and it was hard to think. She consumed less water and food and could hardly sleep. Wrenley kept her eyes on the forest, sure they were being followed or watched. She also felt like she saw shadows out of the corner of her eye, and she would see figures darting in and out of the shadows. One moment they would be there, the next they would be gone. She wanted to tell Bronson and have him reassure her that they were safe, but her pride would not allow it.

~ ~ ~ ~ ~

"She's not eating or drinking, Bronson…" Garrick said quietly as they paused for a break one afternoon. "You need to do something."

"She's fine…" Bronson gritted his teeth, chewing on an apple as he slid down a tree truck to sit on the ground.

"I don't think she is…"

"She's a spoiled brat, Garrick. Plus, she has room to lose a little; she's not a skeleton."

Garrick winced at the harsh words and looked at him, the disappointment in his eyes evident as Bronson looked away. Bronson felt horrible about saying it and knew that Garrick was right. Wrenley was not lean like the women in this dimension just because she ate differently in her world, and the spell that had stifled her looks was still wearing off. Though she was not obese by any stretch of the imagination, she just looked different than women living under the war. The spell would eventually wear off, and her looks would change. He regretted it as soon as he said it, knowing it was his fear talking. Once the spell faded, she would look just like her mother, and he was not ready for it.

"Bronson, that's not fair. She is in a new realm, alone, and needs people around her. She cannot be isolated like this…"

"She'll survive." He responded curtly.

"But I'm afraid she is sick…"

"Garrick, she's fine! Drop it. That's a damn order."

Garrick gave his friend an exasperated look, "You are not a cruel man, Bronson Aughton. It's what I admire so much about you. You may be tough as nails, but never cruel. The way you have been acting lately towards Wrenley is vicious on every level," Garrick's eyes narrowed as he ran a hand through his grown-out red hair. He lowered his voice and ground his teeth, "The woman who disobeyed you on that road was the most royal and beautiful thing I have seen in fifteen fucking years. The people saw it, and though they don't know who they saw, they will soon enough. Her compassion for that one girl will be what our people need to rally and defeat Earnesh once and for all; not violence, not death."

Knowing Garrick was right, Bronson's stomach whirled at his friend's words. Wrenley's words collided with him…the words she uttered to him on the road, *If I weren't a princess, you wouldn't have given me a second look, and that's not how I want to be.* Is that how she truly felt about him, that he was so shallow and callous? Could he blame her? Had he done anything to show her otherwise?

With one last growl, Garrick turned on his heels and strode away. Bronson slumped against the tree trunk he had perched himself against and felt the strain against his promise to protect Wrenley. He had been failing to do that. The distance between them was more harmful than beneficial, and the damage was palpable to everyone. He wanted to stop his friend and apologize for snapping, but he was too exhausted, too tired to care. For now, he would eat and attempt to sleep. He would find Wrenley soon and apologize profusely, probably on his knees. Bronson wanted to avoid it because he genuinely did not know what to say to her, his harsh words still causing grief to swell inside his gut. Soon…he would go to her soon.

~ ~ ~ ~ ~

During the brightest part of the day, they would rest and stay in the woods to avoid being seen. Wrenley dismounted from her horse and groaned, feeling like she had been hit by a train. She noticed a nearby stream; for once, her body signaled that she was indeed thirsty. She felt sleepy, and even though the wind was cold, she needed something more to wake her up. Wrenley usually would not have wandered off alone, but she felt she would not be missed. They all but ignored her now, and once again, she was invisible.

The men were busy settling the horses, Bronson was preoccupied with Garrick, and Wrenley was not thinking as clearly as she probably should have been. She tied her horse and wandered towards the sound of running water, almost as if it were calling to her. Time and space were a blur, and Wrenley was unaware of how long she had been wandering to find the water source. She pushed through the shrubbery on her hands and knees and finally found the stream. She bent down and washed her face, feeling almost numb. Standing back up, she looked around her, disoriented with no idea which way led back to camp.

Suddenly, a dizzying sensation hit her, and she felt fear rippling through her body. Stepping forward and nearly falling, she used the last bit of her strength to grab a tree. Her heart was pounding, and her body was so weak she could barely lift her arms. Wrenly felt the sensation again: eyes on her from somewhere beyond the stream in the thick woods. Looking around frantically, she heard a twig snap or a leaf crunch as she frantically clawed at a tree for something, anything, to hang on to, to brace herself. Something was lurking beyond her sight. It was as if she were being hunted. Before she could catch her breath to call for help, Wrenley collapsed, and everything went dark.

Bits and pieces: she felt a piercing cold envelope her, and she tried and failed to breathe. Ice-cold fluid filled her lungs as she clawed for air. As Wrenley drifted in and out of blackness, she felt herself being lifted out of the cold and wrapped in something warm. She could hardly open her eyes, her eyelids so heavy she just wanted to sleep. Wrenley kept her eyes closed at this point, but she could sense it was dark around her. She had no idea how much time had passed. Usually, she would be afraid, but she was just too sluggish. Was she dead? Was she moving towards the afterlife? She honestly did not care, as long as she was warm…as long as the water did not invade her aching lungs. She felt so sick that she did not have the strength to fight whatever was holding her. She just succumbed to it and drifted out of consciousness again.

~ ~ ~ ~ ~

The dark warrior sat in a tree a hundred yards from the camp, his dusky eyes taking in the routine activity below. He could see they were not dark forces, and his brow furrowed. Why would rebels be this far into the forest lands? He eyed the only female among them with curiosity, intrigued as she nervously looked around her. He concluded she must have been magical because, even with his stealth and ability to blend in, she had sensed him, casting glances toward him and his brother as they hid among the trees. Kage had given up on the camp of soldiers and followed the woman, frowning as he took in her stumbling gait and sunken face. She seemed disoriented, and none of her male companions even noticed her walking off into the woods alone. Male or female, this was no place for anyone to be alone, especially with dusk approaching. With a quick whistle, he signaled to his brother to follow, and they did so to the stream.

He saw her fall in, and without a second thought, he stripped off his weapons and jumped in after her, his brother following on the shore behind. She would have drowned if they had not found her when they did. She had taken several gulps of water into her lungs, and as Kage hauled her out of the icy river and onto the muddy bank, he pumped several breaths into her mouth with his own and turned her petite frame over to slam his hand into her back. She sputtered, and the water escaped her, a coughing fit enveloping her. Kage held her as she coughed, her body convulsing so fiercely he thought she would either throw up or stop breathing. He motioned for his cloak and dropped it onto her, her body almost blue from the cold.

"Is she...what is she?" His brother stood over him, his brow knitting together in worry.

Kage shrugged and cradled the woman, rage simmering under the surface at how these men had just let her wander off. She had not been in her right mind. If this was who he thought it was...he shook his head and lifted her, bringing her against his chest. "She needs Mother if she is going to survive."

CHAPTER 12

The Earth

Bronson jarred himself awake and noticed the sun sinking, darkness settling over their camp. Something was wrong; he felt it. He stood up and stumbled forward, bracing himself on a tree.

"Garrick, where is Wrenley?"

Garrick looked up from his place on the ground by the fire. "I haven't seen her; I thought she was resting somewhere."

Bronson shot up to his feet then, feeling the blood drain from his rough face, "Tell me she is here somewhere."

Garrick disappeared and was back in two minutes, his eyes bulging. He rubbed the back of his neck nervously. "She's not here."

"You lost her?" Bronson snarled, and Garrick held his hands up before him like a barrier.

"I'm not in charge of her! You are!" He snapped back to Bronson, who had lurched to his feet.

Bronson felt his stomach drop when he realized she was not in the camp. Her horse was tied, but she was nowhere to be found, not in her tent, not by the fire, not on the outskirts of the camp. His gut twisted as he followed her trail beyond camp and into the forest. He had been a damn fool for being such an ass and leaving her alone. None of this would have happened if he had stayed close to her. Guilt and shame flooded him at the thought of how he had avoided her, stripped her of any connection or friendship because of his damn ego. Now, he may have lost her…

The reality of the situation was crushing, and he barked orders to fan out into the forest and begin searching…every damn inch of it. The thought of something happening to Wrenley made him want to vomit, and he clutched the scar above his left pectoral muscle as it screamed at him, causing pain to shoot down his arm. He had to find her; there was no other option.

~ ~ ~ ~ ~

"Welcome back, my girl," the voice was smooth and comfortable in her ear. Wrenley stirred on the soft mattress under her, blankets tucked around her face, not wanting to open her eyes. Ruth was trying to wake her up. She must have overslept. She had experienced the most impressive yet awful dream and could not wait to tell her mother. She stretched, opened her eyes, and gasped. Wrenley was not at home, nor was she in her bed. She was not in Missouri.

She froze, her eyes taking in the dirt ceiling above her. It was very dark, but she could make out a warm, orange glow from a fire nearby. She smelled something delicious and heard soft voices in the background. Her first reaction was to bolt, but as she lay on the comfortable bed that felt like a cloud, with blankets piled around her, she did not want to move. If she was going to die, at least it was in a warm place with a ridiculously soft bed.

It then all came back to her: Bronson, the crossing over, the journey to take back some kind of throne, an evil sorcerer wanting her dead, or worse, to sexually enslave her just because of her royal blood. She could only remember fragments…she knew they were traveling somewhere, and she had been sick.

"Careful now, girl…you are not yet at your full strength."

Wrenley jumped at the sound of a female voice to her left. She shifted in the bed and reluctantly took in the woman beside her. She was older, with thick, white hair braided at the back of her head, cascading down to her waist. Her bronze skin was dark and smooth, looking more perfect than Wrenley could ever hope her skin to be. She was tall and slender, dressed in a simple frock made from soft, flowing material. Her delicate, long nose was pointed, her almond eyes rich and deep against her dark skin. She was slightly hunched over, her frail hand touched Wrenley's forehead, and her hand was cool against her flushed skin.

The woman's eyes seemed to relax slightly as she breathed in, still looking deep into Wrenley's face. "We almost lost you."

"Lost me? I don't even know you…" Wrenley slowly raised herself off the bed and onto a chair nearby.

"You had almost succumbed to the forest's darkness before my sons found you. How long have you been here, girl?" Wrenley bristled, unsure what to say or admit to, even though this woman had saved her life.

"I've uh…" Wrenley stuttered, "Like right here or…?" She was trying to come up with a lie, but her mind was blank, still foggy from her apparent dive into a river. She licked her lips nervously and sat up, making her head swim.

"Don't play games with me, child," the old lady chided and pointed a graceful, spindly finger toward Wrenley and wiggled it. "I know exactly who you are and why you are here. Don't you lie to this crone!"

Wrenley felt fear shoot through her slightly as the lady leaned over to her, face-to-face. When the woman moved, the sweet scent of honeysuckle drifted towards Wrenley, and she inhaled it.

"You crossed over from somewhere," the woman said, narrowing her beautiful eyes and tilting her head as she peered into Wrenley's soul.

"I uh…"

"You began to feel it, didn't you? The sickness?"

"Well, I…"

"You are on a quest…an important quest?"

"Listen, ma'am…"

The woman backed up, then raised her arms to either side of her and bowed low, her head almost below her knees. Wrenley sat in complete awkwardness at the show of reverence from the older woman. The old lady straightened again, silver lining her beautiful eyes. A smile broke over the crone's face as she came closer and wrapped her slender arms around Wrenley. Wrenley went rigid at the embrace but could not help feeling a flush of warmth creeping over her at the affectionate gesture. She almost purred from the physical contact. She realized it had been weeks, maybe longer, since anyone had even touched her. It had been weeks since anyone had made her feel like she was an actual human being.

The woman held tight and whispered, "I never thought I would live to see this day. The princess has returned."

~ ~ ~ ~ ~

"My name is Astara, and I am old."

The woman was stunning, and though she was worn with wisdom and age, her beauty was impeccable. Wrenley had the strength to sit at the table with the woman. Astara handed her a steaming bowl of broth and ordered Wrenley to drink it. She did, and it tasted heavenly. Wrenley had a second helping, and a half bowl of a third, groaning in bliss as she pushed the bowl away and fought the urge to rub her belly. She had been living on wild rabbit meat and old bread for days when she ate at all, so this was a delicacy. Astara looked increasingly pleased with every helping Wrenley was able to put into her belly.

"I am Wrenley, and I am…confused."

Astara laughed; it was a deep, hearty sound that echoed off the hut's walls. Wrenley grinned, for it was a rich and joyful melody that rang like music in her ears after she had been so isolated and lonely for weeks. The mirth radiated off the older woman and seemed to simmer in Wrenley's bones, filling her with a new energy. Wrenley had not noticed how weak and tired she was or how sadness had soaked into her very soul these past weeks.

"I suppose you are wondering if you can trust me." Astara got up and became busy, fiddling with drying herbs hanging from the ceiling and clinking jars on a shelf. She moved with a silent grace, flittering like a butterfly back and forth in the kitchen, making Wrenley feel dizzy.

"Yes, well… I wonder that about anyone and everyone nowadays." Wrenley fidgeted with the frayed corner of the quilt wrapped around her, supposing there was no reason to lie.

"Good…that is smart. "After Astara seemed content with her selection of dried herbs, she began to grind them in the bowl, using her weight to crush them. The scent of the powdered herbs drifted to Wrenley, and she inhaled them with delight.

"I am Astara of Ozul. My ancestors have lived within the earth for thousands of years. We remember the old evil. We tried to warn the kingdom it was coming." Astara seemed irritated, taking it out on the herbs in the bowl. "Ever since the king and queen died, the civil war has taken so much from our people and our land. It took my husband…" She paused, and Wrenley saw a wave of pain seem to crash over the older woman. "They took my oldest son. Our ancestors were here when the great deity roamed the land...the evil had disappeared then...but now it is back."

Wrenley slid off the bed and onto a stool next to the kitchen table, empathy for this woman's loss overwhelming her heart. Astara paused in her work for a moment, almost lost in a memory, and then she shook her head as if reminding herself of the present task. Wrenley reached out and touched Astara's arm, "I can't imagine that loss. I am so very sorry."

Wrenley genuinely could not imagine. She had lost her parents, yes, but she had no memory of them. Once again, she had no insight into the horror these people had faced. She had no idea what it was like to lose someone so close to her, and she hoped she never would. Wrenley had almost prepared for some type of jab, but Astara gave Wrenley a weak smile, "You are kind, my lady. Thank you...you have a warm and tender soul."

The crone continued to work on the herbs and spices, bustling about the kitchen at a pace that made Wrenley want to lie back down. "I have kept my family safe for the last fifteen years. We have hidden away..."

"Are you a seer?"

"Hah!" Astara huffed, slamming her mallet down onto the herbs one last time and pouring them into a jar. "I am no seer! I am a smart woman. I am familiar with the elements, and my family respects the earth. In turn, the earth protects us. It covers us with dirt and vegetation. It hides our home. It heals us when we are sick." She shoved the jar of spices across the table at Wrenley, nodding in its direction.

"You were not ready to be in this world. The evil here is powerful and is beginning to wear you down. You almost died when you fell in the river. My sons found you and pulled you out. These herbs will help you regain strength and provide protection. Take a spoonful with your tea every day until they are gone."

Wrenley reached out for the jar and took it, weighing it in her hand. "Thank you... Thank you for doing this for me. It is so very kind..." Wrenley shifted and caressed the lip of her coffee mug with her finger. "Some have not been as understanding of my limitations."

Astara cocked her head, "What has happened to you, my child?

It surprises you that I would be kind?" The crone gave Wrenley a look that made Wrenley want to burst into tears.

Wrenley bit her bottom lip and nodded, "I get it…I've been away and now I am back, and there's so much to do…I hate being weak."

"It's not your fault you weren't prepared, and it is my pleasure to assist my lady! Who were your companions?"

Wrenley did not answer and sipped on her broth. Astara raised her eyebrows and sighed, groaning from the aches and pains as she lowered herself to a stool at the table. "My child, if I wanted you dead, I would have had my sons do it before they even pulled you from the river. If I were to be with the evil, I would have turned you in already. You might as well trust this old woman so that I can help." Astara grasped her walking stick and tapped it playfully at Wrenley's foot. "I won't bite," she said.

Wrenley sighed, avoiding Astara's gaze for a moment. She knew it was true. Astara would have killed her or turned her over to the enemy by now. She must trust someone if she has any hope of finding her way.

"I was with a company…"

"Who?"

"Just some forest people…"

"And a seer?"

Wrenley did not answer and shifted uncomfortably, noticing her hips were only slightly sore. Why was Astara so persistent? It was clear that she already knew the answer to these questions. Astara nodded as if she could read Wrenley's mind.

"You were with Bronson Aughton." Astara leaned back and allowed her hand to fall on the table, creating a thud in the room's silence. She tried not to read into Astara's icy tone.

Astara sighed and rubbed her forearm, "That man was foolish for bringing you back here without the proper precautions. It was risky and imprudent. He is as careless as ever."

"You know him?" Wrenley was intrigued now and leaned forward in her seat.

"Of course, I know him. We all suspected Bronson had taken you, but didn't know where. Before that, he and the king experimented with dangerous, unnatural magic. The rumor was that they attempted to cross different worlds and travel in time; it's why the evil returned. The evil sensed the magic and the power those two were conjuring up, and Earnesh wanted a piece of it." She lifted a hand in the air, finger pointing to the ceiling for emphasis.

Wrenley winced. "Conjuring?"

Astara took a sip of her bowl of broth and coughed, covering her mouth with a handkerchief. "I may be a spooky old lady in the woods who allows the elements to work with and for her, and I may appreciate a good bout of enchantment here and there, but Bronson and the king were doing things…" Astara's voice lowered as she leaned over the table to whisper. "They were greedy for power, and they unleashed an evil. They weren't content with what they had. They had to get more and more. It's their fault the enemy came, and it's their fault the kingdom fell. It's their fault we lost you to begin with…and I lost my husband and son." Astara shook her head passionately, her thick, grey braid bouncing back and forth as she moved, "The queen knew this, and yet they didn't listen to her, and then we lost her in such a terrible way. I blame Bronson Aughton."

Wrenley jumped as the heavy wooden door creaked open, and two young men entered. Astara's face lit up, "Ah! Wrenley, these are my twin sons, Kage and Alcott. They saved your life, my dear. They found you in the river and pulled you out."

Astara stood and leaned on the table for support as if adjusting to standing, and walked over to the young men. Then she reached up, lovingly and tenderly, and embraced the men. The young men did not turn away or look embarrassed. Instead, they leaned down to embrace their mother with a gentleness that almost made Wrenley tear up, treating their mother like some priceless jewel or piece of artwork.

"Thank you," Wrenley stood respectfully, nervously taking in the young men before her. She felt some pain in her legs and groaned as she stood to her feet. They looked very much alike, and Wrenley knew she might have trouble telling them apart at first, so she studied them intently. They were much younger than Bronson was, still in their twenties.

Kage was slightly taller than his brother; the resemblance to his mother was uncanny. He was built like a Greek god, his clothes tight on his body, and she could see his chiseled chest and bulging arms under his clothes. His skin was the same dark copper color as his mother's, his clean-shaven face concentrated, his large almond eyes surrounded by thick black lashes. His ebony hair was long, braided like his mother's, and almost reached his shoulder blades. On his belt was a sword, another dagger in his boot, and Wrenley assumed probably more weapons on him than she could see. He did not smile at her but nodded in acknowledgment, looking down the slope of his nose at her.

Alcott was slightly shorter and had the same features. He covered himself in a long brown tunic that fell below the knees, not showcasing his muscled frame as his brother did. He, too, was armed and looked at her warily, but managed to give her a small smile.

"This is Wrenley, daughter of King Dolion and Queen Adinnil. She has come to end this war and bring peace back to our kingdom."

Alcott and Kage were silent. Wrenley stood awkwardly before them, hands clasped together, and mustered up the warmest smile she could. They observed her with hesitation, and Astara giggled in the background. Wrenley turned back to her with raised eyebrows.

"Excuse them, my dear; my sons are protective of this old woman." Astara made her way around the table to Wrenley's side, gently patting the younger woman's hand. "They have lost greatly in this time of darkness, just as I have…just as we all have in one way or another. If we work together, we can make some things right."

Wrenley nodded, but swayed on her feet, pain shooting down her legs. She thought most of the damage from her disease had corrected itself, but apparently, she was wrong. Astara narrowed her eyes at Wrenley, taking her in with a haughty gaze.

Astara grabbed Wrenley's elbows and frowned, "You are cold…you need more food. You need to rest and feel safe so your mind can heal."

Wrenley could not agree more. She was already sleepy just sitting upright for an hour. Perhaps it was because she felt safe and warm, maybe it was because her belly was full, or perhaps it was sheer exhaustion, but she wanted to do nothing more than sleep. Kage moved from his position by the door and lifted her into his arms. She gasped as he pressed her against his chest. She yelped slightly as his arms encircled her, but she was too grateful to be angry at his impudence. Quickly and efficiently, he deposited her back on the soft bed. She was exhausted, and her legs had been about to buckle underneath her. He then retrieved the intricate, homemade quilt and wrapped it around her shoulders.

She was silent as he worked. Alcott helped his mother in the background, dishing Wrenley food. Wrenley tried to protest when they served her, but Astara's firm look silenced her, and Wrenley clamped her mouth shut out of respect. She was given a heaping bowl of hearty stew and another mug of hot tea. They all stared at her as she ate every bit of the stew, drank the tea with the mixed herbs, and snuggled into her bed. The brothers vacated the small dwelling, and Wrenley fell asleep to the soft and soothing sound of Astara's humming beside her on the small bed that was the most comfortable place she had ever slept.

~ ~ ~ ~ ~

Astara listened as the young girl fell into a deep sleep, aided by the slumbering tonic the crone had added to her tea. The deep purple circles around the girl's eyes were confirmation enough that nightmares and dreams haunted her. Astara knew the only thing that would heal the young woman was uninterrupted slumber. She ensured Wrenley was tucked in, pulled a shawl over her slim shoulders, and stepped into the cool night air.

"It's a risk bringing her here, Mother." Kage's deep voice was respectful but firm, and Astara shrugged her slender shoulders. He had been waiting for her outside to have this difficult but needed conversation.

"I know my son, but sometimes the risk is necessary."

"Will this Aughton seer come and find her?" Kage's nostrils flared slightly as he shared with Astara the state Wrenley had been in before falling into the river.

"Yes, he will…" Astara mused, looking up into the trees and spying stars peeking out from over the canopy of foliage. "Whether we like it or not, he is the only one who can help her back to the throne." Astara withheld the truth from her child, who Bronson truly was, and what he had been hiding in plain sight for the past years. It was not the time to tell her son that his father and eldest brother followed Bronson on the battlefield and were slaughtered like animals while Bronson lived to escape. It was not the time to tell her son that she had felt a whisper in the earth, a message on the wind that change was coming, whether they were ready for it or not. They each had a significant part to play, no matter the cost. Kage would learn this at the right time.

She placed her hand on her son's forearm and said, "In times of great peril, we must take risks, be vulnerable, and be brave."

"We've lost so much…" he murmured, looking down at her with those beautiful eyes, and she spied for a moment the five-year-old that once climbed the trees and built forts in the rocks before the war had raped him of his childhood and innocence.

"And we will lose even more if we do not fight."

CHAPTER 13

Lightning Bugs

Astara explained that the crossing between worlds had impacted Wrenley mentally and physically, resulting in her delirium and confusion. Wrenley had assumed that her body and mind had broken down due to the crossing, the grueling journey, and the magical pressure exerted upon her. Still, Astara's confirmation made her feel…well, validated. Astara explained that it may be weeks for Wrenley to normalize under the conditions of her new world.

Astara was peculiar. She reminded Wrenley of the stereotypical forest witch. Astara had a caldron over the fire, which she would stir with a large spoon. Astara could be heard at all hours of the night, clinking and clanking jars of herbs and specimens, humming and muttering to herself. When Wrenley awoke, she continued to pretend to be asleep. Wrenley thought that the crone mumbled spells or incantations into the darkness. Wrenley could not be sure, but she thought she saw things floating out of the corner of her eyes: a delicate teacup, a heavy book, maybe even a broom. When Wrenley would snap her head to catch it, the teacup sat innocently on the table, the book rested unknowingly, and the broom leaned untroubled. Wrenley swore that the crone did it to her on purpose. Astara's ornery grin was the evidence.

The cottage was nestled under a hill in the earth. There were two small bedrooms, a small common area, and a large fireplace that seemed to be the center of the home. Wrenley observed that the space was so very tiny, but quaint and pleasant. Herbs and different spices hung from the walls and dried on the hearth ceiling from makeshift hangers. Beautiful paintings hung around the small living area that Wrenley could not help but stare at while she lay in bed. Walls of jars decorated the shelves of the small dwelling, alongside books and other unusual artifacts. Wrenley nosily studied every item. Astara shared the herbs and their medicinal properties with her.

Wrenley had observed the twins eyeing her, maybe out of curiosity or outright suspicion. They had grown up in a different world from Bronson and Astara, having been young children when the war began. Unlike Astara, they did not seem to grasp the significance of Wrenley's presence. Wrenley could not blame them; she did not understand it either. They were always at a distance and never engaged with Wrenley unless Astara initiated them.

Wrenley had volunteered to help pick the day's provisions as she felt her strength returning. Ruth had a garden in the backyard every summer since Wrenley was old enough to remember; how different could a garden be here? Wrenley observed that the seasons in this world were much like the seasons in hers, and winter was upon them, with a variety of cold-weather vegetables.

"You are plainer than I thought you would be, for a princess and all."

Wrenley straightened up from her bent-over position in the garden. It had been a week since she fell into the river. Half of that time, Wrenley had been recovering her strength and stamina in bed. She had slept for three days, only waking up to eat and to use the bathroom, then returning to sleep. On day four, she took a bath. Astara pulled out a large, round tub, and the twins filled it with steaming water that Wrenley had melted into. Days five and six were spent by Wrenley having enough strength and courage to venture outside the door and marvel at the awning of forest and vegetation above her. The sun shone through because the foliage was thin due to the leaves falling, but the cottage was still mostly covered. She felt safe under this umbrella of thick forest.

Kage leaned against a tree. Who knows how long he had been standing there watching Wrenley unattractively step over rows of produce and stumble on her skirt. It was warmer here than in the mountains and forest, and he was dressed in a loose shirt and pants. She was reminded how finely built he was, and she gulped, very much aware of her limitations when it came to beauty.

"Thanks? Asshole…" She mumbled and bent back down to pull

a carrot from the earth. Wrenley had concluded that the people in this world were much more attractive than in her world. Everyone, even Astara in her old age, was stunning. Wrenley was painfully aware that her looks were average, which was nothing new. Normal height, typical build, nothing too fancy or alluring. She was somewhat square, not the shape of a goddess from fairy tales. She felt agitated as Kage ventured closer, almost as if he was taunting her on purpose.

"Are you offended?" He asked, a grin tugging at his lips.

Wrenley did not stand, but remained bent on her knees to give the carrots a harder tug. She could tell by his voice that he was closer now. "Nope."

"Then why are you mad?"

"Not mad," Wrenley kept her head down. She slammed the carrots on the ground to remove the excess dirt, tossed them in the basket, and stood, heaving it onto her shoulder. The garden was bursting with color; pumpkins, lettuce, radishes, and other leafy greens were thriving in the mild winter temperatures. Under any other conditions, she would have loved to work in a garden as luscious as this.

"You seem mad." Kage was standing in front of her now, blocking her path between the rows of vegetables.

"I am working."

Kage cocked his head and continued to stare at her, his sharp features unreadable. His dark eyes examined her, and she could feel his eyes traveling over her, almost as if to size her up.

"I sense you are…upset." His voice rumbled, and Wrenley detected a hint of amusement.

"Fine! I am mad!" Wrenley dropped the basket beside her, straightened, and jutted a finger in Kage's chest. He took a step back, seeming surprised.

"I'll tell you why I'm mad." Wrenley took a deep breath, reaching down to smooth the wrinkles out of her skirt before unleashing herself on him. "I am worlds away from my family. I didn't even know who I truly was until Bronson came for me. Hell, I don't even know how long it's been because time is fucked up here. There is an evil deity out there looking for me, and there are people who are counting on me. I don't even know where I am or how to get back to whoever I am supposed to be with, and I don't even know who I should be with or not." She was yelling now, holding her hands in front of her. "I didn't even ask for this shit, and now, you come up and tell me I am plain looking? I am NOT in the mood for this!"

Half of Wrenley felt like she should step back and breathe, as Kage and his family had fed her, clothed her, and kept her safe for a week now. The other half of Wrenley wanted to pop his smug mouth with her fist. Wrenley took a step closer. Kage took a step back as her finger poked him in his ridiculously muscled chest.

"I have been bossed around, taken from my home, almost eaten by a werewolf, and damn near drowned; and, from what I gather, this is just the tip of the iceberg. Not to mention…" She hissed as she fisted the material of her skirt, "…this goddamn dress has almost killed me three times." She held her palm in his face as he tried to speak, "I need you to step the fuck away, please."

Kage froze, eyes wide. Wrenley held his gaze, challenging him, daring him to say one more word to her. He did not move out of her way, though, and Wrenley gasped as Kage took a brazen step towards her and leaned down to kiss her. Her whole body went rigid, and he reached out to grab her chin, not letting her move away from him. His lips brushed hers gently, and his kiss was as gorgeous as he was. She felt a rush of heat wash over her, rapidly dispelling her frustration. She wanted to pull away, but her body had reacted before her mind, and she felt a burst of excitement in her gut. The kiss lasted for several seconds, his grip strong on her chin, but he was not hurting her.

He pulled back and grinned at her, and she finally came back to her senses, wrenching her face away from him. "It's a pleasure to serve you, lady, plain or not."

He winked. His gaze once again scanned her, now focusing on her clothing. "Do you want different clothes? We can't have you dying because of the dress."

~ ~ ~ ~ ~

Everything about Kage was different than Bronson. Bronson was older, taller, and reeked of power, wisdom, and experience. Bronson was also mysterious, often treating Wrenley like a child. There was a dark side to him that Wrenley could not identify, and it put her on edge, but it also made him extremely attractive to her. Kage was boyish and the picture of flirtatious youth and physical strength. He was younger than Wrenley by five years, at least, she crudely calculated, despite the time issues between worlds. He was shorter, muscular, and stockier than Bronson. He was also immature and funny, making Wrenley laugh whenever they were together.

Kage never bossed her around or tried to tell her what to do. He was respectful and treated her like an equal. He asked her questions about herself and her old life. They spent hours together working in the garden, gathering wood, and wandering the pathways along the forest floor as they talked. He treated her like a human being, not a commodity to be won in a war. For the first time since she had been in this obscure world, Wrenley felt she was connecting with someone. She had depended on Bronson to survive, but she was developing a relationship with Kage and his family—a mutually beneficial relationship, with no power struggles or tension, just genuine connections.

Kage was neither a seer nor a magician. He possessed no spiritual or magical powers whatsoever. Unlike his mother, he was a hunter and had only briefly fought in the civil war. He had been fighting since he was a teenager, losing his older brother and father in the war. He and Alcott would fight when the enemy came close to their home, using the forest to their advantage. The soldiers of Earnesh were not used to the conditions, often getting lost, becoming stuck in a bog, or wandering aimlessly and eventually abandoning their posts. Sometimes the best thing to do was to hunker down and hide, not engaging the enemy but observing them.

Astara seemed to speak to the oak trees and sing to the wind. She was a tough lady, no doubt about that, but also extremely gentle with Wrenley. It was obvious she loved her sons immensely, and they would sit together, drink ale by the fire at night, and laugh together. Wrenley envied their relationship and wondered about her parents, the ones in Missouri whom she missed so deeply that it hurt her heart; she would give anything to sit and laugh with them right now.

Alcott was more withdrawn and only spoke when spoken to. He and Kage would joke and push each other around when Alcott forgot Wrenley was in the background. He was polite to Wrenley but did not gravitate toward her as Kage did. Alcott was like a wallflower, tucking in and watching everything around him.

"We are here, in the lower earth lands. You must have come from the eastern mountain and through this forest region," Kage spread a large map over the table, and the four of them poured over it a few nights later. Wrenley noticed Kage's smell…cedarwood and earth. It was not a dirty smell; on the contrary, it was alluring. She tried to focus on the map before her rather than that delicious smell.

"You said you saw wolves?"

"If you could call them that," Wrenley muttered, shuddering at the memory.

Kage nodded, "Then this is the way he was bringing you. This is where I saw you fall in. We are here now." Wrenley's eyes widened, not realizing how far she had wandered alone.

"If we are going to take you to Ailios, we will have to go the long way. We must avoid large populations and enemy troops," Astara propped herself over the map, leaning close to be able to see the small details with her magnifying glass.

"And what good is that going to do, Mother? What about when we get there?" Kage spread both palms on the table. He leaned over, his shirt loose, allowing Wrenley to see the beautifully sculpted pectoral muscles beneath, which were hard to ignore. She blushed and looked away, pretending to study the herbs hanging from the ceiling.

"Brigid has brought her to us. The longer she stays, the more energy she will create. It's safer for everyone if she is on the move. Her rightful place is on the throne. You boys must take her there."

"Who is Brigid?" Wrenley's eyebrow shot up in question.

"She's the Goddess of the Earth people," Astara explained, "She will show us the way."

"We can't fight the entire enemy army by ourselves," Alcott said, seated in the corner, using his knife to cut his apple into slices. "We are not equipped to fight. What is the plan once we get there?"

"Things will fall into place, Brigid will help us," Astara said and groaned, lowering herself onto her stool.

"That's not going to work for me," Kage said, seeming

frustrated at his mother. He was a soldier, and he needed a plan.

"What about Bronson? He has a company of people who can help," Wrenley offered.

Astara sniffed, "I do not trust that man, but unfortunately, we may have to use him."

"That piece of shit isn't getting near you again unless we are with you," Kage stated protectively, rolling the map up and pointing it towards Wrenley. "He almost let you die. He allowed you to wander away alone when it should never have happened. If he truly cared, he would have treated you like the treasure you are."

Wrenley felt defensive at first, then blushed at the compliment. "I mean…it was an accident."

"He let you wander off and fall into a river! With all his powers, he should have known you were sick." Kage shook his head in disgust, his eyes dark with anger. "He failed you."

Wrenley saw Kage's point and could not argue against it.

The family continued debating about the plan, and Wrenley felt helpless. Again, people were making strategies concerning her, and she had no power or opinion. She had no control over the situation; however, she was the key figure that everyone needed. She almost felt used, alone again, and the burden of it was crushing her. She slipped out the door quietly as the three continued to dispute loudly.

Wrenley breathed in the clean, cool air and wrapped a shawl around her. Kage had given her some pants and a shirt with knee-high boots. *At least I will not be tripping over a stupid dress anymore*, she thought to herself with a sniff. She walked out from under the canopy of trees and foliage, looking up. The night sky was crystal clear, with stars twinkling above her. Sadness flooded her as reality set in that these were not the stars her parents could look up to and see. She was so disconnected from them, and it left her frail heart aching. Were they okay? Bronson had said that if Wrenley were gone, they would be safe. She just hoped he was telling the truth.

Wrenley pulled out some herbs Astara had allowed her to take, and a match she had swiped from the hearth this morning. She sat down on the ground, her legs crossed, and lit the dried herbs, setting the bundle on a flat stone. She allowed the scent to fill the air, remembering her altar at home, which had brought her so much comfort and joy. There was nothing like that here…nothing that was truly hers. No sacred place to come back to, no home she could see or touch. She was a nomad, a refugee in a land she had not even known existed. Would this place ever feel like home?

Wrenley thought about Bronson, her heart tugging slightly. Was he trustworthy? Is what Astara said the whole story? Bronson was dark and mysterious, but he never gave Wrenley a reason not to trust him, that is, until he chose to ignore her. She felt a connection with him, and she strangely missed him. She felt out of control and conflicted as a tear slid down her face. The injustice of the situation was heavy on her. On the one hand, this world and this kingdom had suffered greatly, and she had an opportunity — an obligation —to help. On the other hand, she never asked for this. It was not her fault. She was dealing with a problem she had not created.

She felt a pull inside her, something she usually would have attributed to a spirit or a ghost when meditating at home. Feeling it again, Wrenley listened for a moment, closing her eyes. The smoke filled her senses as she breathed in and out. She found herself reaching up to clasp the pendant around her neck as she stilled.

Can you hear me? It whispered in the air.

It was inaudible…but it was there.

~ ~ ~ ~ ~

Bronson snapped his head up from where he hunkered down to the earth, following a fresh trail. He had been following it for a week now, using what little magic he could without disturbing the unseen. He knew she was close; he felt it. Bronson's world had been turned upside down this last week. For fifteen years, Bronson had known exactly where Wrenley was at every moment. He always knew she was safe, and he always knew where to find her; but this — her absence from his life — was unbearable. He had been a fool and a bastard to act as he did. He had been too preoccupied to notice what she needed. He knew her better than that. He should have seen that she was growing weaker. He should have been there when she wandered away…

The trail suggested two other humans, and Bronson breathed a sigh of relief that it was not the tracks of a beast. They were splayed openly in spots, almost as if they wanted him to find them. He ached to lay eyes on her again, to be able to tie her to her damn horse and never let her out of his sight. His chest throbbed with her absence, and he ruminated about all the stupid things he had said to her or about her. He would not rest until she was safe with him again.

Then he heard it again…a whisper on a phantom wind…

Can you hear me?

"I'm coming for you…" He whispered back into the darkness.

~ ~ ~ ~ ~

"A lot to think about, eh?"

Wrenley jumped from her thoughts as Kage sat beside her on the soft grass, one knee propped up with his arm resting on it. He picked up a piece of grass and fiddled with it, not prying any more about her thoughts. They did not speak for a while, and she saw him eyeing her smoldering herbs when she did not explain. Wrenley felt herself relaxing a little with his presence.

"I sometimes feel like all of this is my fault."

Kage turned to her, seeming surprised. "None of this is your fault."

Wrenley drew her knees to her chest and wrapped her arms around them, sighing. "All I have learned so far is how much loss and destruction have been caused since I left. I wish I could have done something different. I wish you hadn't lost your brother and father, and I wish you didn't have to fight as a teenager." *I wish Bronson hadn't had to travel back and forth to watch me. I wish my parents hadn't died, and I could have known them. I wish…*

"Sometimes we have to deal with things that aren't our fault. At least you're here, willing to help," the young man shrugged. "Most people wouldn't willingly inherit a world of problems like that."

Wrenley felt the sadness and understanding in his voice. She shrugged, "I know. It's hard because I don't know who to trust."

"You can trust me."

Wrenley shifted slightly, her cheek resting on her knee as she looked at Kage, taking in his features in the warm moonlight. She smiled shyly, her brow raising almost to her hairline. "Can I? Can I trust you?"

Kage leaned in with a flirtatious grin. "I will not let anyone hurt you."

"You don't even know me…" Wrenley mused, shifting to look back at the herbs that were smoldering in front of her. She inhaled the smoke, bringing its sweet aroma into her lungs. "And you can't promise that anyway. No one can promise I won't be hurt. Despite our best efforts, people get hurt, and they die."

Kage whistled lowly. "That's a grim view of the world."

"Well, the world is a pretty shitty place, this world and mine."

The two sat in silence again, Wrenley's brain recycling all the information she had learned in the last few weeks. It was undeniable that no one, not even Kage or Bronson, could ever promise she would be safe, and she would never ask them to make a promise she knew they could not keep. Anyway, death did not scare her…being alone did.

Kage cleared his throat, "Well, in that case, I promise I will defend you until my dying breath. And when I die, you may die too, but at least you know I tried."

Wrenley giggled and reached out to shove his shoulder. His muscles were like a cement wall, and they pushed her back. She steadied herself, "Why? I haven't done anything for you. I'm just a big problem."

"You are our royalty; we must protect you."

Wrenley snorted, "That's what everyone has been telling me. That they have a duty…" She rolled her eyes and her head back dramatically.

"You also are a friend. You are now part of our family. Mother would destroy me if I let anything happen to you. She scares me more than Earnesh and his cronies any day."

They laughed a little, and Wrenley stretched her legs and arms, "I'm a big hassle for such a plain girl from Missouri. Who would have thought?"

"Maybe plain wasn't the right word to use," Wrenley noticed his voice was quiet, almost a mumble, and she shifted to look at him, raising an eyebrow.

Kage was close to her, seeming to lean in a little more. Wrenley smelled him again, cedarwood and sage filling her nostrils. His beautiful black hair was loose around her shoulders, shining in the remaining rays of the full moon above. His dark, copper skin was flawless, and Wrenley refused to give in to the compulsion to reach up and touch his cheek. She had failed to realize how starved she was for people, for attention, for interacting with others; nor had she realized how sick her mind and body had become. Kage, Astara, and Alcott made her feel part of something again; they had saved her life.

"It has been years since my father and brother's death that I have seen Mother excited about something. You make her laugh…" He leaned in again, taking a deep breath. "And it's been a long time since I could talk to someone who isn't my brother. You can be a friend with me, not just a pawn in someone's game."

*Friend…*Wrenley held her breath as she thought about being Kage's friend. She never had many friends during her childhood. Memories of sitting alone on the basketball bleachers floated in her memory. Dances where no one would look at her because of her legs, and hushed conversations when she painfully passed by. The memories reiterated the loneliness she had felt every day of her existence. It would be nice not to feel so alone, to trust him, to allow him to be someone she could rely on.

Wrenley jolted at something out of the corner of her vision. Her eyes widened, and a smile burst onto her face as she shoved Kage's shoulder again and pointed.

"Look! Lighting bugs!" Wrenley exclaimed, clasping her hands to her chest. She remembered when she and her mother would gather the fireflies in their backyard, put them in jars to marvel at them, and gently release them back into the air. Wrenley would laugh and squeal as she chased the bugs that popped up from the ground. It was a fond memory, one where she had been healthy and happy, unencumbered by the harsh realities of her life or illness.

Kage raised an eyebrow, "Is that what you call them in…Missouri? Lighting bugs?"

"Well, yes, what do you call them?"

Kage dipped his head, grinning widely as if amused. "We call them what they are. Those are foliage fairies."

"What?"

Kage brought a finger to his lips to hush her, then reached his large hand outward. Wrenley gulped as she noticed several lights approaching him and landed on his palm. From Wrenley's perspective, they were almost the size of a small dragonfly from back home. Kage motioned for Wrenley to get closer, and a gasp escaped her as she witnessed the tiny, human-like creature land on his hand. They were unafraid of him but sat nonchalantly on his fingers and palm. They were different pastel colors of pink, blue, and green; their delicate wings resembled a butterfly's.

The beautiful creatures danced with each other and then flew away again. Kage gently grabbed Wrenley's wrist and raised it palm up, his fingers slowly caressing her upturned wrist, which made her blush even more. Suddenly, fairies appeared around them, so many that Wrenley could not count them. They flooded around her, landing on her hands, shoulders, and even in her hair. She could hear them hum and feel them tickle her skin. She sucked in a breath, biting her lower lip in excitement as they made spiraling patterns in the darkness before them. As she leaned her ear to listen more carefully, what had sounded like a hum at first was a song. The fairies were singing, and it was a joyous, happy sound.

"They know you," Kage leaned in and whispered, tucking a stray curl behind her ear, and Wrenley marveled at the sight in front of her. It was as if she were surrounded by a million stars, all singing and humming a beautiful melody that filled her chest with a joy she had not felt in years and years. They were all unique creatures, but moved as one, pulsing and swaying in unison to their delightful song.

"Know me?" Wrenley asked, tears stinging her eyes. She could not explain it, but these little creatures brought her so much joy and happiness in this moment that she felt as if her chest might burst.

"They know who you are, that you are their royalty. They are dancing for you...The dance of the fairies for their beloved queen."

She had never been known before…no one ever noticed or glanced at her when she entered a room. Wrenley snapped her gaze from the little magical creatures to Kage's face. He was so close now, and he leaned in to gently kiss her again like he did in the garden. As if on cue, the little fairies scattered in a million directions like fireworks, and Kage reached over and grabbed Wrenley, pulling her onto his lap. He was gentle but firm, his large arms able to lift her easily. Wrenley was caught off guard and so surprised that she melted into him for a moment, the swirls of fairies still singing around them and the moon now rising and casting a magical light. Wrenley seemed to shake out of a trance, pressed her hands on his muscular chest, and pushed away from him slightly. Is this what friends are supposed to do in this world?

"Listen, I…"

"You what?" He asked hoarsely.

"I've always felt so alone…" she trailed off, watching the little lights float away with a warmth in her belly.

Kage sighed, "You aren't alone anymore, Wrenley. I promise."

"But…"

He hushed her with a finger on her lips, and she wrapped her arms around his neck despite the voice in her head saying to pull away. Against all her better judgment, she reached out one hand to run her fingers down his cheek. What on earth was she doing? This was the most inappropriate time for this. She had only known this man for a week, but something about him was familiar and safe. Was this a real attraction or her need to feel secure? Did that even matter?

At first, Kage's hands had ventured to her hips, then loosely at her waist, but then he wrapped both large arms around her and crushed her into him. She felt his warmth, his tongue gently running along her own as their kiss deepened. She let out a soft moan, and she felt a noise that resembled a purr rumbling out of his chest, his hold tightening.

Suddenly, he jerked away and turned his head as if to listen to something she could not hear.

"What is it?" Wrenley pulled away, still flushed as she studied him.

"Something's wrong."

He jumped to his feet swiftly, lifting her quickly with him.

"Go back to the hut and send Alcott. Stay in there with Mother until I come to get you."

"Kage, what is happening…"

"Go!" he ordered, suddenly sounding much more mature than his youthful face would suggest. She was winded and shaking when she stumbled into the house. Alcott was still sitting by the fire.

"Kage needs you. Now!" She pointed towards the door, bending over to catch her breath.

Alcott did not question her, but grabbed his sword and flew out the door. Wrenley felt as if there was a rock in her stomach. She looked terrified at Astara. The older woman stood, shaking as she leaned on her cane. She suddenly seemed older; the youthfulness almost drained from her. Astara reached out and steadied herself on the table.

"What is it?" Wrenley whispered.

Astara took in a deep breath. "The enemy is close."

Astara was feeling something —an energy—and it was heavy. All Wrenley could think about was that it was all because she was here. She grabbed the small sword Bronson had given her days ago and ripped it from the leather sheath.

"Where are you going?" Astara screeched, and Wrenley paused before she ducked out the door, shaking her head at the older woman. "I am sick of people dying and getting hurt because of me."

Wrenley dashed out, not listening to Astara's protests behind her.

CHAPTER 14

Light

Wrenley made her way down the rocky path, slipping on the dew covering the stones she and Kage had walked on an hour ago. She panted and pushed her body forward, though everything in her screamed to run away from the shouts and clanking of weapons. With the moonlight, she could maneuver her way to the tree line and follow the sounds of battle, her blood chilling the closer she drew to whatever lay beyond the rocks. She headed towards the river, the stones creating a path that led down to the river's edge. She scaled the rocks, careful not to slip and fall to her death. She braced herself and peered down, gasping at the sight before her: Alcott and Kage were outnumbered, cornered into the cliff wall.

Kage was a fierce thing to behold, face set with rage as his powerful arms swung his mammoth sword back and forth. He took out one soldier after another, roaring as she noticed a jagged wound across his brow and blood oozing down his face. Alcott was also covered in blood, but Wrenley could not identify whether it was his blood or someone else's. She marveled at the sight of the twin warriors. Their dark hair drifted around them as they twirled, ducked, sliced, and killed. On their own, they were powerful, but together…god, they were a force of nature.

Wrenley noticed something coming down the riverbed, slinking from the thick darkness. She gulped, shrinking even more at the sight of a large reptile creature. Its long, slender body was low to the ground, but it moved fast. The creature had a short neck with a head sprouting several spikes. Its bulky tale was like a whip, swinging back and forth, devastating to anyone caught in its path. A giant warrior sat atop it. Wrenley eyed them, a chill sweeping over her at the sight of the oncoming duo.

Wrenley jumped over the formations and slipped down the loose gravel leading to the river, the rocks biting into her legs and hands as she slid. No one noticed her; they were too busy with the brothers. She ran full speed towards the creature and its rider, sword up and ready. Before she could make contact, she was hit by something from her left. She felt like a football player had intercepted her, a whole body hit that took her breath away and landed her on the ground and rocks. Legs and arms flailing, she cursed as the pain shot through her. Her sword went flying off into the distance, and she landed on her ass with a thud on the hard ground.

"Fuck…" She spat, trying to catch her breath, pain shooting up her leg and back from the impact. She rolled over onto her belly to see that a soldier clad in heavy armor had hit her. He held his sword and lifted it to strike, but she heard a cry, and the soldier suddenly fell forward, a sword through his neck. Kage pushed him to the side with his foot and pulled his dagger out of the soldier's abdomen.

"What the hell are you doing here?"

Wrenley was unable to answer because of the rush of enemy troops that descended on them. Alcott joined the two, and he and Kage continued to fight the slew of men that seemed never to end, no matter how many they butchered. Wrenley felt the fear sink into her, realizing they were trapped. Frustrated tears rolled down her face; why had she not paused and thought of a better plan? The three of them were backed into the bluff cascading over the river. As the twins hacked away at the oncoming cluster, Wrenley looked for a way out, but there was none. There was no way they could keep this pace, and she had just made it worse. The twins were overpowered and trapped, with no way to retreat from their position on the river's edge.

With one final push, the enemy troops swooped in and disarmed the brothers. One of the soldiers grabbed Wrenley by the hair and dragged her away from Kage and Alcott as she fought and struggled against him. Kage was tackled by four soldiers, still thrashing as he snarled at them. Three other soldiers shoved Alcott down to his knees. Wrenley had managed to wound a few with a sword she had picked up from a corpse, but she was practically worthless with it. Panic enveloped her as the drive of soldiers parted, and the lizard beast crawled to stand before them.

"Fucking Dragon..." Kage murmured, barely audible enough for Wrenley to hear.

The rider on the beast looked down at the three. The man on the beast laughed and pulled off his helmet, revealing his ugly, scarred face. She supposed 'Dragon' was appropriate for the man who towered before them. He must be a giant, two feet taller than the twins; his gigantic chest and shoulders were twice the breadth of Kage's. His skin was pale with a grey hue; his bloodshot eyes had large, dilated pupils, and he took them in with a crazed look. He smiled wickedly, Wrenley noticing several teeth missing in the front and what looked like a long scar from the corner of his mouth up to his cheek.

Dragon had only half of a head of dark, matted hair, looking as if the other half had been lost to an injury or a burn. He held a sword in his arm longer than Wrenley; the other held a spiked mace that could take out a horse if aimed right. She felt the color drain from her face as he approached, devouring them with his predatory gaze. And god, he smelled...her stomach recoiling at the pungent odor that wafted off him like a green, poisonous fog.

"Well, well, well..." Dragon chuckled as he looked down at them, cocking his head to the side to get a good view. "The dark, mysterious twins that have been a thorn in my ass for the last three years. I was beginning to think you were ghosts..."

Kage spat on him. The Dragon stepped back to avoid it, growling in response to the apparent show of disrespect. His eyes then shifted to her, only for a moment, unimpressed.

"I have been waiting for a chance to kill you," He steered back towards the twins, an unpleasant grin still plastering his face. "I may let my men fuck you first and then kill you, one by one. Maybe we will find your mother and make her watch." Wrenley could tell the brothers clenched their jaws, refusing to respond. It dawned on her then that Dragon did not know who she was...he had scanned her and dismissed her.

"It's what I did with your father...your brother," he snickered loudly as the other soldiers who held them shifted. "I killed them slowly, methodically, until they begged and pleaded to die. Then I impaled their mangled bodies on spears and watched as the crows and animals fed on their rotting flesh." The commander closed his eyes as if savoring the image in his head.

Kage roared and surged against the soldiers, but they held him. Dragon sighed then, shaking his head. "As much as I'd like to kill you now, your head is more valuable in the capital city. You will be hanged, you will be cut open, and you will be a spectacle for the entire kingdom…"

Dragon grinned again, "But we can still fuck you. Take the brothers, kill the girl after you do what you want with her." He waved a gloved hand and turned nonchalantly. The men moved the twins away from Wrenley, and she began to scream. Her mind rapidly cycled through scenarios: Dragon was unaware of who she was or why she was there. She was just another woman to him at that moment. She thought fast, her brain calculating what to do with the moments she had left.

"You ugly f-fucking coward! Don't you walk away from me!" It came from somewhere deep in Wrenley's gut. Dragon's spine visibly stiffened at the taunt. He had already pulled himself up on the serpent but turned the animal to face her.

"What?" He snapped, disbelief flashing across his face only for a moment.

"Yeah, you heard me." Wrenley shook off the hands that attempted to grab her and stepped forward, every muscle under her skin shaking. She pointed a finger at the commander, her chin raised defiantly. Pain shot through her back, and her pulse was thudding uncontrollably, but she puffed out her chest then, trying to make herself look as big as possible. "You're a goddamn coward. Maybe you should go fuck your own mother and leave us alone."

Dragon seemed to halt. Wrenley did not know whether he was processing what she was saying or the fact that she was speaking at all.

"Oh, right…I guess to fuck your mother, you'd need to know who she was...but that's hard when your mothers' a whore." Wrenley pronounced the last word slowly and purposefully, leveling him with her eyes.

A collective gasp rippled across the group of soldiers, and she felt them all take a step away from her. Wrenley did not move from her defiant stance, baring her teeth at Dragon in a sneer.

Wrenley found some kind of courage deep inside her, rumbling through her unconscious and pouring out of her mouth. She then raised one hand slowly and gave him the middle finger, accompanied by an additional insult to his mother and whatever sister he had. All common sense left her mind as all she could think about was stalling long enough that maybe Kage had a plan. At least she prayed he did because she was out of resources and ideas. A young enemy soldier pinned her arms with one hand, grabbed her hair, and pulled her head back with another. Dragon dismounted from his beast and strolled up to her, eyeing her like some zoo animal.

"You are spirited, woman."

She spat at him, hitting him in the face. The man holding her shoved her to the ground on her knees and punched her in the gut. The pain reverberated through her, and she groaned, coughing as she hunched over. She tried to catch her breath as another blow landed on her face, feeling her nose and cheekbone crack under the fist... She realized Kage had no backup plan. Three other soldiers held him, and the look he gave her was one of pure rage and hopelessness.

I'm in big trouble, she thought as Dragon leaned closer. His seven-foot frame towered over her, and he reached out to caress her cheek with a grimy hand; his thick, dirty fingers then ran down along her neck to her chest, where the curve of her breasts peeked from under her tunic. He grabbed her by her throat and hoisted her up, her legs kicking in protest. He was tall, tall enough to lift her feet off the ground. She felt his grip begin to crush her windpipe, and she started clawing at him. His arm was so long that she could not even reach him.

Unexpectedly, Wrenley felt a heat in her arms and legs. It was slight, but then it began to build. At first, she thought it was oxygen deprivation and maybe she was succumbing to the blackness, but there it was again—a tingle, an energy that crept up her arms and legs.

"What..." Dragon recoiled, ripping his hand away as if he were burned. He fell backward, scrambling away but still facing her as he cradled his smoldering hand. Wrenley looked down, gasping, realizing she was levitating above the ground. Her fingers began to quiver with more intensity, and she felt the heat radiate out of her fingers.

Everything began to bend together, and Wrenley felt something rise in her that had been dormant for as long as she could remember. Memories of the nights in the house, where she felt the presence of ghosts, swirled around her. In her mind, the colors of the crossing flooded through her, and images of her playing in the old house during the cold autumn days flashed. Then she saw Bronson in the shadows; he had always been there.

As if time had stopped, Wrenley looked down at one hand, the other, and then at Dragon. Wrenley let out a piercing scream, body rigid, her head thrown back and arms stretched out in front of her. The power was all-consuming.

Everything went black.

~ ~ ~ ~ ~

Bronson heard the skirmish long before the company could see it. They followed yells and clanging of swords until they were on the bluff over the ridge. They saw the enemy backing Wrenley and the two men into the corner. Bronson's stomach plummeted, knowing that if they did not get down the bluff soon, Wrenley would not stand a chance. They tried to find the fastest way down, and Bronson heard Wrenley screaming. He listened to the serpent grunt and roar, as well as some muffled voices.

Bronson and Garrick made it down the bluff and forced their way towards the clearing, but it was too late when they broke from the tree line. The large man had Wrenley by the throat, and the serpent was guarding his back. He knew the man standing before him, with his big, meaty hand around Wrenley's throat: his queen's throat. Bronson felt his blood begin to boil at the sight of Dragon assaulting her, her frail body thrashing around, her face pinching and turning blue. He would cut off that hand and shove it…

Suddenly, the hair on the back of his neck stood up as if a current of electricity had shot through him. He noticed something then and thought it was just a reflection of a sword from the torchlight, but it was more than that; it came from Wrenley. He then saw the sparks surrounding her, and her skin began to glow. Bronson was paralyzed as he watched the large soldier release her, his hand burning, falling back in agony. Wrenley stayed in the air, levitating, sparks flying from her fingertips.

Bronson almost stumbled back when she looked up at him, her eyes a stony black, her once-beautiful hazel eyes disappearing. Bronson's body went cold at the sight of her; at the absence of the Wrenley he knew. Then she screamed. It was the most profound and terrifying shriek he had ever heard. Her body went rigid, arms stretched, head thrown back. Light exploded, and a force came forth from her, shooting out of her like wind, rain, and lightning. It knocked the man and his beast backward, and each man holding her companions were immediately thrown back. The explosion caused so much illumination that he shielded his eyes with his forearm and turned his back to it, the force shaking his very bones.

The soldiers were wounded but were able to pick themselves up. Fifteen of them stood, weapons drawn. They were not as cocky now as they cowered at the sight of her. It was silent as death for a few heartbeats…Wrenley's ebony eyes sparkled in the moonlight, and she raised her hands to her chest as if holding something. The light was collecting there, growing, and, as if in slow motion, she raised her head towards the enemy troops.

"Release them."

Her voice was low, like a growl, almost mechanical. Wrenley turned her head slowly towards Kage and reached a hand towards them; the men who had held him began to scream, clutching their faces. Bronson watched in shock as blood began to pour from their eyes, nose, and mouth, realizing she was melting their eyes out of their sockets. Even with their screams and wails, she continued until they all were floundering on the ground. Her body flexed, brightness pulsated again, and members of the enemy army fell over. Dragon was far enough away that he quickly jumped on the serpent and retreated. The rest of the company had caught up with Bronson and Garrick, and they followed Dragon and the remaining men down the dry riverbed.

Kage snapped up from his position on the ground, Alcott behind him, as Bronson rushed up to them. Alcott, Kage, Garrick, and Bronson formed a semi-circle around Wrenley, her back to the cliff wall, like a wild animal caged and ready to lunge. She glowed, her eyes still black and vacant, the force of her power pressing them backward like a roaring wind. She was still slightly levitating a few inches off the ground.

Kage moved to go to her, and Bronson grabbed him by the shoulder.

"Stop! She could kill you," he murmured through clenched teeth.

Kage ripped himself from Bronson's grasp and sneered at him. "She won't hurt me."

"Listen to him, Kage, for Brigid's sake..." Alcott slowly sheathed his sword, put his hands before him in supplication, and started to back away from Wrenley.

Garrick did the same, "Bronson, what is this?"

Kage snapped his gaze to him, "Bronson Aughton?"

Bronson ignored everyone, slowly moving towards Wrenley with his hands outstretched, palms up. His heart thudded in his chest, either from fear or anticipation, he was not sure. She had descended back to the ground, hands to her side. Sparks still escaped her fingertips, and the light was lessening but still beating through her. One wrong move, and she could kill them all, but would she? She had exploded, killing over ten enemy soldiers and liquidating their eyeballs from their sockets without a second thought, but she had shielded all of them. It was as if she knew and was somehow controlling it. Her eyes were still wild, black, and eclectic; she looked down at her hands and then at Bronson.

"Wrenley?" Bronson mustered a cocky grin, and he neared her. "You sure know how to be dramatic." He inched towards her; his attempt at humor did not seem to faze her. She stared at him inanely, but the light dimmed ever so slightly.

"Wrenley..." Bronson tried again, feeling the magic in himself swelling in defense. He could not help it; he had no idea what this was and how dangerous it could be for Wrenley and everyone else. If she were to lash out, would he have it in him to strike back?

"Wrenley, it's me, Bronson." He extended one hand towards her, resting the other on his chest. "You know me."

"You..." Her black eyes flickered to his face and narrowed, her voice deep and cavernous.

It sent a shiver down his spine as he nodded, "I've been searching for you...I'm sorry..." He clenched his teeth, wishing this could be said privately and not in front of everyone, but he had no choice. "I'm sorry, Wrenley. I didn't mean to lose you."

Something flickered in her gaze; a faint recognition, just a sparkle of the Wrenley he knew. Taking in a deep breath, Bronson came to a halt before her, just out of arm's length, holding his hands out, encouraging her to approach him.

"Come to me, Wrenley."

He wiggled his fingers, beckoning her to come. Wrenley looked back down at her hands, and the sparks faded. The light was almost gone now; her skin was returning to normal. Her eyes began to clear faintly, and she looked back at Bronson; her beautiful hazel eyes returning from the blackness that had engulfed them.

"Bronson?" Her voice was hoarse but soft.

"Wrenley? Do you know who I am?" The four men held their breath in unison, waiting for her to answer. Wrenley's golden hair was wild; her clothes were spattered with the blood from the imploding soldiers around her. It appeared she had ripped her pant leg, blood gathering in the fabric there, and another gash on her shoulder. Blood ran from her broken nose, an ugly bruise forming under her right eye.

She paused and nodded deliberately. Bronson inhaled and reached for her with both arms, and she lunged for him. When they touched, Bronson felt something shoot through him. It was magic of some kind, and it was as familiar to him as the sun rising and setting. It spread through him like fire, almost buckling his knees. When Wrenley collapsed into his arms, his knees finally gave way. He clenched his teeth as they hit the hard earth and rocks of the riverbed. She sobbed in his embrace, burrowing her face into his chest, her arms gripping his neck tightly. He held her as she shook violently and looked up at Kage, who stood over them.

Wrenley tried to raise her head, but Bronson held the back of her head against him. "Don't look." He whispered, not wanting her to see the carnage around them, as he snapped his attention to the twins.

"What the hell has happened to her?" Bronson growled at them, cradling her in his arms but trying to twist and face them. "What did you do?"

"We didn't do anything but save her. She almost died thanks to you," Kage retorted, returning his sword to his sheath, his body still tense as he eyed Wrenley with concern.

"Died?"

"Yes, she got sick and fell into the river. You almost let her drown to her fucking death!"

"Sick?" Bronson's mind was reeling as he replayed the last three weeks over in his mind. The isolation, agitation, not eating…all the signs were there that she was unwell, and he had missed it. In his stubborn ignorance, Wrenley had almost wasted away right before him. He gritted his teeth and held her tighter, trying to focus on the conversation and not on the sweet smell of her hair. She continued to sob in his shirt.

"It's your black magic that is hurting her. You are playing with forces you don't understand! And because of that, something happened to her when you brought her here," Alcott held Kage back as he screamed at Bronson, having to use his body to hold Kage back.

"You don't know what the fuck you're talking about," Bronson murmured to the younger man, still holding Wrenley, his hand supporting the back of her head. She was dead weight in his arms. The sight of Bronson holding her was sending Kage into an unmanageable rage, and he suppressed his smirk.

"This is all your fault! You brought this evil onto us!"

Bronson rolled his eyes. "Shut up, you dimwitted brute. Someone get him a muzzle." Bronson waved him away. Alcott and Garrick then advanced to grab Kage again before he pummeled Bronson. Bronson held Wrenley, who was silent, face still hidden in his chest. Bronson felt it then, his magic rearing up to obliterate anyone who would dare to touch her.

"I will only say this one more time before I kill you: Stand down." Bronson's warning was feral, his tone low but deadly. Garrick pleaded with the younger man to walk it off and move away from the seer whose magic was beginning to stir again.

"Everyone, stop!" And everyone did…as Astara wobbled into the group of men with her cane. She moved slowly but gracefully, stopping to stand above Bronson and Wrenley.

"Nothing's happened to her," she said quietly, resting both hands on her cane.

"Of course, something's happened; look at her, Mother!" Kage thrust his hands towards them dramatically. Bronson tensed at the sight of the crone, recognition hitting him.

"No," she waved her son off, keeping her eyes on Bronson. "You know what is happening, Bronson Aughton."

Bronson sighed, freeing his hand to run it through his short black hair. He may know; if it were true, he was a fool for not seeing it. He looked up at the old woman and shrugged, "Astara. You look… the same, as always."

"And you look and smell like hell." She tapped his leg with her cane and motioned for him to follow her. "Come, we have a lot to talk about."

CHAPTER 15

Magical and Royal

"Was he looking for her?" Bronson gripped Kage's forearm, stopping him from exiting the cottage after he had laid Wrenley in the cot and Astara tended to her.

"No…he was after us," Kage's dark eyes went to Wrenley then, and he jerked his forearm away from Bronson. The younger man was now more composed, but his disgust towards the seer was evident. "No thanks to you; she about got herself killed."

"She tends to do that…" Bronson muttered as he rubbed the back of his neck. He eyed the younger man before him, now knowing exactly who stood before him. Bronson could not help but notice Kage's likeness to his father, and guilt engulfed Bronson from the flashes of memories that assaulted him. He did not blame the young man for hating him…but Bronson's leniency for disrespect would only go so far. Even Astara, who hated Bronson, knew Bronson's power and influence in this war and did not dare to provoke him.

Bronson had to find answers about what he had just witnessed with Wrenley. If his suspicions were true, his entire perspective on their mission would have to change. He would need more help, starting with Astara. Bronson braced himself when he looked at the older woman, remembering her collapsing on the earth in front of him when he delivered the news that her husband and son had been captured and killed. He had never heard wailing like that before, her body thrashing and convulsing from grief. Kage and Alcott had been mere boys at that point in the war. Astara had detested him for it, that he survived, and they did not. He hated himself even more; he had failed them all. He groaned and ran a hand over his chin, feeling the stubble growing from days of searching and not stopping to rest. It was not the first family he had failed, and it certainly would not be the last. The reality sobered him, and he frowned.

Dragon had been at that battle too; he was a mercenary for Earnesh. The enemy commander and his men were responsible for most of the senseless butchery in the lands. Garrick's men followed his trail for several miles down the riverbed tonight, but on that beast of his, he moved too fast for them to catch up. However, he left most of his men behind, which was lucrative for them. Bronson knew Dragon had seen everything and would no doubt return to Ailios and report about what he had witnessed or at least send a messenger to Earnesh. Bronson shook his head, realizing things just got more complicated than he would have liked, much too soon. He sighed as he heard the rambling of a male voice next to him. He then realized Kage had been speaking for quite a while, and he had not heard a word.

"You let her wander off, and she fell into the river a mile east of your camp. I followed her there…" Kage's voice was low, yet accusatory. "You didn't even know I was there…and you didn't even notice she had disappeared." His lips curled upward, sneering at Bronson. "I will not allow you to take her again without us. She's too…" his nostrils enlarged. "She's too important for you to be so careless."

Everything in Bronson wanted to smack this kid in the face. Kage had no idea what was happening in the unseen, what Bronson had to do, and what he had done…but Kage was not wrong. Bronson had fucked up, and he almost lost her because of it. He felt the pain in his chest at the realization that he could have lost her if Kage had not been where he was and stepped in. He gritted his teeth, knowing Kage would probably use it against him if they worked together. He shook his head and shoved past Kage, clipping the young man's shoulder as he passed.

~ ~ ~ ~ ~

Here she was again, in that place that seemed to be a dream, yet not. She stirred and looked up from the familiar bed, looking at the dirt ceiling. She was getting annoyed with this whole fainting thing, and she hoisted herself up, groaning at the pain from her tailbone and ribs. The smack to her head and chest left her with a pounding headache, and it hurt to breathe as she sat up with a heavy groan, muttering a string of curses that would have put a sailor to shame.

"I'm glad to see not much has changed…" Bronson muttered, sitting beside her as she allowed him to ease her back down to the soft pillows. She felt lightheaded and was once more frustrated that her body was letting her down. Her attention then traveled to the man beside her, and her heart skipped a beat. The last time they spoke was weeks ago, when she gave that girl the sweater, and she had been so angry at him that she had wished she would never see him again. She had also been so busy with Astara and her sons that she had no time to think about him. But as he sat beside her, his calming presence like a balm to her battered soul, she felt something shift within her as she realized she had missed him. He had been there her whole life, and the past several weeks she had felt out of place with his absence.

"How…why? You found me?" It was all she could think of to say.

"Of course I did; it wasn't hard," Bronson said, handing her some tea with herbs, his voice soft. "Your lightshow back there was hard to miss." Bronson's tone was flat, and Wrenley sucked in breath, memories coming back. "What happened to me?"

Bronson sighed, leaning back on the stool as if to study her, crossing his arms over his broad chest. Wrenley knew that was a sign of frustration for him. He looked tired yet fresh, noting his shaved face, ruffled wet hair, and the beautiful scent. He was dressed in a simple white shirt, black pants, and black boots. His mouth was pursed in a thin line, but she could tell he was attempting a grin for her sake.

"I was preoccupied and distracted when we crossed over. I was so focused on what we had to do that I didn't notice what was happening to you."

"Pay attention to what?" Wrenley sipped her tea, trying to piece together what had happened this time to make her lose consciousness. She remembered being hit in the face by the soldier, she remembered Kage and Alcott restrained…she remembered Dragon. Her stomach recoiled at the memory of the wretched enemy commander, and her hand instinctively went to her throat where he had gripped her.

"To you…" Bronson reached up and tucked a piece of blonde hair hanging in her face behind her ear. "You were vulnerable to things that aren't in your world. That's probably when you started feeling sick and exhausted…you should have told me, Wrenley." His voice was husky and low, his brown eyes looking at her through thick black lashes.

"You weren't exactly available…" Wrenley cut in sarcastically.

"I know…I was trying to protect you," Bronson said. Now, he moved a hand to her thigh, and she felt every point of contact between her leg and his fingertips.

"From what?" Wrenley set the mug of tea down and let out an exasperated huff. "You don't communicate very well, do you?"

He snorted, "I know, it was irresponsible of me. I didn't want to draw attention to us by being so close to you…"

"I don't understand what you are saying to me," Wrenley was getting annoyed at everything she did not understand. She balled her fists in her lap. "I'm about sick and tired of being the victim of things people think I am too fragile to understand."

"It's not that…" Bronson mumbled and moved out of her way, knowing he was unable to stop her as she flung her legs over the side of the bed and hoisted herself up onto her own two feet; she only wobbled briefly.

"Then what, Bronson?" Wrenley was standing up now, fighting the dizziness and angrier than anything. "People are going on about missions, magic, evil, this and that. I'm just trying to survive here. I'm frustrated because my body keeps failing me, and as soon as we get here…" She waved her arms in front of her, "Whatever the fuck this is, you emotionally cut me off. I don't understand what anything means right now."

Bronson also stood, and her eyes widened at how tall he was; she had forgotten how massive he was during their time apart. Slowly, Bronson leaned down, his breath tickling the shell of her ear. "I'm sorry."

He reached for her hand, but she wrenched it away. "Don't tell me sorry, tell me what is happening, Bronson,"

"He thought he couldn't be near you because they could track you if he were."

Wrenley spun around, hand flying to her heart in surprise. Astara sat on her usual stool in the corner by the stove. Her cane now tapped the floor rhythmically as she frowned at them, and she took a pull from her pipe. The smoke escaped from her nose, carrying the scent of tobacco, sweat, and earth.

"Track me?"

"It's because of my magic…" Bronson started, but Astara hit the table with her stick to silence the powerful seer, making Wrenley start.

Astara shook her white-haired head, "It's because of your connection. He felt it and thought it was just an attraction, but it's much more than that. The closer you two get, the greater it grows. The enemy could sense the power and may come looking if they have seers who are powerful enough to notice."

"They do, I'm sure of that," Bronson mumbled, folding his arms and rubbing his brow with his thumb. "They had one who was able to cross over. I dealt with him, but they are more powerful than ever."

"But you made a mistake, young seer. The danger of you being away from her is greater than the danger of you staying close. This entire situation could have been avoided if you had caught it. You still don't know what is in front of your face!" She slammed her cane on the ground with emphasis on each word.

"What is it?" Bronson and Wrenley both said in tandem, and Astara sighed, leaning back in her chair, taking another puff of her pipe, "She doesn't need you, Bronson Aughton, to have claim and power on the throne. She doesn't need any other human to complete her. She is both magical and royal; I don't know how that is possible. In all my years, I have never heard or seen something like this." She narrowed her dark eyes at them, "That is what draws you two together so violently: the magic in her."

"Wait…what?" Wrenley felt the wind knocked out of her, her hands shooting up before her in defense. She tried to process Astara's words but shook her head in defiance. "That's not possible. I don't have any magic…"

"You do…and we all know it, even Dragon now." Astara gave one last puff of her pipe before knocking it against the stones of the hearth.

Wrenley's eyes widened as she whirled on him. "That was your plan? To use me to get to the throne?"

"Absolutely not!" He growled, stepping back from her as if she had hit him.

"But the fact is, Wrenley now has more power than we can imagine. She doesn't need a marriage or a partner; she is just herself. And now, you will know who is loyal to you because if they follow you into this, it is solely to place you back on the throne...alone." She tossed a cold look at Bronson, scowling.

Wrenley stood looking up at Bronson. "Did you bring me back so you could use me to gain power to the throne? Even with the best intentions?"

"No," He did not hesitate, and Astara cackled in the background, "I've never trusted seers."

"Swear it on my mother, Bronson Aughton."

Bronson looked at Wrenley, his chestnut eyes taking her in as his gaze raked up and down her. He gritted his teeth but fell to one knee and reached for the dagger he kept strapped to his muscular thigh. He brought the knife up to his palm, and before Wrenley could react, he slid the blade across his left palm. Wrenley gasped as the blood filled the wound and pooled on his hand. She inhaled quickly as he grabbed her hand with his bloodied one and held it. He then brought his gaze up to meet her hazel eyes.

"Wrenley, daughter of Dolion and Adinnil...I swear my loyalty to you with no intentions of taking power from you. You will be my queen, and I will fight for you in this world and the next." He brought her tiny hand, covered in blood, to his lips and kissed it gently. Wrenley felt a rumble in her bones, and if she did not know better, she could have sworn the hut had shuddered with them, a deep power emanating from the seer. "I swear on your mother."

Wrenley's eyes widened not only at the act of slicing his hand open without batting an eye, but the words he spoke were tainted with power; these were not *just* words, they were an oath.

Did he have secrets? Yes.

Was there something he was keeping from her? Also, yes.

But was he safe? She was no longer sure—not after all of this.

Astara sucked in a breath and shook her head, "You'll have to fight harder than that, Bronson Aughton, for this woman."

"Fight for me?" Wrenley looked to Astara and then back at Bronson, who had shoved his hands in his pockets and dipped his head with a grin. As if on cue, Kage burst through the door, his brawny shoulders filling the frame, tearing through the room like a hurricane. His eyes were dark as he looked at them, standing close together. His nostrils flared as he saw the blood, and he had opened his mouth to speak, but Wrenley cut him off.

"Kage!" Wrenley was so relieved to see him safe, the cut on his brow seeming to scab. Kage swaggered towards her and wrapped his muscular arms around her waist, lifting her away from Bronson, putting himself between them. Bronson stiffened when Kage touched Wrenley, his jaw clenching possessively. Being the gentleman he was, he backed up and put his hands in his pockets, though Wrenley knew something was simmering in those dark eyes. She could feel them on her, like a storm brewing in the distance or a volcano waiting to erupt, and she shuddered.

Wrenley looked over Kage's shoulder to see Alcott slip into the cottage. He grinned, nodding towards Wrenley in silent confirmation, letting her know he was okay. Wrenley allowed Kage to engulf her for a moment, then pushed away and framed his handsome face with her hands, eyeing the cut above his eye with concern. "Are you sure you are okay?"

The young warrior grinned, "Yes. Pissed at you for being so stupid, but okay."

Wrenley reached up, tucked a loose wisp of black hair that escaped his braid, and pushed it behind his ears. "I thought we were dead."

"And I thought you had lost your damn mind."

Wrenley shoved him playfully. "Listen, you didn't come up with any ideas. I was trying to save your ass." Her grin faded as she looked at Kage, Astara, and Bronson again.

"What?" She asked, feeling their gaze on her.

"We can't stay here. We must leave tonight," Bronson said lowly. "Your magic could have alerted any enemy seers in the area. It's safer to stay on the move."

~ ~ ~ ~ ~

Wrenley did not remember the entire event. Once Bronson told her the details of her power emission, she began to reclaim bits and pieces of what had happened at the creek bed. It was like she had a dream but was having trouble recalling it. Bronson explained that crossing over had exposed her physical body to supernatural forces, and after the ordeal with the beasts in the woods, she began to grow weak from the energy being drained from her. Bronson admitted that her weakness may have been manageable if he had caught it and stayed close to her, but he did not apologize again.

But then again, if she had not fallen into the river, she would have never met Kage, Alcott, and Astara. Somehow, they were part of this story; she was unsure how they fit into it yet. Astara's words about Bronson and 'connection' confused her, but she was too exhausted to bring it up. What did they share in the unseen, and why was it so hard to discuss? Why was Bronson so hesitant to give her any information? Did he not trust her?

Bronson was full of mystery, secrets, and even darkness. He was dishonest with her and would selectively choose what to tell her. He was powerful, yes, and he could protect her. He was older and had wisdom that she may never have. He had stayed by her side for the first thirty years of her life. He was not going anywhere. The words of Astara had shaken her to her core at the thought that Bronson may have had motives for bringing her back to the throne, but he had sworn to her with his blood...

Then there was Kage, young and full of life and energy. He had no magic capabilities; however, he was brave and motivated. He was also moody and impulsive, but she was drawn to him. Sometimes, she felt Bronson was so far away, but Kage was right here. She could not help but see how the two men butted heads on almost everything, and the tension between them was practically tangible if they were in the same room for too long.

They had to leave the forest before the enemy flooded the valley, putting everyone at risk. The thought of Astara, the fairies, and anyone else harmed because of her made Wrenley sick. The plan was for Alcott and Kage to join the company as Astara insisted. She explained she was used to them leaving to fight and asserted she could manage on her own. As they packed to head west, Wrenley leaned down to hug the woman before her. She felt tears welling up, as this woman was like the mother she had left behind in her world. Astara hugged the younger woman tightly, her frail hand patting Wrenley on the back.

"Remember, don't let anyone tell you that you aren't exactly what you need," she patted Wrenley's cheek and gently pushed her back. "Believe me, these men will fight for you…But you must fight for yourself." The older lady then slipped something over Wrenley's head, and Wrenley looked down to see an emerald-green crystal nestled in a hand-woven net wrapped around her neck. Wrenley sucked in a breath and was going to protest this precious gift, but Astara held up her hand to halt any objection.

"You will encounter so many unnatural things, my dear. Magic, seers, wizards, witches…but never forget the power of Brigid and the earth. Look to the earth when all that magic fails you. May this stone of Brigid, the Goddess of elements, remind you that you have exactly what is needed when the time is right. Nature will provide a way out…always."

Wrenley gave the woman one last embrace, pinching her eyes shut to keep from crying. Astara seemed to understand and rubbed the younger woman's back gently. "We shall meet again, my lady…I promise."

Wrenley nodded, "And I will keep it safe until we do."

CHAPTER 16

The Lake

"Sail? Like on a boat?"

Wrenley did not like the sound of that at all. She scrunched her nose at the idea, and Bronson grinned against her hair as they rode together since a pack of werewolves ate her horse. Honestly, she did not think Bronson would allow her out of his grasp or sight for the foreseeable future. She noticed the way he gripped her tightly around the waist, sending shivers up her spine, even with her reservations.

"A boat is usually the only way to sail on the water."

Wrenley huffed and elbowed him, "I know that…I just don't know what I think about it."

Bronson chuckled; the deep sound sent goosebumps prickling her skin. She struggled to ignore how solid he was and how sitting against him was…dare she say arousing? She quickly dismissed that thought, afraid that with all his power, Bronson could somehow read her thoughts. That made her flush, and she dipped her head.

"Going across the lake is much safer than around it. Trust me…I've done both."

Wrenley shook her head, still unsure of boarding a rickety old boat and crossing a large body of water. It was bad enough to go on the pontoon boat on Table Rock Lake in the summer with her parents back home…

"Besides, we have to make a stop halfway across."

"Halfway?" Wrenley shifted to look up at him, and he gave a disinterested shrug again, "A friend of mine lives on an island halfway across the lake. He is the oldest and wisest Wizard I know. I think…I hope…he's still loyal to us."

"How will we know if he isn't?"

Bronson huffed, angling his head towards her. "I guess when we get there, we will know. But I have questions about you that we need to answer, and he's the only one I know who can help us. We must take a chance."

The company entered a small, rundown village on the outskirts of the lake before sundown. Within an hour, Bronson purchased passage on the boats for himself, Wrenley, the twins, and Garrick. The rest of the company would have to go a long way; it was simply unwise to travel in large numbers anymore. They would gather information and meet them on the other side. Bronson also secured lodging for the night, and Wrenley looked forward to a warm meal and something that resembled a regular bed since they had been traveling again. She had a small room, and the males shared a room across the hall.

Wrenley grinned to herself as she stepped into the humble room later that evening: she would love to be a fly on the wall in the other room with her male companions. Garrick and Alcott seemed to hit it off swell. Kage and Bronson, on the other hand, still argued over everything. If Bronson suggested it, no matter what it was, Kage fought him over it. If Kage commented, she could feel Bronson's eyes roll mockingly. Several times in the last seventy-two hours, Garrick had to physically get between the two males to avoid an all-out brawl. Wrenley could tell that Bronson was growing weary of the young warrior but was probably extending him some semblance of patience. Whether it was because Kage had saved her life or that Bronson and Astara had a history, Wrenley did not know. Kage may not have known how powerful Bronson was or may have underestimated him. Overall, everyone else was miserable trying to keep the two from ripping each other apart.

Wrenley settled in after a simple dinner of bread, cheese, and some type of soup with a suspicious, unidentifiable protein. She meticulously scrubbed every inch of herself with the provided bucket of water, scoured her clothing, and changed into a nightgown that Astara had given her. Though slightly thinner than Wrenley, Astara had given her several sets of clothes that she had been able to fit into. She noticed her body was changing; her breasts were filling out the clothes significantly. She also noticed that the curve of her spine was receding, her legs were straight, and her back was not curved as it once had been. She kept the weighty green crystal around her neck, not daring to take it off, fearing it might be stolen or lost. The room was sparse, but the fire was warm. She wondered if the others had such luxuries as a fire or if they would be stubborn and insist on toughing it out.

Exhausted and sore, she sat in front of the small hearth and basked in its warmth. She wished she had her library right now, her fuzzy slippers, and the weight of this situation off her shoulders. She brushed her long, golden locks of hair out and noticed they were longer, so she braided them. She assumed it had something to do with the magic of this place that made her body change.

Sighing, she leaned back in her seat, dozing, when she heard a soft knock on her door. She jumped up and peeked out, surprised to see Bronson waiting on the other side. She opened the door just wide enough to see his face, and he placed his hand, palm open, on the door; with the other hand, he held a decanter and two glasses.

"It may not be exactly what you're used to, but I thought we could share a glass..." he grinned lazily at her and added, "For old times' sake?"

She assumed it was a peace offering for the last few weeks. Though she and Bronson had been talking again, things were still strained, and doubt still lingered in the back of her mind. It was still awkward between them, and she shifted her weight from one foot to the other as she nodded. She allowed him in, and they sat together in the winged-back chairs, sipping on the wine together. Wrenley noted it was not a port, but it was not bad either; it was sweet and tasty, making it difficult to have just one glass. Between them, they had drained the decanter of every drop of red liquid in thirty minutes.

"Do you remember when you first met me?" Bronson asked, one leg crossed over the other, sitting like the gentleman she remembered from that first night in the library. He had worn a suit and a white-collared shirt with a tie then, much different from his travel clothes now. His dark button-down shirt was wrinkled from miles of travel, the dust from the road still on his pants and boots. She quirked a brow as she noticed he was slightly tipsy, if his flushed face was any indication. His black hair was rumpled, his eyes slightly hooded. She grinned, biting her lower lip to keep from giggling.

"It feels like ages ago," Wrenley mused, taking another long sip of the final glass, feeling the alcohol also give her a buzz.

"Yes, indeed it does," Bronson sighed, swirled the wine in his glass, and sniffed it. "You were reading that book and drinking wine. Your cat was hunting me in the background."

"Oh, I miss Nyx..." Wrenley moaned as she thought about her cat momentarily, then narrowed her eyes at him sheepishly. "I thought you were suspicious."

"I was pretty suspicious," Bronson chortled and shifted in his seat. "If a stranger tried to get close to you like I did, I'd kill him." Bronson shook his head at the memory and shot back the last of his wine, setting the cup down.

"What happened to that other man...the one you killed?" Wrenley trailed off, blushing. She did not want to make Bronson uncomfortable, but she also really wanted to know.

Bronson sighed heavily, "From the intelligence we gathered, the enemy had known for a while that you were no longer in this world and had traveled to another. It had taken the enemy fifteen years to figure out exactly where you went," Bronson lowered his head, looking at his empty glass, shoulders slumping ever so slightly. "That seer had once been a friend to me, an ally to your father..." Bronson trailed off, and Wrenley sucked in a breath.

"You had to kill a friend?" Wrenley whispered.

Bronson's face darkened, "He was after you...of course I killed him."

Seeming to shut the conversation down, he placed the glass on the table between the chairs and sighed deeply, his black hair falling over his forehead as he leaned forward. "I should go. Your guard dog in the next room will probably come looking for me if I don't show up soon." He jutted a thumb over his shoulder towards the door; his face contorted into a frown.

"He's not my guard dog; he's a good man," Wrenley countered, but could not help but giggle.

Bronson huffed, "He's a boy...not a man."

"He's done a lot of manly things, Bronson."

Bronson raised his eyebrows at her, "Exactly what kind of 'manly things', pray tell?" Bronson then shook his head, "Actually, please don't tell me or else I'll have to kill him too."

Wrenley gasped and reached out and slapped him on the shoulder, "Stop it! You're insufferable…Kage and his family have been nothing but kind to me." She would not utter a word to Bronson about Kage's kiss in the garden.

Wrenley giggled again at nothing in particular, and Bronson chuckled. Suddenly, they were heaving and laughing, unable to form words. Wrenley snorted, and Bronson hooted until his side hurt. They laughed together for a full minute; perhaps it was the wine or because Wrenley enjoyed Bronson, even if she was still mad at him for everything, and her trust in him had faltered ever so slightly…

Bronson looked over at her, and her breath caught in her throat at the sight of him. His large frame took up the entire chair, his broad shoulders dwarfing her in comparison, his powerful thighs spread apart as he lounged as if he had no care in the world. His well-defined chin sprouting dark stubble from days on the road. And his smell…god, it was everything she could do not to lean in to inhale the scent of spice and cedar that wafted off him. Even though she was pretty sure he had yet to bathe or shower, he still smelled so damn good.

She stared at him, running her tongue along her bottom lip as she noticed a heat in her belly that was unexpected. She shifted, clenching her thighs together, very much aware that her cheeks were now flushed with arousal, and she just prayed it was not obvious. She was acutely aware of her heart thudding in her chest as he cocked his head towards her and smiled, "Goodnight, Wrenley."

"Goodnight," Wrenley's eyes fluttered, and she leaned back in her seat, her nightgown drooping down to reveal the curve of her chest, but he did not seem to notice. That made her frown as she hoisted herself up and followed him to the door.

"Wait…"

"Hmmm?"

Wrenley was toe-to-toe with him now, noticing how handsome he looked in the firelight. She felt the buzz of the wine, a glow of excitement traveling down her spine and landing in her stomach. She felt her body reacting to him, and she could feel an ache settle between her legs that was foreign to her. She extended up on her toes to frame his face with her hands and kissed his lips softly.

Wrenley could feel a shudder race through Bronson's body, and she broke away and looked at him, needing him to signal her. Is this what he wanted? Or was this too much? She looked at his face, unable to read him. She also knew she had had a little too much wine.

"What are you thinking?" She asked softly, the buzz of the alcohol stealing away any shyness, replacing it with liquid courage. Her hands slid down from his face to the back of his neck, and for the first time, she heard him breathe. He sucked in a single breath and slowly let it out as if to regulate himself. She knew he was thinking hard; he always thought too damn hard.

"Tell me what you are thinking?" Wrenley whispered, almost pleading, pushing herself up against him now, her breasts invading his space, her arms linked around his neck.

Bronson reached for the hands resting behind his neck and maneuvered them before him, kissing them. "I think you are tired, and you are tipsy."

Wrenley was slightly offended, even if it were true, and she scoffed. "I can put three bottles of that stuff away before I get tipsy."

"I think we need to focus."

Wrenley heard the words coming out of his mouth, but she did not believe them. His body told a different story, and he kissed her hands again gently, leaning forward to where his forehead pressed against hers. She felt him sway a little, probably from the alcohol, maybe from exhaustion...

"I think..." Bronson said gruffly, seeming to lose his train of thought as Wrenley reached up to caress the exposed skin at his neckline. He groaned, moving his head to the side to expose the area between his neck and shoulder. He purred as she ran her nails softly down his tanned skin.

He shuddered again, "I can't do this...anything...with you, Wrenley."

Wrenley was not sure what 'this' was supposed to be, but she raised an eyebrow at him, "Why?"

"I am older than you."

"Hardly."

"I am much older than you. You are young and..."

Wrenley was offended now, pulling back from him, "I'm not

sure what you are saying. I'm thirty-two years old. Are you saying I don't have enough sexual experience for you?"

"Don't do this, Wrenley." His voice was gruff as he reached out and grabbed her wrist. "This isn't a good idea…" He finally shook himself and pushed her away, and she allowed him to. She felt the stabbing pain of rejection shoot through her; disappointment flooded her entire body. His refusal was probably one of respect, but it still felt horrible. She glared at him and crossed her arms in front of her.

"Okay, then go," Wrenley said flatly, shrugging her shoulders. Then, in dismissal, she waved her hand towards the door. Bronson's face was neutral as he turned and opened the door, slipping out quickly. Wrenley felt mortified as she watched him leave. She then felt her hands tingling, and she looked down, gasping: her hands were glowing again, sparks erupting from her fingertips. She looked at her hands and then at the door, wondering if she should follow him and tell him, but her embarrassment kept her feet cemented to the floor.

Bronson…what's wrong with me? Wrenley said in her mind, a tear falling down her cheek.

~ ~ ~ ~ ~

Bronson shut the door and leaned against it, congratulating himself for not only being an absolute ass but being able to tell her no. He saw the way she looked when he turned to leave, and it made him feel as though he had crushed her soul. Wrenley was stunning, alluring, a complete temptation; he wanted nothing more than to give in, but he could not cross the line she had hinted at. He could not care about her like this, could he? Bronson's head began to hurt, and he rubbed his temples, trying to think clearly. He cursed at himself, feeling his arousal press against his pants and imagining her leaning into him as she did. The last time Bronson put distance between himself and Wrenley, she wandered off and almost got herself killed. But there was a big difference between being close to her and…

And what? What did she…they want exactly? Because he had wanted it too, so much so that his magic stirred under his skin. He thought she was clear about it, the way she touched his face and rubbed the back of his neck, making his heart pound in his chest. He wanted nothing more than to give in to that feeling, but what was the cost? What if all the emotions and magic between them erupted into something like he saw the other night? What if the magic overtook her, and she was not herself anymore? He was also impeccably aware that he had held this same person when she was two months old. Her mother had trusted Bronson to get her to safety.

To keep her safe…and up until now, he had done a lousy job of it. Bronson groaned, feeling like a ridiculous fool.

He felt it then. Something…did Wrenley call out for him? He turned quickly, looking at her closed door and wondering if he had heard her call his name. He heard it again, his magic stirring to the point of illumination, and he reached for the doorknob and opened it.

~ ~ ~ ~ ~

Wrenley did not notice Bronson re-enter the room. She looked down at her hands; the sparks, almost like lightning bugs, glittered around the room in a frenzy. They flew from her fingertips as she swirled the light with her fingers. Surprised, she looked up at him as he stared at her. Mouth gaping, she quickly hid her hands behind her back, almost like a child caught playing with matches.

"Did you call me?"

Did I? Of course not, at least not out loud.

"No." She shook her head furiously. He stepped further into the room, shut the door behind him, keenly taking in the room, and then focused back on her.

"Your hands…" He began, but she stepped back, preventing him from seeing.

"Can you just leave me alone?" Wrenley muttered, irritation now bubbling up within her. She was tired of his wishy-washy attitude. She was exhausted and did not want to hurt him like she had hurt those men at the bluff. If he were not in the room, whatever this was could not harm him either. Not to mention the alcohol was wearing off, and her promiscuous courage was evaporating quickly.

~ ~ ~ ~ ~

Bronson closed the gap between them and grabbed her arms, forcing her hands in front of her, and studied them; they were still glowing. Bronson seemed to take it in, looking up at Wrenley and then back down at her glowing hands. "When did this start?"

"Just now, when you left."

Bronson held her tightly, watching the light and sparks dissipate. He kept her hands in his, allowing his magic to probe her. He felt the heat between them, the way she stiffened at his touch, the way she flushed when he caressed her hand. Her sweet face peered up at him as if looking to him for all the answers, and he had none. He would find them, though…he would go to hell and back to get those answers for her.

Bronson steadied himself and inhaled, then exhaled as he analyzed her skin and the disappearing sparks. He felt her pulse thrum in her wrist, the tension between them taut, her leaning away, and gently attempting to pull her wrist from him. He would not let go of it. He allowed a taste of his magic to flush out of him to reach her, trying to study whatever it was.

He felt it—it was something familiar. He sensed whatever was under the skin stir his magic, almost intoxicating him and making his blood warm. He struggled to keep both hands to himself, whether it was her magic, how she looked in that nightgown, or the wine. His large hand tightened around her wrist, and he pulled her towards him, but she resisted, the pain of his rejection moments earlier still evident in those hazel eyes.

"You can go," Wrenley said, her lower lip wobbling as she resisted his pull and squirmed to get free. "I'm fine."

"I know you are," he murmured, noticing her skin glow as her magic was triggered again. Whether it was arousal or anger, he could not tell. If it was the latter, he risks blowing up the whole damn village, but if it was the former...

He lifted her wrist to his lips and kissed it gently. He noticed the light pulsating at his touch, which answered some of his suspicions.

"Bronson, please just go."

Bronson sighed and dropped her wrist, his hands falling to his side, but he flexed his hands at the loss of her warmth. "Why do you want me to leave now and not a moment ago?"

He asked softly, but his heart still cracked as he spied a single tear caress down her cheek.

"I just…" She dipped her head and looked away. "I've never been beautiful to anyone, but you've made me feel more than just…ugly." She shrugged in embarrassment, warmth flushing her cheeks.

"God, Wrenley…" Bronson murmured, reaching to wrap his arms around her and pulling her close to him. He enveloped her, feeling her shudder, and a soft sob came from her. Losing every ounce of control he had thought he possessed, he managed to tilt her face upwards to brush a soft kiss on her rose-colored lips. He paused, feeling her body tense in his arms, but she did not pull away. He then felt her arch against him, and that was all the confirmation he needed.

He lowered his head slowly, brushing his lips against her again. Her mouth parted for him as he reached a hand to fist her hair. Gently but firmly, his other hand reached for the back of her neck, and he drew her into him, enveloping her with his mouth. She let out a soft moan that almost drove him mad. He pressed harder then, pushing her backward until the back of her knees hit the bed, and she nearly fell.

Bronson caught her, holding her close to his chest as they paused to look at each other. He was unsure if it was a minute or an hour, but he was lost in that hazel stare. He felt his arousal, gently grinding his hips against her stomach, and she gasped, placing a hand flat on his chest as if to feel his heartbeat. Bronson felt the urge to rip her nightgown off her, aching to stroke that delicate skin underneath the thin fabric. Bronson took in a shaky breath as he ran a knuckle down her cheek, following her neck and over her chest to the soft curve of her breast. He heard her inhale, and she arched into him again, bucking her pelvis against him. He felt his breath catch as his hand then traveled down to her hip, then cupped her ass from behind. He gritted his teeth as she moaned quietly, grinding harder into him. He knew better, but he just could not fight it.

~ ~ ~ ~ ~

Stupid, stupid, stupid! Wrenley thought of herself as she felt his hardness against her front. She sensed a connection to him in an intoxicating way, as she had been yearning for him all these weeks. She had felt a shadow of it since the night in the library, where they shared a glass of wine and some conversation. It was as if the connection had begun that night but was not yet fully complete.

"I've never…" She whispered, pushing against his chest to look at him. She felt her cheeks flush and embarrassment wash over her, "I've never been with a man before."

Bronson looked down at her thoughtfully. "I know."

"You do?" She said, raising an eyebrow, too breathless to feel embarrassed.

"If anyone had as much as looked at you, I would have killed them." He growled as he again lowered his lips to hers, then trailed from her ear to her neck. He still held her as if trying to decide if he would push her onto the bed or not.

"Oh…" she replied with a grin, and Bronson laughed at her surprised expression, but became somber, "Wrenley, things are so complicated…"

Wrenley did not allow him to finish the thought but reached up and grabbed his face, smashing his lips against hers. He rumbled, and she felt him firm against her thigh. He ground against her even harder, with more and more pressure, to where she felt like she would explode. Her whole body ached to feel more of him, all of him. Bronson reached a hand up to her breasts over the fabric; her breathing became more sporadic as she felt his other hand slide down her thigh and snag a finger beneath her nightgown and underwear. She gulped, looking him in the eyes as if to dare him to go farther.

Bronson gazed down at her, and she could feel the energy pulsing off him. Chest heaving, sweat breaking out over his brow, Bronson reached down between her legs and ran his thumb between them. Wrenley felt her knees buckle at his touch and whimpered, fisting his shirt and yelping in pleasure.

"You're wet for me…" he murmured against her ear, and she all but collapsed from the pleasure shooting through her. He held her up with one arm as his hand gently caressed her folds. She widened her legs for him, and he pushed two fingers up inside her. She squealed softly, hanging onto his muscular forearms, her head now falling back as she allowed him to feel inside her. He leaned down to kiss the exposed flesh of her chest, traveling to the nape of her neck and sucking, leaving a bruise.

"Come for me…" It was a soft but firm command, and Wrenley felt the heat coil between her legs as Bronson continued to stroke inside her with two fingers. She began to feel it building in her core, a flush of heat swelling so powerfully she began to writhe against his touch. So close, she was so close…

"Bronson! Please…"

~ ~ ~ ~ ~

Bronson's body jarred as a loud knock sounded at the door. Wrenley and Bronson froze precisely where they were, Bronson's hand still between her legs, the other holding her waist. They both looked at each other for a moment, wide-eyed.

"Wren? You in there?"

"Fuck…" Bronson released Wrenley so abruptly that she fell backward on the bed. Her eyes widened as the orgasm that had almost enveloped her disappeared, and she moaned in disappointment. Bronson looked down at her, trying to give her a serious look, but she clapped her hands over her mouth, eyeing him up and down.

"I've never seen you move so fast," she said, suppressing a giggle.

"Shit!" Bronson tried to sound mad, but he stared at her for a long moment, taking her in as if imagining what they could have done…

"Shit…" He said more softly this time, his gaze taking every inch of her, and he was keenly aware of her arousal still on his fingers.

"Hide!" She hissed, trying to keep her laugh low. Kage's deep voice bellowed from the other side of the door as he banged again, getting louder the longer she did not respond. Bronson grinned at her one last time and quickly slid under the bed as Wrenley straightened her nightgown and took a long breath to calm herself. She tripped over several items on the floor, made it to the door, and flung it open, her mass of blonde curls in a frenzy around her shoulders.

"I, wow…were you sleeping?"

Wrenley shrugged, "Maybe."

"Are you drunk?" Kage tightened his eyes at her.

"Why?" Wrenley felt slightly offended but then laughed. "Yes, I sure am."

"Alone?"

Wrenley did not miss a beat, saying, "Best time to drink is alone."

"Indeed."

Wrenley and Kage stood in silence for an awkward moment, and she blew air in her cheeks, still feeling the buzz of wine in her head.

"Do you need something?" She asked pointedly, allowing the nightgown to fall slightly off her shoulders as she leaned against the door jam. She knew she was being a flirt, but she calculated that he might leave if she caught him off guard. To her surprise, Kage met her stare without hesitation. He did not move or react, except for his eyes traveling over her, then to the soft white skin revealed at her shoulder. Then his gaze zeroed in on the curve of her breast, where Bronson left a bruise. Wrenley felt herself blush, which seems to be something she has been doing a lot lately. She knew Kage's eyes were studying her, and she shifted, realizing she had failed to make him uncomfortable.

"Is that my mother's nightgown?"

The air seemed to have been sucked out of Wrenley's lungs in an instant, and she just gawked at the handsome man in front of her. Any attempts to connive him were gone, and humiliation took its place. It indeed was his mother's nightgown, and her face turned a shade of crimson. Kage noticed the discomfort and grinned at her; he knew exactly what she was up to.

"I'm looking for Bronson; we have to discuss plans for tomorrow." Kage crossed his muscular arms in front of his chest, cocking his head and smirking at her. With his height, he could peer into her room over her head easily.

"He's not with you?" She muttered, adjusting the nightgown back up on her shoulder.

"No…usually I can find him right up your ass," he retorted.

Wrenley shrugged, pulling the nightgown back on her shoulder and trying to reclaim some dignity. She seemed to sober up slightly, "I don't know where he is either…certainly not here…in here…with me…not up anyone's ass."

"I find that hard to believe…" Kage frowned at her, arms still crossed over his chest, his muscles bulging, and he seemed to be flexing them as he stood before her. He glanced over her head into the room one final time and seemed slightly more convinced when he confirmed she was alone, "You two are joined at the hip most of the time."

Wrenley shrugged again, putting her hands on her hips defensively. "We are not!"

"Well, if you see him, will you tell him I will be at the tavern?"

Wrenley sighed, "I guess… I'm going to bed, though."

"Sure, you are…." Kage gave her one last suspicious look, sneered, and turned to leave.

"I'd ask you to join me, but it seems you've consumed enough alcohol for the night…Lightweight," he threw back over his shoulder playfully as he trudged down the stairs that descended to the dining area. Wrenley stiffened to protest, but he was already gone. She then remembered Bronson, who was hiding under her bed. She slammed the door shut and swung around.

"Are you alright?" She clambered to her knees, laying her cheek against the cold wooden floor to look under the bed, but he was not there. She gawked and shot back up onto her knees, scanning around the dimly lit room; there was nowhere else for him to hide. She searched for five minutes and huffed to herself when she concluded he must have used magic to escape the room undetected through the single window. A swell of disappointment hit her, but she shook her head; the alcohol was wearing off. What on earth had she about done?

CHAPTER 17

Wizard

Wrenley did not like water; perhaps it was more what was under the surface of the water. She clutched the railing of the small ship, white-knuckled as it bobbed up and down with the wake, making her stomach grumble. The lake was so vast that it gave the impression of an ocean; the black, inky water lapped the side of the boat, and a mist rolled off the shore, making visibility difficult. Wrenley could not help but shiver at the eerie feeling that swept over her as she peered down into the black abyss. It was as if something lingered just under the surface, a deep, dark presence that she could not recognize and had no intention of wanting to know.

Bronson had explained it was easier for them to cross the lake by boat than to go around on land. Wrenley would take his word for it…under protest. Wrenley felt herself shiver in the wind and pulled her cloak tighter around her. The air was calmer on the lake, but she also trembled at the memory of last night with Bronson. He had left her room, probably using magic to slip out the window, leaving her feeling like an absolute fool.

"Sleep well?" Kage asked, grasping the rail as she did and leaning forward to look into the water. His dark hair was wet from the lake's spray and pulled back into a knot at the back of his head. He looked energetic as his dark eyes gazed on in curiosity. Had he ever been on a boat before? His question made Wrenley squirm and blush. She had not slept well because her brief encounter with Bronson so aroused her that she lay there all night, wanting him to come back. She also had never pleasured herself before, but at this rate, she would have no other choice.

"I did," she lied.

"Any sea monsters yet?" He bent over the side of the rail even further, and Wrenley reached out and grabbed his shirt.

"Stop! You'll fall over."

"I can swim…good enough to save your ass from the river if you remember."

"And get eaten by a sea creature for breakfast?"

"Sea monsters are just a bunch of stories and legends," Kage said lowly as he turned to her, snatching her hand and holding her wrist. She sucked in a breath as he gently held it, rubbing it with his thumb. He held her gaze briefly, but it was deep and affectionate. His gaze flickered to her breasts as if remembering her in his mother's nightgown the night before. Silence lingered between them for a moment, electricity sparking between them.

"Tell that to the sailors who swear by them," Garrick said as he and Alcott strolled to join them on the deck. Garrick's hands clasped behind his back as he glanced into the dark water, shaking his head, "I hear many things lurk in the depths. Giant squid, see dragons, kelpie…it deserves a healthy respect."

She then noticed Garrick reach out and touch Alcott's arm as he pointed out a bird over the ship, and they shared a glance. Wrenley's eyebrows shot up; was there something more happening between them? They occasionally shared glances and seemed to enjoy each other's company. Some may look at them and assume they were best friends. But… were they?

"We'll be arriving at the island soon, and then we'll travel on foot to the castle in the middle of the island. Let's hope the host is on our side," Garrick's voice brought Wrenley back to the present.

Wrenley asked Garrick, "What are the chances he is not on our side?"

Garrick lifted his shoulders in uncertainty. "Bronson and I spoke to him about a year ago. At the time, he was leading the resistance in this area. Let's pray to any god who will hear that he is still our friend; he's quite a powerful wizard."

"I hope so too," Wrenley murmured, turning away from the group and leaning on the railing again. The freshwater sprayed up at her, and she breathed in intently. Her headache was subsiding now, and maybe even her embarrassment waned. She had avoided Bronson's company at all costs this morning, fully aware that she had pushed him into their interaction last night. Her cheeks heated, and her stomach fluttered at the thought of his hardness grinding against her, his lips ravaging her neck…even in her inebriated state, she had been desperate for him. It was not just his dark, striking looks, but also his immense power and control, that were so attractive. She grabbed the railing tightly now, feeling the splinters rub against her tight grip.

"Careful…you'll split the railing."

Wrenley held her breath at Bronson's voice beside her. His tall frame leaned against the railing, back towards the water. He crossed his arms in front of his chest and looked at her intently, a smile tugging at the corners of his lips, "Your knuckles are looking a little white there…"

She did not answer, nor even look at him.

"Enjoying the lake?"

She avoided his gaze and kept her face looking outward toward the water, wisps of golden hair hitting her face. Bronson turned around and propped his elbows on the railing, dipping down to whisper in her ear, "Do you want to talk…"

"No," She felt his breath against her ear and pulled away. "Are there monsters in the lakes?"

Bronson seemed surprised at how she cut him off, but he took her cue and straightened beside her. "It depends on who you ask, but the ones who sail this stretch of lake say there are."

"Like what?"

Bronson slightly gestured with his shoulders, looking back down at her again, and she finally met his gaze. She was so embarrassed she could barely look at him. She had thrown herself at him and almost taken advantage of him. He would not have been in her room if she had not insisted, if she had not made him feel obligated…why did she not take no for an answer?

She wanted to crawl into a hole and die somewhere. The second-best option was to throw herself in the lake and hope one of those monsters gobbled her up before she would have to apologize to Bronson. After another agonizing moment, she opened her mouth to attempt an explanation, but Bronson cut her off. He had stepped behind her, placing his long arms on either side of her, caging her against the rail. He bent over to whisper in her ear against her golden curls.

"Just so you know, Wrenley of the house of Dolicn…I was

planning to make you moan last night." His breath was hot against her ear and neck, and she felt herself flush. Heat traveled from her ear where he whispered, down her back, to between her legs. Though the air was cool, she was sweating profusely, and she shifted, very aware he now had both arms on the railing with her in the middle, him straddling her, his pelvis pressed against her back.

"…And how you think you could take advantage of me is very enduring."

Wrenley felt her knees buckle slightly, and she was thankful for the railing, or else she would have melted like butter right there on the deck of the ship. Bronson pressed against her backside one last time, causing her to gasp.

"I promise you, my lady…I would enjoy every single moment of whatever you imagine doing to me in that beautiful head of yours, and you have my full consent." She could feel his lips on her ear, goosebumps prickling her arms.

"You don't have to…"

"The concern for my honor is appreciated but unnecessary," he interjected, the last words a seductive growl in her ear, and he pushed off the railing. He sauntered away, throwing a glance back at her with a wink. Wrenley was left panting, eyes round as she watched him walk away triumphantly; he knew what he was doing to her and enjoyed it. That bastard…she felt no guilt at all now.

~ ~ ~ ~ ~

As scheduled, the boat landed on the island at midday, and the group disembarked and proceeded on foot for the remainder of the journey. Wrenley noticed Bronson was stiff and on high alert; the others were more excited and rambunctious. Alcott, Kage, and Garrick were mighty warriors, but sometimes, they reminded Wrenley of a pack of high school boys. They seemed to know the seriousness of the situation and sobered as they advanced closer to the large castle.

The castle was built on elevated ground, perched on a cliff with massive rocks at its base. It could be seen long before the boat landed, and Wrenley heard that boats dared not allow any of their men to set foot on land. The villagers around the lake believed it was cursed. It looked gigantic as she craned her neck to take it in as they moved closer. There was no sign of life outside; however, Bronson kept trudging forward as if he knew exactly where they should go. She followed him meticulously, Kage very close behind her. His hand rested on the hilt of his sword, the gesture sending anxiety rippling through her.

The group finally reached level ground, and before them lay a significant incline paved with stones, large enough for an army to travel on, sloping upwards to a set of giant wooden doors entering the castle gates. They advanced, Wrenley feeling small compared to the immensity of the castle. Bronson pursed his lips as they neared the doors and waved his gloved hand. Suddenly, the door swung open, the creaking sound almost deafening. Bronson looked back at everyone and motioned to follow; they entered watchfully.

The courtyard of the castle was abandoned, its walls deteriorating from erosion. She smelled rain and dirt...the cobblestone beneath her feet was slick. Somehow, things felt wrong, though she was unable to say why or how. They ventured silently through the courtyard, observing the broken-down structures, waning stone statues, and overgrowth of vines and foliage. Wrenley was in awe as she lifted her gaze upward, taking in the tall structures built into the high castle walls. She mused that it must have been a fantastic sight in its prime.

They made their way through the courtyard and into what appeared to be a larger area surrounded by hefty stone towers. Bronson headed towards the left, and they followed him without question. A smaller door into the building's wall was open, barely hanging on its hinges, and Kage and Alcott quickly drew their swords. Though no words were spoken between the men, they entered the building. They returned a few moments later, swords down.

"It's abandoned," Kage stated, raising his sword and resting it on his shoulder. "It looks like it's been uninhabited for a while."

Bronson's murky chestnut eyes shot back and forth, his dark hair wet, and he slicked it back out of his eyes as he took in the scene around him. He went past the brothers as if to see for himself.

"I'm telling you, Bronson, no one's here," Kage held, rolling his eyes as Bronson knocked him in the shoulder as he passed. Wrenley followed, and the three men flanking them. Beyond the door, it looked like it was once a great hall, but Kage was correct: no one was home. It was run-down, with holes in the ceiling and vegetation as thick and lush as it had grown over the years. Bronson stood in the middle of the room and put his hands on his hips, spinning in a slow circle as he took it all in.

Again, something did not feel right to Wrenley, and she reached out to touch Bronson's arm.

"I think we need to leave," she whispered, and Bronson turned back to her.

"We can't…" Bronson responded quietly, not looking at her but looking up.

"Why?" A chill crept over her at his tone.

Bronson finally tore his gaze away from whatever held it and looked at her, "Because I was here a year ago, and this castle wasn't crumbling. We've been led into a trap."

The words had yet to sink in when laughter echoed off the cold walls of the old hall, amusement that made Wrenley's stomach drop. She looked around the space frantically, catching a glimpse of a silhouette floating above them, almost as if it were made of shadows. He appeared before them in complete form then, levitating above the ground, black energy swirling around him. A whirlwind of fog, mist, and shadows ebbed around him. The man was old, dressed in long black and purple robes. He had a large grey beard, long white hair, and a pointy black hat.

"Bronson Aughton!" The older man bellowed, his voice booming so loudly that Wrenley wanted to cover her ears. It echoed off the stone walls and reverberated through the air. "What a surprise to find you at my dwelling."

"Nicolas! We have come to seek your counsel," Bronson bowed, motioning for the rest to follow suit. Bronson dropped to a knee, one hand splayed on the ground, the other behind his back.

"It's a dark time to be seeking me out, Bronson Aughton. How dare you come in here as if we are friends?"

Bronson snapped his head but did not respond, a muscle feathered in his jaw. Wrenley could tell he was thinking, probably planning his escape route if this plan went to shit.

"We may be too late…" Garrick whispered, slowly pulling his sword out of its sheath. "Nicolas and Bronson parted on good terms a year ago. He may be turned."

"What do we do?" Wrenley asked, breathless. The sheer power of this wizard was pulsing around them, and Wrenley could feel it inside her blood. It was as if her magic pulsed with his, and it thrummed in her head, *Thump, thump, thump.*

"Nicolas, I am your friend," Bronson stood his full height, opening his palms flat on his chest over his heart, "You taught me and Dolion many years ago. I need your help now."

The wizard roared and slammed his staff against a pillar that held up what was left of the old roof.

"Enemy! Traitor!"

"No! Please, Nicolas…" Bronson attempted again, but the wizard thundered, and a bolt of light came from him towards Bronson. Bronson waved his right arm behind him, knocking Wrenley and the others back with an unseen force. He swung his left arm above his head as the bolt of light struck him. The light then bounced off Bronson and back at the wizard. This seemed to make the wizard even angrier; he exploded, the wind picking up pieces of old furniture, wood, and rock to carry them into the cyclone. Garrick and Alcott scrambled for something to hold onto, Kage crawling on his belly to put an arm around Wrenley, as the wind was so mighty, it would either pick them up and throw them or hit them with debris.

Bronson stood in the middle of it all, his skin vibrant with light, his muscular arms flexed, and his hands in front of him. Bronson lifted himself into the air, his powers beginning to catch momentum to match the other wizard. Wrenley raised her eyes to see him and felt her breath catch at the power and beauty she saw in him. Bronson's long black coat was waving around him, his gloved hands still outstretched to the sides, his face glowing and beating like the wizards.

They clashed with inhuman power, lights flashing, thunder cracking as electricity shot through the air. Bronson lifted himself higher into the air with his arms outstretched to be level with Nicolas, and the wizard swung at him with his staff. The two pushed back and forth with energy; all the while, the storm around them was becoming more treacherous. Bronson's eyes turned black, sparks and fire coming from his fingers.

"My god," Kage murmured in her ear as he attempted to hang onto her, fighting the suctioning power of the wind. Wrenley was frozen as she beheld Bronson in this state, never having witnessed so much power in her life. He did not even look like Bronson anymore; his form seemed to fade in and out, his body translucent. His body seemed to morph in and out, flashes of another form appearing just for a moment and then disappearing in the fray.

"We need to get out of here, now!" Kage screamed above the raging wind, pulling her beside him as he tried to tug Wrenley towards the door.

"No! We can't leave him!" She shrieked back, fighting against Kage to get closer to Bronson. She could barely see him now; their powers' light, wind, and force were like a massive black wall. It was as if they were in the middle of a gigantic tornado or cyclone of matter, magic, and wind.

"We'll die if we stay!" Kage thundered.

"Then we die!" Wrenley screamed, her rage igniting her magic. Suddenly, a rock the size of a fist flew from the cyclone, hitting Wrenley on the forehead and knocking her and Kage backward to the ground. The moment Wrenley hit the ground, Bronson snapped his head towards her. It was just enough distraction for the wizard to knock Bronson out of the air. Bronson's body crashed to the floor, but he rolled and jumped back up to his feet. Bronson hit hard but could lift himself back up with his power. He lost too much momentum, and the wizard waved his staff, a groundswell of force pushing Bronson down to his knees.

"No!" Wrenley screeched, gaining her wits from the blow and frantically clawing her way toward Bronson as blood gushed from the wound on her head. Bronson's hands were now forced behind him with invisible energy, and he was on his knees, the wind now swirling around him. Bronson began to scream as his body convulsed in pain.

"Help him!" She sobbed and pulled on Kage, but he was still disoriented from the debris that had knocked him down. The utter strength of the wind pinned Garrick and Alcott to the ground. With these conditions, Garrick could not shoot an arrow if he tried. Wrenley used every ounce of strength to stand and watch, and Bronson began bleeding from his nose and mouth.

"Stop! Stop! Stop!" Wrenley screamed, a guttural sound coming from deep down and welling up until every ounce of hate shot out like a bullet from her mouth toward the wizard. Wrenley felt it, but she knew exactly what 'it' was this time and embraced every drop. She felt the fire and heat caress her veins, her arms and legs pulsing, and her skin began to glow. She allowed it this time, permitting it to be unchecked and untethered. Light roared from her in two spinning pillars, and they tore through the cyclone. The scream was like a wave of energy that closed the distance between her and her enemy. It knocked the wizard back, and he paused from his torture of Bronson long enough to identify that she was the source of it.

"What the hell…?"

"Stop!" Her throaty warning was deep and robotic, shaking the ground as she uncoiled her limbs and stretched her arms on either side of her. Wrenley's eyes flashed then, the blackness taking over her hazel eyes, her features transforming. Wrenley exploded as if she pulled all the blackness in and detonated, with light and energy raging out of her body as it lifted her into the air.

Autumn colors. Oranges and red….

Falling…or flying?

Thrashing, pulsing, raging….

She then saw red…was it blood?

Things spun again, and she felt like she was moving but going nowhere.

I will not lose him, she said to herself. *I will never lose him.*

~ ~ ~ ~ ~

As Wrenley blasted upward, the energy leveled everything within ten feet of her except for Bronson. She shielded him somehow from the blow of the energy that came out of her. The wizard was knocked out of the air like a rag doll, and he yelped as he plummeted to the ground on his ass with a thud. He groaned, and the cyclone disappeared almost instantly. Wrenley hovered above him now, balls of fire in each hand, the pillars of fire still circling the little man. Wrenley curled her lips back and bared her teeth at the wizard. Her eyes resembled black stones; power and light pulsated through her and reverberated through the room. It was a deafening, persistent 'hum, hum, hum'. The emotions she felt within her were enough to kill this man where he lay, wizard or not, and she wanted to do it. She wanted to see him die slowly and painfully.

"I will kill you," her voice was calm but thickening as she raised her hands, ready to lash out at him. Her magic was whispering to her to tear him apart piece by piece.

"Wait! Wait!" He said, lifting his shaking hands above him in surrender. The wizard pulled a white handkerchief from his pocket and waved it frantically.

"You win…I know now!"

"Know what?" Wrenley bellowed, her voice echoing against the rock walls of the old buildings. Her body was still suspended in the air, and light continued to cascade from her.

"I know you are not of the enemy, but I had to make sure! Please!"

"Prove it!" She shouted, and he flinched, holding up his arms in front of him as if knowing she could strike him with that power at any moment.

Nicolas snapped his finger, and suddenly, the old, decaying buildings melted away; beautifully kept towers and buildings replaced them. Colors, smells of food, and warmth flooded around them as the spells faded.

Wrenley paused and suddenly felt herself shake awake as if rousing from a nightmare. She lowered her hands, and her body slowly descended back to the ground as the mirage faded. It had been a trick; the wizard had cloaked the castle with a spell to make it appear deteriorated and run-down. She felt her chest rise and fall with her breath, still feeling the itch to catapult a ball of energy at the wizard's head.

This was different from the last time for Wrenley; she knew she had control of her power, but almost lost control of her rage. The thought of this wizard hurting Bronson made her want to slash him apart, piece by piece, dissecting him alive until he could no longer beg for mercy. She felt herself taking deep breaths to calm the wrath inside her. When her feet were steady back on the earth, she ran to Bronson's side as he lay on the ground. He was motionless as she knelt beside him, using her arms to pull him against her. She fell backward, his full weight on her. Kage was behind her and reached out to break her fall, his sword drawn, and he pointed to the wizard, who was now sitting in the dust cross-legged, only feet away. He appeared much smaller now and less scary than moments ago.

"What is this?" Kage demanded, his sword still pointed directly at the old wizard's throat, one hand still on Wrenley's shoulder. "What have you done to him?"

"This is remarkable…" The wizard almost whispered and used his staff to push himself up, not taking his eyes off Wrenley, shoving Kage's sword away with one hand.

"I never thought I'd live to see this day…"

"I've been getting that a lot lately…" Wrenley muttered as she felt Bronson's forehead. He stirred in her arms, and she laid a hand on his chest to feel his heart thumping under her palm. She sighed faintly, relieved he was still alive. She tore fabric off her shirt sleeve and wiped the blood away from his nose and mouth with it, still shaking violently from the fear of losing him.

"What day?" Kage sounded like he was losing his patience as he finally lowered his sword.

"The day our royalty would return to us."

Bronson moaned and tried to sit up, but Wrenley held onto him, murmuring for him to be still. Her hands traveled over his arms, chest, and down to his thighs as if unconvinced he did not have some fatal wound hiding out of sight.

"Careful," he whispered in her ear, "You'll get me excited."

She let out a laugh that was more of a sob, his attempt at humor warming her as she wrapped her arms around him and laid her head on his shoulder. She squeezed him so tight he moaned, and she relaxed her arms. Her gaze flashed to the wizard and then to Kage, "You better get him out of my face before I fucking finish the job."

Kage eyed Wrenley, knowing how serious and capable she was of carrying out that threat. He sheathed his sword and motioned for the wizard to move away, and Nicolas obeyed, muttering to himself. Wrenley turned back to the man in her arms and let out a ragged breath.

"I thought I fucking lost you," she whispered in his ear, taking in his cedar and spice scent. She held him tight, her hands still roaming over his chest, still not convinced he was unharmed. "Never do that to me again."

She shook him lightly as if to augment her command. He chuckled, stirring in her arms, allowing his head to fall against her chest, and grinned up at her. "I will do my best, but no promises."

"Are we safe?" Wrenley uttered, dipping her mouth close to his ear again, running the tip of her nose on the side of his face. She felt his shift, and it took every effort for her not to kiss him. She had never felt such dread in her life, and she never wanted to let him go for fear of him being ripped away.

"From Nicolas? Yes, he's telling the truth," Bronson slowly sat up with a grunt, and she changed positions to hold his shoulders. He continued, "I think our biggest concern is you now."

Bronson grinned at her, and she gasped as she noticed her hands were glowing every time she touched Bronson, leaving sparks trailing behind. She pulled them away from him and twisted to look at the others. When they noticed her glare, Garrick, the twins, and even Nicolas snapped from their staring and pretended the walls and ceiling were far more interesting than the couple before them.

"I don't want them afraid of me," she murmured, and Bronson reached for her hand. "Let them be afraid of you; it's good for them."

CHAPTER 18

Watchdog

"I had to make sure you were not compromised."

The great wizard Nicolas sat at the head of the magnificent table. Platters of pork, roasted chicken, stewed venison, and other delicacies spilled into a feast before them, fine enough for a king. The cold, disheveled castle was a spell, and the wizard revealed the real castle to his guests once he confirmed their identity and mission. The servants were hidden out of sight and showed themselves as soon as the commotion had ended. Bronson was still weak; the beating he took left him physically bruised. He groaned as he reached for food.

"You didn't have to kick my ass, Nicolas." Bronson was stripped down to his pants, large purple bruises forming on his ribs and on his back. Wrenley worked on applying salve to the more serious wounds and was attempting to bind up a broken rib or two. Staff tried to assist, but Wrenley shooed them away politely. Wrenley sucked in a breath as she ran her hands over his chiseled stomach, trying not to notice how stiff his muscles were under her touch.

"Well, what else would you have had me do? What if Bronson Aughton were turned to the enemy side? With your power, we would all have been dead if I had let you in the door and you had turned. I had to get control of the situation."

"So, you put a spell on the castle and waited?"

"As soon as I saw the ship on the horizon," the wizard said matter-of-factly, rubbing his hands together unapologetically. He reached for a large turkey leg and bit into it, the juices dripping from his mouth unattractively. "In this war, it is to kill or be killed. Too many search parties of the enemy have landed on my shores, and the spell usually does the trick. We hide and wait until they leave, or we kill them."

"So, what...were you just going to kill me to find out?" Bronson groaned as Wrenley applied pressure to his ribs and tightened the bandage around his chest.

"You were using magic to cloak yourself...I couldn't see past it. And no, I wasn't going to kill you all the way," the wizard chuckled and continued devouring his turkey legs and washing it down with a glass of red wine. "You would have snapped right back from it, I'm sure. You are a sturdy lad." The wizard burped, padding his mouth with a napkin. "But you brought someone I didn't foresee...." He leaned forward, resting his elbows on the table before him, and pointed the turkey leg toward Wrenley. "You, my dear, were unexpected."

Wrenley had been eerily quiet, still haunted by the sight of Bronson writhing in pain and screaming just hours earlier. She believed she had lost him—really and truly lost him—and that thought was unbearable. She was drained from using her powers again and felt too weak even to eat or drink. She felt nauseous and wanted to vomit, maybe right on Nicolas if she was honest. She hated him for what he did to Bronson, even if he had a good reason.

She gathered up the dirty linens and shrugged, not having the energy to answer. A servant quickly appeared and took them from her arms. Another staff member manifested, pulled out a chair, and motioned for her to sit. She did not know if every guest was treated this way, but they hovered and doted over her, ensuring she had everything within reach.

"That's why we are here," Bronson nodded to Kage, Alcott, and Garrick, and then his eyes drifted to Wrenley, "We need your help."

"When did you find out you have magic, my dear?"

"Days ago, maybe a week," she grumbled, rigorously massaging her temples with her fingers.

The wizard seemed to sit back and think momentarily, and nodded, "We are lucky you didn't kill me."

"I was ready too," she murmured, leaning back in her chair and finally taking a sip of the wine the servants had pushed into her hand. She twirled the liquid, smelling it, "Slowly, painfully..."

The wizard laughed uncomfortably, knowing it was no joke. Kage grinned behind his cup of wine, eyes darting between Wrenley, Bronson, and the wizard. He was waiting for Wrenley to finish the job and probably would enjoy every second of it.

"All right then, I'll help you!" Nicolas clapped his hands in excitement. "Never in all my years have I ever heard of the bloodline of royalty having powers…" He rubbed his chin with his stubby finger and sighed, "What you need most is rest because tomorrow, we will seek the answers to all these questions." He was looking straight at Wrenley now, and she raised her eyes to meet his.

"I'm fine…I want answers now."

The room collectively held its breath at her tone.

"You want answers, but what you need is replenishing."

"I said, I am fine…"

Kage jumped and caught her as Wrenley tried to stand, but her knees buckled. Bronson moved towards her, but was too slow due to his injuries. He halted when Kage swept her up in his arms. Bronson's jawline tightened as he watched Kage hold Wrenley, cradling her gently so that her cheek rested on his chest, his long black hair covering her as he looked down at her.

"Her room is ready; they will show you the way," Nicolas waved Kage in the right direction, Garrick and Alcott on his heels as if to supervise. Wrenley resisted Kage and argued the entire way to her room, with the three men squirming and looking at each other as her protests grew louder and echoed off the stone walls.

~ ~ ~ ~ ~

"Tell me everything," Nicolas leaned forward, "You didn't breathe a word that you were going to get her!"

Bronson shrugged, "It was something I wasn't anticipating or planning. We received intelligence that another seer who had broken the barrier was crossing over to find her." Bronson took a shot of whiskey that his friend had poured him, throwing his head back and wincing from the physical pain and the burn of the liquor.

"It was Alexander…" Bronson's voice lowered, taking another shot of the golden liquid. "I killed him, Nicolas. Without a second thought…I stabbed him in the heart outside the very house she was sleeping in that night. If I had been a day later…even an hour…"

"But you weren't my boy. You were exactly where you needed to be."

"I killed a brother. A friend…" Bronson's voice broke, the fatigue from the day slamming into him.

"A friend whom the enemy had turned. You did what you could to save us all, Bronson."

Bronson sighed again, kicking his feet into another chair, groaning from the pain of the motion. In his head, he knew the older wizard was right, but the number of gruesome things he had done in the name of the greater good was stacking up on him. He remembered the disappointment and repulsion in Wrenley's eyes when he attempted to force her to walk past the starving child. He closed his eyes with the memory and pressed the cool glass against his forehead, noting that it was, by far, the least despicable thing he had done over the years.

It was amusing how he never considered it until Wrenley came along. Suddenly, he cared about what she thought of him and what he did. If she only knew the atrocities, the lies, the manipulations he had performed in the last fifteen years and even before…Bronson poured himself one more glass of the golden liquid and shot it back, slamming the glass on the table.

Nicolas gently squeezed the younger man's shoulder, "Heal yourself, boy. My spells will protect against any unwelcome attention in the unseen. Our enemies will notice nothing that happens here. We need you at full strength."

Bronson leaned back, "I think I'm in love with her, Nicolas."

The older man sighed and rubbed his chin. "Worse things could happen."

"I knew her when she was a child…"

"And things change! Bronson, she isn't a child anymore; she is a powerful woman." Nicolas rubbed his rump as if that reminded him of how she quickly tossed him out of the air onto his ass. "Having a powerful man at her side would make sense as she navigates this difficult journey."

"There's so much she doesn't know…" Bronson sat up and stood, stretching his body and allowing his magic to begin healing, "When do I tell her the truth? About me?"

Nicolas sighed and shrugged, "You will tell her when the time is right."

Bronson snorted, bracing his sore back with one arm, "Never. There will never be a right time."

~ ~ ~ ~ ~

Bronson was slightly tipsy, not enough to forget his worries or evil deeds, but enough to make him stagger up the dark, cold stairs to the second floor. He stopped and turned at Wrenley's door, a warm feeling flushing over him at the thought of them tipsy together only last night, him holding her. He had slipped out the window, leaving Wrenley probably confused and pissed that he had not stayed to finish what he started. He stood there momentarily, toying with the idea of going to her and completing whatever 'it' was that happened in that room. The thought made him even more dizzy than he was, whether it was his wounds, the whiskey, or lust, he could not tell.

"I'd keep moving if I were you."

Bronson's head snapped over to Kage, lurking in the shadows by Wrenley's room. The sudden movement sent a tidal wave of pain throughout his body once again, but he ignored it.

"Don't you have something better to do than play guard dog outside her door all night?" Bronson growled, not even trying to hide his irritation. His head was pounding now. He would knock this fucker's teeth out with no issue if he had to.

Kage stepped into the light of the torches hanging on the walls, "If that means protecting her from…" His dark eyes skimmed Bronson up and down and sneered, "…Well, all manner of evil, it is worth it."

"I'm not her enemy or yours, Kage."

"No?"

"No!" Bronson hissed, taking a step closer to the younger man, "I was fighting this war before you even touched your own cock. I have been watching over her for her entire life!" Bronson pointed a finger towards Kage. "You have no idea what it's like to protect her, to be responsible for her…" *To love her*, he thought to himself, the reality slamming into him.

"Really?" Kage raised his brows inquisitively. "Does she know that you had cursed her body in the other world? Or that you were the one who caused her that pain and emotional suffering? Is that brave? Or honorable? Or even love?"

Bronson felt his right eye twitch, and Kage snickered. "Oh, she doesn't know? My Mother had put it together when Wrenley shared about her infirmity in the previous world. I wonder how her adoration of you would disappear knowing you did that to her?"

"You don't know what you are talking about," Bronson rumbled. Bronson was usually not impulsive, but he grabbed the collar of the younger man's tunic and shoved him against the stone wall. He had moved so swiftly that Kage was caught off guard, unable to defend himself.

"You don't know what the fuck you are talking about," he said again and shook Kage like a rag doll by the shirt. "I've had to do things to protect her and this kingdom that you would never have to dream of doing. You, sheltered in your little hut, hiding away from the torture and pain while the rest of us had to suffer and fight every damn day," Bronson shook him one last time, then dropped him. Kage forcefully shrugged Bronson's hands off him.

Standing six inches above Kage, Bronson leaned down to whisper in the young man's ear, his voice husky. "Your father… and your brother…they were brave men. I was there when they died defending this realm. But until you have proven yourself to be just as courageous as them, don't you fuckin' talk to me about honor. Until you have watched those you love most be dismembered and displayed on the castle gate, don't talk to me about suffering." Bronson leaned back and looked away, "Until you've ever taken a woman to your bed and pleasured her to where she wails your name and comes for you over and over, don't talk to me about love. You are… a…child." He pronounced the last three words slowly and methodically and pierced Kage with one last look.

Bronson pushed off the wall, still looking down at the younger man. Bronson admired Kage's enthusiasm, but it would get him killed, or worse, it would get Wrenley killed. Bronson turned and headed towards his bedchamber, his breath short and his head throbbing with the pain of the day's events.

"Is everything ok?"

Both men froze as Wrenley poked her head out of her bedroom and looked at them. Her hair was tangled around her shoulders, looking like she had been sleeping. Her eyes were heavy, and she yawned as both men straightened, Bronson plastering a smile on his face while Kage clenched his teeth.

"Fine…just headed to bed," Bronson sauntered up to her and reached to tuck a piece of hair behind her ear. Bronson could physically feel Kage's rage behind him, knowing the younger man must be ready to explode. Bronson could not help but feel satisfied at his jealousy; his fingers glowed where his and Wrenley's skin touched. "Everything is fine; go back to sleep."

Wrenley nodded with another yawn and disappeared back into her room. Bronson, feeling particularly smug, turned and smiled at Kage. "Go to bed, watchdog; she can handle herself, even against me," he tossed over his shoulder and winked. "Even though she may not want to."

He could sense Kage erupting behind him, but disappeared into his room with a grin.

CHAPTER 19

Unprecedented

"When did you notice your powers?"

Nicolas wore a typical wizard-looking outfit: a long purple robe, a black tunic that trailed the floor, a pointy hat, and his staff. The next day, he sat at his large desk in his observatory, the desk overflowing with books, manuscripts, and plants that trailed off the desk and climbed up the walls. Wrenley could barely see him behind the piles of books.

"Ummm…a week ago?" Wrenley fiddled with an intricate-looking knick-knack on the edge of Nicolas's desk, shaped like a bird. "I'm not sure exactly."

Deep in thought, Nicolas leaned back in his chair, stroking his long, grey beard. Bronson was sitting next to the fireplace, continuing to flip through a book that Wrenley knew he was not interested in. She noticed that he and Kage were no longer acknowledging each other, and the tension between them was palpable. She felt conflicted between the two but decided it was not something she could fix or worry about. Frankly, she had much more important things on her mind, like controlling this power that lay dormant inside her until it was not.

"The disadvantage for you, my dear, is that we have never had royal blood also be a seer," Nicolas finally said, reaching out and pouring himself a cup of tea. "The good news is, royalty or not, you can control it. I'm just unsure of the implications."

"Implications?" Wrenley felt a little alarmed.

"Traditionally, the royalty must join with a seer for the full effect of the throne's power to be released. For you, you don't need anyone…" Nicolas peered over his spectacles, giving Bronson a look, "You can take the throne yourself. However, the more concerning thing is if the enemy somehow captured you, you could be manipulated to be the most dangerous weapon we have ever seen."

"That won't happen," Kage piped up in the back of the room, leaning against the door frame. He must have just washed, as his dark hair was wet and braided, slung over one shoulder. His brow was lowered in a frown as usual, most likely brooding over something. "I won't allow that to happen."

Wrenley noticed Bronson rolling his eyes as Kage walked past him.

Nicolas scoffed, "I appreciate your bravery, my young warrior. However, this fight will be more than just brute force. There is unprecedented magic here; the kind of magic we haven't seen in a millennium."

"That's why we have him," Kage jutted a thumb towards Bronson, and Bronson snapped the book shut and stood up. "It's not that simple. Even with the most powerful seers, we will be outnumbered. Not only will we need to fight, but also protect Wrenley while we fight."

"And what happens then? We go in, fight, obliterate the bad people, and I sit on the throne? Then what?" Wrenley felt anxiety tug at her; leave it to her to break the molds and test the limits of normal. Of course, this was unprecedented...just her fucking luck.

"That's when the real war begins," Nicolas stood to his full height, which was not much, and limped around the desk. "When you retake the throne, it gives us the advantage to win this war and eradicate this evil once and for all."

Bronson tossed the book onto the table beside him and stood. "Even with my powers, we need more. Wrenley must learn to control hers, and we need her to fight. You saw how she took you out in minutes." Bronson turned to the short wizard and grinned, and Nicolas sniffed, seeming slightly offended.

"I was out of my rhythm. Wasn't expecting that..." Nicolas mumbled, scratching his bearded chin.

"We need more help," Bronson said again as he crossed his arms over his chest, worry lining his brow.

"We have a company of men who will meet us on the other side of the lake in about a week. We have that much time for you to help her," Kage was still inserting himself into the conversation, and Bronson seemed annoyed when the younger man dared to breathe.

"Wrenley isn't the only one needing to tighten things up a bit," Nicolas said as he sat on a stool, slightly groaning as he settled in. "Bronson Aughton, the second most powerful seer I have ever known until yesterday, was distracted long enough that it could have cost him his life." Nicolas narrowed his eyes as he studied Bronson, "You lost focus, and it could have killed you."

Wrenley sucked in her breath, knowing it was her fault Bronson was distracted. She blushed slightly, watching Bronson shift under the wizard's gaze.

"You're right," Bronson said, running a hand over his face and then lacing his hands behind his head. "I am distracted."

"Well, no sense in feeling sorry for yourself, lad!" Nicolas slapped Bronson on the back forcefully, and Bronson groaned. Even with his healing abilities, it appeared he still had a few tender spots.

"What can we do to help?" Garrick's steady but low voice asked, having slipped into the room minutes before. Nicolas pondered that momentarily, then pointed his staff towards Garrick, Kage, and Alcott.

"Rest, strategize, and then train. You all will be stretched to your limits before this war is done."

CHAPTER 20

A Gathering

Wrenley found herself luxuriously pampered by the castle staff. It was uncomfortable for her because she could care for herself, but they certainly treated her like royalty. They drew her a hot bath and let her soak for two hours, replenishing it when it cooled. A short, well-endowed older woman rubbed sweet-smelling perfume on her skin, making it soft after weeks of being cold and drying out. They brushed her hair and wove it around her head like a crown decorated with flowers and jewels. She was given an emerald green dress that fit her like a glove. She peered at herself in the mirror, shocked at how it complemented her figure. She twirled around, feeling almost giddy. She had never truly felt like a princess until now…

She acknowledged that her body changed the longer she spent in this dimension. She noticed her features were sharper, and her form was leaner and more muscular. In her old world, she had tried to be as positive as possible about her body, given that it was the only one she knew. But this…she gave one more twirl, and her eyes landed on her full breasts. She had never had breasts before now, not like this. She wondered if Bronson had noticed the changes in her physical form or if he even paid attention. With how his hands had traveled along her body two nights ago, she suspected he noticed much more than she had initially thought.

The castle was its own city: the apartments were on the east end, and the great hall was on the west. The kitchens below were bustling with activity as they prepared large pigs on spits, freshly baked bread, roasted vegetables, and an abundance of sweets to fill a bakery. It smelled as good as her mother's Christmas dinner at the bed and breakfast, and a tinge of pain hit her then, thinking about Ruth and Jim. She could not be sure, but maybe it was Christmas time in her old world. Did they even celebrate Christmas here?

Wrenley had been pondering everything that had happened since crossing over. The heaviness of the world's responsibility weighed her down. She was worried about her company and her dear friends. She breathed in the air, realizing she had grown so fond of Garrick, Alcott…Kage. The thought of Astara, the fairies in the woods…so many lives at risk. There is so much beauty in jeopardy of being ruthlessly obliterated under the threat of this senseless evil.

And then there was Bronson…Bronson made her flush when he even accidentally looked at her. She had almost choked when his fingers grazed hers as they both grabbed for the same book. She swooned if he accidentally bumped into her in the hall…the memory of his hips grinding against her was intoxicating. She had done her best to avoid him because, apparently, she could not touch him without her magic giving her away to anyone in the room. It was not a good time for anything but the task at hand.

This small island in the middle of the lake was cold, rainy, and covered in heavy fog most days. Wrenley had noticed that the island's inhabitants lived around and worked in the castle. Everyone allowed to live on this land was somehow working for Nicolas. He was a generous landlord and employer, paying his employees considerably, both in terms of money and safety. They had been sheltered during the most brutal parts of the war.

Today, Wrenley noticed a break in the clouds and almost tripped over herself to get outside. She dared not leave the castle walls, but she wrapped herself in a shawl and managed to find her way to the stairs that led up so she could walk along the outer wall. The scenery was breathtaking. She could glimpse the entire island and its lush green color, the village below, and the lake surrounding them. The lake was so large that she could barely see the shoreline of the mainland.

The guards stationed on the wall were polite and nodded in respect as she passed by, not disturbing her silent contemplation as she strolled along the wall. The wind was strong as it whipped against her, strands of hair flying all over, slapping her in the face most of the time. Wrenley still had trouble believing she was here, that this was all real, and that it was not a dream. She missed Ruth and Jim; she grieved her birth parents that she would never know, and she carried the weight of this war on her shoulders and felt as if it would crush her.

She had never been to war, and the reality was she would face it sooner rather than later. She was sheltered in her tiny town in the Ozark Hills. The few encounters she had in the past month made her sure that she never wanted to know what real war was like. But then she thought of Bronson, Kage, Alcott, and Astara…they had suffered greatly from the war. Her mind went to the small, malnourished girl on the road, so much suffering…

"It's cold up here." Wrenley jumped at the sound of Garrick beside her. She relaxed when she realized it was not Bronson.

She smirked, "This coming from a guy who lives in the cold mountain forests?"

Garrick shrugged, "It's a dry cold. This is…wet." He made a face and shivered, and Wrenley grinned. Garrick was always quiet in the group, but he observed everything. When Bronson and Kage were duking it out, Garrick watched them intently as if expecting he would have to pry them apart physically. He trained with the twins every day and by himself at night, as if he were avoiding sleep.

"Do you have a family? A wife? Waiting for you to survive all this?" Wrenley leaned against the wall, looking up at him with genuine curiosity. Garrick sighed and leaned against the wall, looking over the vast land under them. Wrenley waited a few moments while he seemed to ponder the question.

"It's a long story; the short answer is no. I had a partner, and they died."

"I'm so sorry."

Grief flashed through his intense eyes as he scanned the horizon, the same grief that was there when she had asked before. "I'm not sure what it is like in your world…but in my world, the way I want to live, and love isn't very…accepted."

Wrenley's eyes widened when it all clicked together. Pain shot through her as she reached out to cover Garrick's strong hand with hers. "How did he die?"

Garrick held onto the wall with both hands but looked down at his feet. "He was an archer when the rebellion first started. He was on the front lines when we received news about what they did to the queen...he saw her." Darkness replaced grief, and he took a deep breath.

"The queen was a kind, gentle soul who had passed the laws to protect relationships like ours. Love like ours..." Garrick's shoulders now slumped, shuddering. "She was a champion for us. But after they did those things to her..." Garrick quivered, closing his eyes and shaking his head as if to push the memories away.

"They hunted us down like animals. Our village turned on my partner and me. Our village was starving, and they betrayed us for a few coins to buy food for their children. He was taken captive, tortured, and killed. At that point, I left everyone and everything that had betrayed us, and I joined Bronson, who was also loyal to the queen and mirrored her kindness and inclusion."

Wrenley dared not ask anything more about his partner's death. Garrick's handsome face was lamented; his appearance seemed cold, even with his short-trimmed beard protecting him from the wind that nipped at him. Wrenley reached up and gave the man a long hug, and he melted into it, heaving a sigh. "It feels good to have someone listen and to be able to speak about it."

Garrick was still stoic, and he gave Wrenley a slight smile as she pulled back, "I live unapologetically now, and if I die, I die for it. But it's not common to have someone who understands or doesn't condemn me."

Wrenley nodded, "If you need to talk anytime...I am here. My world is just now catching up on all of this."

"I hope in time, you can also be an ally to us and others?"

"Of course I will...I promise." She paused, knowing she was pushing her luck, "So, you and Alcott..."

Garrick laughed, saying, "With all due respect, that is none of your damn business, my lady."

After that conversation, Wrenley felt a little closer to Garrick, honored he had felt he could confide in her—another reason not to cower in fear but to fight.

~ ~ ~ ~ ~

Nicolas was hosting a gathering to announce the return of the lost royal family and garner support. He had sent word to the rebellion sympathizers and seers still loyal to the old kingdom and Ailios. No one knew that Wrenley was alive or even existed, but to unite the rebels, it may be time for everyone to know. Everyone had assumed she was dead or lost. Her arrival in this world would cause an eruption and restore hope and momentum for the rebellion forces; at least, that was the expectation.

Nicolas had given her several history texts regarding the kingdom and her family to pass the time. Her family had ruled the kingdom for as long as the records had been kept. Her family was good and kind, popular with the people, and champions for the minorities. The land had not known war and horrors until the king and queen died fifteen years ago. Small rebellions, pirates, thieves, and uprisings were typical for any kingdom, but nothing compared to the darkness that hovered over Ailios now.

The kingdom consisted of several different types of peoples and cultures: mountain people like Garrick, the forest people who would come to the cities and villages to trade their game, and earth people who traded spices, roots, and medicines. This is where Kage, Alcott, and Astara's ancestors originated, and they have stayed in the exact location all this time. They were known to hide away from the danger as long as possible. During the first few years of the civil war, they hunkered down, but the fight came to them when enemy forces moved into their lands and started to destroy the trees and vegetation that would have pummeled ecosystems for so many, like the fairies. That is when Astara's husband and eldest son died in the war.

Then there were the 'seers' or the magical people. They were most uncommon and would come out of the other populations to learn the needed skills to wield their magic. Nicolas had been overseeing all the seers' official training for the last fifty years. However, Nicolas was banished and forbidden from teaching magical skills when the kingdom fell. Harboring Wrenley and teaching Bronson was a death sentence for the older man and anyone who dared to side with him.

Bronson was one of the last seers to serve under the king before the kingdom fell that they could locate. Bronson and the seers loyal to King Dolion were hunted down like animals. If they were caught, they were either converted to work for the enemy or they were tortured and butchered. Bronson escaped the persecution, but his friends and companions were not as lucky. The seers were mutilated and displayed for everyone to see, sending a shock wave of terror throughout the country. The symbols of power, medicine, and healing were turned into ash. The thought of something like that happening to Bronson made Wrenley want to vomit. She would level the entire city before allowing him to be taken and slaughtered.

Wrenley had not truly understood how much Bronson risked doing what he had done for her…what he continued to do for her. Between crossing back and forth to keep track of Wrenley, he contributed to the resistance and played a pivotal role in leading rebel forces. Wrenley concluded that it was his dark side: one could only take so many years of loss before darkness began to surface. She did not blame him. Wrenley felt ashamed of her attitude, complaining about her hardships when these people had been through so much. How could she be the key to uniting a kingdom and taking down an enemy so powerful when a king and queen were unable to do so?

The sun was setting, and out her window, Wrenley noticed boats arriving and guests entering the castle. Her heartbeat sped up at the thought of so much responsibility; how could she do this? She tried not to let it overwhelm her as she prepared herself for dinner.

~ ~ ~ ~ ~

Bronson greeted guests as they entered the great hall. Most of these people he had known and fought beside for years. There were new faces, and he found himself uneasy and on edge. He had to trust Nicolas's judgment in sending for these people. These were representatives from all corners of the continent who fought in the rebellion, and they would not win this war without their support.

Bronson also could not help but notice how Wrenley had avoided him ever since that night at the inn. Bronson was unsure whether he had crossed a line with her, and he allowed her to take the space away. He also knew she had been terrified when Nicolas handed him his ass when they first arrived. Once they left this castle, they would be practically chained together, so she might as well take the space now. He would not allow her to sleep by herself as far as he was concerned. There was no way he would let her out of sight when they left the safety of these walls.

His chest had tightened as he perceived her blushing when their hands touched at the breakfast table or how she avoided him in the hallways. She kept her face down and made no eye contact, and if he spoke to her, her responses were short and curt. He would admit he went out of his way for those tiny points of contact...even if it were just a touch or a graze. His fingers ached to touch her soft, pale skin; to plunge his hands into her hair. He cleared his throat, not wanting everyone to notice his arousal at the mere thought of Wrenley.

The great hall was the finest of its kind and probably the last of the great halls on the continent since the war started. The ample space was warmed by two gigantic fireplaces on either side of the room, with staff constantly adding more wood to keep up with the dropping temperature outside. The wood ceilings were vaulted up, and the beautiful hand-carved rafters depicted stories of folklore and the history of Ailios. Bright and detailed tapestries lined the walls, also providing a history of the kingdom and its royal family. The table was set for at least fifty people; its rich, velvet blue tablecloth peeked out from under plates of seafood, entire cooked pigs, and other delicacies. Barrels of wine lined the outer walls; jugs of sweetened spiked cider and ale were set up and down the table. Looking at the magnificence before him, his chest tightened at the memory of the great feasts when his king and queen were still alive.

His gaze drifted from one tapestry to another when his breath caught at a familiar-looking depiction on the wall hanging above one of the fireplaces. The beautiful face that looked down at him was that of his queen, his dear friend Adinnil. It must have been created during the months of her pregnancy, as her swollen belly is depicted in the tapestry. The artistry shows her face bright with love and joy, her hand gently resting on her belly. His heart constricted, and he realized that he missed her. She had been the last link to...to home. He still mourned for her, even fifteen years later.

Whispers caught his attention from the guests, and he looked up quickly towards the door of the great hall. Bronson felt the wind knocked out of him, looking at Wrenley as she entered the room with Kage on her arm. She was a spitting image of her mother, and everyone knew it. The group parted as she entered, and Bronson knew she was afraid, even though no one else could probably tell. She had no idea what she represented to these people, and she looked like royalty. Her knuckles were white as she clutched Kage's arm.

Wrenley was dressed in a midnight blue gown that brought out her brilliant hazel and gold eyes. It flowed around her, the diamonds woven into the fabric reminded him of starlight. It was a modest dress with long sleeves and a moderate neckline, not revealing any cleavage but showcasing her lovely neck. Wrenley's hair was swept up with silver combs, and a dainty tiara was placed on her head, her hair woven through it. Her skin was creamy and pale, with a slight blush as every eye in the room was on her. Around her neck, she wore her mother's pendant and Astara's crystal; on her arm, she wore Astara's son, Kage, like a ring or a gaudy bracelet. Bronson's chest stiffened at the obnoxious smile plastered on Kage's face, or maybe it was how he allowed his hand to linger a little too long on her waist when he pulled her seat out for her.

Bronson knew her too well; he had seen her grow and was privy to all her secrets. He was there when she began high school. He remembered worrying when she had her first boyfriend, which he made sure did not last long. He watched her grow from a child into an adult in the last few years; now, she had blossomed into a woman. He opened his eyes to the tapestry again and smiled. Adinnil, his dear friend, would have been so proud of her daughter.

He shook himself back to reality and let out a small gasp as he turned to find the woman who preoccupied his every thought, standing toe to toe with him. His entire universe revolved around her, and he froze as she eyed him intently, giving him a sweet smile. She stood before him, looking like a queen, her blue dress flowing as gracefully as she did. He could smell her sweet scent of honeysuckle and lavender, noticing how her eyes searched his face under those thick, dark lashes. She stepped closer to him, invading his personal space, and he could feel his nostrils flaring and his pulse quickening at her nearness. For a moment, he could only imagine his hands feeling that soft skin and touching the easy blush on her cheeks. Damn, the woman before him was the picture of strength and power. She tipped her head up, almost daring him to say something silly or flirtatious. He was frozen at that moment, and they gazed into each other's eyes for what seemed like an eternity.

"Let's get you seated," Kage, whether on purpose or by accident, broke their gaze and stepped between them distastefully. Bronson tried to ignore him; he was young and had something to prove, but Bronson smiled, knowing that her blush belonged to him.

~ ~ ~ ~ ~

Wrenley sat between Bronson and Kage as Bronson recounted the history of the queen, his taking Wrenley, and the secrecy necessary to keep her safe all these years. Wrenley finally regained her appetite but was careful not to gorge herself in front of the people fighting for her. She nibbled on the succulent pork and roasted vegetables and sipped minimally on the wine placed before her in a goblet. The table was something more magnificent than she had ever witnessed, and she almost felt guilty sitting in such luxury when others were starving and dying beyond these walls.

Many men, who knew more about this war than she ever would, discussed the rebellion, the struggles, and the concerns of the weeks to come. She listened intently as different key players addressed the strategies of the insurgency. They would have to raise an army big enough to conquer the throne city, which would take time. They also discussed funds for the so-called military that they were yet to possess.

"Even if we raise an army big enough to withstand the enemy's defense, how will we take back the throne? It's nearly impossible to get back into the castle walls."

"It was easy enough for them to get in," someone scoffed.

"It was as if someone let them in."

Someone had tossed a suspicious glance towards Bronson at that comment, and Wrenley felt herself stiffen. He sat in his seat, leaning back, an ankle crossed over his knee; like always, he was a picture of calm, power, and almost indifference at the arguing at the table. He said nothing but allowed them to discuss. Though Bronson had taken on a huge burden over the years, these leaders suffered with their people. Wrenley could understand why there was such anger and resentment.

"If the king had minded his own business and stayed away from the dark arts, none of this would have happened," someone else shouted out, and Wrenley physically felt Bronson's irritation, even though he still refused to show it. Her own body went taut, and her back straightened in defense.

"The king was merely developing weapons to keep this kingdom safe. We had no choice…he knew what was out there," a man from the back chimed in.

"But they still came! And he didn't help matters!" An older man stood up and pointed a pudgy finger towards Bronson. "This is his fault."

"It's no one's fault, dear friends…Bronson has done nothing but protect our royalty and assist in reclaiming this kingdom ever since it fell," Nicolas smacked his staff onto the table. "I will ask you all to show a little respect to the man fighting in this rebellion and clocking more hours on a battlefield than any of you!"

The hall burst into an uproar. Wrenley noticed Garrick, Alcott, and Kage were on edge, hands moving to their weapons. She also saw out of the corner of her eye that Bronson still did not speak but listened intently to the arguments that surrounded him and her father's honor and intentions. She felt angry and began to feel herself flush. She knew what this meant; she had felt this coming on before. Without thinking, Wrenley pushed herself away from the table, her chair flying backward so forcefully that it hit the stone wall behind her and broke into pieces. It was probably a little dramatic, but it did the trick.

"Enough!" She bellowed, and the entire table of men went silent, looking in her direction. Up until this point, she had been quiet. She could no longer stand the way the conversation was going. Not only was it counterproductive, but she drew the line when they began to accuse Bronson and her father of treason. She took a deep breath to steady herself, willing her voice not to shake.

"This isn't helping us," she slammed her goblet on the table, placed her hands palms down in front of her to keep them from shaking, and looked at each person in the eye. "This isn't helping us win a war."

"No disrespect, Your Majesty, but you are merely a woman; a

woman who hasn't had to suffer this war for the last fifteen years." The jab came from a younger man to her left, and she turned to him. Kage stiffened, but Wrenley motioned for him to stand down. Wrenley fisted her hands to her sides to collect herself, summoning the courage to say anything to take control of this room.

"You are right, sir; I don't know the horrors you have seen or the price you all have paid during this conflict…I didn't even know about this until a month ago. One day, I was living a simple life and discovered all of this…" Wrenley motioned with her hands to everyone and thoughtfully met each of their gazes.

"You are a foreigner to this land…and we don't even know if you are Adinnil's daughter," the young man was jabbing on purpose, his smug expression evident.

"Are you insane? Look at her!" An older man at his side bumped the younger man in the ribs and whispered, "She's a spitting image of her mother. Show some respect before you get yourself killed."

Wrenley went on as if the young man had not spoken. "Now that I'm here, I want to help. But to do that, we all must realize that this isn't the fault of anyone in this room. It's not your fault, Bronson's fault…" She glanced at him, and he smiled slightly, lounging back seductively, elbow resting on the arm of the chair. She could feel his dark eyes on her. Was it pride she saw in them?

That gave her the boost of confidence she needed to continue despite her shaking: "…but I need your help. We need your help." She gestured to her company around her and clasped her hands at her chest. "I will do whatever I must and go wherever I need to. I will serve you all like my mother and father once did."

"Forgive me for interrupting your heartfelt speech." The same young man pushed out of his chair and mockingly touched his heart, stepping towards Wrenley. She felt Kage and Alcott snap to attention, flanking her as he barely moved in her direction. Their hands were on the hilts of their swords.

He took in the twins and laughed. "You think you have what it takes to win this war? Your father certainly didn't…if he was even your father." The young man narrowed his eyes at her, "I heard your mother was a whore."

Someone gasped as Wrenley saw a blur of blackness, feeling the rush of air as something moved past her. She blinked, refusing to show any more shock than that as Bronson stood in front of her, his decorated dagger pressed against the young man's throat. She glanced at Kage and Alcott; the only indication they were surprised was a single blink from both of them. Bronson had moved in a heartbeat…inhumanly fast. He towered over the younger man, one hand fisting the man's hair to pull his head back to expose his neck, the other holding the dagger.

Bronson was dressed in all black: a black button-up shirt, pants, and boots that matched his marvelous short black hair that had been combed back. He wore his long black coat and leather gloves like always, but Wrenley swore she saw shadows dancing around him. He looked as if he could disappear into darkness if he wished. Nothing compared to the blackness in his eyes, though, as the man cried out.

"Do you fucking know who you are talking to?" He murmured to the man, his voice so cold it made Wrenley shiver. "You stand before Wrenley, heir of Dolion, royalty of Ailios and its continent, daughter of Adinnil." He pulled on the hair with more force and shook him slightly. Bronson's upper lip curled back in a sneer, showing off his perfect, pearly white teeth. "Your inexperience betrays you; if you were in the old court, your head would have hit the fucking ground before you even looked at her sideways."

"Please, he is young and doesn't know…" the old man beside him cried.

"Whose fault is that old man?" Bronson did not take his eyes off the younger man. The young man, as if delusional with fear, chuckled even with the blade piercing his skin. "Are you fucking her too? Just like you did to her mother? Oh, I've heard all about it…"

Wrenley felt her magic stir, wanting to boil his eyes out of his skull, but she did not move an inch. She wanted…desperately needed to see what Bronson would do next. Bronson did not flinch or even blink as he slowly pressed the dagger into the man's neck and throat. The man flailed; his screams were wet with the blood now flowing from his carotid artery. Bronson released him and let him fall to the floor, the man crumbling into a heap as he bled out in front of the whole room. Bronson sidestepped him, dragging his black gaze up to Wrenley, as she felt goosebumps prickle across every inch of her body.

Bronson turned and, to Wrenley's shock, stabbed the older man on the top of the head, blood squirting as he slumped to the floor. Wrenley did not allow herself to gasp, but others did. She even felt Kage and Alcott tense behind her. Wrenley glanced over at Garrick, who was leisurely leaning against the wall, examining his fingernails; if he were surprised, he did not show it.

~ ~ ~ ~ ~

The dark crimson liquid pooled on the floor at Bronson's feet, his black boots leaving bloody footprints in his wake. Gone was the soft man who had held her in the tent when she was freezing, the man who had giggled with her in the room at the inn and scampered under her bed. This… was the darkness that had been there, the dusk she had suspected. The shadows that left little girls on the road to die, who fought in wars and killed countless people. She took him in for who he was, the most powerful man she had ever met, and maybe even a monster. Her throat bobbed as she took every inch of him as he swaggered towards her, not breaking her gaze as he grabbed one of the crisp white napkins off the table and drew it along his bloody blade.

"Let that be the warning to anyone who speaks against you while I live and breathe in this dimension," he said to her, but loud enough that everyone could hear it. There was not an ounce of remorse in him; she swallowed, her throat closing with the sudden heat that pooled in her core at the sight of him. She tried to ignore the arousal, the need to disappear into that darkness and never come back out. She took a deep breath and made her face neutral, even as she pressed her legs together in need and excitement.

"Is that what you'll do then?" she asked, shifting to look up at his towering frame. His brown eyes were almost black with rage, his black hair had fallen over his forehead; he reached up with a gloved hand as his thumb rubbed his bottom lip, the corners of his lips turned only slightly upward as if he knew of her internal struggle. She lifted her chin almost defiantly. "You'll cut the throat of anyone who breathes a word against me?"

She almost felt him rumble as he replied, "If they are lucky…that's all I'll do to them. That bastard is lucky I didn't want to make a bigger mess…"

She should be ashamed of herself for being so aroused at his violence…a fierceness that worshipped her. Such utter darkness, and it was at her disposal? The way he looked at her was confirmation that Bronson Aughton would do anything…absolutely anything…for her.

No one said a word as he stalked up to her, bowing his head only slightly, then leaning in to murmur in her ear so faintly that she was the only one to receive it. "I never loved your mother like that. She was my dearest friend, and she loved your father."

"I know."

That was all Wrenley said, and he straightened, meandering back to his chair and taking his seat. He resumed his position seductively, staring at Wrenley as he leaned back, crossed an ankle over his knee, and grasped a tumbler of whiskey. God, he was magnificent, and she could not ignore the statement he had just made in front of the most influential people of the war. Bronson had meant to do it, sending the signal to anyone considering the court's strength now. He wanted everyone to know exactly what would happen if they even thought about harming his queen or her honor. She realized he had been looking for an excuse to flex that power and fidelity to her, and she tried not to let it make her knees buckle.

"Well…anyone else then?" She asked, turning and raising her chin so confidently that it surprised her. She tried not to look at Bronson as he watched her, a grin playing on his lips as he sipped his liquor. She shrugged, and then, with one movement, she ignited her magic, using her arms to make a sweeping motion in front of her. With the movement, a mighty wind cleared the table of every ounce of food and drink, the plates and food crashing into the far wall, and everyone gasped.

"Enough eating then; we need to discuss strategy. And clean them up…" She waved to the dead bodies on the floor. The twins flanked her like shadows as she returned to her seat. The great hall was so inaudible that one could have heard a fairy fluttering. The group looked at each other in shock as Nicolas cleared his throat, "Well, you heard her! Let's talk strategy!"

CHAPTER 21

The Closet

The meeting lasted late into the night. Wrenley excused herself from the meeting after the fifth round of drinks and desserts was served. The inhabitants of the room started to get louder as more liquor was consumed, and Wrenley's head began to pound. Although the meeting started with two dead bodies and Wrenley leveling off the entire dinner table, it transitioned into a robust strategic planning session that incorporated diverse perspectives and experiences. Kage, Alcott, and Garrick were in the thick of it, poring over maps and discussing battle tactics and campaign approaches. Even Nicolas elbowed his way to the table, making sure to throw in his opinion. Kage was incredibly excited, and she could not help but grin at his youthful enthusiasm as he almost crawled onto the table in eagerness as he discussed various military tactics.

After the incident, everyone was the picture of respect and courtly protocol—at least, that is what Wrenley expected protocol to look like. The crowd parted when Wrenley approached; heads bowed respectfully, and all parties ceased to speak if she opened her mouth. She could tell the younger men had a more difficult time, nervously shifting if she spoke with one of them. The older men had served under her parents and seemed comfortable with it. Exhausted, she slipped away after she caught herself dozing off in her seat, almost spilling her tea.

She escaped into the dark hall, hands clasped behind her back, deep in thought about the tension of the evening. She felt herself struggling internally, as the judgments and concerns of the group collectively were the same ones she battled within herself. The task was almost impossible, even with Bronson, Nicolas, and herself.

The road before them was treacherous, and their chances of survival were slim. Some of them would most likely die, but without that sacrifice, thousands of others would undoubtedly perish. Was she willing to make that sacrifice? The evil would eventually crush everybody, with or without her. She could not let that happen; if there was a chance, she must take it.

"You disappeared."

Wrenley knew he was there before he spoke a word. Bronson fell into stride beside her, hands shoved in the pockets of his pants. "I can tell there's a lot on your mind."

Wrenley pulled her shoulders in, unsure what to say, so she whispered, "Yes."

"Wrenley," Bronson put a hand on her arm and turned her to him, "I need to apologize…"

"No, you don't." She reached out to graze Bronson's shoulder with her fingertips, shaking her head at whatever he was about to say. "You apologize for nothing."

He exhaled, closing his eyes as her other hand traveled to his cheek, roaming to his chin, then down to his chest. "I don't want you afraid of me, Wrenley, ever. What I do to protect you…"

She pushed herself up on her tiptoes and kissed him, capturing his face between her hands. Bronson groaned, pulled her close, and returned the pressure of her kiss. He buried his face in her neck next, and she rested her head on his shoulder, allowing her tears to stream onto his shirt.

"I love you," she whispered to the fabric of his shirt, letting her self-control slip as she took in a deep inhale of his scent. She had been falling in love with this man her whole life and knew how dangerous that was for him… for her. She knew she wouldn't be able to do what needed to be done without fully and unapologetically loving this man. She would be fractured without him, only half of what she was meant to be. At that moment, she realized he completed her—what she had been searching for her entire life—and she wanted it to be filled with countless experiences and unforgettable moments with him. She could feel his heart racing as she lay her cheek against his shirt, his shoulder now soaked with her salty tears. Then she felt her own heart crack under the weight of his loyalty, the sadness she saw in his eyes. What he had done, what he continued to do, and what he had promised… she did not deserve it. She had not earned this, but he gave it freely.

"You…you deserve so much more." She felt his body shift when she assumed he registered her words. "You deserve to be happy…"

"Wrenley…"

"No, Bronson…" she pulled back, placing both hands against his broad chest and tipping her head up to look at him. "You shouldn't have to give everything because you knew my parents. You have suffered so much…" She felt him tense, something almost shattering on his face as he looked down at her.

"Wrenley…" he said softly again, and she loved how her name rolled off his tongue. She pulled back from him to search his face, and he smiled and then surprised her by kissing her eyelids, lips, and chin. "I'm not serving you because of your parents or some fidelity to the realm; I'm serving you because I know you better than anyone in this world or the next. I believe in you; you are the path of hope for us. For me…"

She took in a shuddered breath and then hid her face in his chest again, pressing deeper into his trunk, squeezing him so hard she could not believe he was still breathing. She wanted all of him, for his essence and energy to swallow her up so no one could know where she ended and where he began. She wanted that beautiful, thoughtful side. *But god*, she was greedy for the darker side. The side of him that slit a man's throat without a second thought, and never took his eyes off her. She felt something shift in her as she fisted his shirt in her hands and pulled his face to her, kissing him again, pressing her body into him as temptingly as she could.

~ ~ ~ ~ ~

He felt a shift in her…something transitioned from sadness and brokenness to hunger and need as she pressed her body flush against him, and he groaned. This should not have happened; he had a responsibility—an obligation—a promise to her mother.

"What do you want, Wrenley?" he breathed, his hands traveling down her ribs and torso. He dug his fingers into her hips and took in her scent, that sweet smell he would come to worship.

She strained to look up at him and shook her head, "You,

Bronson; I just want you. I need you."

Bronson sighed to smell her hair again, then cupped her face to kiss her lips gently. Every fiber of his being screamed at him to push her away, to retreat like he always did. She was too young, he was too broken, and there was too much at stake for this to happen. The kisses grew firmer, and he pushed her up against the cold stone of the dimly lit hallway, her back thudding against the wall.

Wrenley began to explore him with her hands, moving to his chest, down his upper body, and to his pant line. He groaned as she attempted to reach around his thighs and touch his ass. Bronson's breath began to quicken as he pushed his tongue into her mouth and reached for her breasts, but her damn dress was in the way. Without thinking twice, he reached up and ripped the neckline of it, exposing her shoulders and the beautiful curve of her breasts.

Bronson felt the force of his arousal hit him, and he gasped. Wrenley looked up at him with those hazel eyes under thick lashes, and he felt his heart nearly explode. He knew she had never been with another man before…he had ensured that. He may or may not have been responsible for several unfortunate events involving boys who had less than honorable intentions with her. Taking her in this moment was a decision that could change the entire course of their world. It would connect them fully, and then the dimensions separating them would become one. For years, Bronson had lived in the gray, not entirely in this world but also unable to stay in hers. His heart desired to find an oasis where he understood every dark and ugly part of himself.

Bronson had sex with many others through the years, but what he felt for Wrenley at this moment was something he had never experienced before in his long, miserable life. No, not just this moment…but for a while now. He had been in the presence of kings, queens, warriors, and gods…fucking some of them…but never had he felt so awestruck as with her. He had never felt love, nor believed it existed…at least for him.

"What do you want, Wrenley?" It was almost a plea, hoping she would give him a different answer, a sign that he should push her away and not look back.

"You. Goddamn it, Bronson, I just want you," she breathed.

It had undone him; he knew now that no matter what, there was no stopping him. Bronson considered himself an educated and well-evolved male, but the pure, primal need to fuck her and claim her was almost overwhelming. He could not think above the pounding of his pulse in his ears or the way he could hardly catch his breath. He grabbed Wrenley around the waist and dragged her to a door off to the side of the hall, kicked it open, and threw her inside.

~ ~ ~ ~ ~

Wrenley had fallen backward against a table with a surprised gasp, knocking over dishes stacked before the evening festivities. She immediately tried to keep them from falling, but was not fast enough, and the pile of expensive-looking crystal dishes (the kind her mother had in her cabinets at home) crashed to the floor. She gulped and glanced at Bronson in the doorway; her breathing labored as he stood between her and the rest of the world. His presence and power filled the room as he took one step inside.

Her breath caught as he moved closer, one foot in front of the other, his boots crunching the broken glass on the floor, his gloved hands flexing at his side. His eyes were dark, almost black, as they traveled over her as she clung to the table's edge, panting. A shiver raced through her at the sight of him, and she was suddenly very much aware of how dry her mouth was as she licked her lips.

"This is your last chance, Wrenley." His voice was a deep rumble.

Wrenley swallowed the lump in her throat, clutching the table tighter to keep him from seeing how her hands trembled.

"Last chance for what?" She whispered, feeling the heat pool between her legs as he took yet another step towards her.

"Last chance to tell me to turn around and walk away; because if you don't, I will fuck you so hard you won't remember your name…" he paused and took in a shuttering breath. "If I fuck you now Wrenley, I will never let you go again. Are you ready for that?"

Was she? She tried to be reasonable and think past the lust, the attraction, the innate desire to feel his length inside her. She surveyed him, eyes widening at the impressive outline of his length that was constrained by his black pants. She felt her cheeks heat, afraid and excited in the same breath, the thought of joining with this man something she absolutely could not live without.

Finally, she raised her head and nodded confidently. "I am ready for that, Bronson Aughton."

~ ~ ~ ~ ~

He prowled up to her, shrugging off his coat and tossing it, reaching a gloved finger up to his perfect mouth and biting it, peeling it off with those flawless white teeth. Unbuttoning his black shirt next, he took his time. She gaped at him as he pulled off the shirt, revealing even more of his chiseled chest. Her eyes trailed his muscles down to his hard abdomen and the delicious V-shaped muscle at his waistline dipping below his belt. He did not break his gaze with her once, watching her face change and eyes grow wide as he took his time with each button, watching her squirm with arousal and need. He closed the space between them, pausing as he lowered his forehead against hers, his hands moving to her waist once he discarded the shirt on the floor. No words were spoken, but they both knew exactly what was happening; their magic sparked between them, their skin glowing in the darkness as Bronson caressed her neck with his tongue, and she shuddered.

~ ~ ~ ~ ~

He began to unlace her midnight blue dress, working around her ripped bodice. He tarried in the motions, gently untangling the mess of strings and ribbons, and Wrenley caught herself closing her eyes and moaning softly every time his fingers brushed up against her flesh. She was still backed up against the table, her hands holding tight to the corners as he removed layers of clothing. He paused occasionally to gauge her reaction, as if looking for a sign to stop.

He removed the outer dress first, tossing blue fabric to the side, inhaling sharply when he tore his gaze from her face to look down at her chest, still crammed tightly in her corset. Using one finger, he hooked it at the front of the corset and ripped it off her, breasts releasing. Bronson seemed to marvel at the sight of them; he cupped them both in his hands, using his thumb to tease the end of her hard nipples. She arched back at the soft caress, his hands massaging her breasts as he stroked.

With every touch, Wrenley felt dizzy as sensations flashed through her. He took his time discovering her, kissing her slowly after every piece of clothing was discarded. As much as she enjoyed this, all she could think about was him on top of her, his magnificent body naked against her, pushing inside her. She felt a heat rush to her cheeks and between her legs again at the thought of it, at the potential sensation of his length inside her. He must have sensed her reaction, chuckling in her ear as he leaned down to kiss her neck.

Bronson reached behind to grip her ass, then spread his hands on the part of her belly right under her navel. His breath caught as he sucked gently on her nipples again, his tongue teasing as she curved her body and whimpered against him. She coiled back, clutching his arms, not able to keep herself from crying out in desire. Without warning, he quickly reached up to catch her throat with one hand and pushed her back.

"Bronson!" she gasped. He was firm, but he was not hurting her, though she still struggled out of reflex.

"What…" He asked almost impatiently, still shoving her backward on the table. Somehow, while kissing her, he removed his boots and discarded them with the rest of his clothing, only wearing his tight black pants and belt, which were unbuckled now. "Will you shut up for once and let me…"

"Wait!" She said breathlessly, pushing him back with both hands, and he stilled. He towered over her, looking at her like he would kill anyone or anything that interrupted them, but he still stopped when she asked.

"I've never…" she blushed and dipped her head in embarrassment, "…I've never had sex with anyone…I don't know what to do."

Wrenley had made out before; she also indulged in rough 'petting' and groping when she was a teenager, like the time Jim from tenth-grade English shoved his hand down her pants during barn warming. Yet, she had never had sex or made love. She was not even sure if she knew the difference between the two. Right now, she did not give a fuck which one Bronson did to her as long as he did something soon before she went mad.

He stood still as death, like a predator after her outburst. His tussled dark hair fell into his eyes, a muscle feathering in his jaw as he looked down at her, and she detected he was fighting a smile. One side of her wanted to run at that look; the other one wanted to open up for him and let him devour her. But what if he was disappointed? What if he was looking for someone more experienced than her…

"Wrenley, one word from you, and I will end this right now, but if you tell me to continue…" It was a growl that thundered from him. His magic ebbed and flowed around him, warping the air and space in the room. "I will fuck you, and I will start easy…but it will end with you screaming my name as I pound you as hard as I can without breaking you in half."

Wrenley's eyes widened, her tongue darting out to lick her lips again, and she drew the bottom one in; she was terrified but also so intrigued that she nodded.

Bronson looked at her incredulously, brushing a curl away from her face. "I need you to say it."

Wrenley took in a breath and released, "Please?"

Bronson smiled then, pressed both hands flat on the table on either side of her, and leaned down to softly growl in her ear, "Please what, Wrenley?"

"Please…" she trembled, goosebumps breaking out along her arms and down her back, "Please have all of me, Bronson."

Too much? Was that more than what he was looking for? She could not tell as Bronson dipped his head again, his hair tickling her breasts, shoulders tense, hands still pressed on the table on either side of her. She observed a shudder running through him and shifted uncomfortably as he seemed to take several deep breaths. Was he going to reject her? Would he chastise her for being too serious at this moment? Maybe he just wanted sex; maybe he just wanted to hook up and leave? Perhaps she should apologize…maybe she should…

She squealed as he shoved her down on the table, hoisting her ass and pelvis up with one hand to level with his hips, freeing his length, "Relax, and I'll be gentle…at first."

~ ~ ~ ~ ~

Every ounce of common sense screamed at him to stop and walk away, but he simply could not. As she sat there before him, naked and trembling, there was no way in hell he would leave this room without taking her for himself. She had told him she consented; she wanted it just as much as he did...didn't she?

"It's okay..." he said tenderly now, noticing how she shock and wondering if it was anticipation or fear. He pulled out his length then and aligned it with her entrance, splaying a hand flat on her stomach and applying pressure. Sparks erupted from her at the expectation; he knew this intimacy would stir their magic. He was aware of her inexperience, but also, physically, she was so small and delicate under his large body. It took every ounce of control for him to go slowly, inch by inch, and she whimpered when he entered her ever so gently.

"Do I need to stop?" he asked softly, inching into her as she writhed on the table in front of him, making him almost mad as a thrill shot up his spine.

"No...d-don't stop," she moaned, trying to find some traction to grasp on the table. He felt her pushing away from him slightly, so he seized her hip, pausing his descent until she adjusted. Bronson gritted his teeth, trying to keep himself from pushing harder. He wanted to consume her, to feel every inch inside and out. He felt her quake again as he was almost entirely inside her. She jolted under his weight, and he pulled away to look at her. She gazed up at him with those large hazel eyes, and he knew that they could not finish this here. He was very aware that they were in a place where the servants might need access, and the last thing he wanted was to be interrupted again. It had happened once at the inn; he would not let it happen again.

~ ~ ~ ~ ~

"Let me take you upstairs..." he said hoarsely.

"No! Please, Bronson!" She wailed his name, finally finding the table's edges and clasping them. Wrenley held back a gulp at his size, trying to shift and adjust around him. "I don't want to wait one more moment without you..."

Wrenley gasped when he pulled out and asked, "Are you ready?"

"Y-yes…. for what?"

Before the question was fully out, he thrust his entire length into her, and she felt her body and magic explode. It hurt, but the pain was like ecstasy, and she bit her lower lip to stop herself from screaming his name. True to his word, he went slowly, and she knew he was being gentle despite his own growing need. He was so loving to her, but greedy, almost making her weep as he began to increase his rhythm and rammed inside of her over and over.

"Are you in pain?" He asked lowly, and she shook her head. With her response, he grabbed both hips and pulled her towards him while he drove into her, and she fought a scream.

"God, Bronson!" She wasn't sure if it was her magic or hormones, but she felt every inch of herself tingling as they were entwined together. In the back of her mind, she thought about how inappropriate it was for them to fuck when everything was falling apart around them; on the other hand, she would rather die than stop. They had to be one to win: it was just that simple.

~ ~ ~ ~ ~

Bronson gently pressed a splayed hand to her chest so that she was lying flat on the table, and he continued to penetrate her, purposefully and harder. He reached out to touch her hips and her legs, and she moaned every time he did. He should not take her here…he should carry her upstairs and finish with her in his bed. But…he could not pull out or away. He scooped her up off the table surface, still inside her, turned around, and sat on the table with her facing him, her legs wrapping around his waist. She began to breathe heavier as she enveloped his neck with her arms, her body fully pressed up against him.

"I'm in love with you, Wrenley…" Bronson rumbled in her ear. She felt sparks around her as she noticed a growing pressure in her pelvis and belly. She had never had an orgasm before and wondered if she was doing it right. There was so much more than a physical response; it was as if her soul had searched for this her entire life. For thirty-two years, she had wandered, searching for someone to see her, love her, accept her…and now it was as if her soul was melting into this man she held in her arms. She felt her magic roaring inside her and prayed that she would not blow up the entire castle.

As if sensing her turmoil, Bronson said, "I've got you, Wrenley…I always have."

She could only think about it for a second, and then it hit her with a magnificent force, her body raging, sparking, and shaking against him. Her climax was enough to send Bronson over the edge as he came inside her, his moans muffled against her breasts as he held her tight against him. It was a wave of pleasure so intense she could never have imagined it before, her entire body feeling as if it were on fire. She tensed as she felt him, and a new burst of power erupted like fireworks around them in the dark room. She cried his name again, and he held her through her peak. She then went limp against him, and he had her there, caressing and stroking her hair.

~ ~ ~ ~ ~

Bronson did not care who saw them as he carried her to his room. Wrenley was loosely covered in his black shirt, Bronson bare, except for his pants. His knee-high black boots were discarded in the closet downstairs with every stitch of Wrenley's clothing, and he tried not to grin at the scandal it would cause when the staff found them in the morning.

Bronson took her to his chamber, laid her in his enormous bed, and covered her with a heavy feather-down quilt. She was still limp and breathless; her smell was intoxicating, and her skin glowed softly as her magic calmed itself. They lay there together, Bronson removing the last of his clothing so they could touch as much as possible. He wrapped his arms around her and pulled her tight against his body, her ass pressed against him, and he fought the impulse to take her again.

"Why does this happen?" she asked softly, motioning towards their glowing skin. Sparks still appeared when their flesh rubbed together.

"Love, sex, intimacy…it stirs the magic in us. We don't know why. Many seers don't marry or make love or even have sex because it expends power."

This confused Wrenley because she felt very powerful after what they had just done. She frowned. "That seems like a lonely life."

Bronson shifted, lacing his fingers through hers. "It can take much magic. It also creates a disturbance, allowing other seers to sense the energy. So, they can remain secret or 'invisible' in the unseen by not having a connection or a partner."

"What about you? Are you not worried?"

Bronson sighed and rested an arm behind his head. "Some would argue it is irresponsible of me to allow this." He leaned over to kiss her neck, "Nicolas probably already knows, but he has a shield around the castle, so..."

"He what?" Wrenley shot up with an alarmed expression; Bronson laughed, catching her waist with his arm.

"This is how it is, Wrenley. I am powerful, but you are even more, so there will be a disturbance in the unseen that others will notice. Nicolas has spells covering the castle, so no one outside can detect us...or anyone inside, for that matter, if they don't know about the spells. But to stay away and fight this connection would only be more harmful to us both. It's a risk that I believe is worth it."

"What a risk..." she retorted, and he chuckled, caressing her breast with his index finger.

Wrenley sighed and lay back beside him, her back arching again with every soft stroke of his finger.

"What about when all this is over? What happens to us?" Wrenley whispered.

Bronson sighed. "You get to decide if you want me around or not."

Wrenley grinned and leaned over to kiss him. "I do?"

Bronson kissed her nose, and Wrenley sucked in a breath as he reached to touch between her legs. Bronson then leaned over, his lips brushing her neck and ear. She held her breath as he began to move down her body, from her breasts to her navel, then to her lower stomach, finally arriving between her legs. Wrenley laced her fingers in his hair as he lingered down there, and she could barely keep herself from screaming as he unleashed his tongue on her.

CHAPTER 22

Keeping Secrets

"Those loyal to you will spread across the land and recruit troops. Hopefully, we can gather a force large enough to have a chance at breaching the city." Nicolas scratched at his big white beard as he pored over the map the following day. He looked troubled, removing his pointy hat and tossing it on the table before him. He continued gravely, "I am concerned about any siege that will be held against the castle."

"Why?" Wrenley leaned forward in her seat, intrigued by the concern in his voice. She winced slightly, flushing at the ache in her stomach and between her legs, not glancing at Bronson. After making love most of the night, she was sore, especially since it was her first time. She pulled her attention back to the wizard, hoping he did not notice.

"The castle sits in the middle of the city, on top of a hill consisting of solid rock, much like this one. There is no way to climb the sharp incline without being slaughtered. The way into the castle is through the front gate, which will be heavily guarded."

"I don't understand; if the castle was so impenetrable, how did the enemy get past the king and queen's defenses in the first place?"

Bronson and Nicolas exchanged glances. Bronson cleared his throat and stood, crossing his arms before him, "Your father and I were working on a project."

"Project?" Wrenley eyed him, noticing how he seemed almost uncomfortable.

"We were trying to perfect traveling between dimensions. We had done it once, and I suspect the enemy noticed that powerful shift. Your father and I didn't know how risky it was...or maybe we did."

"It had to be done, Bronson, by us or them," Nicolas said, rubbing his sore knee.

Bronson nodded, regret still etching his eyes, "We had no idea the enemy would descend on us so fast. Our magic had created such a shift in the atmosphere, and unseen, all the seers who would normally have sensed the danger thought it was our activity. We don't know how they got in…"

"Wait…if traveling causes such a disruption, why haven't they found us by now?"

"They probably know about us, but that's why we keep moving," Bronson rubbed his chin, and Wrenley noticed the stubble beginning to grow again. She could understand why he looked tired since they had made love all night. She once again flushed, ducking her head to sip her tea, and she was sure Bronson was trying not to grin at her. "Every time we use bursts of energy, it has the potential to disrupt the unseen and draw unwanted attention."

"It's not the only thing that causes disruptions…" Nicolas muttered to himself, and Bronson shot him a look. Nicolas huffed and continued, "We must surprise them when we attack, and I'm just not sure how to do that yet."

"What could be done to create such a distraction that they wouldn't notice?" Wrenley looked at the two most powerful seers in the kingdom for answers. Bronson and Nicolas both shrugged their shoulders simultaneously, and Wrenley rolled her eyes. "Well, that's just great."

"Unfortunately, that's the least of our problems at the moment," Kage announced as he burst into the study, pushing the heavy wooden doors open so forcefully they slapped against the walls. "We have received word that enemy soldiers are snooping around the inn we stayed at before setting sail. It's only a matter of time before they show up here." Kage stopped next to Wrenley and Bronson, eyeing them. "We need to leave."

Wrenley noticed Kage's young, handsome face twisting in apprehension as he reached out and pulled Wrenley up from her seat, and she groaned slightly at the sudden jerk. "Pack your things; they could arrive here at any moment."

Bronson nodded. "Go help Wrenley; I need to speak with

Nicolas privately before we leave."

~ ~ ~ ~ ~

"She's not ready." Bronson paced back and forth in front of Nicolas, feeling a wave of uneasiness washing over him. "We needed more time for you to begin training her."

"We must improvise, Bronson." Nicolas propped his feet up and leaned back in his chair, sipping hot tea as if he had not a care in the world. "Besides, we have time for our forces to be gathered; we will meet again before it's all said and done. But for now, you must keep her on the run and safe until the time is right."

Bronson glowered at him, shaking his head. "It's going to be very hard to keep her hidden with how powerful she is; not to mention, she can't control it."

"Really? You are certainly not helping matters at all," Nicolas tried not to smirk in his mug. Bronson snapped his head towards the older man, "I'm doing the best I can here. No need to remind me of how I am failing...again."

"Now you listen, young seer! Don't have that attitude with me!" Nicolas set his teacup down forcefully and rested an elbow on the desk, pointing a bony finger at Bronson. "You will never be able to keep your head on straight if you don't stop blaming yourself for all this."

"It was my fault, Nicolas!"

"We both know that's not true!" Nicolas hit the desk with his fist. "You may have been influential with the king, but nothing would stop him from practicing this magic. You could have refused, and he still would have done it. The enemy would have still come; they would have still died. It was fate that you were there to save her."

"But I should have known something was wrong," Bronson hung his head and dropped into a chair across from Nicolas, "If I couldn't save her parents, how could I possibly think I could keep Wrenley safe?" Bronson's voice dropped into a whisper, "If only Dolion had told me the truth..."

"Speaking of truth, does she know about you yet? Or are you still keeping secrets?" Nicolas wiggled his eyebrows, and Bronson sighed deeply, rubbing his red eyes with the palms of his hands.

"No, I can't tell her, she's not ready for that yet either."

"War tends to force our hands, whether we are ready or not. I implore you, young seer, telling her sooner rather than later would benefit you."

"Her father wasn't ready…" Bronson muttered.

Nicolas puffed, "If she's ready to be in bed with you, at least you owe her the truth."

Bronson sent the wizard a seething look, and Nicolas held up his hands, "Easy lad…I just need to remind you to be careful. Wrenley is not her father or mother, and now there are things at play that we did not expect to happen. She is our miracle, Bronson…our god sent miracle."

CHAPTER 23

Just a Scratch

The group headed east once they arrived on the mainland of the lake. They traveled light and stayed out of sight, moving by night and hiding during the day. It was now a waiting game, as recruitment for the rebellion was spreading. There was no advantage in breaching the castle before reinforcements arrived; it would be a slaughter. Bronson's task was to keep them moving and invisible to the enemy as long as possible while their forces gathered across the kingdom. The rest of Garrick's men were sent in all directions to deliver messages, recruit troops, and gather information.

The road was still tough on Wrenley, though she would never admit it. She was still adjusting to this world, and though her mind was catching up, her body was still brutally behind. She often felt sick, lightheaded, and fatigued. She took turns riding with each of her companions; Garrick was quiet and somber as they traveled, lost in deep thought. Wrenley did not have the heart or courage to interrupt his ponderings.

Alcott was just like his brother; however, she did notice Kage seemed to hold her tighter. She caught him looking down at her several times as she sat flushed against him, his body heat keeping her warm against the dull drizzle that constantly seemed to pervade this world. She noticed him looking down at her again and finally furrowed her brow. "What is it?"

Kage shrugged, holding the reins to the horse with one strong hand, the other around her waist. "You look terrible."

Wrenley snorted and covered her mouth as she yawned, "I know I do; I feel even worse."

"That's what I am afraid of..." Kage steered his horse to the side, avoiding a low-hanging branch. "I wish we could return you to Mother; she'd know what to do."

"You miss her."

It was not a question, but she felt Kage's chest heaving slightly at the words. His arm tightened around her in response, "I do."

"I'm just adjusting," she said nonchalantly, waving a hand aimlessly to reassure him. Wrenley shivered, leaning harder into Kage. He had draped his heavy cloak over them both, and she was beginning to feel sleepy.

"You're sick."

"Maybe…" She yawned and burrowed deeper into his cloak. "I'm about tired of all this changing business. I want to be able to function like a human being."

"Well, my lady, you will never 'just' be a human being around here."

Wrenley did not know how to respond to that and instead fell silent. She knew he was right, and the weight of her obligation and the barriers ahead were never far from her mind these days. She felt its weight like a rock between her shoulder blades, and a headache formed at the base of her skull.

Wrenley tried not to enjoy Kage's wonderful scent or how comfortable he was to ride with, and she felt terrible for almost falling asleep several times in his arms. Bronson never brought up the night they made love, even though it had been over a week, not that they had any private time to process it. Bronson was on high alert, always listening not only with his ears but with his magic. He was focused on everything and anything around them when they were on the move; she loved him and resented him for it.

"You've never really said much about your world…where you came from. Do you miss it?"

Wrenley shrugged, a wave of gloom washing over her at the mention of her former life, "I do miss it terribly. It's much different than here; we have electricity, central heat, and air…"

"I have no idea what that even is."

Wrenley giggled, "You push a button in your house, and it warms up. Our clothes are different…"

"Did you have a lover back there? Anyone that misses you?"

Wrenley reddened at the memory of her and Bronson making love. Kage noticed her blushing and misread it. "I guess that's my answer."

"No…really no….no one missing me…" Wrenley quickly looked to her side and noticed Bronson riding beside them now. He was so close that his gloved hand brushed against her thigh, and she felt a jolt of electricity through her. He looked at her and grinned, but his features turned somber, almost possessive and longing. The expression was so intimate and erotic that she felt her heart skip a beat. She watched him ride before them and wondered what was so heavy on his mind.

~ ~ ~ ~ ~

Wrenley woke from her deep sleep on her hard bedroll to a hand on her shoulder. She sat up quickly, shaking, disoriented, but thankful that she was not wet from the rain. She peered up to see Garrick hover above her, pressing his finger to his lips, and motioning for her to follow. Wrenley obeyed and trailed him to a deep ditch covered under thick foliage behind a tree line where Bronson, Alcott, and Kage hunkered down, watching something and talking in hushed voices. She felt her senses prickling, the hair on the back of her neck rising. Wrenley noticed it was dusk, meaning she slept most of the day. She crawled up beside Bronson, and he motioned for her to stay silent. Then, he nodded his head towards the road.

"There has been an increase in enemy patrols. We may not be able to move tonight," Bronson leaned down and whispered in Wrenley's ear, and her heart sank at the news. Every day they were unable to move was another day they were losing ground. She tried to conceal her disappointment and nodded. Bronson positioned himself behind her as she peeked out from behind the large fallen tree, with him kneeling behind her, and she allowed her back to rest against his chest. Her stomach fluttered slightly at the sensation of his breath on her ear, feeling his warmth, and inhaling his scent. He had put both hands on either side of her, grasping the log, caging her with his body. It was an internal battle not to imagine him grabbing her hips in much of the same way. She leaned into him, wishing they could have just a moment of peace and quiet between them.

"They may stumble onto us, though…if we don't get out of

here. There is so much activity," Kage uttered under his breath, and the decision was made to move deeper into the woods to ensure they went unnoticed. They had been creeping along the tree line when suddenly they stumbled into a clearing without warning. Kage was the first to venture out and was followed by the others when they heard something at the far end of the clearing.

"State your business!" Someone yelled, and Wrenley's body became rigid. Bronson came up cooly beside her, reached to lift her hood over her head, and quietly said, "Don't say a word. Don't even look at them. Let us do the talking." It was a small patrol with only a few soldiers, nothing like their encounter on the other side of the lake. She wished she could be as calm as Bronson…

"We are just traveling to the highlands…have some family there we wish to visit," Kage said flawlessly as the soldiers approached with no apparent suspicion. Kage made several vulgar jokes and commented on the weather, resulting in the soldiers laughing and snorting, and Wrenley had to force herself not to roll her eyes. She was impressed as Kage wove an intricate story about the family in the western forests, a dying aunt, and their search for lodging. For a moment, Wrenley thought they might disperse soon until one of the guards noticed her.

"Hey, who is she?" One of them asked, pointing to Wrenley with a gloved finger. He was a middle-aged man, short in stature, and missing a front tooth. Wrenley only glanced up and then back down again, and Bronson stepped beside her, "Leave her be. She is a special creature and can't speak."

"Huh, pretty little thing to be dumb…shame," another soldier exclaimed, and he stumbled towards Wrenley. She could smell the alcohol on his breath and inwardly groaned, pressing closer to Bronson.

"She's simple. Please don't get too close…" Bronson warned, and Wrenley could not help but send a glare his way. *Who is he calling simple?*

"Oh, mates, she's just a girl in a woman's body…" Kage laughed and clapped one of the soldiers on the back, but Wrenley noticed he was getting tense as the two soldiers stood before her, eyeing her up and down like a plate of food. Garrick and Alcott were also stiff, hands moving to the hilts of their swords. Wrenley saw Kage shift his position.

"She's good enough," one of them said, "If you let us fuck her, we'll let you pass with no trouble."

"That's not going to happen," Bronson said lowly, stepping in between her and the two soldiers, standing to his full height. The two men had to crane their necks to look up at him.

"We don't want any trouble," he continued. "If you allow it, we will be on our way, but there is no way in hell you will touch the girl."

Wrenley sensed it, the magic stirring under Bronson's calm exterior, and she almost winced. These men had absolutely no idea what they were getting into. Yet, she found not an ounce of empathy for them as they continued to speak.

"Then maybe we need to visit the outpost…" One of the men reached around Bronson and grabbed Wrenley's arm. In reaction, Bronson drew a dagger from his boot, the same one that killed the man at the gathering. The dagger almost whistled as it sliced down, dismembering the limb from the body. Blood spattered, and Wrenley stood there for only a moment, gaping at the detached arm still clasped onto her forearm. It was as if time was paralyzed, the arm falling in slow motion to the ground at her feet, the blood splashing her. She gasped, then pulled her gaze up to the rest of them.

The next moments hit as quickly as a lightning strike; one soldier pulled his sword and swung at Bronson. Kage and Alcott came up from behind and dismembered them with three blows. Alcott swung, taking off another arm, while the soldier plunged a dagger into Kage's side. Kage didn't falter and took the last lethal strike and swiped the man's head off his body. Bronson and Garrick slaughtered the remaining men with ease. The confrontation was over in a moment, but Wrenley could not help but yelp as Kage fell to his knees.

"Fuck," he groaned, holding his right side near the ribs forcefully. He was bleeding heavily now, and Wrenley quickly knelt beside him and covered the wound with her hand. The bleeding continued as she pressed harder.

"That's not good…" Kage choked out, and Wrenley looked up to Bronson, color leaving her face. "We need the bleeding to stop."

"I'm fine," Kage muttered, but the color was also draining from his face when Wrenley assessed the wound. Bronson kneeled beside them and swore, barking at someone to get him clean clothes or a bandage.

"Just a scratch, no big deal…" Kage inhaled sharply as Bronson stuck two fingers into the wound and packed it. Kage shuddered, "Fuck…you are doing that on purpose."

"I'm trying to save your life, you asshole." Bronson tore another cloth with his teeth and continued to bandage the young warrior.

"Use your magic!" Alcott roared uncharacteristically, his fear catching up with him as he watched his twin writhe in agony. Wrenley winced, never hearing him raise his voice before. She raised her hand to try to summon her magic, but Bronson snatched her hand before she could allow any magic to escape her.

"No, they will feel the shift so close…I am using all I can to shield us and dull his pain. We need to get deeper into the woods and then tend to him, or else we are all as good as dead."

"He is losing too much blood!" She hissed, attempting to pull her arm free, but was unable to.

"We need to move now," Bronson's voice growled, and Wrenley hated him for being right.

Garrick and Alcott stashed the bodies in the tree line, and Bronson and Wrenley helped Kage onto his horse. Wrenley pulled herself up behind him, taking the reins, allowing the warrior to slump onto her. She gritted her teeth as his weight almost crushed her, but she held on. The darker it got, and the farther they went, Kage began to grow weaker, moaning in pain at every bump they hit on the road.

"We must help him!" Wrenley pleaded. Bronson came up beside her to check on Kage. The charismatic, energetic young man was now pale and limp, almost leaning his whole weight against Wrenley. Bronson could tell she was struggling to manage the horse and his weight, so he grabbed Kage's shirt and hoisted him over to his horse.

"We keep moving," Bronson gritted his teeth and dug his heels into his horse to plow forward. Panic engulfed her as Bronson galloped through the forest, the sense of urgency hitting the company like a tidal wave. Wrenley knew that if they did not get help soon, Kage would die. She kept her eyes on Bronson then, noting the tightness in his jaw, his eyes darting back and forth as if trying to see something. She kept silent, knowing her questions would do no good as the young man fought for his life. Wrenley also noticed Bronson was urgent but not panicking. He was looking for something, and his pace and direction were intentional. The realization hit her that he was headed in a purposeful direction, not just aimlessly riding. The thought gave her some hope to keep pushing.

They pressed through the thick forest until they landed in a clearing in the woods. In the clearing was a small cottage; its windows were warmly aglow, and smoke rose from the chimney. The cottage was made from rustic logs with a thatched roof; overgrown flowerbeds littered the walkway paved with crumbling stones. It looked run down and old, and Wrenley sensed a magic in the air, hers stirring as they neared.

Bronson slid off his horse and lifted Kage onto his shoulders with brute strength. He headed towards the cottage door, carrying the almost lifeless man on his shoulders.

"Wait!" Wrenley panted, sliding from her horse and catching up to him, grasping his arm to try and stop him, "We have no idea who's in there."

"We don't have a choice…" Bronson said hoarsely, winded under the dead weight of Kage. Bronson used his foot to kick the door, and Wrenley could feel her heart thud in her chest as they waited. She held her breath, the reality hitting her that this could end them if this person were an enemy. The group paused as the door swung open, a young girl on the other side.

She was hardly a woman, her pale face lit up in the moonlight. Her emerald eyes took in the group of travelers; she cocked her head to the side, raising her brow in question. Wrenley shuddered, the girl reminding her of a haunted doll. Wrenley felt her body tingle, knowing that this girl had some magic.

"Interesting…" she mused, her eyes vacant and unblinking.

"Help us," Bronson pleaded, resting his palm against the door. His body shook from the warrior's weight on his back, and his brow dripped with sweat. As if she had been waiting, the girl threw open the door without hesitation and motioned them to come in. Bronson carried Kage over the threshold, followed by the other three companions. The girl cleared off the table swiftly with her arm, jars and other items crashing to the floor, and motioned for

Bronson to lay the wounded down.

"I have hot water and clean bandages." She did not even wince at the sight of the wound as she lifted the cloth covering it.

"I will also need some yarrow..." Bronson stripped off his black jacket and leather gloves, then began rolling up the sleeves of his black shirt. His skin was already glowing as he moved to pull the packing out of the wound.

"Don't have any...some horsetail?" The girl squinted her eyes as Bronson pulled out the cloth, blood once again oozing out of the wound.

Wrenley was familiar with some of the names because Astara had taught her. The herbs mentioned were used to clot blood and stop bleeding.

"That will work," Bronson and the girl began working as if they had done it for years, gracefully moving and weaving between each other as if it were some dance.

"Alcott, I need you to fetch more water." Bronson took a seat on the stool, not looking up at the twin.

Alcott warily received directions from the young girl and took a bucket outside in search of the creek nearby. Wrenley proceeded to cut Kage's shirt, peeling the blood-soaked garments off and cursing at the amount of blood.

"He's lost too much blood." The girl studied the wound and then said, "We need to get fuel inside him; otherwise, his body won't be able to produce more."

Wrenley was helping Bronson unclothe Kage, but she watched the stranger out of the corner of her eye. She delicately put on a kettle in one fluid motion and grabbed five bottles of herbs and a bowl. She then began to pound out some concoction in the bowl and poured the boiling water over it.

Wrenley's stomach churned as Kage whimpered in pain when Bronson began inspecting the wound. Wrenley had forgotten that seers were also healers...not just in magic but also in skill. Bronson began cleaning it, and without a word, the young girl handed a bottle of some alcohol to him. He first gave Kage a swig of it and then doused the wound, causing the patient to convulse in agony.

"That will need to be cauterized..." The girl said softly to Bronson, laying a hand on his shoulder. Bronson nodded grimly to her, pulling his knife from his knee-high black boot and handing it to the girl.

"Will that help with the pain?" He motioned with his head to the liquid in the steaming mug, and she nodded. They then focused on getting the tonic down Kage's throat. During this interaction, Wrenley realized they had plenty of water, but Bronson must have sent Alcott away so he would not have to see his brother in this state. As they struggled to administer the concoction to him, the girl held the knife over the flame until it glowed red. Kage screamed as Bronson brought the red-hot knife to the wound, and Wrenley held back vomit from the smell of burning flesh.

"Dammit, he keeps moving. Hold him down!" Bronson barked at Wrenley, and she obeyed. Tears fell from her eyes as she leaned her entire body on him, the young man screaming and writhing in pain. She held him with all her strength, whispering and laying her head on his chest, Garrick at his legs. She felt her body grow warm, and before she could stop it, a soft glow escaped her and covered Kage. As soon as the warmth covered him, he fell silent, as if he were in a deep sleep. Bronson snapped his head up at Wrenley, giving her a warning look as if to say, "Not too much."

By the time Alcott stumbled back in from searching for water, his brother's midsection was being wrapped tightly to immobilize the ribs as best they could.

"Put him in my bed..." the girl threw open the bedroom door, and Bronson carried Kage in and gently laid him down. The girl then sat beside the warrior on the bed, lightly putting another bowl of tea to his lips and encouraging him to drink.

"This will restore your strength..." She whispered, and Wrenley stood outside the bedroom door and looked around her, dazed. The smell of burned flesh still clung to the air, and the sight of blood still covered the table in front of them. It looked as if a massacre had happened...Kage could have died. It was all too overwhelming. Wrenley was barely able to make it to the door to open it and projectile vomit outside.

"I take it you aren't used to the healing arts," the young girl smirked, wiping the blood from her hands with a towel as she shut her bedroom door.

"No," Wrenley moaned as she wiped her mouth with the back of her arm and straightened up, "I'd watch where you step out there."

"My name is Gwyneira," the girl slumped on a stool beside the fire. "Sorry, I don't eat a lot...you'll have to fend for yourself if you get hungry. There is plenty of hot water and tea. No sugar...hasn't been sugar since the war started."

"That's no problem. We thank you for helping, and we have supplies to share," Bronson wiped his brow, his shoulders sagging. He washed his hands in the water basin provided and unbuttoned the shirt he was wearing, drenched in Kage's blood. He shed it to mop up the remaining blood from the table. The small group silently cleaned up the mess while Gwyneira sat before the fire, mesmerized by the flames.

Wrenley watched her out of the corner of her eye, and she noticed Gwyneira was a funny little female. She was probably older than she appeared, having barely entered womanhood. Wrenley also noticed several cats hiding in the shadows...up on the bookshelf, under the bed, one hiding under Gwyneira's skirts. Wrenley observed shelves of odd commodities, such as potions, dried herbs, and the occasional animal skull. Astara's kitchen was that of an old medicine woman, but this looked like something very different.

"Yes...I am a witch."

Wrenley jumped, so consumed in studying the items on the shelves that she did not hear Gwyneira come up behind her. Wrenley knocked over a jar full of some potion and immediately set it up right again. "That's cool. I was a witch for Halloween once..." Wrenley internally shuddered at her awkwardness and wandered away without offering any explanation.

"It was an honor to work alongside you, Bronson Aughton." Gwyneira turned to Bronson. Her jet-black hair shone in the firelight, and her pale, almost white face showed little emotion as she spoke to him.

Bronson nodded, "Thank you for taking us in. I saw the shifting above your cottage, and we had no other choice."

"The word of your company is spreading. You will find you have many allies here in these woods."

"And even more enemies," Bronson breathed, leaning his hip against the table for support. "You will have to be very careful. I don't want any trouble coming to you because of us."

"I'm always in trouble," Gwyneira laughed and reached down to scoop up a black cat in her arms, nuzzling its silky fur with her petite nose. "They fear me, so the soldiers don't come in the woods this deep. Tales of an old witch prowling the woods keep them a good distance off. The last one who showed up seemed to combust internally with no warning. Unfortunate luck…" She chuckled, and Wrenley shivered at its sound.

"Your skill is remarkable…" Wrenley added, feeling her strength leave her, and lowered herself to the ground in a heap. Out of nowhere, a large, fat tabby cat sauntered into Wrenley's lap and flopped down. Alcott joined her on the floor, the warrior collapsing from the trauma of his brother being wounded. Wrenley accepted a blanket from Gwyneira and extended the blanket around Alcott's shoulders, putting a comforting arm around the devastated twin and rubbing his arm. Gwyneira stood up in front of Wrenley and just stared at her deliberately.

Garrick excused himself to tend to the horses, but Gwyneira did not move from her spot. She just stood there for several long moments, head cocked to the side, staring at Wrenley. Gwyneira was short and had large almond eyes that took in every inch of Wrenley to the point where Wrenley began to squirm under her gaze.

"You are not as dumb as you look," Gwyneira finally said, still watching Wrenley as she stroked the purring cat in her arms. Bronson choked on a cup of tea he had helped himself to and snorted. Wrenley shot him a look.

"My apologies, my lady; it took me a moment to realize who you were. Your seer companion had put a spell on you that even I didn't catch at first."

"He had?" Wrenley shot him another glare, and he shrugged at her, sipping his tea.

"You have some stuff to work on…" Gwyneira mumbled, setting the cat down on the ground and straightening back up. "Like it or not, you must stay here for a few days. Not only to let the activity die down, but he'll need to heal and replenish his blood supply before he can travel…" She nodded towards the bedroom.

Gwyneira was certainly not warm and fuzzy, but she was competent. Unlike Astara, who gushed with motherly affection and hospitality, Gwyneira had fewer social skills and a lesser desire to comfort or please anyone, except her cats. She did, however, express some tenderness when nursing Kage, assisted with his dressing changes, and managed his pain. Gwyneira and Bronson had discussed using magic to speed up his healing, but decided against it. They both were using powers to not only cloak their surroundings but also to detect anyone coming close. Any more magic would exhaust them and possibly cause a disturbance in the unseen. Kage was young and healthy, and he could manage his healing.

"He's a nice, healthy specimen; he'll heal quickly," Gwyneira mused as she pulled off his dressing and smelled it, which made Wrenley want to vomit again. Gwyneira shrugged at her. "What? Just checking for infection."

"She called me healthy," Kage rasped, trying to grin at the girl but wincing instead. "That's pretty close to handsome, right?"

Though Gwyneira struggled with basic people skills, Wrenley could pick up bits and pieces of her story as they got to know each other during the next few days. Wrenley may not be a powerful seer or witch, but she had run a bed and breakfast for years…she learned to listen. Gwyneira had just turned nineteen; her mother and father had left to fight in the rebellion when she was younger. They never returned. She had been living with her cats, collecting medicine and herbs, and practicing her craft ever since. Though Gwyneira rarely showed any emotion, Wrenley could sense some grief passing through her eyes when she spoke about her mother and father. She was an only child, and they were all she had.

"The enemy moved in last year. They take land, they rape women. They kidnap and torture people. They kill any men who could fight back and keep the vulnerable for their perverse agendas. Their darkness also spreads over us, preventing things from growing and causing animals to leave. They make life painful and difficult. But they don't bother me often…they tried that," Gwyneira said matter-of-factly, and Wrenley did not ask for her to explain further. "The worst part is, they catch the cats and use them for cruel amusement. That's when I started setting the bastards on fire."

CHAPTER 24

A Witch

W renley found herself restless again in the next few days. Bronson, Alcott, and Garrick were busy making plans, observing the enemy forces as they moved in and out of the area, gathering supplies, and hunting. Gwyneira tended to Kage, though he complained most of the time, and flirted when he was not complaining. Wrenley did her best to keep him entertained while he healed.

Wrenley needed some time alone, away from Kage's complaining, Gwyneira's unnerving glances, and Bronson's avoidance. She slipped out one evening after the simple meal of roasted rabbit stew, hoping to find some cedar or other plants to burn. She would have tiny rituals to comfort her back home, such as lighting candles and burning her herbs, among other quiet things. Her intuition seemed hyper-alert, and she sensed it yanking her along the path. The trees seemed to whisper to her, and the rocks had laid a path for her to follow.

Wrenley came to a clearing in the woods not far from the cottage and noticed a fire burning in the middle. Wrenley hid behind a tree and peered into the clearing to see Gwyneira standing before the fire. The young witch's hands were raised above her head as if praising the magnificent full moon. She was dressed in a black lace nightgown, nothing underneath, her body on display to whoever happened upon her. Gwyneira's hair cascaded around her slim shoulders; her porcelain face was turned upward as she chanted something in a language Wrenley did not understand. The wind tugged at the witch's hair, and the moonbeams swelled around her in a sparking spiral. Wrenley was mesmerized by the beauty of the young woman.

"You don't have to hide; I know you are hovering."

A blush swept over Wrenley's face, and she cleared her throat.

"You can join me by the fire," Gwyneira didn't turn around but maintained her position, her delicate face still upturned towards the moon and stars. Wrenley approached, slowly, moving into the firelight.

"What are you doing?" Wrenley asked.

Gwyneira sighed, seemingly annoyed. "I gain strength from the moon goddess."

"How?" Wrenley also turned her face upward, feeling the moonbeams brush her cheeks.

"Witches and seers have much in common, but witches depend on the elements around them to give them strength, courage…comfort. We worship the Goddess Selene…who gives us our power." Gwyneira finally turned to Wrenley, giving her that stare again, which made Wrenley uncomfortable, "What are you doing here?"

Wrenley shrugged, "I guess I just needed some time to think."

"You are clumsy and weak. You must get stronger to protect your company."

Wrenley felt herself bristle and snapped her head towards Gwyneira, "Excuse me?"

Gwyneira sniffed, "You are like a rare bird or pretty jewel. You are a priceless commodity that the winning side needs to have. Your power and bloodline are too…" Gwyneira tilted her head for a moment in thought, as if choosing her words carefully. "…attractive to some people. You need to learn skills to protect yourselves and them." She motioned with her head in the direction of the cabin.

Wrenley felt the puncture of her words and looked down at her feet.

"You will get them killed if you don't master your fear and skills," the witch continued. "They would follow you to the ends of the earth if you asked them, but it's not you they follow…it's your mother and father's memory," Gwyneira said the words with a vacant expression, without emotion in her tone or face.

Those words…god, they held something so deep and painful, and Gwyneira had done a good job of masking them, but she was not fooling Wrenley. Those words were of a scared child who was afraid. Those were the words of someone who was hurting.

"Why are you telling me this?" Wrenley asked gently, not taking offense but invoking curiosity.

Gwyneira shrugged, bending down to retrieve her heavy cloak and wrapping it around her shoulders, "Somebody should; they all tiptoe around you like you'll break."

"I hear the pain in your voice and the resentment in your heart," Wrenley said gently as Gwyneira turned toward the cottage. "You may blame my parents for the death of your own. Rightly so…I blame my parents for many things. I don't even know who the fuck they are."

Gwyneira did not turn around as she spoke, "My parents died a horrible death in this war that your parents started. You will bring nothing but chaos."

Wrenley chuckled then, but it sounded more hysterical than mirthful. She rubbed her face with her hands, "God, I don't know what I am doing here! I don't want to be here. I'd much rather be home in my library with my books and cat. I want to listen to the October rain on my bedroom roof while I sleep in my cozy bed. But here I am! In the middle of the end of the world, everyone believes I am some answer to this whole problem. And you know what? I owe that to all of them. My parents got us all into this fucking mess; the least I can do is show up and try to make it right."

Wrenley's voice had elevated, and she slammed her fists onto her thighs, allowing her anger to spill out. She felt tears sting and looked down, her breath catching as her hands began to glow, sparks starting to fly from her fingertips. She quickly hid her hands in her pockets, hoping Gwyneira did not notice.

Gwyneira had moved on, trudging through the woods, calling behind her, "Keep up, princess. We don't want you to get lost…"

Wrenley huffed and hoisted her skirts to hurry after her, not sure if she was angrier at the little witch or herself.

~ ~ ~ ~ ~

"What happened?" Bronson eyed Gwyneira as she slunk into the cottage, then landed his gaze on Wrenley as she trailed behind the witch. He leaned against the doorframe, taking a step to block

Wrenley from following Gwyneira inside. He looked down at her, and she knew he had noticed her red-brimmed eyes.

"Nothing." Wrenley attempted to push him out of the way, but he grabbed her arm, pulling her a few yards away from the door.

"Talk to me...I know something's wrong," he said firmly, and she jerked her arm away.

"No."

"Why not?"

"Because after I let you fuck me, you don't seem to have two minutes to sit down and check on me...to have a conversation with me. This is the first time in days you've acknowledged my existence. If you want to talk, it's too late."

Bronson looked at her, his brows knitting together, "Wrenley, that's not what happened."

She stepped away from him. "That's what it seems like to me."

Bronson sighed in frustration, pinching the bridge of his nose. "There has been so much going on...I never meant to make you feel like that. You should have told me."

"Well, you did make me feel like that. When have you been available for a chat?" Wrenley pushed past him now, but Bronson reached for her arm to keep her from passing. It surprised her, and she gasped, quickly pivoting. She raised her hand, and an unseen force shoved him three feet back, sparks flying everywhere as Bronson skidded in the dirt. Gaping at her, he regained his balance from the push. Within a heartbeat, Bronson flicked his wrist, and Wrenley felt her arms and legs freeze into place.

"You are restraining me?" She hissed at him, and he approached as she struggled. He grinned at her as she tried to wiggle free of the invisible bonds, prowling at her like he was a predator playing with prey.

"If I weren't afraid of drawing every enemy bastard to our location, I'd kick your ass Bronson Aughton," She spat out, and Bronson chuckled, knowing she meant every word of it. He towered over her, reaching to run a knuckle down her cheek. She stilled at his touch, and Bronson bent down to lightly kiss her lips. His nostrils flared, inhaling her scent and snapping his fingers; the invisible bonds fell off her, and she huffed as she was released. Bronson then seized her, both of his hands gripping her waist as he leaned to press his forehead against her possessively. She dared not move; she could hardly breathe at the feeling of his fingers digging into her hips.

"I want to talk about everything…and we will, when we get into the highlands where we are safe…" Bronson said lowly, his dark eyes taking her in. "But I won't risk anything happening to you on the road…and if I start talking to you about how I fucked you on a table in a closet and made love to you all night after…" He drew in a shaky breath and reached up to grab a fistful of her hair, pulling her head back, exposing her neck as he brought his mouth so close to hers, "I will not be able to control myself."

She panted and then groaned as he kissed her forcefully, his tongue forcing her lips apart, and he took her whole mouth for himself. He released her then, and she shrugged away, a fit of curses pouring out of her mouth. She topped it off by giving him the middle finger; whether he knew that reference or not, she did not know or care.

Bronson shoved his hands in his pockets, cocking his head disdainfully. "The next time you try to use your powers on me, I will bind you up and do unspeakable things to you…unless that's what you want."

Wrenley swallowed, knowing he meant every word of it. He winked at her and turned to stalk away. Wrenley noticed his hand shot up to rub the back of his neck. He did not look back at her as he trudged into the cottage. Wrenley stood there dumbfounded, trying to ignore the heat spreading in her gut at the thought of him doing exactly what he threatened.

~ ~ ~ ~ ~

"You look better."

"I feel better."

The next day, Kage sat on the edge of the bed, attempting to move his arms and torso. His eyes lit up when Wrenley came in and sat on the bed next to him. He smiled and stretched slightly, testing the pain.

"I'm sorry that happened to you." Wrenley was so short her feet did not touch the ground when she sat and scooted up onto the bed, so she swung her legs nervously. "I feel like this whole thing is my fault."

"Why on earth do you think that?" His eyes darting to her face, "What's wrong with you? This doesn't sound like the Wrenley I know."

Wrenley tried not to cry as she shrugged, "I am very much aware how this whole thing is my family's problem. And I feel like there isn't a lot I can do to help. I feel like I rely on you, Alcott, Garrick…Bronson, a lot."

Kage rolled his eyes, took his good arm, and draped it around her shoulder, squeezing her gently. "And despite having no control over it, feeling like you must depend on everyone else, facing tyranny, war, and battle…you are still here. That must count for something?"

Wrenley looked up into Kage's eyes and smiled at him. He smiled back and gave her one last squeeze. She was relieved to see his spirit returning; his dark hair was tied back, and the flush was returning to his handsome face. Kage's strength had almost been completely restored. Bronson had unbandaged him, so he had more freedom to move. Wrenley was beyond relieved that he was recovering.

"Try and avoid swinging your sword unless you have to," Bronson mused when he examined the wound for a final time. He looked closely at the wound, feeling around the site. "It will scar, but I think you'll live to fight another day."

"And what happens if you get ambushed? One more heavy skirmish and he could rip open that wound," Gwyneira protested, straightening up from her bent-over position in front of the hearth. She tossed the last of the wood into the fire and faced the men, hands on her hips.

"We will have to avoid it at all costs," Bronson replied, motioning Kage to put his shirt back on. "We don't have a choice."

"You'll need me to help you," she stated.

"I can't ask you to do that," Bronson began, but Gwyneira raised a hand to quiet him. "I have nothing else to do. And she isn't much help…" Gwyneira jutted her head towards Wrenley.

Gwyneira stood confidently, her hands on her hips, hair wild around her shoulders. Bronson surveyed her, his brows furrowing into a frown as if to consider her ridiculous request. Wrenley knew that they could use her, despite how annoying Wrenley found the younger girl to be. Wrenley also saw conflict; allowing her to come would endanger her. Finally, Bronson drew in a breath and rested his elbow on the table, massaging his temples with his thumb and forefinger.

"I can't promise you'll be safe…" he started, but was interrupted by Gwyneira's huff.

"No one is safe," she shrugged, her face vacant of emotion, "Everything I've ever loved has been ripped away from me.. there is nothing left to lose."

CHAPTER 25

Highlands

"Where are we even going?" Wrenley yawned five days later, her body aching. She knew everyone must have felt the same: tired, cold, and utterly exhausted. Gwyneira was equally drained and grumpy, muttering as she rode with Kage. He pretended not to enjoy it but flirted occasionally, a telltale sign he was feeling better. The witch was bundled in her heavy cloak, with only a small opening for her eyes.

"Better be somewhere warm…" Garrick's words were muffled with the heavy scarf wrapped around his head to protect him against the bitter wind.

"It is…" Bronson murmured, clutching the reins with his leathered gloves, his arms around Wrenley's midsection. They still hadn't replaced her horse, and he refused to let her ride with anyone else. Bronson had led them up into the forests of the highlands, where Nicolas had offered them one of his hidden holiday homes to hunker down in for a while. They had to catch their breath; they were exhausted. Bronson explained that the home was located so far up the mountain that the enemy was unaware of its existence.

"It's spacious, safe…it has everything you will need to stay for a while. It has staff and spells to protect and hide you if you don't do anything crazy," Nicolas had given Bronson an incredulous look and then glanced at Wrenley over the brim of his reading glasses. She had blushed as he continued, "Go there and wait for the spring. Our forces will be ready for you when the snow melts."

The house is a small castle built into the side of the mountain, camouflaged by trees, but facing downward and allowing its occupants to see for miles. Wrenley gasped as they cleared the thick forest and looked up to see it towering over them.

"Spacious? This thing is huge…" Wrenley whispered, and Bronson smiled. "Nicolas has always had a luxurious side, and he's wealthy. This is one of his secret holiday homes. I stayed here after I took you…" Bronson stopped, and Wrenley turned in her seat to look at his face. His handsome features were sad as he looked up at the castle, like a million memories had flooded him.

"What?" She asked softly, and he shook his head as if returning to the present.

Bronson swallowed, lowering his gaze to hers, "This is where I hid after I left you with Ruth and Jim…to mourn."

Somehow, the staff at the castle knew they were coming. The castle gates were lowered, and the group was welcomed with open arms. The horses were whisked away to be watered and fed in a warm stable. The maids took Gwyneira and Wrenley to a conjoined bed chamber with rooms and private baths. Bronson, Garrick, and the twins were also shown their accommodations.

The castle was ancient and magical; the walls were lined with oil paintings of past kings and queens. The décor was rich and expensive; most of the furniture was adorned with red velvet and gold. Wrenley took in her room with a gasp: the gigantic bed, the clean white sheets, and the feather-down black quilts were magnificent. The room also had a full closet, dressing room, and bathroom. The bath was large and spacious, enough to submerge her entire body. Wrenley was sore, exhausted, and chilled to the bone; her whole body ached so badly that she was afraid she might be coming down with a sickness. She allowed the staff to peel off her wet clothes and prepare a bath for her. Wrenley was submerged in sweet-smelling rose and vanilla water, bathed, and then slipped into a soft nightgown before crawling into bed.

Though her stomach was screaming for nourishment, Wrenley was so fatigued that she was unable to move, much less eat. She felt the sheer weakness of her body, the cold still lingering in her bones even though she had soaked in a hot bath for an hour. There was so much to do, yet she could not bring herself to do anything. Despite the many plans whirling in her head, she fell into a deep slumber as soon as her head hit the soft pillow.

~ ~ ~ ~ ~

Wrenley felt as if she had died and come back to life. She could not believe the dream she had experienced… it seemed so real. She stretched, feeling the sun coming into her window above her bed. She smelled breakfast drifting up from the kitchen, which meant it was time for Wrenley to get up and help her mom. Guests would be coming out of their rooms and needing coffee and tea before breakfast was served. Wrenley opened her eyes and allowed them to focus. She yelped and jumped up, hitting the backboard of the bed. In front of her was a face she recognized…and she groaned.

"Oh shit…" Wrenley moaned, covering her eyes with her hands, "It wasn't a dream."

"Afraid not," Gwyneira stood beside Wrenley's side of the bed, barely two feet away from Wrenley's face. She was dressed in an ebony nightgown, her jet-black hair so long it was braided and slung over her shoulder, coming past her breasts. She stood above Wrenley, her arms crossed in front of her.

"You snore," she said blankly, tapping her foot on the floor.

Wrenley rubbed her eyes, "Dear god, can I just wake up from this?"

"Unfortunately, no. You should let me help you with your snoring; you sound like a dying cow."

Wrenley huffed and tossed her covers off, hurling her feet over the side of the bed.

"We could break your nose and reset it; it may help with the snoring." Gwyneira was serious, arching an eyebrow at Wrenley's shocked expression.

"No! You are not breaking my goddamn nose."

"I'm not sure I can tolerate your noises moving forward," Gwyneira put her hands on her hips, but her face was still expressionless. She shifted her weight from one foot to the other, her emerald eyes narrowing at Wrenley.

"Close the damn door if you don't want to hear me snore," Wrenley snapped and suddenly felt dizzy as she sat up. She must have moved too fast after sleeping for so long. Gwyneira produced a bowl before her as if on cue. Wrenley vomited up what little was left in her stomach and dry-heaved the rest.

"This is interesting…" Gwyneira mused as Wrenley's body convulsed on the side of the bed, holding the bowl as Wrenley planted her face in it. Gwyneira did not comfort her; instead, she watched Wrenley dry heave so violently that her body shook.

"Do you want something?" Gwyneira asked blankly. "I realize that some people may find it socially appropriate to hold a person's hair when they vomit. Do you want me to hold your hair while you vomit?"

Wrenley finished dry heaving and wiped her mouth, looking up at Gwyneira with a death glare, "I want you to get out of my fucking room."

Gwyneira paused and touched Wrenley's brow with her delicate, cool fingers. Wrenley tried not to relish the cold on her forehead and the gesture that almost signified caring from the younger woman. But as quickly as she did, Gwyneira pulled away again.

"Hmmmm…that's interesting too," Gwyneira mumbled again, moving to set the bowl on the table beside the bed and wandering back into her chambers. Wrenley fell back into bed and shuddered, unsure if it was from the cold or absolute exhaustion. Everything came flooding back to her: the journey, her parents, the dark enemy taking over the kingdom, Bronson…Wrenley moaned and brought her legs up to her chest, feeling miserable. She would give everything to go home so her mother could care for her.

Wrenley managed to get up and dress herself before any of the staff came in. She was new to the servant thing, which still made her uncomfortable. She did not know how long she had been asleep, but it must have been for more than twelve hours. She peered outside the castle window. The sun was shining, and a new blanket of snow had fallen.

She found her way out of the chambers, down the hall, and then down a cold, steep set of stone stairs, steadying herself against the wall. Her body was weak from throwing up and not eating for who knows how long. She felt her limbs shake, her head pounding from the pressure of vomiting. She followed the smell of breakfast, though her stomach would not allow food consumption. She finally came to a large hall with a robust table filled with different breakfast foods.

Alcott, Kage, and Garrick sat and whispered amongst themselves as Wrenley entered the dining room. Plates of fruit, eggs, and different pastries decorated the table; coffee and tea were replenished by staff regularly. Bronson sat at the head of the table, intently reading some map or manuscript; of course, he did not look up. Gwyneira also found her way down and sat across from the other group members. Gwyneira picked at the food, scrunching her nose as she stabbed some sausage and sniffed it.

Wrenley observed the company and noticed they all looked refreshed. Kage still favored his wounded side but seemed energetic and in a good mood. Bronson also seemed reinvigorated; his dark hair had been trimmed, his face had been cleanly shaved, and he wore a new set of clothes. He looked up from his work, finally noticing Wrenley, and shot up as she approached.

"We were beginning to think you'd sleep another day away..." Bronson said casually, as he eyed her repeatedly, examining her. Wrenley wore leggings and a sizeable sweater-like tunic she found in the closet, with satin slippers on her feet. Her golden hair was pulled up on her head in a messy bun.

"How long have I been out?" Wrenley rasped, taking the seat Bronson pulled out for her next to his spot at the head of the table.

"A full day."

"Jesus..." she mumbled as she steadied herself in her seat. The servants came around offering Wrenley food, and she politely declined, internally trying not to vomit again. She took coffee with cream and sugar and hoped it would not come back up. Bronson noticed, his eyebrows shooting up in question.

"She threw up this morning," Gwyneira said in a monotone voice, and Wrenley shot her a hot look.

Bronson leaned back in his chair and tossed the manuscript aside, still studying her.

"Has this happened before?"

"I mean...it's kind of been a rough couple of days," Wrenley sipped on her coffee and avoided the question, and Bronson continued to scrutinize her. Wrenley was constantly feeling sick or lightheaded, so this was nothing new. She was tired of always being the 'weak' one.

"She also snores. I could probably fix it if she'd let me..."

"Would you shut up? You're not breaking my nose!" Wrenley snapped, slamming her coffee cup down so hard it broke. The group jumped in unison; all eyes turned to Wrenley. Bronson was the only one whose features remained unchanged; he leaned back in his seat, one elbow resting on the arm of the chair. Kage paused his fork piled with eggs midway to his mouth, looking between them. Wrenley took in a shaky breath, lifting her hand to reveal a deep cut from the broken glass. She grabbed a napkin and wrapped her hand in it, her companions still frozen.

"What? She's like a creepy possessed doll that moves around, and you never know where she will be," Wrenley huffed and stood, scooting the chair forcefully away.

"I'd agree with that…about the doll," Gwyneira said nonchalantly, not bothered by Wrenley's outburst as she ate her pastry.

"You need to eat," Bronson said lowly from his position, but Wrenley stood with an agitated huff and stomped out of the room, blood soaking the napkin wrapped around her cut.

"I think this is more than just about Gwyneira…" Garrick murmured to Alcott, the younger man also raising his eyebrows as their royalty left the room.

"Excuse me…" Bronson pushed away from the table and followed Wrenley out of the hall. Kage eyed Wrenley and Bronson as they left. Garrick and Alcott continued their breakfast, seemingly very interested in their eggs and fruit.

~ ~ ~ ~ ~

Bronson made it out of the hall and hit the corridor in time to see Wrenley lean over and vomit again, although there was not much to throw up at this point. Wrenley fell on her hands and knees, her body convulsing, holding her stomach. Bronson immediately went to her side, put an arm around her, and held her. By this time, the commotion had gained the attention of the house staff, and several flocked around them, offering to help. Her hand was bleeding profusely now, saturating the napkin Wrenley had used to wrap it up in.

Someone suggested calling for a doctor, but Bronson politely declined. He was more skilled than anyone within a hundred miles. Bronson managed to get Wrenley back to her feet, and she pulled away from his touch.

"I can manage," she said, and Bronson's jaw tightened.

"Let me help you," he said with a growl, which irritated

Wrenley even more. He had said that before…Since then, he had ignored her, commanded her around, fucked her, and did not have the decency to talk to her about it.

"I don't need your help," she hissed, shoving past him. He began to protest but paused when Kage had sauntered past him, hands casually in his pockets, giving Bronson a smug smile as he followed Wrenley. Bronson stood in the hall watching after them, his fists curling as they wandered out of sight.

~ ~ ~ ~ ~

"You can heal yourself, you know."

Wrenley whirled at Kage's words and gasped slightly; she had not realized he had followed her into her washroom. One of the young staff members bravely moved around the washroom, providing her with a bandage and some supplies. Kage filled the door, lifting his arms to grasp the top of the doorframe, and leaned towards her. His black hair was pulled back in a knot behind his head, his almond eyes scanning her intently.

Wrenley started, "I thought I wasn't allowed to use magic…"

Kage snorted, pushed off the frame, and fully entered the washroom. He ventured to where Wrenley stood, pulled up a stool, and sat in front of her, motioning for her to sit on the edge of the bath. He gently took her hand and studied it as if it were the most interesting thing in the world. After what seemed like minutes, he shrugged and looked up at her.

"Being the son of a healer, I can help you bandage this up. Or you can use your magic to heal your wound, which I have also seen done."

"But Bronson…"

Kage rolled his eyes and reached for the clean, wet washcloth the staff member handed him. He began to clean the cut tenderly, "He uses magic all the damn time. It's the big bursts of energy he is avoiding…" Kage finished and slanted his head to her. "Look at it and will yourself to heal it."

Wrenley wrinkled her brow but did as he said. At first, she noticed nothing but sharply inhaled as her hand began to glow. Slowly, the rugged edges of her cut began to move as they darned themselves back together, leaving a soft pink scar in its place.

Without even catching herself, she let out a laugh of delight and looked up to see Kage beaming at her.

"Remember what my Mother said, my lady…" Kage stood, lacing his fingers with hers and squeezing gently. "You don't need anyone to complete you. You lack nothing in yourself except truly believing it." He reached down to flick the green crystal between her breasts, the one Astara had given her as a reminder.

Wrenley breathed, realizing what a friend Kage had become to her during these struggles. He was like the younger brother she never had, and without warning, she threw her arms around his neck and crushed the younger man in an embrace. He stiffened, surprised at first, but she felt him chuckle, and he wrapped his arms around her and gave her a gentle squeeze. He groaned just a bit when she squeezed him too tightly, his side still tender.

She knew he was right, that she had the power within her. Fear kept her bogged down: the fear of hurting people, failure, and attracting the wrong attention. Her anxiety had made her lock up and become paralyzed. Kage always seemed to be able to call her out and kick her ass if she needed it. No longer would she be afraid of what was inside her. Layer by layer, she would tear down the walls that fear had built and begin to discover the treasures that had been dormant for too long. She hugged him one last time and released him, patting him on the cheek.

"Would you help me?"

If Bronson would not empower her, she would find someone who would.

~ ~ ~ ~ ~

The company found its routines in its new residence. Every need was taken care of for them, and every luxury was provided, so much so that Wrenley felt uneasy living with her needs fully met while the world outside struggled to survive. There were books in the library, games in the sitting room, and an area for them to train and exercise in case of inclement weather. That is where the males spent most of their time: training, sparing, and keeping themselves as fit as possible, even with the snow and icy conditions. Weather permitting, Alcott, Garrick, and Kage would run bundled up in the snow for hours; Bronson joined them when he was not busy in the library or locked up in the study.

Wrenley had taken to discovering her powers out of the watchful gaze of Bronson and Garrick. The generational differences between the four men were undeniable. Bronson and Garrick knew 'the old ways and what things looked like before the war'…Alcott and Kage did not. The twins treated Wrenley like a sister, and Bronson would reprimand them for being too rough or casual with Wrenley. To Bronson's annoyance, the twins usually ignored him.

Wrenley would sneak to the conservatory to practice small bouts of magic. She supposed she was not doing too much to bring unwanted attention in the unseen, or Bronson would have noticed and yelled at her by now. She would sit on the cold marble floor and summon bits and pieces of the light inside her, testing it. She would feel it stir under her skin, flushing her with warmth as she practiced summoning it.

One day, as Wrenley sat on the floor in the conservatory, bathing in the warm sun that poured through the large windows, she sat by the fishpond that trickled water through the room. She played with a small ball of light, bending, twisting, and working on sending it out, then recalling.

"You don't have to hover," Wrenley said through gritted teeth as she sensed someone behind her. Gwyneira shuffled out from behind a large potted tree and trotted to stand next to Wrenley. Gwyneira said nothing but tilted her head and watched as Wrenley worked the soft ball of light in her hands.

After ten minutes of silence, Gwyneira spoke, "I could teach you… or something."

Wrenley paused her exercise and shifted her body to look at the small woman. Wrenley's eyebrow darted up in question and even suspicion. "Why?"

Gwyneira shrugged, "Our magic is different, but we could at least share what we know and learn from each other…since we have nothing better to do." Gwyneira pushed her black bangs out of her eyes and sighed, "And I refuse to run for hours like livestock outside with the boys."

Wrenley could not help but grin, scooting and motioning to the spot beside her. Wrenley thought she detected a hint of excitement in those emerald eyes as Gwyneira hurried over and plopped down beside her. Wrenley began explaining her magic and how she summoned it, and Gwyneira listened intently. Wrenley noticed how young the other woman was, prompting questions in her mind about her past. Still, Wrenley did not ask; it would only cause the younger woman to pull away.

That moment began the friendship between Gwyneira and Wrenley. Gwyneira listened in fascination about Wrenley's old world and asked countless questions about cars, electricity, science, and medicine. Wrenley could not believe how good it felt to talk about her old world to someone else. Wrenley gleaned every bit of information on magic from Gwyneira, even if witches' magic differed from a seer's. The elements of it were very similar, and Wrenley grew into some resemblance of comfort and familiarity with the power under her skin. Wrenley and Gwyneira mustered the courage to insert themselves into physical training with the twins.

Wrenley gasped as she ducked out of the way of Kage's practice weapon, a wooden sword that had been provided to them for training. Gwyn, Alcott, Kage, and Wrenley had taken up the gym area and worked together for several hours now. Wrenley was soaked with sweat, stripped down to a lightweight shirt and her pants. Garrick sat on the opposite wall in a chair, eyeing the company's younger members as they trained. As usual, Bronson was locked in his study, writing letters, reading, or whatever nonsense he preoccupied himself with these days. Despite his promise to talk with her about whatever happened between them, he avoided her. She took her anger at him out in the ring.

Kage and Alcott were machines; stripped down to their pants, their chiseled, muscular chests did not hold an ounce of fat, complete with the defined V-shaped muscle that dipped down into their pant line. A thin coat of sweat covered their beautiful copper skin; their bodies were built to move and fight. Kage's hair was pulled back into a knot, while Alcott's was braided. Wrenley recognized that Gwyneira had shot the twins a glance or two. They moved with such elegance and power that Wrenley was initially intimidated to enter the ring with them. They were enormous compared to her, but Wrenley felt a little easier when Kage swaggered up to her as she stood off to the side. She flushed at his gaze that blatantly raked over her, an ornery grin tugging at his lips.

"Ready?"

Wrenley licked her lips as she tore her gaze from the beautiful man before her and turned to the ring where Alcott was prepping Gwyneira with a practice sword. The smaller woman did not look afraid; instead, she grinned as she held the weapon and weighed it in one hand.

Wrenley finally shrugged, "I guess so."

Kage's face broke into an enormous grin, and he motioned for her to follow him to the weapons rack where the others readied themselves. She chose a medium-sized practice sword, wincing at how awkward it felt to hold it.

"Don't look so excited." Kage took up space behind her, reached to position her shoulders, and then went for her thighs to maneuver her legs.

"Not so handsy, kids!" Garrick called out, frowning at them. Kage snorted and rolled his eyes.

Wrenley shook her head and sighed, "I'm not excited…I can't imagine having to kill someone with a weapon like this." It made her sick to her stomach.

"The hope is you will never have to, but if it comes to it, you need to know how." Kage straightened and sauntered over to retrieve a practice weapon. He and Alcott used real blades when sparing, but she was thankful he would not with her. They began going through simple motions. After an hour of balancing and stretching, Kage began to push Wrenley harder. Wrenley panted, and Kage did not relent, coming at her to the point where she felt her body moving too fast and her brain not catching up.

She tripped and tumbled forward at one point, her hand shooting out to break her fall. Kage was already in a downward strike position and could not call off the blow he thought she would avoid. In a heartbeat, a pulse of power came out from her, and she closed her eyes, waiting to fall face flat on the floor, crunch her wrist, and take a blow to the back by the wooden sword…but it never came. She opened her eyes to notice that her magic had softened her fall, and now a soft shield enveloped her. Kage's sword had just bounced off it, pushing him back several feet.

Kage skidded to a stop, surprised at the shield, and gaped at

Wrenley as she turned over, the shield pulsing around her. Garrick almost fell out of his chair, and the group gathered around Wrenley. Gwyneira reached out and inhaled as her hand hit against the invisible shield, grinning at Wrenley. Wrenley released it, afraid she had done too much already, and hoisted herself back up to a standing position.

Kage gave her a lopsided grin, "Now that is a good trick."

"Shit," Garrick seemed impressed, tossing a glance at Alcott, and the younger man grinned.

Gwyneira crossed her arms over her chest. "Can I do that?"

"Only one way to find out," Kage tapped Wrenley's shoulder with the wooden sword.

"Again."

CHAPTER 26

Concerns

Bronson had been in his office when he felt it; a pulse from the unseen, just light enough he would have missed it if he were not in a silent room. He raised his head slowly and tilted it as if to listen; nothing. He stood, shoved his chair away from the desk, and narrowed his eyes. Where was Wrenley? What was she doing? He could not remember and would admit he had been so preoccupied with other things that he had not recently paid much attention to her. Returning to the first level, he heard a commotion from the gym area.

Garrick stood outside the circle where they were sparring, his arms folded tightly, watching. Bronson sauntered up and stood next to him, his eyebrows knitting together.

"What the fuck are you allowing them to do?" Bronson muttered, and Garrick glanced at his friend as if he had just realized Bronson was beside him.

"I'm getting too old to argue with the young folk…" Garrick muttered. Bronson cringed as Kage and Wrenley sparred, alarm growing in his chest as he saw her duck and weave in and out to avoid Kage's blows. He knew Kage to be a powerful enough warrior that if one of those blows landed, even with a training blade, it could do damage.

"Widen your stance!" Garrick yelled at Wrenley but winced as his friend scowled at him and clamped his mouth shut.

Bronson growled, "You shouldn't encourage the kids to fight." Bronson was only fifteen years older than Wrenley, putting him almost twenty years older than Kage in this world's time. Though still in his prime, the mental ageing this war had put on him was heavy. He stood next to his friend and watched their companions spar in silence.

Wrenley was fast, and Bronson was taken aback by how skilled she had become with her blade. How long has she been practicing without him realizing? He took in her toned body, the muscles replacing the weaknesses she had arrived with months ago. Wrenley jumped to tap Kage's ass with her blade, and he roared in competitiveness, lunging at her with his entire body without reservation. She gasped, not expecting it, and his large body had knocked her out of the air. She yelped and flung her shield out. Bronson winced again at the surge, realizing that is what he must have felt in his study.

Wrenley's shield padded the impact of her fall, but she failed to calculate enough to protect herself from Kage's weight as he landed on top of her. She groaned, and he pinned her down, his muscular thighs on either side of her torso. He drew his dagger from his boot, using his other forearm to hold her neck down to the ground. She was pinned, and he brought the knife to her throat. Wrenley gasped, eyes wide as she looked up at Kage in surprise. Kage grinned at her, and she blushed, realizing he held her captive.

It took every ounce of restraint for Bronson not to roar at Kage and rip him off her, his fist clenching at the sight of Kage's body covering Wrenley's. The thought of any man being so close to Wrenley made his magic stir…but he fought it. Bronson knew she had to learn how to fight, get away, and even kill when the time came because it surely would.

Kage grinned down at her, the metal blade still close to her throat. "Pinned. Do you submit to me, lady?" Kage's voice was a low growl, his eyes sparking with amusement. "If I win, I get a kiss."

Bronson tried to ignore the flirtation in the younger man's voice. Wrenley's face was flushed, whether from the flirting, the weight of the massive warrior on top of her, or the physical energy she was expending…he could not tell. Bronson suddenly realized that he was jealous; jealous of Kage's proximity to her. He was jealous that she worked and laughed with the twins like they were close. And whose fault was that? His. For being so busy that he had avoided the conversation he knew they should have had when they arrived. He ached for her…desperately.

Wrenley panted, "Pinned, but not dead…" She reared back and, with every ounce of strength, wiggled her right arm free and punched Kage between his legs. Kage screamed, then groaned and slumped off her. In a flash, she was up, disarming him and holding his blade to his neck.

"Pinned...and wishing you were dead," Wrenley beamed triumphantly at Kage, and Alcott and Garrick almost doubled over with laughter.

"And no kiss," Gwyneira chanted in a sing-song voice.

"Men are babies," Wrenley chided as Garrick and Alcott applauded and Gwyneira snickered. Wrenley flipped the blade and handed it back to the grating warrior. Kage moaned and accepted it, pulling himself up on his knees, one hand on the ground and one clutching his manhood as he waited for the pain to lessen.

"If you ruined my chance to reproduce...I'm telling Mother."

"That a woman landed you on your ass? Sure, you go ahead." Wrenley was laughing so hard she bent over now, hands resting on her thighs as she took deep breaths.

Wrenley raised her head to meet Bronson's gaze, and her eyes narrowed. He held her stare and grinned at her as she came sauntering up to him, her clothes drenched in sweat as she downed a glass of water from a nearby table. It was as if she were expecting him to disapprove in some way. She held his gaze as she sucked dry every ounce of liquid, set it back down on the table, and wiped the remnants with her sleeve.

God, she looked different, and he felt the confidence oozing off her. He noted the swagger and how she held her body. She did not look at him for approval but in defiance. Something in his gut twisted at the thought, finding her newfound confidence so attractive he could hardly keep himself from reaching out to her. When she was weak and vulnerable, every ounce of him wanted to protect her...she needed him. But this, this was a woman who needed nothing unless she wanted it. He should be thankful for the changes and celebrate her growth; he did, but it was new. This Wrenley was uncharted territory, and he was unsure how to proceed.

~ ~ ~ ~ ~

Wrenley wrenched herself from a fitful sleep and threw herself out of the bed, emptying the contents of her stomach onto the floor. Her body convulsed and shook as she shamefully allowed the puke to spill on the floor. She did not care; she just wanted it over so she could collapse back into bed and pray it would subside. She puked for several minutes, finally panting and falling backward to where she sat on the floor, her head resting against the side of the bed. The staff always attempted to be inconspicuous, as did the young girl who entered the room and quietly cleaned up the mess.

"I'm so sorry…" Wrenley whispered, and the girl's pretty face turned to her.

"My lady, there is nothing to be sorry for, truly…" The girl finished cleaning the mess, washed her hands, and retrieved a cool washcloth. The girl padded over, gently washed Wrenley's face, and sat beside her nervously.

"What?" Wrenley asked weakly.

The girl shifted. "My lady, may I fetch Bronson…?"

"No!" Wrenley did not intend it to come out as sharp as it did. She tried again, "No, but thank you. You have been very kind. I am okay now, so there is no need to bother anyone else." Was she fine, though? Wrenley felt like death, her whole body weak as she trembled on the floor, hardly able to get herself back up in bed. She glanced down and noticed her hands glowing. Her magic stirred as it probed her body for the source of the illness.

"Your heaving is even louder than your snoring."

Wrenley jumped and cursed, slightly turning to look up at Gwyneira. Once again, the younger girl was like a shadow, her dark hair a mess around her shoulders, and dressed in a lacy undergarment.

"Sorry…I didn't mean to wake anyone."

Gwyneira did not respond but lowered herself onto the floor next to Wrenley and felt her forehead. Gwyneira then kneeled in front of her and, without hesitation, reached a hand to lay on Wrenley's cheek. Gwyneira's eyes slid shut for several moments. Wrenley stayed still but studied the strange little woman before her, realizing that Gwyneira's presence was comforting. Gwyneira's eyes jumped open, and she removed her hand as if Wrenley's skin had burned her.

"What?" Wrenley asked, slightly alarmed.

Gwyneira did well schooling her features, the vacant expression returning to her young face. "I think you may have some stomach bug...I would avoid training until Bronson can properly assess you."

"Well, that's just great."

"You promise you'll talk to him tomorrow?"

Wrenley groaned in response and allowed Gwyneira to help her back into bed. She was finally able to drift off after there was nothing left to throw up. The next day, she avoided breakfast, the nausea still lingering. She did join the others in training and made sure to drink water when she could. She was surprised to see Bronson in the gym the next day but ignored him, her focus being set on not projectile vomiting while Kage proceeded to kick her ass in the ring.

~ ~ ~ ~ ~

Bronson and Garrick leaned against the gym wall the following day, watching the regular sparing matches between Kage, Wrenley, Gwyneira, and Alcott. Bronson had things he could be doing, but he did not dare skip after Gwyneira had come to him this morning with her concerns. He carefully watched Wrenley, noting she was not as energetic as usual. Her movements were sluggish, and he saw her wince several times when Kage did not hold back the blows. To her credit, Wrenley took them in stride, but Bronson detected she was not using her shields like normal.

"Have you noticed anything odd about Wrenley lately?" He murmured to Garrick, Bronson's chestnut eyes not leaving her face as she moved around the gym.

Garrick sighed and shrugged, rubbing his face with one hand. "She's a little withdrawn...and pulling to her left when she swings."

Bronson frowned. "What does that even mean?"

Garrick watched her, crossing his arms and stroking his trimmed beard with his thumb and forefinger, "She is in pain; something is hurting her."

Bronson watched as Wrenley fell back, thudding on the floor with no trace of her magic easing her fall. Probably unaware, Kage returned to land a decisive blow, assuming she would raise a shield to protect herself. She did not. Instead, she raised her practice weapon weakly, panting and breathing heavier. Kage noticed and halted, confusion blanching his face as Wrenley dropped her sword and fell back, her chest heaving in difficulty as if she could not breathe. Within a heartbeat, Bronson had pushed past Kage and knelt over her.

"Wrenley?" Bronson asked firmly, but she did not answer. She lay there, panting, her eyes rolling to the back of her head. Gwyneira was at her side immediately, those emerald eyes glancing at Bronson for guidance or command on how to help her friend. Bronson reached down and tore her shirt open, looking at her chest for any sign of swelling, rashes, anything that could explain. He then lowered himself onto a plank and rested his head on her chest, listening to her lungs and heartbeat for several moments.

"What's wrong with her?" Kage asked frantically, his fear evident as he towered over Wrenley's still body.

"Her magic is diverting itself..." Bronson murmured to Gwyneira, and the witch raised an eyebrow.

"To where exactly, and why?" Bronson and Gwyneira held each other's gaze for a long moment, then, without another word, Bronson scooped Wrenley up in his arms.

"I need to examine her more thoroughly." He carried her quickly up the stairs to her room and settled her into bed with Gwyneira's assistance. By then, Wrenley's breathing was returning to normal, and some of the fight was returning to her.

"I'm fine," Wrenley waved him off, trying to sit up in bed, but still weak from the episode. She argued with Gwyneira, the staff, and anyone else within two feet of her. Bronson ignored her protests, worried that perhaps this was a residual effect from her issues earlier this month. He had thought she was adapting well, but he could have been wrong.

"I need you to undress, please," Bronson said sternly, motioning for Gwyneira to exit. She complied without question. Leaving them alone, Wrenley looked up from her position on the bed and looked at him with shock. "Absolutely not!"

Bronson exhaled with relief as he noted the fire back in her eyes. He rolled his sleeves up to his elbows and washed his hands in the bowl of clean water on the table next to the fireplace.

"Good grief, I'm not going to rape you. Either I examine you myself, or they call a country doctor from one of the villages to come over and tell me what I can diagnose in five minutes. And the bright side is…"

"Oh, please tell me the bright side…" she whimpered.

"I've seen you naked before."

Wrenley snapped her gaze up at Bronson and noticed a hint of a smile on his face.

"You haven't even spoken to me about that in weeks."

Bronson sighed, "I know…but we are here now. Let me help you."

Wrenley would not argue anymore. She had no strength to fight after battling for breath only fifteen minutes earlier. She slipped her leggings and sweater off, quickly tossed them to the side, and pulled the covers over her, her cheeks burning. Bronson was thorough but discreet, examined her quickly, and kept her covered when he could. He noticed some swelling in her knee and bruises on her arms, legs, and torso, which she attributed to training. He asked her to lie down flat and pulled back the sheet, exposing her breasts and stomach. He gently felt her abdomen, palpating her neck, shoulders, and breasts. She winced and pulled away slightly.

"Does that hurt?"

She nodded. He continued to palpate around her breast and up into her neck again, and she held her breath, noticing how sore her breasts had been. Nothing he did was sexual; he was focused on something, and she could not tell what he was in search of. He then felt for her pulse in her neck and counted, doing the same with her breaths. Finally, he laid his palm on her stomach. She sucked in a breath quickly and shot up from her lying position, jerking to the left just as Garrick had predicted.

"Does it hurt?" Bronson asked again, holding his hands before him, noticing Wrenley's reaction.

"No, I just…felt something…what's wrong with me?" She grabbed the covers and held them to her chest again, her face flushed, her body shaking.

Bronson's eyes darkened, his voice lowering as something like a growl escaped him. "Can you please trust me and be still?"

Wrenley nodded and leaned back as Bronson pulled the covers down again, laying his hand on her stomach, pushing gently around her abdomen. Wrenley felt it again, but did not jerk away, gritting her teeth as Bronson's broad hand splayed on her stomach, keeping her from moving. He pinned her down with one hand as his other hand felt around, and she squirmed. She noticed Bronson's hands glowing; sparks started to snap around his hands.

"What is it, Bronson?" Wrenley was feeling panicked now as she noticed his brow furrowing. Bronson's face was neutral; she could tell he was schooling his features for her.

"It's…unexpected."

"What?" Wrenley sat up, but Bronson did not remove his hand from her stomach. He seemed to be deep in thought, his head tilted as if he was listening for something. He was firm but gentle as he forced her pelvis back on the bed, another hand moving to the center of her chest as it glowed with his magic.

"What is wrong with me?"

Bronson moved his hands away now, assisting her with covering herself again.

"Wrenley, I think you are pregnant."

~ ~ ~ ~ ~

The words hit her like a sledgehammer. Wrenley looked at Bronson, then down to her stomach, and back to Bronson again. She felt dread swell in her chest, and she leaned back into the bed, feeling her face go numb. Bronson assisted her with pulling her clothes back on and tucked her in. He sat awkwardly beside her for several minutes. She did not know what to say. Finally, after the wave of nausea passed, she cleared her throat.

"I'm fucking stupid."

Bronson appeared preoccupied but quickly snapped out of it, looking at her with raised eyebrows.

"I should have known better…this is all my fault!" She felt tears coming on, and one spilled down her cheek.

"What do you mean, your fault? Wrenley, this is…this is…"

"What is it, Bronson?" She snapped at him and ripped her hand away when he tried to reach for it. "This is an absolute nightmare. This is dangerous enough as it is. I've almost been eaten by a wild dog, killed by enemy troops, and now we are headed right into the eye of the storm…now this." She motioned to her stomach with both hands and buried her face. She began to cry now, her sobs shaking her shoulders, and she allowed Bronson to reach for her. Quickly, he lifted her into his lap and cradled her as she sobbed, letting the exhaustion, fear, and grief escape her body.

She cried for almost an hour, soaking his shirt. She then rested her cheek on his chest for a while after the tears dried, listening to the steady beating of his heart. Her thoughts were reeling, clanging, and clattering so fast that she could not speak them. Finally, she took a shaky breath and sat up. She wiped her snot away from her nose with the sleeve of her shirt.

"When I was young, they diagnosed me with the disease and told me that in the rare chance I could conceive a child, I would never carry it. I would never carry a baby…" Wrenley broke out into sobs again, and Bronson slipped an arm around her as she leaned on his soaked shoulder again.

"I know," he murmured to her.

"It was just a dream, you know? To have a baby, a family…and now that…" She placed a hand on her stomach, her hands glowing and sparking. "Now that I can, there is so much danger. So much at risk…it's another person to lose."

Bronson caressed her forehead, pressing a kiss to her temple. "I won't let anything happen to you or this baby," he murmured against her hair.

Wrenley sniffed. "You can't make promises like that."

Bronson exhaled, lifted her off his lap onto the bed, and slipped onto the ground, kneeling before her. He grasped her hands, "As long as I am alive, I will protect you and this child."

"A child," Wrenley said, looking down at Bronson, fear tugging at her heart. "It's your child, too…are you…happy about this?"

Bronson seemed to take a shaky breath and hoisted himself to where he could slip into bed next to her. He pulled her close and grasped her chin with his thumb, forcing her to look up at him.

"You have no idea how this is an absolute miracle for me."

She knew he was telling the truth and almost thought she spied a glisten in his eyes as he looked at her. The words sank into her, and she sighed as Bronson leaned down to capture her mouth with his.

She pulled away then. "I just don't know how…"

"Wrenley, this is my oversight. I should have known that you…" He struggled with the words, and she raised an eyebrow towards him. He cleared his throat, "I just wasn't thinking about anything like that. I had thought that the shock of your body adjusting to our world would have prevented a pregnancy…"

"But it didn't."

Bronson sighed with a lopsided grin… "No, it didn't."

They sat silently for several moments, and Wrenley grinned slightly, giggling as she tried to muffle her laugh with her blanket.

Bronson frowned. "What?"

"Does this mean you can't tie me up and do unspeakable things to me now?"

Bronson groaned, catching her in his arms and depositing her in the middle of the bed. Yelping, she struggled as he crawled on top of her, pinning her down gently.

"I never said that…" he said lowly, and a delightful shiver raced up her spine and spread through her body as he lowered his head to kiss her.

~ ~ ~ ~ ~

Wrenley stayed in bed for the next several days on Bronson's orders. The others were under the impression that she had caught a virus while traveling. Wrenley felt like Gwyneira knew more than what was said as she hovered in the background, watching Wrenley. Though Wrenley still had difficulty with her sometimes, Gwyneira had become a friend, one that she was beginning to count on. They did not necessarily talk, but they could sit silently for hours…reading books before the fire in the library, playing with their magic by the fishpond in the conservatory, or frowning at the boys as they guffawed at ridiculous jokes.

Bronson and Wrenley still had not had any deep conversations about what exactly this was between them, especially now that there was a baby. A baby…Wrenley would break out into a cold sweat whenever she thought about it. It felt unreal, and how could they be sure anyway? It was not as if they could buy a test at the drugstore. But Bronson knew…his magic had known for sure when he had placed his hand on her stomach. Wrenley could imagine Bronson wrestling with all these things; maybe that is why they had not discussed it yet.

Bronson and Garrick would come and go from the estate. They

traveled to nearby settlements and gleaned information about the enemy and relevant news. The only traffic in and out of the secure location was the servants who went for supplies and returned to provide information to Bronson. Lately, reports of activity near the lake border were increasing, and Garrick had shared with Wrenley that enemy outposts along the lake were moving westward towards Ailios.

Wrenley could tell the company was restless; the twins were ready to crawl out of their skins with pent-up energy despite their daily training routines. With more snow moving in and the weather turning harsher, everyone, even Bronson, was restricted to the estate while the snow blanketed the land around them. The most recent blizzard lasted several days.

Wrenley awoke that morning to the sun peering in her window. She mustered enough courage to defy orders and venture out of her room, hoping to make it to the conservatory to sit in the sun. She slipped on pants and a sweater and tiptoed down the narrow staircase. Once on the main level, she quietly passed the sitting room, where she heard Kage, Alcott, and even Gwyneira talking in hushed tones. She was not sure if she heard Bronson among them. She had an idea for a quick walk outside. Her mood had been so low recently that some fresh air would do wonders. She stood and contemplated it momentarily, shifting her weight on one foot and then the other, mentally calculating the risks and benefits her audacity would cause her. She decided it was worth the risk.

She slipped past the sitting room and avoided the house staff as she stole a heavy coat, scarf, and gloves. She ducked out the back door, the one servants had to use to bring in goods and supplies. She was so eager that she almost tripped out the door, sucking in the cold fresh air, thankful for the sun that was peeking out from behind the clouds. She knew that if Bronson discovered she was outside the dwelling, he would lock her in her room and throw away the key. That is why she was determined not to get caught.

She was not going far; just a short walk to the loch beside the estate, the usual route Alcott and Kage took when they ran and trained. It was a small loch of water, and she could walk around it without problem. She felt her body ache from being stationary and knew it would benefit her. Wrenley trudged through the new blanket of snow, feeling her lungs burn from the exercise, but she also felt the energy released from her. She tingled from head to toe and felt much better halfway around.

As she stomped through the snow and felt it crunch underneath her, her mind wandered to home. Her thoughts went to Ruth and Jim, and she wondered what they were doing now. She did not know the season in Missouri, and the disconnect from everything familiar cracked something in her chest. Wrenley felt an overwhelming sense of grief overtake her, the intensity of it stopping her in her tracks.

She stood alone at the other end of the loch, a sob escaping her throat. Ruth, Jim — they would not know. She needed them so desperately, and they could not be a part of this with her. They would have been so elated at the news of a baby. Wrenley had dreamed of the day she would get married, have a baby, and see Ruth and Jim as grandparents, even if the dream would never be a reality. Wrenley's tears flowed freely as she crumbled in the fresh snow.

Why do you cry so?

Wrenley heard it as a whisper and paused in her weeping.

So much sorrow. So much heartache.

The soft voice wafted around Wrenley, causing her to startle and stand. She looked around her, the hairs on the back of her neck standing on end.

"He-hello?" She managed to squeak aloud; her voice was still shaky.

Do not be afraid, dear girl. The voice was soft and playful, like a lullaby. Wrenley felt gooseflesh break out over her arms. "Who's there?"

I know what you carry. The voice was getting closer, more audible now. Wrenley frantically looked around and gasped as she turned to the loch. A beautiful white horse stood at the bank of the water, drinking lazily. The horse was the most magnificent creature she had ever seen, its white mane glistening in the sun, its coat fresher than the snow that had fallen during the storm last night. The horse's eyes were a beautiful gold, its long lashes blinking at Wrenley.

Come closer.

It was speaking to her, though not out loud. Wrenley rubbed her palms against her pants and took a step towards it. Something drew her closer to the creature standing by the water's edge, and her hands tingled to feel its softness.

Do not be afraid, young one. Do not be distressed… It seemed to croon at her. The voice was so silky that it almost made Wrenley sleepy.

"Wrenley, please come to me."

Wrenley was jolted from a trance; the words snapped her awake long enough to look behind her. To her surprise, Bronson stood about ten feet away from her. She gaped at him, noticing that the sun was dropping to the horizon. She blinked, confused, as the sun had just risen when she ventured out. How long had she been out here?

She panicked and glanced towards the water's edge. The horse was still standing there, drinking lazily from the water. She just had to touch it before it ran away…

"Wrenley, come with me. We need to go," Bronson calmly reached a gloved hand for her, but Wrenley felt she was cemented to the ground. She had failed to realize she was not an arm's length away from the beautiful creature. She could almost touch it…just a few inches now.

Where is home for you, dear one? The voice tutted again softly. The horse's mouth did not move, but Wrenley knew the voice belonged to it.

"Wrenley, you need to step away from the horse. I'll explain everything."

Wrenley felt herself growing frustrated, jerking herself again and realizing the sun was almost setting on the horizon. Bronson stood far off, his hand extended, the horse so close now. So, so close…she just wanted to feel something, to feel that silky softness and bury her face in it.

"Wrenley, please. You need to trust me. Come here, take my hand, and I will explain. Please trust me."

Trust him? Why would she trust him? He took her away from Ruth and Jim and everything she knew. He kidnapped her! He wanted the throne for himself. He was using her…

"Wrenley, come here now!"

Wrenley had reached out to touch the horse but froze as she felt movement in her womb. The baby! She was pregnant with his baby. He would not do anything to hurt her. It took all her strength to retract her hand and move backward from the horse, now flaring its nostrils at her. She was so cold, and the beast seemed so warm and inviting.

But you are so lonely… The horse whispered seductively.

"No, I'm not…"

So, unfortunate…a sad, sad girl.

"I'm not…I'm…"

Another voice then came to her, one that she had heard in her dreams. It was like a whisper, a wind that kissed her ears, saying, *Come find me…*

Wrenley gasped as she felt Bronson's strong arms grab her around the waist and heaved her behind him, drawing his sword and pointing it toward the horse. Wrenley gasped as she collapsed in his arms, turning to see the beautiful horse contort into an older woman. The woman was covered in pale, gray robes, one eye in the middle of her face as it peered at Wrenley. She smiled, teeth sharp as she hissed towards them.

"Cailleach." Bronson dipped his head at the creature, maneuvering Wrenley behind him, his sword still pointed towards the crone.

"Such a pretty prize, young seer."

Wrenley shivered at her words, and Bronson took several steps backward away from her. "She is…and she's mine."

The crone's eye widened as she smiled, "Pity, I would have loved to eat her." She shrugged her long, slender shoulders and flipped her pale blue hair back as if tempting Bronson. "Such power in such a little creature."

"Yes, more powerful than you realize."

The crone cocked her head to the side. "Let's make a bargain; you give me the girl, I'll give you something you want."

"And what would that be, Cailleach, Goddess of Winter?"

Wrenley's eyes widened as she peeked over his shoulder, taking in the old woman. She was thin and tall, her pale robes cascading around her, skulls and bones of different shapes and sizes decorating her garments. Her single eye was an icy blue, her pale hair blowing in the wind.

"You give me the girl, and I give you a way into the capital."

Bronson hesitated, "You know of a way in?"

The goddess chuckled, pointing a spindly finger towards them.

"I do know a way…And I will show you if you give me her."

Wrenley felt Bronson tense, shaking his head. "Sorry, not this time, Cailleach. I've grown rather fond of her."

Cailleach hissed, and she played with a bone that decorated the hem of her cloak. "Another gift, then? I do love gifts."

Bronson's face was stone, and he shook his head again, backing farther away from the goddess. "Maybe next time. Go back to your watery depths, goddess." His voice was firm, but Wrenley felt him tremble ever so slightly.

The creature looked at them and shrugged again. "Fine…but I am here if you change your mind."

Then the crone seemed to melt before their eyes, turning into some type of beast that was part woman, part fish. Wrenley thought it resembled a mermaid, but it was so horrifying she almost had to turn away. Cailleach's robes disappeared, bearing her breasts as her legs turned into fins. The one eye took them in, the teeth still sharp and gnarly as she grinned and pulled herself back into the loch's murky depths with her forearms.

CHAPTER 27

Could Not Save Them

Bronson burst into the front door, commanding the group's attention in the sitting room to the left.

"I need hot water in a bath and warm clothes. Now!" Bronson barked the orders to the staff, and everyone snapped into motion. Bronson was filled with so much adrenaline that he took two stairs at a time, entered Wrenley's room, and began to peel her clothes off her frozen body. She had lost consciousness fifteen minutes ago, and Bronson was afraid she was hypothermic.

Kage and Gwyneira were now flanking him, with Alcott and Garrick behind them.

"What the hell happened?" Gwyneira asked, wide-eyed as Bronson slapped Wrenley's face several times. "Wake up, goddamn it!"

"She is almost frozen!" Kage spat as he helped Bronson undress her, her blue lips and pale skin contrasting with her usual rosy hue. Kage's features were alarmed as he assisted Bronson with lowering her into the warm bath, and Bronson nodded, "She's been out there all day."

"What? Why?" Garrick spoke from behind them, worry etching his voice.

Bronson did not answer as he checked Wrenley's pulse, cursing. It was too low, and her breathing was shallow. He looked at Gwyneira, "We may have to use more magic. Her pulse is very weak. Her magic is being rerouted to the baby..."

"What baby?" Kage snapped his head from Wrenley's face to Bronson, and rage filled his eyes. Bronson ignored the younger man as he stripped off his gloves and jacket.

"Gwyneira, your magic is not as detectable as mine since your power comes from the moon. Nicolas has spells, but I don't want to risk anyone tracking us. But I'm afraid we will lose her if..."

For the second time in Bronson's life, he felt a wave of helplessness wash over him as he looked at Wrenley's pale form slumped in the tub. Her face was ashy, her lips ghostly white, and her eyes, open just a bit, glazed over vacantly.

"If we can get her temperature up…" Gwyneira shoved her way past Bronson and met every man's gaze in the room. "If you aren't healing her, move back!"

The small woman's loud voice made everyone take a step backward. Gwyneira reached out to place a hand on Wrenley's chest, feeling for the heartbeat.

"Oh god, I can't lose her," Bronson was sobbing now. He did not care who saw him. He did not care who was in the room. The all-encompassing fear of losing the woman he loved was crashing around him. He struggled to breathe. Tears began pouring from his eyes, and his low body temperature began to take a toll on him. He had been out there with her this whole time…

Gwyneira placed a calm hand on him, "It's going to be ok. I will help her."

Bronson felt Gwyneira's small, warm hand on his cheek, and she reached out to put the other on Wrenley. Bronson heard himself weep, but he was numb and frozen in place. He was useless, utterly useless, at the sight of the woman he loved almost dead before him. He could not remember his skills, his powers…all he knew was his love, his life, his baby… was dying before him, and he was too frantic to think.

~ ~ ~ ~ ~

Keep her safe, my friend.

The words still echo in his mind every time he closes his eyes.

Bronson felt his muscles ache as he pushed his way upward toward the royal rooms, his sword slicing enemy troops as he moved methodically. He had lost count of how many; it was all just a blur by now. The blood that ran down the stone steps did not faze him as he sloshed through the gore to reach her. His body felt the fatigue of hard fighting, and most of the castle guards were levels below, holding the line as Bronson raced for Adinnil's bedroom. Though they had fought bravely, he knew they had been overrun. It was not a question of defending now but escaping.

Outside in the large courtyard, the blasts of magic shook the castle, one after the other, as Dolion took one last stand against Earnesh. An eruption knocked Bronson over from the left side, and he heard the cries of soldiers being crushed under the falling debris of the crumbling tower. Bronson was knocked into the wall but gritted his teeth, only momentarily stunned by the power of the blow.

Bronson hit the final level and dashed across to the bedroom, darting around dead bodies, the blood still trickling across the floor and down the stairs. Bronson noticed the door was open, and his heart sank. He propelled himself forward, sword drawn. He quickly but carefully entered the room to see Adinnil slit the throat of an enemy soldier, the young man falling into a bloody heap at her feet as she looked up. Relief filled her eyes at the sight of her dearest friend, and Bronson jerked his head to the sound of a baby crying from the crib in the corner.

"It's time to leave, my lady." Bronson eyed Adinnil as she hurriedly scooped up the babe, holding it tightly to her shoulder and softly kissing Wrenley's head.

"Yes, it is time for you to leave."

Bronson almost did not catch it, but he eyed the queen as she hurried to him and pulled the baby back from her shoulder. Her lip trembled slightly, and she leaned her face down to smell Wrenley's hair and kiss the sweet, chubby face. She handed the baby to him, and he awkwardly sheathed his sword, taking the baby in his bloodied arms. He had never even held a baby before, let alone the sole heir of the kingdom.

"You will take her away from here, now..."

Bronson felt shocked as he received the command. He cradled the tiny baby as it whimpered for her mother and squirmed in his arms. His queen drew a sword, holding it up and placing a hand on the flat side of the blade, exhaling and closing her eyes as if to center herself.

"No..." he whispered, his voice breaking as Adinnil's face changed, his friend disappearing, his queen emerging.

"You will follow the plan, and I will remain here to assist with evacuating my people. That is an order."

"Adinnil…" Bronson started, but she silenced him with a look of steel.

"No matter what you see or hear, you will go and not look back." The queen was relentless, her voice a steady beacon amidst chaos and ruin. Bronson was afraid, and he felt useless. All his power and training meant nothing; it would not help him save her or Dolion now. Bronson was built for war, not for running. The cries and shrieks of those being butchered rose to them, making Bronson's stomach tighten. He had known war, but this was no war; this was a slaughter.

Adinnil was not frightened but embodied valor and strength. Her eyes locked on him for one last time, her golden hair a mess behind her head, and she smiled softly. She reached out and pressed a hand on his cheek, sadness flashing only momentarily in those hazel eyes.

"Bronson, I give you the love of my life. Please protect her until you have no more life in you. Love her…promise me?"

Bronson felt a tear roll down his cheek. "I promise."

"Be her guardian angel, Bronson."

"I will…" He felt anger heat his face.

"Fight for her; bring her back to her throne; kill this bastard and see her crowned…swear this to me, Bronson?" She pressed the silver pendant necklace into his hand. "Swear it!"

Bronson took in his queen and nodded. "I swear it."

~ ~ ~ ~ ~

"Bronson? Bronson!" Kage grabbed the man's shoulder and shook hard. "Wake up dammit!"

Bronson catapulted up, realizing he had been on the ground. He had awoke from his dream; his body finally stilled after convulsing for minutes. He still smelled the smoke from the fires, heard the blood dripping off the stones, and felt his people's fear as a wall of black had overcome them so quickly. He had to shake himself back to reality, looking up at Kage and Gwyneira to ground himself.

"I thought I had killed you," Gwyneira said dryly as she helped him to his knees.

"Wrenley?" He clawed at them, still frantic, pulling himself to where he looked over the lip of the tub.

"It's okay…" Gwyneira helped him over to the bathtub. Wrenley's blue body was now returning to a standard color, her shallow breaths returning to deeper ones.

"Wrenley? Please wake up!" Bronson, fully clothed, climbed into the bathtub and sat behind Wrenley, submerging himself around her naked, limp body. He held her so tight he was afraid he might break her, but he could not help himself. The flashbacks devoured him as he began to shake again, and he buried his face in her golden curls and sobbed.

~ ~ ~ ~ ~

Gwyneira felt her heart break as the seer continued to cry in the crook of Wrenley's neck, his body rocking with such sorrow that it was difficult for Kage and Gwyneira to watch. Gwyneira leaned over, felt Wrenley's chest, and rechecked her pulse.

"Bronson, she's coming back," Gwyneira whispered in his ear. Bronson laid his chin on Wrenley's shoulder, murmuring to her in a tongue she did not recognize.

"You aren't losing her. She's okay…she is coming back." Gwyneira quickly assessed Wrenley's hands and feet for frostbite and other complications, moving to her stomach, palpating it gently, and laying a palm on it. Her eyes flicked upwards to Kage as if to say, *Can I get some help here?* Kage was no help, to her dismay, and his feet seemed glued to the floor. She huffed and turned back to Bronson.

"Baby is fine too," Gwyneira's voice softened as she laid another hand on Bronson's shaking shoulders. "She's coming back, Bronson. She is safe now…You saved her."

"I couldn't save them both…" He wept, and Gwyneira shot Kage a worried look. Thankfully, Garrick appeared, moving to the side of the tub and clasping Bronson's shoulders. Out of them all, Garrick had known Bronson the longest, and he murmured something in Bronson's ear as if talking him through what was happening, offering reassurances and soothing words.

Gwyneira knew without a doubt that this was more than Wrenley at this moment; she had seen the effects of trauma on the mind many times. Her chest constricted at the pain and agony Bronson had dared to show them, being vulnerable for the first time since he had shoved his way into her little cottage in the woods. She straightened her shoulders, concluding she was going to have to take charge here since Kage stood there like a fuck-nugget. Alcott could not stand to look at a naked body, and Garrick was busy with Bronson.

"Let's get her dressed and warm…both of you move now!"

Garrick lifted Wrenley from the bath and assisted Gwyneira in drying and dressing her. They then laid her flaccid but warm body into the bed. The staff surrounded her with heated blankets. Alcott and Kage assisted Bronson with his clothes. Bronson was almost limp as he sat on the side of the bed. There was no embarrassment or awkwardness as Garrick and Kage tended to the man who had been caring for them, leading them, fighting for them since the beginning. They gently undressed, assisted him with dry clothes, and tenderly covered him as he lay beside Wrenley.

Gwyneira's heart throbbed at the sight of him; the desperation and anguish in the sounds that escaped the man were something she had only heard one other time, long ago, after she had lost her parents. She had truly understood the gut-wrenching noises, the prayers he had recited, and then he had seized…or was it something less physical and more spiritual? She could not be sure, but it scared the hell out of her.

Before he accepted her into this company, Bronson had told her he needed her to be there to aid Wrenley, but he never specified how. Now, she knew without a doubt that this woman was carrying the only other living heir to the throne of Ailios. Bronson had allowed Gwyneira to join their company, offered to pay her for her skill, and be by Wrenley's side. It all made perfect sense now that the moon and stars had aligned so that they could be together in this moment. She watched as Wrenley moved into Bronson, curling herself against him. Unconsciously, he had reached for her and pulled her to his chest. Garrick had assisted Gwyneira in applying warmers to different bed areas to maintain their temperature. Kage and Alcott had left, giving them as much privacy as possible. As she took them all in, she felt a sliver of her broken heart heal, and she snuggled into the bed on Wrenley's other side. She had justified it by determining her warmth would help Wrenley, but the truth was, she could not leave these people who had come to mean so much to her. With that realization, she fell into a deep sleep, the deepest she had since her mother died.

~ ~ ~ ~ ~

Wrenley stirred where she lay, feeling like she was awakening from a dream. All she could remember was a beautiful white horse, Bronson, and a hideous creature…oh no. Wrenley shifted slightly, realizing she was not alone in her bed. Bronson was sleeping beside her, and she turned in surprise as she looked at him. He was so handsome, looking almost boyish. His arms were around her waist, his head resting on her stomach.

"Do you try to get yourself killed on purpose, or is it just terrible luck?"

Wrenley fought the urge to jump; she was too afraid she would wake Bronson. She turned her head marginally and sighed at the hot cup of tea Gwyneira offered her. Wrenley gently maneuvered herself to a sitting position to reach for the steaming cup without waking Bronson.

"I don't even know what the fuck happened…"

"Ahh, well, it's not exactly your fault," Gwyneira waved a hand towards Wrenley, her face still vacant, her black hair swept up on the top of her neck. She retrieved her mug of hot cider and sipped.

"The horse…I was outside…"

"That was a Kelpie, a form of the goddess Cailleach."

Wrenley furrowed her brow in confusion, "A what?"

Gwyneira sighed, "I forget that you are new around here. A Kelpie is a creature that lives in the lakes and lochs here in the highlands. They like to seduce people who are vexed or grieving. She probably heard you crying and took the opportunity. The goddess loves to snatch pretty things."

"But I was just out there for an hour…"

Gwyneira rolled her eyes, "Bronson discovered you had snuck out of the house right away and followed, but Cailleach had found you first. An eight-hour standoff between you, him, and the winter goddess unfolded. He could not come close because she would have also entranced him. He stood with you for eight hours, and I think you subconsciously fought it, or else you would have touched the beast immediately."

It was slowly returning to Wrenley, "I felt the baby, and I heard

Bronson, and I moved away…"

"Far enough away that he could grab you and break the beast's illusion."

"What would have happened if I touched it?" Wrenley wasn't sure she wanted to know.

Gwyneira shrugged her thin shoulders, taking another sip of her cider, "Not that anyone has touched Cailleach and lived to tell about it, but they say once you touch her, she drags you down to the depths of the lake, drowns you, and eats you."

Wrenley was right…she could have gone without knowing that for the rest of her life. She shuddered, "Then what? I don't remember anything."

Gwyneira sighed, setting her mug down, "You were almost frozen to death; we almost lost you…" Gwyneira trailed off momentarily, her unoccupied eyes scanning Bronson's sleeping form following Wrenley. "I had to use magic to bring you back."

Wrenley tried to steady her breath, fear gripping her gut. She had compromised them because she was restless and stupid and had to get fresh air. She had almost killed herself, killed Bronson, killed…

"The baby?" Wrenley jerked herself so hard she spilled the tea, and she cursed as the hot liquid scorched her fingers. Bronson's eyes fluttered open, and he sat up instinctively, still seeming dazed. It took a moment for things to sink in, and then his eyebrows raised at Gwyneira sitting on the bed, almost on top of Wrenley, knees touching the other woman.

"The baby is fine."

Wrenley fell back onto her pillow, able to breathe again as Gwyneira grabbed the cup from her.

"Though I am bursting with curiosity about the conception of this fetus, I suppose we can wait to discuss that when you are rested," Gwyneira said dryly, rising from her seat. "I can't wait for that family meeting."

"Do I need to tell you how babies are made, Gwyneira?" Bronson's groggy voice was music to Wrenley's ears as he ran a hand through his black hair, throwing himself back down on the pillows, covering his eyes with an arm.

Gwyneira did not flinch. "That is unnecessary. We had goats before the war started. I assume it's the same concept. I'll leave you two alone." Gwyneira sauntered out of the room and shut the door behind her.

~ ~ ~ ~ ~

"Bronson, I am so sorry!" Wrenley threw herself onto him, and he groaned, wrapping his arms around her and lying back down with her.

"I am so stupid. I just wanted some air. I was so lonely…"

"I know," He murmured, caressing her hair.

"I've compromised everyone, all of you."

"I just can't leave you alone ever again," Bronson stated matter-of-factly. Wrenley did not think it was funny, but she felt a rumble in his chest that she interpreted as laughter.

"Gwyneira had to use her magic…"

"Yes. Nicolas has spells around us…I don't think Gwyneira's energy will trigger anything with them in place. I'll send Kage and Alcott out later to ensure our location wasn't compromised."

"You could have been hurt…"

"I was terrified I had lost you…When I saw your blue, lifeless body in that tub…" Bronson held her tighter, "I will never allow that to happen again."

"The baby…" Wrenley began but trailed off.

"Our baby is safe."

They sat silently for several moments; both hearts had much to say but did not know how.

"What now?" Wrenley looked up at Bronson.

"Well…I literally cannot ever leave you alone again. Kage saw you naked, and now they all know you are pregnant."

Wrenley groaned and covered her face with the sheets, a giggle escaping her. Bronson lay flat on his back next to her, his bare chest rumbling with his chuckles. The two began laughing at the ridiculousness of it all. Wrenley was crying, laughing so hard that tears were streaming down her cheeks.

"So, I am six weeks along?" Wrenley finally managed to ask.

Bronson shrugged, "Technically, but I don't know. Things happen differently in this world than in yours. Your body is more powerful and healthier here. The baby may take nine months to grow, maybe less. It depends on your magic and mine. It also makes you more trackable because your energy is more potent."

"What are we going to do?"

Bronson leaned down to place his face near her stomach, "I don't know. We could hunker down and wait for the baby to be born, but that's so much more time the people will suffer, allowing Earnesh to grow his forces."

"No, I meant about Kage seeing me naked."

Bronson exhaled heavily, flipping over on the bed onto his stomach, hoisting himself up on his elbows, and reaching up to rub her stomach again, "I guess I'll just have to kill him."

CHAPTER 28

Family Meeting

The next day, the five companions sat in the drawing room together, an untouched tea tray between them. The tension was thick, and Wrenley squirmed in her seat, wishing she could be anywhere but here. No one said a word to one another. The silence was equally as copious that Wrenley was sure they could all hear her heart thud in her chest. Wrenley sat on the sofa next to Gwyneira, and Alcott in a wingback chair across from them. Kage glared at Bronson from his position at the hearth, and Bronson stood at the window, hands clasped behind his back as he studied something outside. Garrick was out scouting for enemy activity, clearly avoiding the meeting about to unfold. She did not blame him; she would rather meet the enemy head-on than have this conversation.

Gwyneira cleared her throat, reaching out to pluck a fruit tart off the tray. "Is someone going to talk?"

Wrenley elbowed her friend in the ribs, and Gwyneira hissed and swatted her away. "What? We are wasting time just staring at each other."

Kage continued to scowl at Bronson, and Bronson continued to study outside while Alcott, Wrenley, and Gwyneira looked at each other.

"I am so sorry!" Wrenley finally blurted, wringing her hands. "Everything is my fault...I-I am to blame..."

"That's bullshit, and you know it," Kage snapped at her, not tearing his gaze from Bronson's back. "I'm sick of you taking the blame for everything."

She flinched at his anger even though she knew it was not directed at her.

Alcott blew air out of his cheeks, finally moving to pour himself a cup of tea nervously. He kept his voice light as he said, "Well, let's all agree that none of this is anyone's fault. This war is not our fault, and that's why we are here." He clinked the spoon daintily against the cup and slurped the liquid. Wrenley noticed his hand trembling.

"Yes, exactly, brother!" Kage pushed himself away from the hearth, stepping towards Bronson. Kage's dark eyes danced with fury, and he postured towards the seer. "You are absolutely right! We are here to fight a war, not chase pussy and fuck the princess."

Wrenley gasped and clapped her hands over her mouth, Gwyneira paused with a fruit tart halfway in her mouth, and Alcott spewed his tea across the table at his brothers' words. Bronson whirled around, nostrils flaring, magic sparking around him like fireworks. "Don't you have a bone to go chew on?"

Kage's face scrunched and turned such a deep shade of red that Wrenley was afraid his head might explode. He pointed at Bronson, fingers shaking now with pure rage. "I'm not the one getting her pregnant now, am I? You didn't have enough foresight past your dick to realize you have made things so much more dangerous for her! Not only does the enemy want her, but they will want this baby. You did that!"

Kage was toe-to-toe with Bronson now, eyes wild as he bared his teeth. "You took advantage of her. She was vulnerable, scared, and she was relying on you, and you fucked her!"

"Hey! No one took advantage of me!" Wrenley wriggled between the two men, trying not to be insulted by Kage's words. He was talking about her like she was not sitting in the room, and she wanted to throttle them both. She placed one hand on each chest and pushed with all her strength, magic beginning to glow from her. "Stop this, both of you!"

Bronson snatched her hand from his chest, never taking his eyes off Kage. "I don't want to hear shit from you; I have been with Wrenley her entire life…you met her a month ago. You have no idea how to take care of her."

Kage threw his hands up. "Oh, well, you sure know how to care for a girl, including knocking her up."

Bronson shook with ire, "Don't pretend you haven't been ogling her ass whenever she walks in the room. You've wanted her ever since she fell into that river, you horny bastard."

Alcott raised his hand sheepishly from his position in the chair. "I, for one, have done no ogling."

"You're old enough to be her father," Kage derided, finally shoving Wrenley aside. The two men erupted then, screaming at each other as Wrenley tried to keep them from throwing punches. Alcott nervously leaned forward and poured another cup of tea. Kage shoved Bronson, but Bronson grabbed his shirt collar and shook him like a ragdoll. Wrenley was finally being pushed out of the fray as she sat back on the sofa beside Gwyneira and covered her face with her hands in exasperation.

Gwyneira shifted in her seat and leaned over to Wrenley. "I never held a baby before."

The entire room froze. Bronson and Kage halted their arguing to shift toward Gwyneira as she shoved another fruit tart in her mouth. She shrugged at the attention, brushing a crumb off her breast onto the floor. "I mean, it's not ideal, sure…but there is so much death in this world…" She tilted her head nonchalantly; her expression was still flat. "I can imagine each of us has seen so much death; it would be nice to see life. I am kind of excited about having a baby around."

The room fell into an eerie silence, the awe from the little witch's musings resonating with each of them. Wrenley fought the urge to reach out and feel Gwyneira's forehead for fever while battling the impulse to cry. Gwyneira had never shown emotion or feelings toward anyone since they met that night in the woods. Though they had grown closer these past weeks, she did not know what was going through her head most of the time.

Gwyneira continued, oblivious to the shock of her company. "When I was healing Wrenley, I saw something; The baby saved her mother from giving in to the goddess. It was almost as if she was trying to hold on until Bronson could save them, like the baby knew help was coming." She waved the cookie in the air for emphasis.

Wrenley stared at Gwyneira for a long moment, trying not to break down into a sob at the tenderness of Gwyneira's voice. Bronson moved to the front of the sofa, kneeling before the small, odd woman with pale white skin and long black hair.

He raised his large, powerful hands to frame her face, "What did you say, Gwyneira?"

The witch raised an eyebrow at him, but did not pull away from his touch. "The baby was protecting Wrenley…"

"No, Gwyneira…you said 'she'?"

Gwyneira looked at them blankly, then motioned her lips into a silent 'oh'. "Why yes, the baby is a she. That is probably why she almost killed you after you nearly froze to death. Female babies steal more power from their mothers than boys in times of distress."

~ ~ ~ ~ ~

Kage was still activated and stomped out of the room, clipping Garrick's shoulder as he entered, returning from scouting. Kage did not acknowledge the older man, and Garrick held his hands up to let him pass. Alcott followed behind slowly, hands in his pockets, giving Garrick a look that screamed, *I'll tell you later.* The two followed the twin, probably making sure Kage did not do something irrational or stupid. Gwyneira awkwardly wandered off, muttering about a full moon tonight and creating a bonfire on her balcony. Bronson and Wrenley sat cumbersomely on the sofa, and Wrenley was not sure what to do next.

"What now?" She whispered, wringing her hands in front of her.

Bronson looked over at her, his handsome face like stone, his dark hair falling into his eyes as a muscle feathered in his jaw. "Well, I guess it could have gone worse."

Wrenley chuckled, covering her mouth with a hand. She knew she was laughing because she was anxious, and Bronson reached out to grasp her hand.

"Can I marry you?"

Wrenley snapped her head towards him, opening her mouth and closing it again without uttering a word. If this were his idea of humor, she would box his ears. To her surprise, Bronson knelt before her, holding her hands in his.

"It's not just because of this baby…" Bronson reached up to tuck a blond curl behind Wrenley's ear. "Wrenley, when I saw you almost dead in that bathtub, I couldn't breathe. The thought of not having you…" He closed his eyes and lowered them briefly but raised them again to meet hers steadily.

"It's complicated, Wrenley, because I held you in my arms when you were…a baby. And I watched you grow from an infant into a child, a teenager, an adult, and then a woman. It wasn't until the last few years of your life that I knew I was falling in love with you. I don't ever want an existence without you, Wrenley."

Wrenley felt a tear slip down her cheek and gasped as something slid on her finger. She looked down at a simple engraved ring with a delicate pattern on the golden band. She let out a breath as she looked up at him.

Bronson took a shaky breath. "This war has ripped everything I have ever known and loved away from me. I have managed to hide you away for almost a lifetime, and I'm tired of keeping you at arm's length. Marry me, Wrenley? I will follow you to the gates of hell and put you on that throne. I won't ask for a single thing. I don't want any power. I don't need a single treasure. I want to be the one you come to bed with, that you cry and laugh with…and trust with your life. I will protect you and our daughter until my last breath leaves my body, and then I will protect you from the grave and beyond."

Wrenley looked at Bronson, then at the ring on her finger, and back at him. She took in his sight and reached out to caress his short black hair, pushing it away from his eyes. She traced his handsome face with her fingers and drew a line down his neck, arm, and finally, his hand. Holding it gently, she pulled his hand up to her chest over her heart and rested her cheek onto it tenderly, a tear escaping down her flushed cheek.

"I don't ever want an existence without you either." She shifted, noticing his eyes darkening as he looked up at her. "But marriage? Is this the time for anything like that?"

Someone had to be the voice of reason in their mess. No matter how much she yearned for something like this, the chance to have a family, what if it was all just a pipe dream that would be ripped from her? What if it were just another thing for Earnesh to take and pillage? Then it dawned on her that Bronson was the only link to the family she never had…to her mother and her father…to the world where she came from but may never see again. She had been searching for her whole life and finally found it…she finally found him. What if he were taken away?

Bronson pushed her legs apart, still kneeling in front of her, so tall that he was eye to eye with her. He framed her face with his large hands and pressed his forehead against her. "Do you have a better idea?"

Wrenley released a shuddering breath, feeling his warmth as he lowered his hands to grasp the back of her neck and head, still pulling her against him.

"Maybe when we are safe? Maybe when it is all over? Maybe…"

Bronson kissed her, his mouth enveloping her own as she moaned softly while his tongue dipped into her mouth. He broke away again, "Why are you so afraid?"

Wrenley felt her lip trembling, and Bronson leaned back to take in her face, his chestnut eyes looking on in concern. "What is it, Wrenley?"

She shifted. "If I marry you, I want it to be because you love me, not because, without being married, I could be used as a weapon against you."

Bronson's face softened as he sighed and placed his hands on both sides of her. She felt the magic stirring within him, her magic slithering across her skin, her fingers tingling, and her hands aching to run through his dark hair. They had one night together. That was it, at least romantically, but he had been there, in the shadows of her world, just out of sight and reach for her entire life. He knew her better than anyone ever had, maybe better than she knew herself. Though he was still such a mystery to her, she knew him too; something subconscious and profound, buried deep within her, just waiting to come out.

"Whether I marry you or not, Earnesh will still use you. And…whether you marry me or you don't, I will still protect you. Either way, I am bound to you forever, with or without the baby." Bronson's voice was husky as he leaned down to whisper in her ear, his warm breath making her shiver. "Maybe I am selfish, but I want you to be mine, and I want others to know they can't tear us apart."

Wrenley's breath hitched as she bit her lower lip, looking at him under her thick lashes. Slowly, she leaned in to kiss his cheek and murmured, "I am yours, and nothing will ever tear us apart. Of course, I will marry you, Bronson Aughton."

He smiled, his features turning feral as he reached for her waist and pulled her onto him, her legs wrapping around his waist as he crushed her against his chest. She was not sure what the future looked like, how they would make it out the other end alive…but she was willing to fight for it. Even if she were only married to him for a day…she would still fight for it.

~ ~ ~ ~ ~

Bronson felt his chest tighten at her words, and somehow, he felt the broken shards of his heart slowly weaving and mending themselves together again. With all his loss and heartache, she was the last thing he expected. He had never pictured his life going this way, and now…it was all he wanted. A life with her, with their child, with his people that he had come to know and love all these years. He loved this realm, this world, and he had been able to put his old one behind him and make a home here. It never felt quite complete…until this moment.

Bronson kissed Wrenley, his hand slowly working down her body until he found the hem of her sweater and pulled it over her shoulders. She gasped, her eyes wide in outrage, as she struggled against him. Her adorable nose wrinkled, and she tried to push away.

"We can't do this here!" She gulped, slapping his arm as he chuckled, pulling her against him and biting her neck. She melted into him and cried out as his teeth pierced her skin, not in pain, but in ecstasy. "If someone walks in…"

"I've cast a net with my magic…no one will set foot in here without me knowing."

Wrenley's eyes fluttered open, her mouth still pursed in a frown, but he could tell her eyes were filled with need. "I won't let anything in…" he murmured against her skin, and he felt her body relax on him.

"Okay…" she whispered back softly. "I trust you."

Bronson shifted and grabbed her waist, flipping her around to where she was on her knees in front of the couch, her elbows braced on the cushions, and Bronson kneeled behind her. Pulling her leggings down around her thighs, he groaned as his hands cupped her ass and released his length from his pants. Wrenley had reared back as if to argue, but he grabbed her neck and firmly but gently shoved her into the couch cushions as he entered her from behind.

Wrenley's back arched as he filled her, Bronson moving his hands down to her hips as he used his thumbs to caress soft circles into her flesh.

"I love you more than life…" he purred as he watched her reach out and grasp the throw pillows as if that would give her some traction. He smiled and thrust into her, and she moaned again, the sound driving him mad as he continued to plunge into her. "You are my queen. My love. My everything…" A thrust accompanied every word, and Wrenley pushed up in her elbows, pushing back against him and rocking with his movement. Bronson growled at her movements, his pace quickening as he felt Wrenley's magic ignite inside her.

In a heartbeat, he withdrew his magic that was keeping watch and pulled it in tight, Wrenley's enchantment snapping out and bouncing off his shield. It reverberated over them as he held them in a cocoon of energy to keep the power from escaping. Wrenley cried out as her release enveloped her, her body convulsing as Bronson held her hip with one hand, his other sliding up her back to between her shoulder blades. When the energy dissolved back into her, Bronson chased his release, trying to contain his roar as he grabbed Wrenley by the waist and held her against him as he came.

They sat there for a moment, Wrenley shirtless and enveloped in his arms, his length still inside her as he buried his face in her neck. Out of breath, they held each other, Wrenley groaning as Bronson peppered kisses up her neck to her ear, using a hand to turn her face back to him so he could kiss her.

"You are enchanting…" he whispered, and she giggled as she pulled away from him and retrieved her sweater that he had discarded onto the floor. After fixing her leggings and pulling her sweater over her head, Bronson fixed himself as she crawled back to him. Knee to knee, she rose and wrapped her arms around his neck.

"You are diabolical, taking me in the sitting room while anyone could walk in."

Bronson chuckled against her mouth as they kissed again. "I

don't care who sees us."

"Well, I think Kage would probably blow a gasket."

Bronson snorted as he stood, pulling Wrenley up and wrapping his arms around her. "I'm trying with him, Wrenley, but that kid is going to get himself killed if he can't learn to control himself."

"I know," Wrenley said, allowing Bronson to take her hand as they moved out of the sitting room and towards the second level. She was exhausted, and as if he read her mind, he pulled her behind him up the stairs. "What are we going to do about it?"

Bronson shrugged, "He'll learn, I just hope he doesn't burn something down in the process."

CHAPTER 29

Compromise

Wrenley spent the next several weeks in the rather extensive library, full of manuscripts and records of her family's heritage. Wrenley had found abundant history books about the kingdom of Ailios, lapping up every bit of information she could about her ancestry. Wrenley could not find out much about her father. She recalled Bronson mentioning that Dolion came from an influential family of seers, but she was unable to locate any solid records of his family bloodline. She would have to ask Bronson about it when he returned from his trip to the lowlands. Allowing him out of her sight was challenging, especially now that they had an understanding...but not as tricky as him allowing her out of his. Perhaps that was why Garrick was always within earshot of her. Even now, she sensed him sitting right outside the library door, talking in hushed tones with Alcott.

Wrenley studied the musty-smelling pages of a history book when she flipped the page and gasped. The picture almost leaped from the sheet as she reached to touch it softly. It was a portrait of a beautiful blond-haired woman standing majestically by a throne, a golden crown placed on her head. She was stunning, and Wrenley recognized the slight smile on the queen's face that resembled her own. The queen had a large sword on her hip, looking much more like a warrior than Wrenley had imagined.

"Mother..." She whispered, resting her palm on the piece of paper. To the queen's left, almost in the background, was a handsome man dressed in black, flanking the queen as if watching over her.

"Father?" Wrenley stared at it for a moment, not sure what she felt as she finally could see the image of them. She had imagined what they looked like a thousand times, but here they were, even more gorgeous and regal than she could have ever imagined.

"She was a lovely person…"

Wrenley jumped in surprise as the housekeeper dusted the shelves in the library's background. She knew it was a feeble attempt to keep an eye on her. The housekeeper nodded towards her mother's picture in the book. "She would come here when she was pregnant, you know…to escape all the castle stress. She would stay here for weeks by herself. You look just like her."

Wrenley shifted in her seat. "What was she like?"

The housekeeper's face was thoughtful. "Outspoken, but always polite. She never raised her voice at anyone except the court. She was also fearless…" The housekeeper's face saddened, and Wrenley could only imagine why.

"She was a warrior for those who had no voice. She spoke up for people, and she was also a free spirit. You remind me of her…" the woman trailed off.

Something inside Wrenley warmed at the words, knowing this older woman in front of her had known her mother. She had so many questions and opened her mouth to begin their barrage when she was interrupted by a commotion from the foyer. Wrenley snapped the book shut and jumped up from her seat; more concerning was how the male voices were getting more intense by the moment. She gritted her teeth, knowing precisely who the voices belonged to.

She followed the raised voices until she saw the cause of the disturbance and confirmed her suspicions. Kage stood before Bronson, eyes wild with rage, hands clenched in fists by his side. His turbulent black hair was pulled back, and he looked like he had just returned from training. Bronson was still in his riding gear, a long black coat over his heavy wool clothes; he must have just returned from a trip to the village.

Bronson looked calm and contained; however, she noticed his skin was slightly illuminated. Garrick and Alcott skirted alongside Bronson, eyes traveling between the two males, hackles obviously raised.

"Kage, we need to think about this for a minute. I know this is hard…" Bronson began, reaching a gloved hand towards the young man, but Kage ripped his forearm away.

"Hard? Damn you! They have my mother!" The cry from the young man almost broke Wrenley, and her stomach sank as she registered the words. Wrenley slipped in between the two men now, and she gave Bronson a warning look as she turned to Kage and placed her hands on his forearms, rubbing them gently.

"What has happened? What are you talking about Kage?"

"They have her..." He choked out, nostrils still flaring, pupils dilated with ferocity. Kage grabbed her forearms out of instinct or desperation and pulled her closer to him. A lump formed in Wrenley's throat as she tried to digest this information. "What? You mean Astara..."

"We don't know if they have her or are trying to bait us. Either way, they are trying to flush us out." Bronson's voice was calm, deep, almost unfeeling...but Wrenley felt his furor as his breath deepened. "Rumors are traveling that they took her from her home several days ago; Dragon's cronies."

"How did we get this information?" she demanded, allowing Kage to hold onto her even if his fingers were digging into her flesh, probably leaving bruises.

"I received the report today that they have her and are transporting her to a central outpost by the lake."

Wrenley's stomach knotted up, panic trying to rise in her chest. She looked at Kage and then over to Garrick. "What is an outpost?"

Garrick's face was grim. "It isn't good. It's where they take prisoners of war."

"Well, that doesn't make sense...Astara isn't a soldier."

"But her sons are..." Garrick sighed, his gaze then flickering to Bronson.

"Well, we need to go now!" Wrenley crammed her neck to Bronson, keeping her hands gently on Kage, allowing him to hold her close to him. "There is no question. We must leave now."

Bronson's growl reverberated as he ran his fingers through his dark hair in obvious grievance. Wrenley knew he was struggling to remain calm. "I understand, Wrenley, but this enemy is trying to find us...find you."

"And it's fucking working," Wrenley turned fully to him now, her small frame toe to toe with his. "I will not stand by and let anything happen to her." Wrenley's hand instinctively went to the crystal that hung between her breasts, the stone almost warm to the touch.

"They know if they can get us out of hiding, they have a chance at capturing us. We can't move from our secure location here. Especially now…" Bronson's words trailed off.

"I will not stand by and watch them brutalize my mother." Kage's voice was surprisingly quiet but deadly.

"We'll go, Bronson. Kage, Alcott, and I will go and retrieve her." Wrenley winced at the offer from Garrick, and a part of her prayed Bronson would shoot his idea down immediately.

"We can't afford to lose any one of you…" Bronson exhaled and turned away, putting his hands on his hips. He dipped his head, shaking it as he said, "I will go. You three stay here to protect Wrenley, and I will get Astara."

Kage opened his mouth to argue, but had not expected Bronson to offer himself. Wrenley bristled as she spun around to face him.

"You will not go alone!" She was appalled at the mere suggestion.

"Well, someone has to go."

The four turned at the sound of Gwyneira's calm voice. Her simple back dress swished as she approached, her jet-black hair pulled into a braid over her slim shoulder. Her vibrant green eyes were again emotionless, and Gwyneira folded her arms over her chest. "We have lost enough mothers, enough fathers. We cannot lose another; Wrenley and I will retrieve her."

The males in the room erupted in a fury of arguments, but in the midst, the females looked at each other in understanding. Silent communication traveled between them, both knowing this needed to be done, and the men would spend precious hours arguing. Wrenley was tired of being the odd person out, of everyone treating her like she was made of glass that would be shattered. What Gwyneira and Wrenley lacked in brute strength, they more than made up for in magic and wits. Wrenley, finally sick of the bickering, balled her fists and flexed her hands. A shock of energy was discharged from her, almost knocking the unsuspecting men over. Wrenley straightened, head high, standing with more confidence than she felt.

"Enough, everyone!" She barked at them, and they hushed. Wrenley was so sick of Bronson and Kage's pissing contest that she was ending it here and now. "Gwyneira is right. There is no way they would expect Gwyneira and me, especially if we catch them on the road. My magic is less noticeable in the unseen; Gwyneira is practically off any radar. Where is this outpost from here?"

"A day's ride from here, between us and the earth borders." Garrick eyed the women and then the men. "Say the word, my lady, and I will take you."

Wrenley nodded. "We leave within the hour, then."

"You absolutely will not!" Bronson bellowed, using every inch of his six-foot-six-inch frame to tower over Wrenley, but she did not flinch. "You will not encourage her, Garrick. That is an order!"

Wrenley opened her mouth to retort, but was surprised when Garrick stepped between her and Bronson. Wrenley blinked in surprise as her friend stood straight and tall, face to face with the seer.

Garrick reached out and grasped the seer's shoulder, squeezing it tightly. "Bronson, you are like a brother to me, and I'd step in front of a sword for you, you know that. But it is time for you to accept Wrenley's position with us. You can't have it both ways; you can't preach that she will rule from the throne and step over her whenever you get scared…not in times like these."

Bronson growled, balling his fists to where his leather gloves groaned. "My only purpose in this life is to protect her. There is no way I am letting her leave here to skirmish with an enemy patrol. There is no goddamn way I will let you or our child be in that kind of danger." His voice was low now, sidestepping Garrick, reaching out his hand, and gently grabbing her forearm. His breath was hot on her ear as he leaned down to whisper. "I won't lose you."

Wrenley smiled thoughtfully, knowing full well she should be more afraid, but when she thought of Astara and rescuing her, she had no fear. She also could not help the tingling that shot through her body at the way he wanted to protect her, to save her…

"I know," she uttered softly, reaching up to pull his forehead down to meet hers. No one would ever have known it, but he trembled. She then wrapped a hand around the back of his neck. "We can compromise on this…you can be close by, but they know Kage and Alcott will be together, and you are the most wanted man on the continent. They will never suspect Gwyneira and me.

You take us close enough to ensure we get there safely, but far enough away so you aren't detected. Gwyneira and I will be in and out before they even know. I'm already in danger, Bronson, every moment of every day…but we can't allow them to take any more of us, not while we can help it."

Bronson swore under his breath, grabbing Wrenley and pulling her close to crush his mouth against hers. He fisted her hair, using his other hand to press her lower back and pelvis toward him, consuming her as much as he could with an audience around them. She melted into him, moaning slightly as she smelled the familiar scent of cedar and spices on him. She grinned against his kiss as she noticed Alcott, Garrick, and Kage avert their gazes, keenly interested in the walls. Gwyneira just stared at them, eyes vacant, her arms crossed in front of her, tapping her foot as if waiting impatiently for them to finish. They both knew they must go after Astara and knew the men would be compromised much faster than the females.

As hard as it was for him to admit it, Bronson knew this was their best plan. He finally released Wrenley, his hands lingering on her hips as he spoke to the rest of the company without taking his eyes off her. "You heard your queen, we leave within the hour."

CHAPTER 30

Another One

The company rode out solemnly, pondering the tasks ahead. Wrenley felt cold despite the heavy cloak, wool clothes, scarf, and black riding boots she had chosen carefully to protect herself against the frigid temperatures. Since nearly freezing to death, she had never felt warm unless in bed with Bronson, who held her and shared his body heat. Wrenley contemplated their next move, pushing down any apprehension that may try to creep up on her. Her thoughts then drifted to Astara in the ruthless hands of their enemy, and it was enough to make Wrenley want to vomit. The enemy would not kill Astara; she knew that, but they would do other things, especially if Dragon was in charge. Astara could be freezing, unfed, and beaten. She could be locked in a cage. She could be…

"It doesn't help."

Wrenley jumped with a start at Bronson's low voice next to her. She rode with him, but she had been lost in thought.

"What?"

"Thinking about all the unknowns, all the things that could happen…it doesn't help anyone." Bronson was stone-faced, but Wrenley felt like she detected a shudder in his voice. "Stay focused. Don't allow your mind to travel to those things. Try not to use any power until you need to."

She managed a wobbly nod.

They rode silently for a while; then night fell on them faster than the delicate snowflakes that covered their path as they trudged forward. It took them several hours before emerging from the highlands, and Garrick had ridden ahead to scout the pass that led them from the highlands to the lowlands. Garrick returned to them, sliding out of his saddle as soon as he made it under the canopy of thick trees.

"You're not going to like this," Garrick said grimly as he tied his horse. His short red beard was sprinkled with the snowflakes that now flew, almost invisible due to the darkness. Alcott and Kage posed as if ready for battle; their broad, muscular shoulders were covered with heavy woolen cloaks like hers, their swords strapped to their backs. Wrenley could not ignore the worry etched on their handsome faces.

"They have taken her to the catacombs."

"Shit!" Bronson rubbed his bottom lip with his thumb, turning away as if to digest the information Garrick had just presented. Kage, Alcott, and Wrenley looked at each other, confusion crossing between them.

"What are the catacombs?" Wrenley asked lowly, her eyes darting back and forth.

"They are an ancient system of tunnels that run along the lake. Before the war, the catacombs were home to some of the most ancient and deadly creatures in Ailios. After the war, the enemy took them over and now use them as a prison and barracks." Bronson swore again, putting his hands on his hips, ducking his head to the ground, and kicking a loose rock away. "It's where they take prisoners of war to torture and kill them. They also keep valuables and supplies there…it is heavily guarded."

Wrenley sucked in a breath, and Alcott and Kage stepped forward, hands on their weapons.

"We will seize it then! Go in and get her." Kage's rage radiated off him.

"It isn't that simple, Kage. The catacombs are an intricate system that neither Bronson nor I has ever dared to go into. Even before the war, darkness was under the lake in those catacombs that were said to swallow anyone venturing in. Now, the enemy is so far inside it, we wouldn't even know how to get to them, let alone escape." Garrick's voice was low.

"And my Mother is in there," Alcott said evenly towards Garrick, and Garrick's shoulders seemed to drop slightly.

"I know she is Alcott; I know," Garrick replied softly, understanding drawn in his voice. He reached out to grasp the young man on the shoulder.

"There isn't anybody who knows the way through them?" Wrenley asked in exasperation. She turned to Bronson, reaching out a freezing hand to grab his wrist, her eyes pleading him to think a little harder, to dig deeper.

"Wrenley, there is no…" Garrick began but was interrupted.

"There is someone…" Bronson's eyes were still focused somewhere on the ground, one arm crossed over his midsection, and an elbow resting on top of it so he could rub his brow with a thumb and forefinger. Wrenley eyed him and narrowed her eyes. "Who, Bronson?"

"There is another one who knows the way, but…we haven't spoken in a very long time."

"Who?" Wrenley and Kage asked in unison. Wrenley could barely manage the adrenaline surge that shot through her body.

Bronson looked up at Garrick, his face cold, his lips in a thin line. "Johnathan Wendo."

Wrenley looked back and forth between the two men, starting to feel irritated.

"Enough with all the secrecy! Who is Johnathan Wendo, and where can we find him? We don't have much time!" Again, Wrenley shook back the images of what they could do to Astara as they stood here discussing it.

"Name the place, and we will ride to him now." Kage was just as impatient and stepped closer to Bronson and Garrick, halting when he noticed Garrick's drawn face.

"I'm afraid that's impossible," Bronson said again quietly, giving Wrenley a sideways look. "Johnathan Wendo was a friend of your father and mine before the enemy invasion."

Wrenley raised her eyebrows but remained silent. Bronson spoke softly, holding her gaze as if she were the only one who needed to hear this. "He crossed some lines with his magic and was banished. The ultimatum was given that he either cross over or your father threatened to kill him. So, Johnathan crossed over, and he's been elusive ever since…mostly."

"Crossed over where?" Wrenley was confused now, goosebumps starting to flush over her.

Bronson grinned ever so slightly, sending another tremor through Wrenley's body, and he looked into her eyes again. "The last sighting I know of is Alaska."

Alaska. Wrenley felt it like a punch in the gut; home, he was at her home…or at least in the same dimension.

Gwyneira shoved her way through the group, cocking her small head, her jet-black hair swishing back and forth. "What the fuck is Alaska?"

~ ~ ~ ~ ~

The decision for Bronson and Wrenley to cross over was met with some resistance, mainly from Kage. Though he habitually argued with everything Bronson suggested, he had some valid points to present to the company. Finally, Bronson calmed Kage enough for Kage to accept the plan. Garrick, Alcott, and Kage would move ahead to the mouth of the catacombs and wait for Wrenley, Bronson, and hopefully, Johnathan Wendo to arrive before moving in. This Johnathan Wendo had extensive knowledge of the catacombs, and he could get them in and out; at least, that was the best-case scenario. The only hiccup was that Johnathan Wendo was in another dimension.

Bronson brushed up against Wrenley; she could not tell if it was an accident or on purpose. He leaned down to talk into her hair, reaching for her chest. Not sure where he planned to grab, she held her breath as he plucked up the green crystal Astara had given.

"I need to borrow this."

Wrenley shot a look up into his eyes, wanting to protest, "Why?"

"Because we need a beacon to guide me to where I can cross back over. While you were out of this realm, I knew where to cross back and forth because I had made the trip so often, but to travel to where we need to go now and come back safely…I need to be precise. You must charge the crystal with your power so I can follow it."

Wrenley pulled the crystal over her head and covered it with both hands. "How do I do it?"

Bronson enveloped her hands in his, covering them and the crystal. Wrenley felt her breath catch. Bronson was beautiful standing before her, his dark hair tossed in the wind, his eyes so dark they were almost black. He stepped into her personal space, leaning down to speak softly in her ear.

"You know how you feel when we make love?" He whispered to her now, and she felt her face flush as she nodded. He smiled against her ear, "It's the same energy, but you will contain it to the stone."

Wrenley felt his hands over hers and the crystal underneath. She noticed his breath by her ear and remembered how he held her that night during the gathering as he carried her up the stairs, naked and in his arms. She gasped slightly as Bronson leaned down and gently grazed her ear with his teeth and lips. She felt herself heat, thoroughly flushed, and allowed that heat to escape.

"Careful, not too much," Bronson whispered seductively, leaning his head down to rest his mouth above her ear. She was still clasping her hands and gasped slightly at the discharge of energy she felt from her fingers. She opened her hands, smiled at the glowing crystal, and then at Bronson.

"Perfect!" He exclaimed and looked down at her again as if he wanted to say something more...do something more...but it was not the right time. He released her, straightening to his full height, and turned to Kage and Alcott as they awkwardly watched them. He dangled the crystal between them.

"Who will carry it?" Bronson asked no one in particular, ignoring the glare from Kage.

Kage stepped forward, and Wrenley gently reached above his head and slipped the crystal necklace around his neck, over his thick head of black hair. She smelled his earthy, pine scent and stepped back to look at the crystal glisten on his chest.

"Take care of this until I come back?"

Kage did not smile but looked at her longingly, "Of course I will."

"We will get her back, Kage...I promise."

Kage did not acknowledge her promise, probably because Wrenley did not know if she could keep it. But she would try...she would try like hell to make it back and rescue Astara. She was willing to risk the lives of herself and her baby to save her friend's Mother... to save her friend.

"The crystal should hold enough power for three of our days here," Bronson told Garrick and Alcott as they pulled themselves onto their horses. "Find the opening of the catacombs and wait under cover until we get back. Do not engage or attempt to enter until you hear from me." His voice was commanding, and Garrick nodded.

Bronson reached out and grabbed the arm of his close friend, and Garrick, likewise, grasped his.

"Bronson, the things you told me about Johnathan…" Garrick shook his head and smiled wryly. "It takes some balls to go after him and ask him for help."

"It's going to take more than that…" Bronson murmured, glancing over at where Wrenley stood. The two friends nodded at each other, and Bronson released his arm. Kage unexpectedly grabbed Wrenley and hugged her, pressing a kiss to her temple.

Wrenley turned to Gwyneira, whose eyes were still hollow and emotionless. Wrenley gave Gwyneira a nod and quickly hugged the young woman before Gwyneira could push away. Gwyneira hissed and stiffened as Wrenley finally released her, then the company parted. Gwyneira, Kage, Alcott, and Garrick mounted their horses and traveled to the catacombs. Wrenley watched them go; her heart skipped, and her chest heaved. She watched the crystal's light disappear as Kage slid it under his shirt against his chest near his heart. She just hoped they would make it to Astara in time.

Bronson stood before Wrenley and shrugged, "Are you ready to return to your time?"

CHAPTER 31

Wendigo

She never supposed she would get used to it; the twirling and falling, darkness and colors. She knew enough to hold tight to Bronson's neck, hoping she would not faint this time. She knew her power had developed more since she first crossed, and she had grown physically stronger. Her hips had healed entirely, and no limp or wobbling was evident.

Though it felt like hours…in a matter of minutes, she felt the blood rushing to her head as a flash of cold air pelted her face. She gasped at the cold, even as Bronson engulfed her in his arms. It was dark, but she looked up and gasped at the stars' brightness in the sky.

"Where are we?" She asked breathlessly, noting the tall, dark trees that surrounded them.

"Somewhere in rural Alaska, emphasis on rural."

Wrenley breathed in the air, and it felt different in her lungs. Her ears rang with the roaring of the wind that whipped at them, trying to find her bearings and look at the world around her. She lifted her head towards the sky, taking in the moon and stars above her. She held her breath; these were the same celestial bodies Ruth and Jim may be looking at right now. It brought her some comfort, at least.

Bronson and Wrenley began walking, trudging through the knee-high snow and deadly wind gusts. She dared not speak. She was so cold she could hardly feel her face, hands, or feet, even with her heavy clothes. They slogged for at least thirty minutes until a small, shabby cabin appeared in a clearing. Wrenley could only make it out with the help of the moon and starlight, her eyes still adjusting to the dark. She would have cried with relief if she had not been afraid of her tears freezing to her face.

Without a word or glance in her direction, Bronson walked straight up to the cabin and tried the door; it was locked. Wrenley winced as Bronson lifted his knee and used his foot to break the door with one powerful thrust. He turned to her nonchalantly, motioning to move with one arm, "After you, my lady."

The cabin was not what Wrenley had expected. On the outside, it appeared to be a run-down shack in the middle of the harsh Alaskan tundra, with no life to be seen. Bronson ushered Wrenley in and shut the door, using a nearby chair to help it close since he almost took it off its hinges when he kicked it in.

Bronson quickly started a fire in the small hearth, and Wrenley felt the warmth immediately. She then surveyed her surroundings, using the firelight to take in the small room. It was not a dilapidated shack; it looked like someone's home. The one-room dwelling had a small fireplace with a mantle and a golden clock that chimed softly at the top. In front of the fire stood a red velvet armchair, seemingly worn from frequent use. There was a small round table, enough for four people, with a mismatched, chipped teapot sitting atop it. Bookshelves lined the room's walls with trinkets such as globes, maps, clocks, a stuffed bird, and other eccentricities. Delicate but outdated curtains covered the windows. In the corner was a bed with what seemed like a patchwork quilt. No, this was not just a cabin but the home of the mysterious and outcasted Johnathan Wendo.

Wrenley was pulled to look at everything, but she needed warmth first. She hurried to the fire and sat on the floor before it. Bronson stoked it and worked to build it up.

"This cabin is…"

"Johnathan's…" Bronson did not look at her as he worked. "Jahnathan Wendigo's."

Wrenley had wide eyes. "Where is he?"

Bronson finally leaned back, shedding his coat as the fire began to emit more heat. "Probably hunting somewhere."

"At night? This cold?"

Bronson grinned slightly, allowing himself to fall back on his heels and sit next to Wrenley, crossing his legs in front of him as she was. He took his cloak and covered her legs, noticing her teeth chattering,

"Wrenley, there are some things you need to know about Johnathan…" He trailed off, rubbing his face with his hand, "But you need food first."

Bronson made quick work of dinner, pulling out bread and cheese from his pack. He then found a kettle, filled it with snow, and efficiently put it on the fire. Wrenley was unsure how he could function with it so cold; all she could do was sit and shiver. After clanking around the small kitchen, Bronson found some tea and distributed the teabags to their cups. Finally, they were content.

"Johnathan Wendo was my friend. Though your father and I had known each other first, Johnathan joined us in training shortly after, and we learned about our powers together."

"He's a seer?"

Bronson nodded, blowing on his hot tea and taking a small sip, "Yes, but in a different way. Your father and I were focused on time and space, what you would call 'physics,' and applied it to magic. We were trying to discover the ability to travel between worlds and through the veil between. Johnathan was more of an alchemist. His specialty was changing objects and materials in one dimension."

"But he can cross over?"

"Yes. He worked with us and assisted us in overlapping theories and practices. Then something happened…" Bronson trailed off, seeming to drift off into thought for a moment. "He crossed a dangerous line; people got hurt. Dolion gave him two choices: cross into this dimension and stay away forever…or be killed. I wasn't sure who would win in that scenario…your father or Johnathan. They were both extremely powerful. I had advocated for an ultimatum instead of Johnathan's execution. I begged your father to show mercy, to agree to send him away, and I pleaded with Johnathan to take the offer." Bronson closed his eyes and grimaced slightly, almost as if the memory was painful.

He shook his head and set his tea down. "I lost both of my best friends that day. Johnathan was banished, and something changed in Dolion. He…" Bronson glanced at Wrenley, "Something happened to your father then. He began throwing himself into his work and nearly became lost in it. It wasn't until you were born that I felt he snapped out of it. But the damage had been done, and the enemy had already sensed the powerful work your dad and I were doing. I had warned him…I even tried to stop him…"

Wrenley reached over and placed a hand on Bronson's knee, looking up into his pain-filled eyes. "You were put in a terrible position."

Bronson shrugged. "I had warned your father about the potential implications of his projects. I petitioned him to allow Johnathan to return. I felt he didn't hear me in those last months…it was almost as if he went mad."

Bronson shifted to face Wrenley. "You must prepare yourself when you meet Johnathan. He is…very different from you and me."

What could surprise me? Wrenley mused to herself but nodded.

"And you must do exactly what I say when we encounter him. I haven't seen him in probably three years, in this time."

"You kept up with him?"

Bronson nodded, "Very loosely, sometimes he was receptive to my checking in. Other times, he was not. I would bring him gifts," he motioned to the shelves.

The two sat silently for several moments, food in their bellies, and at least for Wrenley, she was beginning to thaw out. She sucked in a breath as her hand shot to her stomach, a sharp feeling going through her. It was not a pain…it did not hurt, but it was very evident something was happening.

Bronson was on his feet and effortlessly pulled Wrenley up with him. She felt it again and doubled over, and Bronson quickly removed her cloak and guided her to the bed. He laid her down flat, lifting her sweater to see her stomach. She had worn a tunic-type sweater and fleece-lined leggings, so he could easily slide his hand under the waist of the leggings to her lower stomach. She sucked in again, not because of the feeling but because his hands were freezing.

Bronson was silent momentarily, turning his head towards her as if listening. She felt it again, and his eyes flicked over to hers. He smiled, "That is the baby. It's moving."

"Moving?" Wrenley shot up on her elbows, looking down at her stomach, his palm still on her skin. "But it's so early…"

"Remember, Wrenley, in our world, things happen differently, even in pregnancy. We used a lot of energy traveling over to this dimension, and the baby is reacting to that power."

"Huh…" Wrenley tried to process that information, but still felt uneasy, and Bronson grinned. "It's okay; nothing's wrong."

Wrenley let out a breath, her shoulders loosening as she remained propped up on her elbows. Bronson kept his hand on her stomach, and she was acutely aware of how close it was to the waistband of her leggings, how he pressed down on her stomach, and how he seemed to have no intention of moving his hand anytime soon. She felt herself flushing, the room suddenly warmer than a moment ago. She knew it was ridiculous and inappropriate, but she wished his hand would slide down a little farther…

Bronson looked up from her stomach to her face and angled his head at her. "Are you okay?"

No, I'm not okay, she thought, feeling the need for him growing every moment. She wanted to feel him against her; she wanted him to touch her like he did on the night of the gathering. She wanted…God, she wanted so much from him. Bronson said nothing, but she could tell he was thinking. He was always thinking…that beautiful brain always planning and weighing the consequences of every move. He had taken on so many burdens and responsibilities that he could not afford to be sporadic. He was built and created to survey the threats, protect others, and be the barrier between good and evil…at least for Wrenley.

Without thinking it through, Wrenley reached for his hand, gently pushing it farther down her pants until it was between her legs. Bronson was silent but allowed it, and she could tell by his fingers gently grazing the flesh between her legs that he was not opposed. She inhaled sharply as his fingers brushed her wetness. She could tell, however, that he was still assessing, calculating, and considering whether to go along with her. They were in the middle of the Alaskan woods, searching for a long-lost, dangerous seer… with lives at stake.

But…

Bronson removed his hand from her pants, and before she could be disappointed, he lifted her to a sitting position on the bed. He then knelt in front of her, and she was breathless as he pulled off her boots, one by one, tossing them to the side. He then gently pulled off her leggings and threw them on the bed. Wrenley was still sitting on the edge of the bed, Bronson kneeling on the floor between her legs and gently reaching to the inside of her thighs to spread her legs farther apart, and her breath caught.

She moaned slightly; just the soft touch of his hands on the tender flesh of her inner thighs was enough to make her cry out. Gently, Bronson reached up to push Wrenley back on the bed, back flat, but he was still between her legs at the end of the bed. Bronson lightly put one hand on each thigh, his thumbs making a soft circular motion on her skin. He stared at her sex for several heartbeats, then suddenly lowered his head.

Wrenley's back arched when his mouth and tongue began to explore the vulnerable flesh between her legs. She moaned, lifting her head slightly to see him, but then falling back onto the bed, almost dizzy from the pleasure that was shooting up through her body. Ecstasy burst through her as her pelvis bucked against his tongue, his large hands now holding her hips tightly so she could not scoot away.

She was unsure if it was hormones or because this was all so new to her, but Wrenley was infatuated with any touch Bronson gave her. She reached down to fist his black hair, guiding him where she wanted him. He groaned against her, his tongue finding its mark, causing her legs to shake. She yelped as she felt him slide two fingers into her, curling them ever so slightly, causing her to cry out again.

"You are beautiful…" he murmured against her. She could not respond coherently.

"You taste…God, you taste good." He was breathless, as his chest also heaved with anticipation. Wrenley felt her pleasure peaking and with one last lick and his finger curling at just the right angle inside her, Wrenley felt an explosion in her belly that traveled outward to her hands and her feet…sparks flew from her as she mewled. Bronson relentlessly kept pace with her, holding her as she shook and shuddered.

Bronson pulled away momentarily, and Wrenley heard him moving just beyond her legs. She did not budge. Though her instinct was to cover herself, she did not want to. She knew he was looking at her, and she did not care. Her embarrassment quickly melted away as confidence took its place. Of all the women in two separate dimensions, he had chosen her. With that realization settling in, she lay motionless as he finally leaned over her, then grabbed her thighs and pushed her farther on the bed as he straddled her, maneuvering her so that her legs were on either side of him.

"You are...intoxicating." He said gruffly, hands placed on the bed on either side of her head, his hips brushing the insides of her thighs as she felt the heat from his body.

"Prove it..." She gave him an incredulous look, reaching a hand up and gently stroking his chest over his shirt.

"I don't want to fuck you right now."

Wrenley's spine went stiff, and her brow furrowed in confusion. "W-what?" Maybe that confidence was too inflated after all?

"I don't want to just fuck you," he said again, trailing his fingers up her legs. "I want to make long, passionate love to you for hours. I want us to be able to lie in bed all day, naked together. I want us to be able to talk about the future, this baby..." He pulled a slow, steady gaze over her body, which landed on her stomach. "But we don't have time. I am so afraid we don't have enough time, Wrenley...when we were apart, all we had was time, and now, together, we are running out of it."

Wrenley felt the regret in his voice. She had been pushing back the same thoughts as danger surrounded them, the unknown and unpredictable future crashing into them from all sides, not to mention the threat that would be walking in that door at any moment. Would they live through all this danger and peril to live a life like that? To meet their baby and lie in bed all day together? At the end of it all, that is what she truly ever wanted...a simple life, with her family surrounding her...

Wrenley shrugged then, a grin pulling at her lips, "Then I guess a fuck will have to do, for now."

Bronson chuckled as Wrenley shakily unbuckled his pants.

"For now..." he murmured as she managed to release him. She caressed his magnificent length, and he moaned every time she stroked him. She gently sat up and motioned him to lie on his back, climbing onto him. She hovered over him shyly, and he grasped her hips and plunged himself into Wrenley, pulling her pelvis down to meet him. She inhaled, arms reaching down as she clutched his back muscles as he continued to grind up inside her. He groaned as he continued to drive into her, and Wrenley felt herself growing hot, either with hormones or magic, she could not tell. She held onto his arms as he continued, slowing at times and then thrusting deep again, enough to make her gasp every time. God, she loved the feeling of him inside her.

Wrenley felt the magic begin to escape from her and Bronson, and she noticed his skin was glowing in the room. Her own was as well, her hands shimmering and sparks spitting from her fingertips as she ran her fingers through his thick hair. She leaned over, and they were chest to chest now, her hands investigating every ripple and muscle on his arms, pectorals, abdomen, and neck. She could not get enough of him; his beauty stunned her.

"I love you," he said in her ear and then climaxed, and whether it was the feel of him coming inside her or the growl that escaped him, Wrenley felt heat and energy exploding from her again, washing over her entire body. Her cry echoed off the cabin walls as she cried his name in the darkness. He roared in response, thrusting even harder as he poured every bit of himself into her.

She shuddered from it, Bronson holding her as she trembled and moaned, and then she went limp on top of him. Bronson, still inside her, wrapped his arms around her and hoisted himself up into a seated position, where she sat facing him, her legs wrapped around his waist. She was still flaccid from her climax, and he rested her against him. She could tell he was smelling her hair as he kissed her exposed neck.

"Not to ruin the mood, but with all that disturbance, Johnathan will probably be back sooner rather than later." Wrenley groaned in protest, not wanting to move from this spot against him, his length still inside her, his body still molded with hers. He chuckled and dipped his head to kiss her thoroughly, running his hands up and down her back and cupping her ass.

"Someday, we will take our time and enjoy each other. For now, we have work to do. I think he is nearing us."

~ ~ ~ ~ ~

As always, Bronson was correct. Thirty minutes after Wrenley was dressed and had swept her hair back out of her face into a messy bun with a ribbon, she felt the magic approaching. She glanced at Bronson, standing at the hearth, features masked, but she could tell he was tense.

"Remember, do exactly as I say."

Wrenley took a position back by the bed, hunkering down in a small nook out of the light of the fire, leaving Bronson completely visible and exposed in front of whoever entered the cabin through the door. Her heart thundered as a presence outside the cabin door grew more extensive and prominent. It was not human but grander by the sounds of the creaking, shabby steps out front. She heard a deep growl coming from outside; the only thing between them and the growl was the broken front door. Wrenley threw another look towards Bronson, his features still unchanged. He did not seem frightened, which was good; Wrenley was scared enough for both of them.

Like a flash of lightning, the door blew off the hinges and flew by where Bronson stood near the fire. He did not wince. The door missed him by three feet, at most. He was like a statue, arm resting on the mantel, an easy grin on his face. Wrenley stifled a cry, covering her mouth as someone…something…filled the doorway.

Whatever 'it' was had to bend down to enter through the door, maneuvering its massive form to be able to fit. It breathed heavily as it ducked one muscular shoulder through the doorframe, pulling itself through. It attempted to stretch up as far as possible when fully inside, but the ceiling was too low. Its body was lean but muscular, like a skeleton covered in dark, leathery skin. Its body was familiar to that of some beast: skinny, toned legs meant for speed and agility, but broad, muscular shoulders and arms meant for ripping bodies to shreds. The arms were as long as the legs, brushing the floor as the creature bent over slightly. Its head was almost like a horse's skull, with a rack of black, glistening antlers on top of its head.

It snorted like a beast, but then Wrenley recoiled when it began to chuckle; a deep, evil gurgle that seemed to cast a tangible shame into the room. It relaxed from standing upright, with its arms in front of it, resting on its knuckles. Wrenley supposed it used all four limbs to run, and she guessed it was fast, judging by the looks of the rippling muscles.

"Who has invaded my home?" It was an unnatural voice, not one of a man, but otherworldly.

"Wendigo, I am in search of your master, Johnathan." Bronson was the picture of calm, but Wrenley felt like pissing herself from fear.

Wendigo laughed, warbling as it shifted its legs on the wooden floor.

"Bronson Aughton," it finally breathed, filling its lungs as if taking in the scent of him. "It has been many years."

Then, the beast used his space in the cabin to pace back and forth, reminding Wrenley of a caged animal ready to pounce. Wrenley was cemented to her nook, ass on the floor and knees squeezed to her chest as if that might somehow protect her from the beast. She smelled it, too, death and decay filled the cabin as the beast moved around.

"Yes, it has been several years. I must speak with your master now, Wendigo. It is important. Can you fetch him?"

Wendigo shook his head, his large antlers shimmering in the firelight. He screeched as his big chest was inhaling and blowing out the scream. Wrenley covered her ears with her hands and hunkered farther in the shadows. Bronson turned to the beast now, and magic ignited in his hands.

"Wendigo, it doesn't have to be like this. I need you to retrieve Johnathan. I don't mean to harm him, but I need his help."

"Help?" The creature bellowed so loudly that Wrenley felt the vibrations in her bones. "Where was your help when my master was thrown away like trash? You are a filthy, weak little human." The beast was escalating now, his nostrils flaring and his eyes glowing red.

"Call upon your master Wendigo, and we shall talk. Please…"

The simple word froze the beast momentarily, taking it off guard long enough for Bronson to push it back with a wave of energy and light. The beast roared as it flew backward, through the wall, and into the cabin's front yard. Bronson leaped after it. Wrenley sat for a moment, stunned, looking at the hearth where Bronson and the beast stood moments before and at the absence of a wall. Where the hell did they go?

Dust and crumbling pieces of wood mixed with the snow as it fell. Wrenley weakly pulled herself to her feet and stumbled out of the giant hole in the wall, gasping at the path of carnage and trees in front of her. Bronson's blow must have catapulted them deep into the woods. She could follow the trail of broken foliage to guide her to them…she guessed.

"Don't bother. You won't survive long enough to find them."

Wrenley swirled around and gasped, just noticing that the sun was peeking up in the east and dawn was approaching. In the light, Wrenley strained her eyes to see a man leaning against the cabin's outer wall. He pushed himself off it, strolling towards her as if he had all the time in the world. As he approached, she took in his older face, short salt and pepper hair, and trimmed gray goatee, his sharp blue eyes looking at her intensely. He seemed almost familiar…

Wrenley could have screamed for help, but what good would that do? If Bronson were fighting that thing in the woods, he would not be able to get to her in time. No, she was going to have to save herself.

"Your escort is a powerful seer…" The man narrowed his eyes at her, looking her up and down curiously. "But to leave the daughter of Adinnil, especially the daughter with so much likeness to her mother, deep in the woods…is a foolish decision indeed." He tilted his head to the side, studying his fingernails nonchalantly. Almost catlike, his handsome features reminded Wrenley of a predator taking in every inch of his prey.

"Who are you?" Wrenley started to put distance between them by backing away slowly, and the two moved in a circle across from each other.

"My apologies," the man said, shoving his hands in his pockets. "My name is Johnathan Wendo, and I assume you are with the seer who removed my front door?" He flicked his hand towards the smashed-up cabin.

"Maybe…" Wrenley did not avert her eyes.

He chuckled, "You found me…so what now?" Johnathan reached into his blazer, pulling out a pack of cigarettes and a lighter.

"Smoke?" he offered.

Wrenley shook her head, eyeing the stranger intently and watching every move of his hands. Johnathan was a handsome man, but much older than Bronson. His face was aged, maybe in his fifties. She watched him use his cupped hand to light the cigarette and draw deeply.

He pushed the smoke out of his nose and groaned. "I didn't know about cigarettes until I came to this shithole of a dimension. You and I are much more alike than you might think," he tapped the cigarette to remove the ash and took another pull. "You and I have lived in this world almost the same amount of time. I was banished about six months before you were born…" His eyes seemed to dim slightly as he continued to suck on the cigarette, eyes narrowing. "We should compare notes."

"I doubt it…." Wrenley pulled her hands from behind her back now, balls of fire in each. Johnathan was taken aback by the sight, cocking his head, "You don't say…"

Curiously, he took a few steps toward her, hands outstretched, palms up, and a cigarette still dangling from his mouth, "You have magic?"

"Back it up." Wrenley did not answer his question, her voice unwavering. The balls of flame hid her trembling hands. He was not listening, and she knew he could disarm her if he could move fast enough. She weighed her options, knowing that unleashing on him was a gamble, but she would rather take that gamble than allow him the chance to swoop on her. She knew he was a powerful seer with weapons…like the Wendigo.

She chose in an instant, firing two handfuls of fire at him. Surprised, he stepped out of the way as the fireballs flew by his face. She fired on him again, sending all her fury and energy towards him as he raised a shield. She pummeled him for five long minutes until he fell back. Wrenley paused, chest heaving, ready to fire off again as she stood over him.

Astonishment crept over his face as he sat in the snow, looking up at her. Slowly, he reached a shaking hand to retrieve another cigarette, as if needing every ounce of nicotine it could provide. He then said, "My God…just like your mother."

"You have no idea."

Wrenley did not move from her fighting stance. Her eyes zeroed in on Johnathan, but she was also aware that Bronson emerged into the clearing from the mangled woods, hands casually in his coat pockets. He came to stand between them, a grin on his lips as he surveyed Johnathan sprawled on the ground.

"It's okay; he's not going to hurt you. His beast, maybe…but not the man."

"Oh, sorry about that," Johnathan shrugged his slim shoulders, hoisted himself up, and flicked the cigarette butt on the ground. "I wasn't sure what company had come to call. I thought sending in

Wendigo first would be an appropriate response. You can never be too careful."

Wrenley glanced towards Bronson, then Johnathan, and then to the wreckage and mangled trees they had flown into when Bronson and Wendigo burst from the cabin. Had Bronson killed it? Mamed it? Where was it?

"Come in, have some tea." Johnathan shook Bronson's hand and peered over Bronson's shoulder at Wrenley. "And then you can explain to me why you have brought the daughter of our queen to grace my humble abode in this dimension in the middle of Alaska."

~ ~ ~ ~ ~

Wrenley supposed Johnathan was a polite man. At first glance, Wrenley would even be gracious enough to call him a gentleman. He sat in his worn red velvet armchair before the fire, legs crossed, pouring himself a cup of tea. Wrenley stepped through the hole in the wall, shivering as the cold wind entered with her. Johnathan glanced up, lighting another cigarette.

"Oh heavens, excuse me." He waved his hand above his head, and suddenly, it was as if time had moved backward, and the wall had put itself back together. Wrenley's eyes were wide, and she glanced at Bronson.

Bronson grinned back at her, "As I said, Johnathan's studies were more of an alchemist nature."

"What can I do for you, old friend? I suppose you look as young as ever, aging like a fine wine," Johnathan mumbled, sipping his tea.

"We need your help."

"What could you possibly need my help with? The last I heard, the kingdom was going to shit, and now you show up with…her." He glanced at Wrenley, eyes narrowing as he brought the steaming cup of black tea to his lips in a delicate floral teacup. "Looks like you have everything under control."

Bronson explained the situation, and Johnathan almost choked on his tea, "You mean to tell me you came all this way to recruit me to help you rescue an old woman who is probably dead already? Doesn't sound like your style, Bronson."

"She isn't just an old woman," Wrenley hissed through clenched teeth, feeling her muscles tense. "She is our friend."

"Either way, I'm surprised."

"What do you mean?" Wrenley felt defensive, but maybe a little curious.

Johnathan sighed, drained his teacup, and then flicked his cigarette butt into the fire.

"My dear friend Bronson here is a strategic man. He is also a great leader, which makes him more of the 'sacrifice the few for the needs of the many' kind of guy. Going after an old woman is uncharacteristically civil of him." Johnathan cocked his head, "How interesting."

Wrenley bristled. "You have no idea what he's been through!"

Johnathan threw his head back against the velvet headrest of the chair and laughed at Wrenley. She stepped back, and the laugh made a chill sweep over her body, goosebumps prickling up her arms.

"And you do? Please, you've been hidden away from the atrocities of this war in your little bed and breakfast, oblivious to all the suffering and carnage raging all because of you, or rather, the lack of you."

"Careful, Johnathan," Bronson snarled from his seat across from the older man.

"You knew where I was?" Wrenley asked.

"It wasn't hard to figure out. I knew Bronson's magic, and when it kept popping up in a little town in Missouri, it wasn't hard to put two and two together."

"This is your chance to come home."

Johnathan paused, meeting Bronson's gaze, dramatically touching his chest. "Are you saying that if I help you go through the catacombs to rescue your old lady, you will break my curse and allow me to come home to be free?"

Wrenley shifted in her chair, glancing at Bronson. She had to assume that whatever Johnathan did to get banished in the first place must have been horrendous. Was Bronson willing to take that chance just for Astara?

"It's not up to me, but to her."

Wrenley stiffened, feeling a flush of heat running down her spine at Bronson's words; her hand automatically flew to her stomach over her womb. She blushed at the movement inside her, glancing at Bronson.

Bronson continued, "Wrenley is both magical and royal. She doesn't need a partner to take back her throne. That makes her the queen and the only one to break the curse over your miserable head." Bronson leaned back and crossed his arms, and Wrenley could tell he was fighting off a smirk on his face.

Johnathan's eyes shot to Bronson, then to Wrenley. He let his guard down briefly, shock and awe filling those cold eyes. Wrenley was stunned by them and felt something so familiar in those eyes that held her own. It only lasted momentarily, and Johnathan gave her a wry smile.

"So, my lady…If I help you through the catacombs, will you release me of this curse of banishment from your kingdom?"

"There are conditions," Bronson interjected, and Johnathan cursed. "I'm talking to our goddamn queen, seer. Know your place!" He turned back to Wrenley, resting an elbow on the arm of his chair and propping his chin on his hand, "My lady?"

Wrenley turned to Bronson with a startled look. "Conditions? Please explain?"

"He does not have a say in this matter…"

Wrenley raised a hand to silence Johnathan. "He has been my protector for my entire life and has made countless sacrifices for his people and royalty. Unlike you, whose crusty ass has been sitting in Alaska for the last thirty years. I'm deciding he has a big goddamn say!" Her voice was raised now, anger burning her eyes, which she did not hide. The words seemed to cut through the awkwardness of the room as they landed on Johnathan. He seemed dazed for the first time since they had met him, his face draining of color as he looked at Wrenley and then at Bronson. All facetious intent disappeared, and he sat back in his chair, bowing his head in silent apology for interrupting.

Wrenley's face warmed due to her outburst, but she raised her eyes at Bronson, nodding at him to continue.

"Wendigo stays here. He can't come back with us."

"You know, wherever I go, Wendigo can be summoned," Johnathan clapped back at Bronson. "We will need him in the catacombs. There are intricate paths in that darkness; he is the only one to manage it. If he doesn't go, then I will not either."

Wrenley and Bronson looked at each other, and Wrenley raised her eyebrow at Bronson. He sighed, rubbing the back of his neck, "Johnathan was banished because, in his magic, he had mastered the power to summon Wendigo. It was uncontrolled…"

"Experimental. I know exactly how to control him now…"

Bronson spoke over him, "…Uncontrolled chaos and a lot of innocent people died. Wendigo was on the loose for weeks in the catacombs, eating people, dragging them into the darkness, never to be seen again. When we captured him…when Dolion captured him…" Bronson's eyes darkened at the memory, "Johnathan and Wendigo were banished to this dimension."

"I have had thirty years to perfect Wendigo. Trust me, he will be our greatest asset in this war. Allow me to beckon him when we need him, and I will ensure you get back on that throne. My beast and I are at your disposal, my queen…if you allow him the ability to come back to the kingdom, I promise he will behave." He presented Wrenley with the most charismatic grin, leaning forward in his seat.

"Also, throw in some land, a fortune, and a title, and I am all yours."

"Wait just a minute…" Bronson started, but Wrenley's hand shot to his thigh. Wrenley again looked at Bronson, and the unspoken message on his face screamed not to allow it. But Johnathan had a point; they may need Wendigo by the time the war ends. If he pledged their service to them, it could be a tool to save the lives of those she loved.

Wrenley attempted to make herself look bored. "Fine. You can bring your beast, but if he so much as hurts one living thing for fun or sport, you will be right back here, freezing your ass off in Alaska. You follow Bronson's orders or mine. Is that clear?"

"Crystal clear!" He saluted her, and she rolled her eyes. "You will also use him to fight beside us and protect our company during this war."

"Agreed," Johnathan clapped his hands in excitement, grinning at Bronson, who looked unhappy with the bargain.

"And I will give you land, a fortune, and a title of my choosing," Wrenley rolled her eyes as the words almost choked her. At this point, Wrenley did not care if Bronson was displeased with the deal; he would have to cope. Astara was on borrowed time, and they would need the beast to get through the catacombs and back out again. Wrenley also knew that as the baby grew, she would need more protection, and every beast would count.

"Lord Johnathan Wendigo has a nice ring to it…" Johnathan mused, reaching into his other pocket and pulling out a silver flask. He took a long drink and offered it to them, but they both declined.

Wrenley felt the exhaustion of the last day washing over her like a tsunami. She was drained as the adrenaline left her body from the crossing, the cold, the sex with Bronson, the Wendigo, and all of this…She slumped in her seat, and a sigh escaped her.

Johnathan's brow spiked, and he shot what seemed to be a worried glance at her and then at Bronson. "Well, this has been a pleasure; when do we leave?"

"Preferably now," Bronson muttered as he rose to attend to Wrenley.

"Splendid! Twelve hours it is." Johnathan waved his hand again, and it seemed his small cabin came to life in slow motion. Magic swirled in flashes, and a large black caldron appeared, simmering over the fire in the hearth. The smell of delicious beef stew with rosemary filled the air as it bubbled, a large wooden tub in the corner instantly filled with piping hot water, and more quilts were piled on the bed.

"Please help yourself to dinner. And help yourself to…everything." He waved towards the bed. "I must go feed Wendigo before the crossing. You two may use my cabin and not be disturbed for the next twelve hours." He stood and straightened his jacket, glancing again between the two, his eyes narrowing slightly. "I'm sure you can manage."

"Thank you," Bronson nodded in respect, which seemed enough to halt the apparent questions from Johnathan that simmered in his eyes.

~ ~ ~ ~ ~

Wrenley ate three heaping bowls of stew, peeled her clothes off, washed in the old bathtub, and slid into bed. Bronson bathed and shaved, prepared the bed, and tucked her in. She groaned as she fell onto the lumpy mattress, not caring at all and just thankful for the opportunity to rest in a warm place.

"I'll sleep on the floor…" Bronson murmured as he tucked her in, brushing a stray hair away from her eyes.

"Don't be ridiculous. We had sex on this bed; we might as well sleep in it together."

"That's the problem; I'm afraid we won't get any sleep."

Wrenley rolled her eyes as she patted the pillow beside her. "I'll take that chance, I guess," she added as he grinned, pulled his heavier clothes off, and slipped beside her. Wrenley unapologetically snuggled up to him as he wrapped his arms around her, pulling her tight to his chest.

"Are we safe here? I mean…to sleep for a few hours?"

"Yes," Bronson yawned lazily, resting his head on the pillow. Wrenley studied him lying next to her; she noticed he looked tired. He was always on the move, thinking, planning, and protecting… She hardly ever saw him sleep. Yet, even with his powers, he was a man with flesh and bones. He ached and hurt and grew hungry with the physical and mental burdens of their reality, or at least she thought. He lusted and craved attention…so much so that the memory of them on this bed hours earlier flashed in her mind.

"Despite the cocky attitude, Johnathan and Wendigo will not allow anything to even come near us in the next twelve hours," Bronson murmured against her.

"Hmmm…I guess that is comforting."

Within minutes, Bronson was asleep, gently snoring next to her. She could feel his body going slack in deep slumber, his breathing heavy and steady. She spent the next hour studying him, watching him rest. His childlike features were more prominent in respite, and she wondered what it would be like to exist with him without the threat of war, destruction, and death. What would it be like to live and have fun with him? What would it be like to raise a child with him? That thought made her stiffen slightly, as she had never asked Bronson what he planned to do when the baby was born. She knew he had pledged to keep her safe, but would he also be a father to this baby? As if knowing it was the target of her thoughts, the baby moved in her womb so forcefully she gasped a little, then smiled. She sighed, imagining what that life would look like, and fell fast asleep beside him.

CHAPTER 32

Rescue

The trio stood outside the cabin twelve hours later. Johnathan joined them, looking refreshed, no beast in sight. Wrenley's eyebrows arched, but she did not dare say anything. Things were tense between the two men, and she did not want to start an argument. They had used words such as 'summoned' the day before; perhaps Wendigo was not something one physically had to move, but he just appeared? Was he some supernatural being?

Bronson seemed equally revived after sleeping for a few hours. His eyes were brighter, and he had more energy than yesterday. Wrenley slept until Bronson woke her up an hour ago, having no idea when he had left her side. She was still groggy and muttering as they gathered in the clearing before the mangled pile of brush and trees from their first encounter with Wendigo. Johnathan looked refined, wearing a dark wool coat, leather gloves, and an ivy cap. Wrenley smirked at him, and he held up his hands in defense, stepping out of her way as she passed. She almost hissed in his direction; her mood was so foul she would end him with one sideways glance.

Wrenley watched as Bronson began crossing over, noting that when he did, he seemed to age just slightly. She knew it took a toll on him. She was somewhat worried about him crossing over with three of them, but Johnathan piped up, almost reading her mind. "I assume I will be crossing over on my power, surely?"

Bronson nodded, "Yes, if you can handle it."

It was meant as a dig, and Johnathan balked at it, muttering something under his breath. "Of course, I can handle it…

"Stay with me. We have a beacon on the other side that will guide us to where we need to go."

~ ~ ~ ~ ~

Bronson crossed over quickly and took them to the crystal. The company was hidden in the woods on a hill overlooking the mouth of the catacombs. Alcott estimated that enough soldiers were stationed in the outpost to constitute a small army.

In her usual fashion, Gwyneira gave a judgmental glance toward Johnathan, her eyes appearing unimpressed. "Who's the old guy?"

"Johnathan Wendo, at your service…" He bowed dramatically, Gwyneira's expression unchanged. The young woman cocked her head and arched an eyebrow at him, pursing her lips.

"So, you are the prized secret weapon that will get us in and out of there…alive?" Kage asked hesitantly, taking in Johnathan with reluctance. God, he looked so tired; Wrenley supposed he had not slept at all since the word of Astara's abduction had reached them.

"Me and my many talents." He flashed Gwyneira with another grin, obviously flirting with her. She turned to Wrenley, "He smells like an old man."

"It's probably his…pet." Wrenley gripped Gwyneira's arm tightly, tugging her away before she said anything too damaging to Johnathan's ego.

"No, I smell the beast on him, too. But he smells like mildew…"

"All right! What is the plan?" Wrenley cut in, ready to start this rescue mission. Garrick lowered his head to muffle his chuckle. Wrenley gritted her teeth, shaking the young woman again as if that would make Gwyneira read the room.

"We don't need a plan. I take Wendigo in, and he clears it. Someone come with me to collect our prisoner, and we shall be home free." Johnathan clapped his hands enthusiastically and rubbed them together.

"It isn't that simple!" Kage interjected, "They have forces that will overpower you. Besides, I'm not allowing anyone to go in without me, now that we know Mother is in the catacombs."

Bronson and Johnathan exchanged glances, and Wrenley detected that the men held back grins.

"Let's just say, numbers are not an issue," Johnathan smirked.

"But fine, who's going with me? It's your funeral."

The plan was for Johnathan to summon Wendigo and take Gwyneira, Wrenley, and Kage to retrieve Astara. Bronson would stay back to avoid attracting unseen attention if enemy seers were in the outpost. Alcott and Garrick would remain at the mouth of the catacombs, ensuring no one else entered or existed. If, by some unfortunate calamity Johnathan needed assistance, Wrenley was the most powerful beside Bronson.

They crept down to the trees, the mouth of the catacombs only a hundred feet away. In one conjoined movement, Garrick and Alcott advanced to take out the guards. Johnathan, Kage, and Gwyneira quickly made their way inside. As Wrenley was ready to leap over a fallen tree trunk to follow, Bronson grabbed her arm.

"If you feel anything off, get the hell out."

Wrenley nodded in agreement, both knowing it was a lie. Bronson knew she would do anything to get Astara back, but he just had to say it. She peered up at him, his dark eyes full of trepidation, his handsome face blank of emotion except for the muscle feathering in his jaw. He leaned down to kiss her, and she bolted after her companions, swinging herself over the log with ease in her pants and lightweight shirt. She knew, without a doubt, she was not coming out of this place without Astara, even if it killed her.

~ ~ ~ ~ ~

The first thing Wrenley noticed was the smell; it hit her as soon as she entered the mouth of the cave. It was thick, and Wrenley was unsure if it was feces, death, or both. It wafted around her, filling her nose and mouth until she almost gagged. There was something sinister about it…as if it held a deep, dark enchantment. The second thing she observed was how penetratingly dark it was as they ventured deeper into the maze of passageways. Even though the tunnels were lit with torches, the blackness was so intense that Wrenley could barely see beyond Kage in front of her. She almost preferred the darkness; it was better if she could not tell how small the tunnels were or how they might close in around her.

Lastly, she heard the noises. This outpost was designed to hold prisoners of war, and Garrick explained it might have at least dozens, more likely hundreds, of resistance soldiers. She heard them wailing and crying from somewhere, maybe underneath or above her. Wrenley could not help but wondered if it came from in the rock itself, the souls of those tortured and killed still trapped there?

Johnathan walked briskly, charging ahead as if he knew exactly where to go. This concerned Wrenley, as she had thought the whole reason for retrieving Wendigo was to have him help, and still, there was no beast to be seen. They encountered some random guards, and Kage killed them with ease and dragged their bodies out of the path. A million scenarios played out in Wrenley's mind: What if Johnathan had brought her here to leave her and take the throne himself? What if he had forgotten where to go, and they wandered on forever? What if enemy soldiers overcame them, and she was thrown into a dark, cold cell and left to die? She squeezed her eyes shut and grasped Kage's tunic tighter, trying to manage the panic growing inside her as they pushed forward. Step after step, the path led deeper into the earth, and all the while, Wrenley's nerves tingled with anxiety.

Wrenley tried to ignore the far-off wails, the clinking and clanking deep within the stone walls. It was as if someone was trying to call for help... Wrenley felt her magic relocate to her womb, protecting her baby from whatever evil lurked there. Wrenley knew that before the enemy had used these catacombs, magical beasts dwelled within the black abyss of the caves. Wendigo had been one of them...

Can you hear me? It whispered on a phantom wind.

Come find me… It echoed back.

"Keep your wits about you, ladies. There is heavy magic here." Johnathan leaned over and shook Wrenley's shoulder, sensing her growing confusion and paranoia. He then grabbed Gwyneira by the scruff of her shirt and heaved her between Wrenley and Kage. One look at the younger woman and Wrenley knew she was struggling in the same way she was, her green eyes wide, face pale and confused. Kage was untouched since he had no magic. Johnathan put a finger to his lips and put his other hand up for everyone to pause.

He listened intently and said, "We are getting close to the main prison area. It will be heavily guarded. Things are about to get fun," Johnathan grinned self-confidently.

As if on cue, shouts were heard ahead, the tunnel winding to the left. Torchlight and voices were approaching as the tunnel spilled into a large cavern. Kage shoved Gwyneira behind him. Johnathan positioned himself in front of Wrenley. His chivalry surprised her as she ducked behind him, peeking over his shoulder. A group of guards came into view and outnumbered them three to one. Wrenley gasped when they wielded large, dog-looking creatures that were snarling and pulling at the leashes of their masters. When the soldiers finally saw the four, they released the dogs, and the animals barreled forward with their fangs on display.

"Now would be a good time to have your beast join us..." Wrenley whispered. Johnathan was silent, and she shook his shoulder.

"Hey! Did you hear me?"

"Shut up! I am concentrating."

"You're what?!" Wrenley hissed in his ear, her grip tightening, nails digging in. The wild dogs were yards away now, crossing the distance between them with fierce ease.

"I may have underestimated the summoning process..." Johnathan mumbled.

"What the fuck does that mean?" Gwyneira snapped, the dogs coming closer and closer. They were feral, gigantic beasts, their fangs gleaming with saliva, their eyes crazed and wild.

It happened fast; the dogs were on them in an instant. Luckily, Kage was ready and began hacking up the monstrous canines with precision and skill. He swung hard, cutting the head off one, pivoting to slit the throat of another with his dagger. Like a cyclone, Kage spun and slashed at the wave of animals on top of them. Wrenley felt her magic coiling under her skin, her hands beginning to glow.

Gwyneira tossed Wrenley a look, "Save your magic for the last...if we can help it." Gwyneira then took a confident step forward, closing her eyes. She did not appear to be doing a thing, but Wrenley looked on in amazement as the dogs began yelping and writhing in pain, blood bursting from their eyes as they hit the ground. The soldiers were close behind their canines, and Kage and Gwyneira stood between them and the heavily armed fighters.

"Johnathan, for fuck's sake, do something!" Wrenley screamed as she summoned her magic, flames appearing in her palms. It was a last resort, but she would not let Gwyneira and Kage die. The soldiers continued to batter them, and she felt the rush of wind as they charged toward her and her friends. More and more came, wave after wave, as Kage and Gwyneira took down one soldier after another. The small tunnel opened into a dimly lit chasm, and the three stood at the edge, ready for the onslaught of chaos and bloodshed to hit them. Kage stood with his sword drawn; Gwyneira stood emotionless in the center, her hands stretched out in front of her. Wrenley flanked her, magic summoned and poised for when another wave of soldiers crossed the vast space before them.

Wrenley was waiting for it, the fear to rip into her and cause her to crumble. To her surprise, the fear did not come. What arrived inside her chest was anger, fury, and a deep-rooted need to kill the enemy before her. She knew they would hit them like a train. They were outnumbered, but she did not care. She widened her stance just like Garrick had taught her, holding up her hands, ready to unleash her powers onto her enemy. Sparks and light curled around her, and she felt heat flush through her. They were closer now, running at full speed across the vast area between the two tunnels. Swords drawn, they neared closer now, so close...

Bronson and her baby flashed into her mind's eye...Bronson's handsome face was marred with grief and confusion, and a beautiful child in her arms that she may never get to hold. Finally, Astara...hidden in the dark and suffering unbearable pain. Is this how Wrenley would die? Underground and separated from the man she loved and the baby she had dreamed of, fading away into nothing as if it never existed? Watching her friends be cut down like wheat in a field before they finally reached her?

No. This is not how she would die. Even if this were her final stand, her last breath, she would go down fighting. *You lack nothing in yourself*; Astara's words returned to her. In her old world, a room of doctors told her how she would die, and she had no power to stop it. Here in this moment, with a wave of darkness rushing towards her, she would not allow anyone to ever tell her how she would die again. If this were the day and the hour, she would die fighting, thrashing and slaughtering the darkness that decided to pick a fight with her. She would not give into the fear that had been crippling her for so long. She would stand and fight for the hope of something better.

Something hit like a boulder before them, knocking Wrenley back with force. She sat up soon enough to see Johnathan stand between them and the army as the soldiers skidded to a stop before him.

"What's he doing?" Gwyneira asked, reaching for Wrenley to help pull her up. Kage still perched with his sword ready, and Wrenley strained her eyes in the dimly lit cave. Johnathan turned to her then and winked, "I forgot to mention, my lady, I actually don't summon Wendigo…"

His form began to shift, his skin seeming to melt away as something appeared from underneath the shell of a man. He huffed and snorted, shaking his head as if it was painful. Wrenley flinched at the sound of muscle and bone snapping and popping in and out of place, flesh stretching, and things growing. He was crouched over but turned to look over his shoulder at Wrenley. Red glowing eyes met hers, and he said gruffly with a deep, guttural voice, "I am Wendigo."

The beast exploded from Johnathan, clothes and skin flying in every direction. Johnathan's human frame was replaced by the eight-foot-tall monster she had met in the cabin yesterday. It shrieked as it manifested before them, the enemy looking at it in horror.

The reality dawned on her…Wendigo was not its own entity. Somehow, because of the magic, Johnathan and the beast were one within themselves. The beast rose to his full height, the soldiers cowering back, and Wrenley saw several of them piss themselves. The beast roared, a defining screech that echoed off the cave walls and down the tunnels, warning everyone that a monster was in their midst and ready to hunt. Wendigo charged forward and began slaughtering the soldiers, body parts and gore flying in every direction. Kage offered Wrenley a hand and pushed the girls forward, following behind Wendigo as he cleared the way for them.

Wendigo made quick work of it, clawing, ripping, swiping, and eating through the masses of soldiers in the outpost. They reached the first cell block, and the three quickly searched every cell. They freed all the prisoners, and Gwyneira volunteered to lead them back to the entrance. They still had not found Astara. Gwyneira gathered the group and led them back to where they came. Wrenley hoped Gwyneira could find her way out; the little witch seemed confident.

"We have to go to the next cellblock," Kage said, panting. His muscular body was balking against the intensity of the fighting. The beast paused, down on all fours since the tunnels were so small, a severed arm hanging from its powerful jaws. He approached Kage and Wrenley, looking at them, his red eyes wild, spitting the limb on the ground.

"Do you have a trinket?" His voice was a deep growl, coming closer to smell them.

"A trinket? Oh! Something of Astara's?" Wrenley looked at Kage and slapped his shoulder. "He needs something to help track her."

"I don't have anything…" He said frantically. Wrenley grabbed him and tore the neck of his shirt, revealing the crystal.

"Here!" Wrenley retrieved it and shoved it in Wendigo's face, the beast taking a deep breath, filling his lungs with the scent. He then roared and turned to dart down another tunnel, and they had difficulty keeping up. Even with its immense size, Wendigo was made for these tunnels. He could easily crouch down and speed through the catacombs like a bullet being shot from a gun. Wendigo came to an open area and slowed, sniffing the air. This cave was large enough for him to stand at full height, and he growled as he looked around.

"She's here…" he muttered.

Wrenley came up behind him, her lungs burning, her legs wobbling like jelly underneath her. She leaned against the cool stone wall momentarily, catching her breath. Kage, less winded than she, began working on breaking down the first door in the room.

Wrenley took a moment to observe her surroundings, estimating the room to be at least five hundred square feet. Different doors, cells, and rooms were scattered around, all surrounding one large door in the center. Nearing it, Wrenley gasped softly as she craned her neck to take in the height of the door, its breadth over ten feet wide. The door seemed normal enough except for its uncharacteristically enormous size, but with closer inspection,

Wrenley noticed different carvings on the doors that caught her attention.

"Something isn't right…" Wrenley whispered, reaching out to touch the door. She jumped back as the door reacted to her, almost burning under her fingertips.

"It's encrypted…" Wrenley said breathlessly, going from one carving to another. A moon, a star, a swirling pattern…

"We are running out of time!" Kage said desperately, coming to stand by Wrenley. Wrenley heard it then, a whisper coming from the very fabric of the door as it seemed to groan and beckon her.

Can you hear me?

The door shuddered, and Wrenley felt its force pulse out, but she had thrown up a shield. Alive…this door was alive, and it knew she was there.

Come find me… the voice said again, trailing on a phantom wind. Wrenley began to feel dizzy as she reached out again to touch one of the symbols on the door. Her fingers shook, and beads of sweat trickled down her brow. The door vibrated, and Wrenley heard a swooshing sound in her ears as she brought both palms to rest on the wood. Her magic recoiled at first but slowly crept back toward the point of contact between her and the door. She felt something dark and ominous on the other side, like something was trying to break through. *Boom! Boom! Boom!* It thundered repeatedly, and Wrenley gasped as she ripped her hands from the door.

"Wrenley, we have to find her!" Kage shook her shoulder as if waking her from a trance. She did not know how long it had been, but she curled her hands at her chest, breaking her connection. In a frantic rage, Kage went to the nearest door and began kicking it down. Wrenley winced, her magic flinching with every blow Kage made to the door until…

"Kage no!" Wrenley shrieked and extended her hand outward, but it was too late. Kage cried out as a swarm of black creatures erupted from the door, knocking Kage backward onto his ass. Wrenley knelt and covered her head as the swarm flew past her, shaking uncontrollably at their screeches and decaying smell. When they had passed, she jumped up and raced over to Kage.

She helped him to his feet as he cursed, "One of those fuckers clawed me."

Before Wrenley could respond, Wendigo shuffled back into the room, cradling a body under one arm. Kage and Wrenley looked at each other in surprise; it was Astara.

Forgetting his scratch, Kage shrugged, "Let's get the hell out of here."

CHAPTER 33

Just Another Journey

True to his word, Wendigo led them through the catacombs, winding in and out of passageways so crooked Wrenley had thought they were going in circles. Wendigo took them so deep into the dark that she doubted any mortal man had ever breathed this same air. Wrenley had never felt darkness like she did in those tunnels, and she felt the magic of the ancient air press down on her. There were no torches or lamps because this was uncharted territory…Wendigo's red eyes were the only light that cast a soft glow for them to follow. Wrenley clamped herself onto Kage's forearm so hard he had to pry her fingers off several times.

Wrenley shuddered at the door's memory; its presence seemed to linger with her even as they moved farther and farther away. It had tried to speak to her. There was something behind it, something trying to get out. If those creatures from the other door were any indication, she did not want to know or find out what that door held at bay.

After what seemed like hours, Wendigo came to a dead end and chuckled, kicking the wall with his large leg. The dead end gave way quickly, and moonlight filtered in. Wrenley fell out of the opening, gasping for air, tears streaming down her face as she wept out of relief. She had honestly thought they would die in the shadows, and she struggled to hold herself up with her arms on the ground. She remembered Astara and forced her body to get up. Wendigo laid Astara on a soft, grassy area and crawled away into the night. Wrenley threw herself on the ground next to the woman, Kage, by her side. Wrenley felt her stomach drop and her heart sink as she looked at the older woman. A sob escaped her as she reached out to tuck a stray strand of white hair behind the woman's ear.

Astara's once beautiful face was bloodied and swollen, and it looked as if one eye was missing from the right socket. Her clothes were shredded, and a deathly smell wafted to Wrenley's senses. She recognized it as rancid, rotting flesh. Astara had wounds of all shapes and sizes on her limbs, and Wrenley could see that they had tortured her relentlessly, infection now setting in. Tears welled in her eyes as she allowed Kage to push her aside and bend down before his broken Mother, a cry escaping from him, a deep, guttural scream that slaughtered Wrenley's very soul. The son reached down gently and cradled his Mother in his arms, shock still covering his handsome young face.

Gwyneira had found them now, and the girl knelt on the other side of Astara, sucking in a deep breath as she placed a cool hand on the woman's burning forehead. Wrenley looked up at the young witch, and Gwyneira shook her head. "I'm not powerful enough...we need Bronson."

Not knowing how long they had been sitting there or where he came from, Bronson appeared, kneeling beside Kage and placing a hand on the younger man's shoulder.

"Let me..." Bronson uttered softly, took the woman into his arms, and held her against his large chest. Kage was howling now; his thick, muscled shoulders were ravaged by grief as he let go of his Mother. Knee to knee with Bronson, Kage chanted something in a tongue Wrenley could not understand.

"Please...save her. Save her!" Kage begged Bronson and placed his large hands on Bronson's knees to look into his Mother's face again. "I can't lose her!"

Tears fell as Wrenley witnessed Bronson's skin beginning to glow. He murmured some prayer or spell, pressed his face against the older woman's head, and rocked her back and forth so tenderly it broke Wrenley's heart. Bronson rocked the woman in his arms for several frozen moments, speaking lowly in her ear as power and light radiated off him in the darkness. There was so much darkness that Wrenley could hardly bear it.

"My sons?" Astara whispered and stirred weakly in Bronson's arms. Alcott, who had arrived with Bronson, kneeled and gently transferred the woman from the seer's arms to his. She looked up at her two children, and suddenly, Wrenley noticed the glint in her eye and the grin that crept onto her face. It was still Astara underneath that bloodied, broken body. Her spirit was still there...

"Y-you...you came for me. I knew you would." Her voice was raspy, and Gwyneira was there in a heartbeat, allowing Astara a cool drink of water from her canteen. Such a simple thing, but Astara looked as if it were the most cherished thing anyone had ever given her.

"Of course, we did..." Kage choked out, looking at his brother, Alcott's shoulders shaking as he kissed his Mother's forehead. "We would never leave you, my Mother."

"I told you, my sons, we all had a part to play...and somehow this is mine." She rasped out, and Kage sobbed into her matted hair.

Wrenley sat beside them but said nothing, allowing her gaze to meet Bronson's for the first time. His face was grim, and he gently shook his head at her. Bile rose in Wrenley's throat as tears began to well and pour from her eyes freely now. She knew Bronson had done all he could with significant cost, knowing they would have to move soon, so the enemy could not track his power to them. Wrenley's heart skipped a beat when she realized Bronson knew he could not save Astara all along; he had brought her back long enough to say goodbye to her sons.

"My queen..." Astara choked, trying to turn her head to look for Wrenley. Wrenley mopped tears and snot away from her face with her sleeve and crawled next to Kage, giving the older woman the biggest smile she could muster. She felt the weight of a million words on her chest and reached to take Astara's limp hand into hers.

"Yes, my dear friend?"

Astara smiled faintly, "It has been a pleasure to meet you, my lady, and to see hope again with my very own eyes."

Wrenley held back a wail, her body shaking as she nodded to her. "You have been so good to me, my friend, and I thank you so much. You have given me love and kindness, and you have given me the most faithful men a queen could ever ask for..."

Astara chuckled and then coughed, blood escaping her mouth. Gwyneira tore a part of her dress and handed it to Kage. He murmured soothing words and wiped the blood gently away from his Mother's mouth. Astara gasped, reaching unquestioningly for

Wrenley's other hand. Wrenley took the mangled, broken fingers into her own, kissed them, and held them near her heart. "What is it, Astara?"

"A princess…" Astara said, shifting to look at Wrenley and then at Bronson. "You are going to have a baby."

Wrenley felt her brain begin to shut down, the pain of this moment too much for her heart and her soul. She gently patted Astara's arm and leaned to kiss her head. "Yes, and she will know your name. She will know the Earth and the fairies, and be kind to them… she will talk to the rocks and the trees. She will listen to the wind and rain and hear its secrets…" Wrenley said, kissing the woman's hand and sobbing now. "Just like you…she will be just like you. I swear it."

What else could she say when there was a lifetime of things that would never be uttered? When there was so much that she wanted to share with Astara? It was as if Wrenley's soul had not had enough of her yet, and it was searching…not ready to let go or say goodbye.

Astara nodded, a single tear trailing down her bruised cheek. "You are good, my queen, kind, powerful, and enough. You are always enough."

Wrenley knew that it was moments away before this soul passed into the afterlife to be with her husband and older son. Was that why there was so much peace on her broken face? Why does her very presence soothe the collective pain of this moment?

"I give you my heart, Bronson Aughton…" She whispered to Bronson, who nodded and squeezed the older woman's hand, a tear sliding down his handsome face.

"I promise I will take care of them all." He glanced around at the group of people, and Astara understood he meant every single one of them, including her sons. "With my life, I will; I swear it."

"Tell her…tell her the truth…" Astara began coughing now, and a death rattle in her lungs began to overtake her breathing, her words becoming jumbled and disorganized.

"We will give you some time," Wrenley said gently, squeezing the woman's hand again. Bronson helped her up and almost had to carry her away from this family that had been so ravaged and broken. Her grief was indescribable as she sobbed into his chest, and he held her tightly, keeping his eyes on the brothers.

"We have to move Bronson," Garrick said lowly as he stepped beside them. "Your magic most definitely caught attention."

Bronson blew an exasperated breath, laying a cheek on Wrenley's head. She felt his body ripple with something, and she was unsure if it was power, grief, or both.

"Fuck it all. I will obliterate anyone who comes near them before they have a chance to say goodbye," Bronson growled, and Wrenley knew he meant it.

Gwyneira stayed near the brothers as they whispered to their Mother, and Wrenley knew that the odd, vacant little witch used her power to surround the brothers and their Mother with a gentle mist of peace. It was subtle, like a moonbeam or starlight, a soft magic to ease the pain of the woman's final moments. It was as if Gwyneira had seen this before, and Wrenley watched as the girl reached over and closed the woman's eyes, signaling that Astara had passed.

Kage wailed as he looked down at the woman's lifeless body in his lap. It was a sound that Wrenley had never heard before, the sound of love...of grief...of a child who had lost a Mother. Alcott was silent, but Wrenley saw tears descending down his young face. Gwyneira removed her cloak and gently laid it over Astara, her magic covering the woman as her sons crumbled at her side. Gwyneira did not move but sat with them as they wept, holding space for the pain, allowing it, maybe even welcoming it. She did not balk of the pain or emotions; she sat with them in it. Garrick sighed next to Wrenley, kicking a rock on the ground and shaking his head.

"Shit..." Garrick breathed, his voice cracking as she heard him heave a sob, just one. Then, he ambled to Alcott and kneeled beside him. Wrenley felt her heart almost explode when Garrick reached to envelop the younger man in his arms and pulled him to his chest, and Alcott turned to sob in his shirt.

Wrenley did not know how to breathe; she did not know how to move or speak. For the first time in her life, someone dear was taken from her, and the void left in the wake of death was palpable. Wrenley snapped to attention as she noticed a soft blue glow lift from Astara's skin, and it drifted up above the woman and her sons as they mourned. Did they not see it? Wrenley squinted, turning fully, and took a step closer. The blue glow turned into a floating blue light and swished above them. It traveled over to Wrenley and whooshed past her ear.

"*Look to the Earth…*" it whispered, and she gasped, so surprised that she stepped back and bumped into Bronson's chest.

"What is it?" He said, gripping her forearm as he stood behind, trying to steady her.

"You didn't see it? Did you hear?" She turned to him and watched over his shoulder as the blue orb gently floated over the grass, caressed by the wind, and then shot up into the sky.

"See what?" Bronson turned to look, confusion knitting his brows together.

"After…I saw something leave. I think it's Astara's soul…" Wrenley breathed as she watched, straining her eyes to avoid missing one movement. Could she catch it? Could she keep it close? But her body would not move, and she knew it was not meant to be kept; it was intended to be free.

The blue light danced around, reminding Wrenley of the fairies she had seen dancing that night with Kage in the forest. She breathed softly as the light dissipated into a million sparks. They floated upward like a million stars in the sky, now beyond her sight.

Bronson inhaled sharply and looked at Wrenley lovingly. "Of course, you can see her…You always have been able to…to see the ones who travel." Wrenley strained for any last glimpse of the blue light, but it was gone now.

"Where is she going?" Wrenley asked softly, raising one hand as if she could touch Astara…maybe she could have one more touch…

Bronson shrugged, "No one knows…" his voice was rough, and Wrenley knew this must have brought up so many emotions for him. She ached for him, too, his bleeding heart undoubtedly ripped open by this blow.

Bronson took a steady breath. "I would like to think death is not the end of life…it's just another dimension we travel to, all of us in our own time. No one can escape the journey." Bronson wrapped his arms around her, and his hand dropped to her belly. Wrenley felt the baby move when his hand rested over her.

"Just another journey," Wrenley whispered against the darkness.

CHAPTER 34

Alone

The days following the raid on the catacombs were a blur for Wrenley. They took Astara's body into the woods and burned it, then scattered the ashes back to the Earth as was the custom of her people. Wrenley watched as the flames engulfed her beautiful friend, wrapped in Gwyneira's cloak. She glanced at the twins. Both had contained themselves now, faces indifferent, standing straight and proud, singing some ancient melody as the flames roared around the body of their beloved Mother. Wrenley felt goosebumps flush over her forearms, and she felt a soft rumble from Bronson's chest as he held her. He knew this song, she realized, and he chanted softly along with the twins as they mourned.

The shock of their loss enveloped them as they traveled slowly and silently back to Nicolas's residence in the highlands. They took the long road, ensuring they were not being followed. Wrenley did not notice the cold or discomfort as they rode on and on into the night. All she could feel was grief and guilt at the extraordinary loss they had experienced. It was because of her; all of this was because of her. It was because of her that so many people had suffered—her birth parents, Bronson, Garrick, Astara, and the twins. Even Gwyneira had lost her parents to this awful war that had been raging, ripping families apart and brutalizing any resemblance of civilization in this dimension.

Wrenley felt like she had no right to grieve over anyone. She had lost the least out of their company and would not allow herself to mourn like the others. But she could be, would be, strong for everyone else. She would be the one to take care of them as they mourned. Johnathan finally appeared after four days, catching up with the party before they arrived back at the cabin. He mumbled something about Wendigo being uncooperative, or was it an excuse to avoid the tidal wave of pain that hit them? Even though he did not know Astara, he was respectful and quiet as they traveled.

~ ~ ~ ~ ~

It had been a week since they arrived at the highland residence. The silence in the castle was deafening, and Wrenley felt everyone disappear to process their grief in their own way. Wrenley had not seen Kage or Alcott since they arrived back. She did not know where they had gone, but gave them their space and did not seek them out. Bronson was also distant, and Wrenley knew all too well that this event had triggered a deep sorrow for his king and queen, whom he had lost fifteen years ago. She allowed him time to process and grieve as well. Johnathan stayed out of the way and drank large amounts of wine; if she had not been pregnant, she would have joined him.

Gwyneira was like a shadow, drifting in and out without being noticed. Garrick and Wrenley seemed to be the most functional of the company, ensuring everyone ate, bathed, and rested. Garrick and Wrenley took turns bringing food up to the twins' door, leaving it outside for them. Wrenley was often left to herself, conflicted and torn about the reality of everything. Wrenley slept alone in her room, not knowing where Bronson was sleeping or what he was doing. She was too distracted to support him in this time of angst. When she had inquired about him to one of the staff, they shrugged, "He's been gone, my lady...for several days now."

Wrenley did not know what was expected between her and Bronson. He had asked her to marry him, but then everything happened, and now he had left the castle without saying a word to her. Had he changed his mind? She felt disgusted even thinking about them compared to what Kage and Alcott had just gone through. Her hand went to her stomach as she felt a flutter and realized it was not too much to ask Bronson to make up his goddam mind. He could at least communicate with her before he just up and left.

Nonetheless, Wrenley dug deep within herself, poring over the books about her mother and father. There was little current literature because the war did not allow many manuscripts to be duplicated. She focused more on the history of Ailios. She read about one mighty army of immortal peoples that had shown up thousands of years ago to fight the reigning deity. This deity defended his land and sent the armies back to where they came from, but it took such a toll on the god that he retreated, never to be heard of again. That is when the royal line was established, and humans have ruled ever since. For two thousand years, Ailios had been a developing world. Why, then, fifteen years ago, did it all explode?

~ ~ ~ ~ ~

Wrenley tossed and turned that night in her bed, her thoughts racing. She sat in the dark room, feeling like she could crawl out of her body. Even the ordinarily soft silk sheets felt overstimulating to her. She finally gave up and tossed the covers off, slipping on her shoes and grabbing her robe. She could not bear to lie in this bed alone for one more moment. She had no idea if Bronson was alive or dead; her friends were suffering, and everything pretty much was going to hell.

Wrenley silently crept downstairs to the kitchen, making herself a cup of tea since she could not drink wine. She then found some shortbread cookies and stole a few before going to her favorite part of the castle: the library. She settled into her favorite overstuffed chair, pretended not to notice the staff following her, and they silently lit a fire in the hearth. She never wanted to be a bother, but she was very grateful. She was still chilly, even with her robe and blanket on her lap.

"Can't sleep?"

Wrenley almost threw the book in Johnathan's direction as he chuckled, coming up behind her and sitting across from her.

"No," she said, shutting the book and sighing.

He nodded, "A lot of that going around."

The two sat in silence, Wrenley not feeling pressured to start a conversation with the man. She glanced across at him, taking in his handsome features. Johnathan was the same age as Bronson but had aged because he had been banished to her world. His salt and pepper hair was short, and his goatee distinguished him. Tonight, he was dressed in blue pajamas with brown house shoes, making him look older than he probably was; he reminded Wrenley of Jim. Even at night, a cup of tea appeared from one of the hovering staff; Johnathan took it, reaching into his front pocket to pull out a flask. He poured the contents into the tea and took a sip.

He offered it to Wrenley, and she shook her head.

"Sorry…forgot about the baby and all. In all the magic and science, we haven't made the connection that alcohol isn't good for pregnant women yet."

Wrenley watched as Johnathan took a long sip of his tea and sighed. He caught her watching him and shifted so he could look at her thoroughly.

"You look like you have something to say."

Wrenley shrugged, sipping her tea. "I do have questions."

"Oh lord."

Wrenley chuckled, "I just want to know about your history with Bronson."

Johnathan exhaled deeply and set his tea down, crossing one leg over the other, folding his hands in his lap as his elbows rested on the armchair. He seemed to contemplate the subject for a long moment.

"Bronson, Dolion, and I worked together. I had met Bronson shortly after he and Dolion met, but I still consider us the 'original friend group,' I guess you could say."

"What was he like? Before all of this?"

"Bronson? That man doesn't change a lot. When Dolion and I had our…" he seemed to weigh his words, "Disagreement, Bronson was young and naïve. I feel that Dolion took advantage of him sometimes…No, I knew it."

Wrenley sat up a little straighter. "How so?"

Johnathan shrugged his slender shoulders. "I was under the impression that the work Bronson and Dolion were doing was almost too much for Bronson. He had made several attempts to convince Dolion to stop, to take a moment to think, and to take a goddamn breath before undoing the very fabrics of this dimension to travel to others," Johnathan shook his head. "Dolion was the king, and Bronson was a good friend and an even more loyal subject. So good and loyal that it blinded him to the truth: that

Dolion was power-seeking and dangerous."

"What's the real story? About him banishing you?"

Johnathan chuckled and raked a hand through his salt-and-pepper hair. "I, perhaps, pushed some boundaries. I had just mastered the art of becoming Wendigo and didn't fully understand how to control him. I may have accidentally eaten some of the king's constituents."

"But it was more than that?"

Johnathan paused and glanced at her, grinning. "He was a jealous bastard. I had befriended the queen, and when he was so obsessed with his work, he had neglected her. I just happened to be more…" He tapped his fingers on the arm of the chair, almost nervously. "Well…I was there when he wasn't."

Wrenley's eyes widened, "Did you and her…?"

"Enough of this talk," Johnathan waved his hand, his body bristling. "It's no one's business, not even you, my lady."

Wrenley grinned at his discomfort and nibbled on a cookie as they sat in thick silence again. Wrenley gathered the courage to ask another question before losing the opportunity.

"What kind of a man is Bronson? He's still…difficult to read."

Johnathan snickered, stretching his long legs, "My dear, good luck with that. Bronson is powerful. Never underestimate his silence for weakness. He is calculated, smart, and can be ruthless. He's the smartest son of a bitch I know."

She knew all too well; the memory of his slicing the throat of that man at the gathering still haunted her in her dreams. Johnathan continued at her silence and pondered, "You forget, my dear; he has been in the throes of war for fifteen years. War makes people do things they would never do, and Bronson has done his fair share."

Wrenley let that sink in, but did not want to think about it much. It made her stomach churn a little, and fear edged into the back of her brain.

"You two…" He asked nonchalantly, and Wrenley sighed in frustration.

"I don't fucking know what we are anymore. He leaves without speaking to me, even though he asked me to marry him a week ago. I have no idea what is in that man's head."

Johnathan nodded in understanding, standing up from his seat and putting a hand on his back. "Sounds about like Bronson, my dear. The man is brilliant, and sometimes, he folds inward into that big brain of his. He's going to have to get his shit together before that baby comes. If not, it's up to you."

Wrenley reached out to massage her temples, hearing every word and realizing Johnathan spoke the truth. Bronson was such a complicated man, but she had to make sure this baby was safe and that she focused on this task. She felt the tea kick in, and suddenly, exhaustion hit her like a bus.

"Hey, you got this, kid," Johnathan said as he squeezed her shoulder and passed her. "He's not the only smart one around here...remember that." He winked at her and disappeared into the darkness.

~ ~ ~ ~ ~

Wrenley finished her tea and cookies, feeling the fatigue wash over her. She knew she would be lucky to make it up the stairs to her bedroom before her legs gave out. She gathered her books, returned them to the shelves, and left the library, her eyes growing heavy. She pulled herself up the cold wooden stairs and sighed when she reached the second floor.

She neared her bedroom when she heard something, feeling a presence behind her. She turned sharply and breathed a sigh of relief when she realized it was Kage. She relaxed as he strode up to her.

"What are you doing up? Are you okay?" She said, putting her hands on his forearms as he stumbled slightly.

"I could ask you the s-same thing," the young man slurred, and Wrenley stiffened when he faltered again, tumbling into her and using her to steady himself. His voice was unusual, and it alarmed her. She recoiled at the smell of alcohol on his breath and tried to lift him off her, but she had forgotten how massive he was.

"Kage, you need to go to bed," she said as she tried to bring his arm around her shoulder to steady him. She gasped as he pushed her and suddenly felt a 'smack' on the back of her head as it hit the cold stone wall behind her. She saw stars but did not lose consciousness.

"Kage, stop it!" She yelled, struggling to push him off her. He pressed his body against her, placing his palms against the wall on either side of her. She began to tremble, fear beginning to take hold. There was something wrong…this was not right.

"My lady…" he whispered, lowering his head to her ear, and then grazed her neck with his lips and teeth. Wrenley sucked in a breath, placing her arms firmly on his chest.

"Kage, you are drunk…"

"I may be drunk…" he growled, bringing one hand to her face and running a knuckle down her cheek, down her neck, and to her chest. "But I know that you still desire me."

"Kage, you need to go to bed!" Wrenley hissed, but he pressed himself tighter against her, reaching to grasp her chin so she had to look at him.

"You aren't stuck with him, you know. Just because you both fucked, and you are pregnant, doesn't mean you have to be with him. I'd take care of you both…" He whispered, dropping her chin and reaching both hands to grasp her hips. He growled as he allowed his hands to travel to her ass and squeezed her, her face flushing. She whimpered as he withdrew a knife from his waistband and dragged it upward, resting the tip on her cheek.

"Kage, you are drunk. You are grieving. You miss your Mother…"

"Don't fucking talk about her!" He demanded, shoving her against the wall again by her hips again, but this time, she kept her head from thudding against it. He had bent down, pressing a hard kiss against Wrenley's lips. He tasted like wine as he forced his tongue into her mouth, his hands still holding her waist as he ground himself against her.

Something snapped in Wrenley, and anger replaced the fear she had felt in her chest. This bastard thought he could get away with this! She knew he was grieving and maybe was out of his mind, or perhaps he was just that drunk. It was the last straw when Kage's hand cupped one of her breasts as he pulled away from her mouth to kiss her neck.

"I will ask you one last time, Kage. Get away from me," she breathed lowly.

He didn't.

~ ~ ~ ~ ~

Bronson pulled off his coat, shook off the fresh snow, and handed it to the waiting staff. Peeling off his leather gloves, he hurried through the corridor to the stairs that led to the second level. All he could think about was crawling into bed with Wrenley, feeling her warmth against him. He had left without a word to her; she must be furious, scared, hurt…

"In a rush?"

Bronson paused on the first step, his hand still on the wooden banister. He groaned and turned stiffly at the sound of Johnathan's voice.

Johnathan sauntered up to Bronson, taking a swig from the silver flask he had retrieved from the breast pocket of his pajamas. It looked as if he had come in from the back, probably smoking one of those horrendous cigarettes.

"Would you tell me the truth if I asked where you've been?" Johnathan was nonchalant, looking up at Bronson and raising an eyebrow.

"I am struggling to see how that is any of your damn business, Johnathan."

The older man shrugged lazily, "Oh, it isn't technically. However, when I find a beautiful young lady who happens to be pregnant with your child, sitting alone in the library, not being able to sleep because she is thinking of you and your mysteriously absent ass…" Johnathan dropped the flask back into his front pocket. "Then it's kind of my business."

"Stay out of it," Bronson rumbled.

"I would, but you see, I was here when you weren't, offering her some emotional support." Johnathan stepped up, now level with Bronson, looking the younger man in the eyes, "And that is saying something…." Johnathan drawled, and Bronson stiffened as he almost detected a red glow in the older man's dark eyes. Johnathan exhaled through his nose, "…because emotional availability isn't a strength of mine."

"What do you want, Johnathan?"

Johnathan's eyes narrowed, his face scanning Bronson up and down before saying, "I suggest you get your head out of your ass and pay attention to what's right in front of you. Let the past go,

Bronson, and get her caught up to the same damn page as you. Tell her the truth before it's too late."

Bronson was about to punch Johnathan's smug face when he heard a scream from the second floor. Bronson and Johnathan snapped their heads towards the sound in unison, and Bronson was the first to dash up the stairs, taking two at a time. Heart pounding at the scream, Bronson turned the corner in the stairway, skidding, and rounding to see a light flash, an energy pushing him back slightly. He could make out the silhouette of a man flying across the foyer and landing on a table, his weight crushing it.

"Wrenley?" Bronson rushed to the source of the light, and slowed as Wrenley stood in her nightgown, her skin glowing and light palpating through her. Bronson swung back towards the man in a heap on the floor and felt anger surge through him as he recognized Kage's significant frame attempt to stand up.

Bronson took a moment to breathe, fury filling his entire being as he put the pieces together.

"Bronson!" Wrenley yelped, running to him and grabbing his arm. He looked down at her, her robe undone, breasts almost hanging out. Bronson's rage only intensified as he noticed her swollen lips, his eyes honing in on a bite mark on her neck. She was panting, shaking violently, and Bronson gently reached for her forearms.

"Johnathan? Please escort Wrenley to her room." It was not a request but a command. Bronson's voice was calm and cool, giving Wrenley a gentle squeeze before he released her, and Johnathan ushered her away.

Bronson cracked his neck as he stalked over to the young man, who was now on his knees, trying to pull his drunk musty ass up from the ground. Bronson smiled slightly, knowing Wrenley had undoubtedly taken care of herself. Kage was bleeding from somewhere, but not enough for Bronson to care. Bronson picked up Kage by the shirt collar as if he weighed nothing and slammed him against the wall.

"What…the fuck…do you think you're doing?"

It was not a question as fury dripped off every pronounced word. Bronson's voice was a low snarl, and he saw fire. Every fiber of his being wanted to unleash a dark, unspeakable magic on this prick. He smelled the wine on the younger man and cursed, pressing his muscular forearm against Kage's throat. Kage began to writhe in panic, scratching at Bronson's arm, attempting to release himself, gasping for air.

"Do you know the penalty for assaulting a queen, you dumb fuck?" Bronson's voice was low as he whispered in Kage's ear. He put more pressure on Kage's throat, enjoying the sounds of his wheezing.

"You would be hung, drawn, and quartered in front of the entire court. You would be dismembered, piece by piece, sometimes when you're still alive," Bronson released the pressure slightly, slapping Kage across the face with his other hand and grabbing a handful of dark hair, "And that was if you are lucky. But you, my friend, are not so lucky…you know why?"

Kage was frozen, not responding as his large eyes took in every bit of Bronson's wrath.

"You not only just assaulted a queen, *my* queen…" he shook the younger man by the collar of his shirt, "…but my fiancée, who's carrying my child."

Bronson felt his magic stirring, and he knew that whatever he did to Kage, he could not do it with magic, even though he desperately wanted to cast some unnatural spell on the boy to teach him a lesson he would never forget.

~ ~ ~ ~ ~

Wrenley felt her magic dissipate as she sat on the edge of her giant bed. Johnathan led her in, sat her down, and gave her a once-over. His gaze slowed at her neck, where the bite mark began to bruise, and he inhaled slowly.

"Are you okay?" He asked slowly, kneeling before her, looking into her eyes that resembled his own. Wrenley shuddered as she took a breath and let it out, nodding sluggishly. She felt her face flushing, unsure if it was from relief or embarrassment. He gently reached for her chin and turned her head to the side, and she gasped as she realized blood was dripping from the back of her head now onto her nightgown. It must have been where she had hit her head against the wall.

Johnathan did not react but gave her a reassuring smile, "If you can manage for a few minutes, I'm going to collect your fiancé before he blows this entire castle into bits."

~ ~ ~ ~ ~

Bronson felt a hand on his shoulder.

"Wrenley needs you, Bronson. Go to her; I'll handle this."

Bronson froze, deciding whether he should kill Kage where he stood or walk away. Every muscle in his body was aching to pummel him, and Bronson felt himself press his arm against Kage's throat again.

"Bronson!" Johnathan's voice was sharper now, "This can wait. Go to Wrenley; I'll get Gwyneira and Alcott. Your healing services are needed sooner rather than later."

~ ~ ~ ~ ~

Wrenley swatted Gwyneira's hands away as the young woman whistled at the sight of the large gash on the back of Wrenley's head. Wrenley sat on the edge of the bed, leaning forward. Bronson had rolled up his sleeves and examined the wound.

"It's fine…" Wrenley felt queasy, primarily because of the sight of blood on the towels they had used to clean her hair and the area around the wound.

"It will need stitches unless you want to heal it." Gwyneira's voice was low as she spoke with Bronson, and Wrenley could feel him tense above her.

"I can't afford to use my magic…but the pain and stress of sewing it up would be equally harmful."

"I can handle it…" Wrenley tried to lift her head to interject, but Gwyneira shoved her head back down with one hand, making Wrenley grunt.

"I could use my power enough to numb the area, and you can stitch it. I'm not powerful enough to heal it all the way, but I can help with the pain." Bronson nodded in agreement, then barked orders to sterilize equipment and to bring clean linens. Though usually, healing the wound would have been fine, the burst of energy Wrenley had produced was enough to risk it for one night.

"Guys, I think you are exaggerating this."

"If we don't sew it up, it will take longer to heal and risk infection, which could harm you and the baby," Gwyneira replied dryly, and Wrenley clamped her mouth shut.

Wrenley was still looking down at the floor as she felt Gwyneira touch her head, a warm tingle sensation flushing over her entire body. The ache in her head disappeared, and she heard Bronson wash his hands and shuffle metal objects on the table next to them. Gwyneira assisted with cleaning the wound and Wrenley's blood-caked hair.

"Tell me if you feel any pain…" Bronson murmured as he began to stitch up Wrenley's scalp methodically.

"I think it will be fine…ahh!" Wrenley jerked her head as a sharp pain invaded her senses. Gwyneira and Bronson held her still.

Gwyneira snorted, "Sorry, I got distracted for a minute." The warm, numb feeling returned.

Bronson's skilled hands flew as he sewed her up, and within fifteen minutes, he was done. Wrenley was finally allowed to sit up and stretch her neck. Gasping, she noticed Johnathan, Bronson, and Gwyneira staring at her.

"Stop it, all of you! You all can't act like this when something happens to me… It's not like I had a concussion or anything…just a cut."

The three stood still, and Wrenley sighed, "You think this is bad? Just wait until I have to push out this baby. Only then do you have permission to worry about me. Until then, everyone goes away," Wrenley waved her hand and added, "And thank you."

Gwyneira and Johnathan shuffled out of the room, but Wrenley raised an eyebrow as Bronson shut the door behind them and locked it, shedding his shirt that had been covered with Wrenley's blood. She found herself shy as she took in his sculpted chest and stomach, now convinced the lightheadedness was because of how beautiful he was and not because of her head injury.

"What are you doing?" She tensed as he sat on the bed and fell backward, staring at the ceiling.

"I'm going to bed with you."

"But you've been gone…" She stammered, and he rolled over, propping his head on his hand, elbow resting on the bed.

"Yeah, I know. I'm sorry, Wrenley."

Wrenley finally felt the adrenaline ease out of her body,

replaced with emotions. Unsure if it was just because of tonight's events, she burst into tears and covered her face with her hands. Hard sobs pulsated over her body as Bronson snapped into action and pulled her onto his lap on the bed.

"It's okay," Bronson murmured in her hair, and she cried harder, her breath so shallow she began to gag.

"You left without a w-word," she finally said, shoving her hands into his chest and pushing him away. He did not budge, stilling as she struggled against him.

"We had such a terrible loss, and you just fucking left!" She yelled at him now, looking up into his dark eyes.

"I know. I'm sorry."

"What am I supposed to think, Bronson? You want to marry me, we have made this child together, but you can't even talk to me before you disappear for days?"

Her words stung; she could tell it by the way he winced.

"I can't do this, Bronson. I cannot live with the fear that you will pull away from me, disappear, or…"

Bronson silenced her by covering her lips with his, kissing her deeply. She struggled at first and then relaxed into him as he reached for the back of her neck carefully.

When he finally pulled away, Wrenley sniffed, wiped the tears away from her face, and pointed towards the door.

"Leave."

Bronson pulled away from her to look her in the eyes, "What?"

Wrenley backed away from him on the bed, tears silently falling down her face, "I need you to leave me alone."

She could see the muscles tense in his jaw as he took a deep breath and pinched the bridge of his nose with his thumb and index finger.

"Wrenley, I know you are upset…"

"No! I don't think you have any idea," she said, angry now, her face flushed as she noticed the throbbing in her head intensify. She reached up to massage her temple, "You have been doing this ever since you brought me here. You pull away, and bad things always happen. You never talk to me before you go inward and live in whatever world you've got going on in your head."

Wrenley waved her hands circularly towards him, "I was grieving, Bronson. I lost the only parents I knew, you pulled away from me, and I almost drowned in the river. You ordered me to bed and refused to come to me after you found out about this baby. When I wandered out, I almost died; and when my dear friend is kidnapped, and I have to enter into enemy territory to save her, to see her die in front of me..." She began to sob now, her small hands clenched in her lap, and she screamed at him. "I'm not saying it's your fault, but I need something more than you bobbing in and out of hard situations!" She motioned to her stomach, her hand resting on it.

"I can't do this anymore, Bronson. I can't be afraid you will disappear and not even tell me what you are doing. I can handle what you share with me. I'm tough enough for that, but I can't stand this wall you put up between us whenever things get uncomfortable or hard. My heart can't handle it."

Bronson looked as if she had kicked him in the balls. He looked away, and she saw his jaw flex in anger. She could tell he was masking the raging storm behind his beautiful brown eyes, and she desperately wanted him to offer this to her freely, without her having to pry it out of him. Without a word, he hoisted himself off the bed and stalked out of the room, slamming the door behind him.

CHAPTER 35

Promise

Bronson fell back into the hot bath and groaned, allowing the water to cover his head as he let his body sink to the bottom. He sat there momentarily, totally submerged, wondering what it would be like to stay there forever and not have to come back up for air. He reluctantly resurfaced, inhaling oxygen as his lungs ached from holding his breath for so long. He embraced the pain, maybe even deserved it.

Bronson was miserable and knew he had no one to blame but himself. Wrenley was right; all the things she had catapulted at him hours before had knocked the wind out of him. He shut down and walked away when things got hard. He had not been there when she needed him the most, which had a steep cost. He should have told her where he was going but did not think about it. He was so consumed with so many things that he forgot her needs…

"Does she even need you?" He said it out loud, aware that Wrenley was more powerful than anyone had ever anticipated. She needed no one beside herself on the throne to rule, but she wanted him beside her. He exhaled as he ran his hands down his face, feeling the stubble growing on his chin. The way she touched him, the way she looked at him, the way she exploded with energy when she thought he was dying, he knew that she wanted him in her life. And like a fucking, goddammed idiot, he was pissing it away.

The wounds and scars he had collected over the years were building up, building walls so tall that soon no one could get in. The years of war and fighting began constructing barriers around his heart and soul, and Wrenley pressed on them. He realized they still hurt, and it was not her pressing that was the problem, but that he had never been able to heal from all the tragedy that had overcome him the last fifteen years…maybe even for his entire life. This was his chance to recover for the first time in his lifetime. Even before the fall of the kingdom, these wounds had been festering. When Wrenley came into his life, he began to hope again. And now their child…

He groaned at the thought of him being such a prick that he had walked away from her tonight. He should have stayed and talked with her. He should have gritted his teeth, sat with the discomfort, and allowed her to force her healing energy into these festering parts of him that he allowed no one else to go. She was the only one he could trust to do it, the only one powerful enough to do it, yet he rejected her repeatedly.

Astara's words had ricocheted around in his head for days; the same brave look, the same smell of death, the same reality that he could not save them. It had overwhelmed him, so much so that he fled. He had traveled to several rebel camps, mindlessly checking in and gathering information that could have waited instead of facing his grief. Wrenley did not need to see him bruised and damaged…did she? And now the charge he promised to protect and look after was on the chopping block because of assaulting a royal…his fiancée, whom he also was supposed to protect; he guessed he had failed everyone all at once.

"Tell her the truth…" Astara had whispered, but no one else had heard. He groaned; the thought of telling Wrenley his secrets made him feel physically ill, but if he did not, he might lose her.

Bronson's bathtub was positioned to the east, and there was a large window overlooking the loch, the same loch that Wrenley nearly died in when the Kelpie almost abducted her. The night was ending, the sun was cresting over the calm water, and he knew he had to talk to her eventually. Raking a hand over his hair, he was unsure which was worse; finding Wrenley and apologizing or dealing with Kage, but both situations were inevitable.

~ ~ ~ ~ ~

Wrenley stiffened as she felt someone brush against her at the breakfast table. She did not usually eat with everyone else, but she had spent most of the night in the library and decided to pop in since it was close, and it smelled so damn delicious. The staff knew she loved sweets and coffee and had baked her blueberry scones with sweet cream and butter. Wrenley was on her third scone as she looked up from her book, tensing as Bronson sat at the head of the table, only a space away from her.

She was still so angry with him that she did not acknowledge his presence. She knew the staff had served him coffee and breakfast but forced herself to continue reading her book.

"What's so interesting?"

She did not look up to him; his dark, rich voice was making her body react.

"It's a history book."

"Hmm."

They sat in silence again. Wrenley finished her scone and sipped her coffee. Her face was flushed, and she blamed it on the heat of her beverage, but she knew it was because Bronson's eyes were on her. Finally, she slammed the book shut and whirled around at him in her seat.

"What?" She snapped, her nostrils flaring as her pent-up frustration slowly rose.

Bronson shrugged, "Nothing."

Wrenly narrowed her eyes, "Stop breathing so heavily, and stop looking at me."

Bronson looked at her and sighed, leaning forward in his seat, hands clasped together in front of him, resting on the table. "Wrenley, we need to talk."

"I don't want to talk to you," she said through clenched teeth, tossing her napkin onto her plate.

"We have to talk sometime; it might as well be now."

Sitting across from them and eating his breakfast, Garrick shoved his chair back and held up his hands, "I can't handle when mom and dad fight, especially not this morning."

"You can talk to your damn self since you like being alone so much," Wrenley barked, standing up from her seat abruptly. She was so angry at Bronson for walking out on her last night that she could have kicked him in the nuts, even if she had demanded he leave. She was going to remove herself before she erupted and obliterated him.

Unexpectedly, she winced in pain as her lower stomach

spasmed. Letting out a yelp, she doubled over, one hand on her lower stomach, the other bracing herself at the table. Her books flew to the floor, and she groaned.

"Damn!" She wheezed, holding her breath as the cramp ran through her body. Bronson was beside her in a heartbeat, his hands now feeling around her lower stomach.

"The baby…" She gasped, clutching his shirt in a panic.

"Has this happened before?"

"N-no," She sensed terror spread through her, knees wobbling as she ruminated on different worst-case scenarios. Bronson felt around her stomach and then looked at her face with concern. "Is it happening again?"

Wrenley did not answer immediately and paused to tune into her body. After a few moments, she shook her head slowly and said, "No…it's subsiding."

Bronson pulled back from her, his brow furrowing in thought as he once again felt her lower stomach. "I don't think it was a contraction. I think maybe you may have pulled something in your lower stomach. Any spotting or bleeding?"

"No," Wrenley whispered, worry etched in her voice.

Bronson shook his head, his hand glowing where it rested on her bump. "The baby is fighting against something…or in distress."

"Distress?" Wrenley grabbed the front of his shirt with alarm.

"Not inside you…not something wrong with it. But it is sensing something, and your magic is diverting to it again. I think you need to rest and drink water. You didn't sleep at all last night."

"Whose fault is that?" Wrenley hissed, pulling away from him and kneeling on the floor, gathering her books in her arms again.

"Why are you being so damn difficult?" Bronson reached for her arm, pulling her upright from her bent position.

"Me? Difficult?" Her heart thrummed from anger. "How dare you!"

Wrenley felt herself flush, heat rising from her core into her chest. If she looked down right now, she knew her skin would glow in pure anger, just like last night. She jutted a finger into his solid chest. "You are the one who is emotionally unavailable and…"

Wrenley had no warning: Bronson pounced on her, wrapping a

hand around the back of her neck and pushing her against the wall, crushing her lips with his, cushioning the impact with his other arm.

~ ~ ~ ~ ~

Bronson could not help himself; she might implode with anger, but he was willing to take the risk. He had to be close to her, and he had to feel her against him. He had to bridge the gap between them again before it ate him alive. Every day, as the harshness of life hit them repeatedly, it wedged them apart until it felt as if they could not find each other anymore. He was determined he would never let that happen again.

Bronson pushed her back against the wall, kicking her books out of the way as he kissed her deeply. She fought it at first and then melted into him, reaching her arms around his neck and stroking his neckline and hair. Bronson inhaled sharply as she touched him, and he pulled away from her, drinking in her flushed face and messy hair after he had run his fingers through it.

"I can't live without you," he whispered breathlessly, lowering his forehead to rest on hers. "I know I am an absolute asshole sometimes, and I know you need more from me. I can't promise to fix it all overnight, but I will try. If you allow me into your life, I will do anything."

Wrenley was breathless as she looked up at him, her eyes wide, arms still wrapped around his neck.

"I-I…am so confused," she whimpered, lowering her hands so they rested on his chest. He fisted her hair, gently lifting her head to look at him, her neck exposed. It took every ounce of self-control for him not to devour her.

"I will always be here, Wrenley. My life's purpose is to keep you safe and always catch you. I know you don't need me. I know how powerful you are, how strong and capable, and how stubborn you are…But I want you to find joy in me, Wrenley. I want your world to be better because I am in it."

He meant every word of it; in all the lifetimes, past, present, or future…this was the one promise he would never release.

~ ~ ~ ~ ~

Wrenley was breathless at his words. She pushed up on her tippy toes to kiss him again, and Bronson pressed her against his body, pinning her to the wall and finally consuming her. Wrenley gasped as she felt his hardness through his pants, his hands now under her sweater and traveling up towards her breasts. She realized she could not stay mad at him, feeling her desire overcome any grudge she had tried to hold against him for some ridiculous reason.

"Let's go upstairs," he said breathlessly, and a thrill shot up her spine. She felt herself squirm, heat beginning to build between her legs as she felt him grind against her. She was lost in his essence, smelling his musky pine scent, feeling his rough hands cupping her breasts under her shirt. Bronson nuzzled her neck and began kissing her softly, avoiding the bruise from Kage's attack last night. She moaned and arched into him, pushing her pelvis towards him.

Someone cleared their throat, and it finally registered in Wrenley's foggy brain that Garrick was still in the room with them. Wrenley felt Bronson freeze, his body tensing as he released a low curse. Bronson propped himself up with both hands against the wall on either side of Wrenley, not taking his dark eyes off her.

"What?" He snapped, still looking at her as she covered her mouth with both hands. She looked up into Bronson's sharp face, his hair tussled, his button-down black shirt only complementing his olive-toned skin. Wrenley buried her face in his chest in embarrassment, quite sure she would die of humiliation.

Garrick looked away, rubbing the back of his neck. "Not sure what's worse, you two fighting or making up."

Bronson exhaled, still not looking away at Wrenley, "Give us the room for a minute, please?"

"Sure…a minute," Garrick's voice was laced with amusement as he sauntered away, hands in his pockets.

Wrenley thought she would melt into a puddle if she had to face Garrick again. Bronson chuckled as he kissed the top of her head, her face still buried in his chest, hands grasping the front of his dark shirt.

"Fucking hell," he groaned again, leaning into her, Wrenley still backed against the wall. "You don't have to be here for this…" He whispered, and she knew exactly what he was talking about.

"No, I need to be here."

Bronson leaned in to kiss her again, and she did dissolve then, wishing they could ignore everything and go to his bedchamber and make love all day.

"This isn't going to be pleasant, Wrenley."

"I know, none of this is."

"This is uncharted territory for us…when your mother was queen, there was a way we had handled things like this. Punishing members of the court wasn't a pleasant affair, and sometimes she and Dolion let me handle it."

"I understand, but I am not my mother, and this isn't her court." Wrenley reached out and rested her hand on his cheek, pulling her lower lip between her teeth before saying. "I want to do things my way."

"Of course you fucking do…" he leaned down to graze his teeth over her ear, and then down her neck towards her chest. "You want everything your damn way."

Bronson released her finally, pushing away from her using the wall and swinging around to meander out of the room. "I've got to take a five-minute walk…without you. If that doesn't work, then a cold shower." Bronson threw his hand over his shoulder, reaching up to rub the back of his neck. Wrenley covered her mouth with both hands again to stifle a grin, knowing exactly why he had to take a walk. She bent over to pick up the books that had fallen to the floor. She tensed then, realizing the next several hours would not be easy for her or anyone else.

CHAPTER 36

Moloch

K age had been taken away by several house guards last night and locked in a cell in the basement. The memory of last night was still fuzzy, alarming, and heartbreaking, but she was more concerned about what lay ahead. As she ruminated about it, she felt the dull ache of the wound on the back of her head, a stark reminder of what had happened. It had all been such a blur, and uneasiness engulfed her as she pondered the events and realized something was wrong. She was very aware of Bronson's capabilities, and she supposed it was a miracle he had not slit Kage's throat on the spot.

Wrenley gulped as two of the house guards shoved Kage into the meeting room, his large body tumbling to the floor before them. Wrenley sat in the middle of the semi-circle, flanked by Alcott and Garrick on one side, Bronson and Johnathan on the other. She pulled herself up from her seat in shock, gasping as she took in Kage's bruised face. Trembling from the sight and smell of him, she stepped forward and reached for him, but a large hand grabbed her shoulder.

"Don't touch him," Bronson said lowly, but she shrugged the hand off her shoulder and glared at him.

"How dare you…" she hissed, looking up at him disgustingly. "He is our friend."

"A friend who assaulted you," Bronson gritted his teeth.

"I am well aware of that," Wrenley barked, shaking her head and looking around at the men in the circle. "What are we even doing? This isn't us, Bronson! We don't treat our people like this."

"We must decide what we are going to do with him," Johnathan said, sprawled in his chair almost like he was enjoying this. He picked a piece of flint off his black shirt sleeve and folded his hands on his leg.

Wrenley twirled to the older man. "Excuse me?"

Johnathan stiffened slightly to sit up straighter. "To have a proper court, you need rules. Your parents predetermined these rules…and their parents. This is the way it has been for centuries."

"Who died and made you the Pope?" Wrenley snapped out.

"What's a pope?" Gwyneira leaned over and asked Garrick; he brushed her off.

"There is royal etiquette to follow…" Johnathan began, but Bronson stepped in.

"I'm afraid he's right…" Bronson said softly, still standing beside her, ready to block her, but his hands were clasped tightly behind his back. "Kage assaulted you. It's a crime punishable by death according to our old laws."

Wrenley's eyes widened, looking desperately at Alcott. "Say something!"

She begged the twin first, then twisted toward Garrick. "You've seen him protect me. He saved my life; his family saved my life!"

"You do not understand our ways, Wrenley," Bronson said firmly, standing toe-to-toe with his queen as his skin began to glow. The room collectively winced, bracing themselves for a clash of incredible power.

"The penalty for a person assaulting anyone is serious, but to do it to you, royalty…" Bronson took a deep breath, steadying his voice. "We must uphold our laws if we are going to make this kingdom function again, starting with our own company."

There was no excuse for what Kage had done; Wrenley knew that. She looked at the man kneeling on the floor; the life had drained from his handsome face, and his characteristically bright eyes were hollow. Had they not all been through enough? She glanced over at Alcott, the twin sitting back, his knuckles white from squeezing the arms of his chair. Something was wildly off, but she could not place it. She felt it in the pit of her stomach.

"What do you have to say for yourself, Kage?" Johnathan asked, tapping his fingers on the arm of his chair impatiently.

"Fuck off Johnathan!" Wrenley tossed out at him, feeling her magic rising. She was ready to blow him into pieces with one wrong word or move.

"Wrenley…" Bronson moved to her.

"No."

It was that one word that sent a rumble through the room. The word carried a guttural sound outward from her, her magic rippling as it traveled from her lips into the air and, as a phantom breath, caressing everyone in hearing distance. The room paused to absorb it; the word was palpable and alive among them. Wrenley felt something stirring deep inside her chest, gut, and fingertips.

You have everything you need inside you… Astara's words appeared in her mind, fighting against the darkness that hovered in the room. She realized then that this was the darkness: the tradition, the etiquette, and 'the way it has always been'. How many years and centuries have people been the victims of traditions and rules only because finding another way was so much more difficult? She was looking at two different generations: one of the old ways and one of the new. As she took in Johnathan's superior smugness, she felt her fists tighten and her lips curl, showing her teeth.

In an instant, she was transported back to a time sitting in the doctor's office, and they told her, "This is just the way it is now." She had begged for another opinion, devastated that they could accept her life being cut short without even trying to fight. She floated back to when they said she was crazy for seeing and hearing things because they could not understand or see beyond their interpretations of the world around them. Then she saw the face of that child on the road, discarded and left for dead because she was not worth the time to save. The injustice burned at her, and she trembled with vehemence.

The reality of that injustice came tumbling down on Wrenley; for her entire life, she had lived in the confines of the expectations of 'this is just how it is,' and it sickened her. Never again would she allow another entity (time, space, dimension, or man) to limit her because of their superficiality. She was unsure whether she had allowed this because of her fear or faith, but it was time to break the cycle of ambivalence. It started with her creating a world where she did not have to walk away and leave others behind.

There was no excuse for hurting another. There was no excuse for Kage to force himself onto her and do what he did purposefully. However, she was going to assess everything before deciding to take a life. They were so ready to assume Kage was evil…but what if…

"You will fail…" Kage susurrated, bringing her back to the present as she shook her head and inclined towards him, meeting his hollow gaze. Something dark and cold peered at her as if it were reading her mind.

"What did you say?" Wrenley whispered back at him.

"You will fail," Kage droned again, shifting to look at her with an unoccupied glare.

Wrenley moved to approach the young man, Bronson, trying to grab her hand, but she spun around and held up a calm hand, "Stop."

That word again made Bronson stiffen, and he halted his movements towards her. Wrenley leveled him with a cool glare, daring him to challenge her. "From this time forward, we will do things my way. If you try to control me again, Bronson Aughton, I will unleash on you. I swear it."

Bronson's face faltered for the first time since she had known him, and she detected a current of fear passing through his dark eyes. She turned her back on him and knelt before Kage. She fought tears as she reached out and pushed his dark hair away from his eyes. She did not want to know what they had done to him for the hours she had been ignorant in her selfish world. Taking his bruised and battered face in her hands, she whispered, "What did you say, Kage?"

Kage looked at her now, but she did not recognize these eyes. The hollow sockets suddenly filled with rage, flaming with something that made her blood run cold.

"Annihilation…" Kage said so softly that Wrenley had to lean in to hear him. His jaw tightened as he angled his chin up towards her. "The star will fade and grow dark."

Wrenley's mind began to spin, flashes of images rushing her as she held Kage's face in her hands and rummaged through the nuggets of information stored in her head. Her brain hurried back to the tunnel, the room with the door…a door with a star. It meant something…but what?

She almost missed the slight shift in Kage's expression, his pupils dilating, and he lunged at her neck like a wild animal. She gasped but shoved him away, not hearing the yells and chaos that were ensuing behind her. Kage fell onto the floor, writhing and screaming, a voice escaping him that was not his own. Bronson had rushed before her, putting himself between her and Kage.

"This isn't right..." Wrenley panted, watching Kage thrash on the floor, even the house guards shrinking back at the sight.

"Bronson..." She said, grabbing his muscular forearm with both hands. "I don't think this is Kage."

Bronson snapped his gaze to hers and then back to the body on the floor.

"When did this start?" Bronson turned quickly to Alcott, who was standing nearby. The twin's face was pale, and his body was visibly trembling from seeing his brother on the ground.

"He hasn't been himself since Mother died."

"How long has he been saying these things?" Bronson was now yelling at the house guards, and they cowered back slightly.

"Ever since we took him into custody when he assaulted the lady."

Wrenley squeezed Bronson's arm in reassurance and stepped toward Kage. As she took steps closer to him cautiously, his convulsions intensified. He was bleeding from a cut above his eye. Her gaze moved to the cut on his arm, and she looked on in horror, the cut now swollen, red, and oozing with pus. It must have been the smell that she noticed a few minutes ago.

Wrenley reached towards him, sparks erupting from her hands, and she gasped as a surge of light left her fingers and shot into Kage's chest. He screeched, and to her horror, he broke the cuffs that had bound his hands behind his back, flipping over unnaturally as he landed on his hands and knees. Wrenley did not balk but generated another ball of light in her hand, this time shooting it forward toward him but keeping it connected to her. She held it, now using both hands outstretched as Kage was lifted off the ground by the light. He began to scream again.

"I will kill you, like your mother! I will tear that bastard from your womb!" He yowled now, his voice booming. It was as if Kage's skin and bones were warping, now twisted into an ugly, translucent beast with tattered wings. Wrenley panted but held him there with her light; the creature was writhing as it began to detach from Kage's body. Wrenley could also feel Bronson beside her, his power reaching the beast with hers. Its head almost swiveled entirely on its shoulders as it smiled, three eyes decorating its forehead, its snout-like mouth stretching into a smirk, revealing long, razor-like teeth.

"Who are you?" Wrenley commanded an answer, and the beast thrashed around, almost see-through as it detached from Kage's physical form, solidifying when it was entirely separated from its host's body. Kage fell to the ground, but the beast stayed in the air as the light seemed to burn its inky skin.

"Who are you?" Wrenley screamed again, and it laughed. The sound was deep and ominous…the creature finally looked at her with those three eyes. He curled his lip back to reveal large fangs growing from a bull's head with horns.

"What a pretty little queen." his voice almost shook the room, his wings, arms, and legs stretching, doubling in size. "I see you are delicate."

"I see you are struggling…" Wrenley mocked, and the demon hissed as she pushed more energy into him. He hammered against her with his mighty wings, but she kept him in place.

"You will fall, just like your mother and your father. You will die…" The demon chuckled at its size but was still locked in Wrenley's power.

"Who are you?" Wrenley said again; a flick of her wrist sent a jolt of heat into the creature.

"They call me Moloch," he groaned, the sound sending a wave of nausea through her.

"What do you want, Moloch?" Wrenley asked, noticing Bronson had stilled, his eyes focusing on the creature. Moloch growled and stretched his body and wings again, his leathery skin cracking and grinding as his muscles bulged with the movement. This creature was the epitome of power, rage, and darkness from the pits of hell itself.

"I am not just one…But I am many. I want the blood of your children," he said, grinning again. "If I extinguish the star, I am promised all the children I could ever want." The demon began to laugh, and suddenly, Wrenley felt heat travel down the light trail into her hands. Pain seared through her body with such intensity that it brought her to her knees.

"Who is your master?" Wrenley absorbed it, clenching her teeth as she fought against the demon's black power.

It snorted. "He is already here. Your seer knows who he is…" The demon nodded his ugly head toward Bronson. The seer stood firm, light radiating from him. Wrenley only momentarily looked at Bronson and then returned to the monster before her.

"What does your master want from us?"

The creature tusked, raising a large hand and balling it into a fist, "Annihilation."

That word again; he had said it before, and her brain was reeling. Whatever this thing was, it was not afraid of her, of Bronson…God, was this what was on the other side of that door in the catacombs? He must have entered Kage somehow through the wound on his arm…had it been feeding off of her friend this entire time, and no one noticed?

Alcott had slipped behind the beast as it focused on Wrenley. With a nod from Bronson, the young warrior took his sword and leaped in the air, plunging it deep into the demon's back. Black blood squirted out of Moloch, and it waved its long arm backward, making contact with Alcott. The young man was thrown to the floor with a crunch.

Bronson moved with lightning speed, one hand wielding his power and the other reaching for his dagger in his boot. With the sword still in Moloch's back, he could not move out of Bronson's reach soon enough. Bronson leaped, stair-stepping up the demon's body and landing his blade on the top of its head. Moloch slumped and crumbled to the floor, Bronson quickly propelling himself off and landing only feet away.

Wrenley gasped as she pulled her hands back, the light retracting as life disappeared from the demon's dark eyes. The room seemed to freeze for a moment, Wrenley falling backward onto her ass and scrambling away from the creature, as its black blood began pooling towards her. She could not look away from it as its large, protruding eyes looked up at her lifelessly, the energy fading from its gaze. Her breath was shallow, and her mind was reeling from the information she was now piecing together like a jigsaw puzzle in her head.

"Wrenley!" Bronson was beside her, trying to scoop her up in his arms, but she shoved him away. "Stop it; I don't need to be carried." Wrenley was on her feet instantly, dashing to where Kage's body lay motionless on the floor. She flung herself next to him and pulled him into her arms, Gwyneira behind her.

"Help him!" she yelled to Bronson, and he knelt beside her.

"He's alive…" Bronson said breathlessly, and Wrenley bit back a howl.

"Kage!" She shook him, and the young man moaned and stirred slightly in her arms. Alcott was beside her, and they all held their breath as the young warrior opened his eyes and looked at them.

"I saw something…" he rasped, and Wrenley could feel him tense in her arms.

"Rest, Kage, don't move." She jerked her chin at Gwyneira, and the young woman dove into the middle, pushing Bronson and Johnathan away.

"We still don't know if more of that thing is in there…" Johnathan protested.

Wrenley threw him a warning look. "From now on, you don't speak or even look at my people. Whatever could be possibly left over in him can't be half as bad as the monster in you."

Her words hit home, and Johnathan stepped back.

"I want us to use any magic necessary to heal him, you hear me?" She stood and tossed the command at Bronson, and he raised his eyebrows at her.

"What?" She growled, ready to fight anyone who dared to get in her way.

"Nothing…" Bronson shrugged, kneeling and laying his hands on Kage's head to evaluate the damage. If he were going to make some smart-ass comment about being aroused, she'd kill him.

"I saw an army… thousands and thousands…" Kage grabbed the front of Bronson's shirt and shook it. "So many of them, just like him."

"Of those things?" Garrick asked, pointing to the demon's corpse.

"Yes, and worse. So much worse…" he passed out as Bronson began healing him.

Wrenley shook her head, the reality sinking into her bones and making her want to purge the contents of her stomach. She had felt something beyond that door, but it had not felt evil. Ancient but not cruel. Moloch's words clanked around her skull until she snapped her head up.

"Bronson! The library…" Wrenley used Bronson to propel

herself forward and heaved her body to a standing position, darting out of the room towards the library where she had spent most of her time these past weeks. She heaved, her head tender, her pulse throbbing as she ignored Bronson's shouts for her to wait for him. She dashed across the foyer into the library and knelt by the stack of books on her chair, which she had deposited earlier.

"Wrenley?" Bronson was behind her, but she did not respond. She tore through the books until she found a large, leather-bound book, picking it up and holding it to her chest.

"Bronson, I think I understand now," she met his gaze after several minutes of searching the text. "I came across this a few weeks ago, before Astara…" Wrenley slammed the large book on the table in the library, opening it and turning frantically through its thick pages. "But then, the night we went to get Astara, I didn't get to talk to you about it…" Wrenley felt the pain of it hit her again, but she pushed it away. "We came into a cavern in the catacombs. It was a room about this size with a large wooden door. Do you remember, Johnathan?"

The older man shrugged, "Maybe? I'm not sure…" Wrenley paused, arriving at the chapter she sought, and shoved the book towards Bronson.

Johnathan shook his head again, "I'm sorry, I can't remember when the beast is present sometimes…"

"What are you saying?" Bronson's brow furrowed in thought as he studied the pages. She felt something change in him, like he had schooled his features, but she pushed the feeling aside and continued.

"I don't know how it all fits…but this book is folklore. It describes a door in the earth, one with a star…"

"What in the hell is the folklore behind the door?" Garrick placed his hands palm down on the table, leaning over to catch a glimpse.

"According to this book, it's a portal…" Wrenley's face drained of all color then, and she fell silent. She took a slow breath and stepped back, swallowing the lump that had suddenly clogged her throat. Kage had broken the smaller door in the catacomb; black, ugly creatures came flying out. She realized they looked precisely like Moloch, only they seemed…underdeveloped? Younger? She then remembered one had injured Kage as it flew by, perhaps being the entryway through which the demon had gained access to him.

"What if these things came from a different world? That they are being brought here…" Wrenley did not want to finish the thought. Alcott cursed behind her.

"It can't be…" Bronson muttered, raking his hands through his dark hair. "I thought these were…" He trailed off, pinching the bridge of his nose with his thumb and forefinger. He seemed to think for a long moment, and Wrenley could not read the emotions that flashed over his face.

"Think about it: there must have been some truth to them because you and Dolion found a way to travel without these doors. We know without a doubt that there are other dimensions. Why is it so hard to believe that maybe there are doors to them?" Wrenley said.

I am not just one…But I am many. The words returned to her, and her whole body shuddered at the implication.

"Jesus Christ…" she breathed. "Bronson…is it possible?"

"Yes, this is possible," Bronson finally admitted, bracing himself with a hand on the table as if it had stolen the breath out of him.

The group collectively paused, each member deep in thought, each in their own way trying to piece things together. Bronson cursed softly, his muscular shoulders sagging in a position that reminded Wrenley of defeat. He breathed and looked at her. "I need to speak with you, Wrenley…alone."

~ ~ ~ ~ ~

Bronson was somber as he watched Wrenley undress in his room. His eyes were distant but also longing as she threw her dress aside and warily stepped into the bathtub to wash Kage's blood from her. He was sitting on a stool in the corner of the washroom, shoulders collapsed as he leaned forward, elbows resting on his knees.

Wrenley caught a glimpse of her naked body in the full-length mirror, and she gasped, a hand flying to the defined bump of her stomach. She inhaled sharply and looked at Bronson, and he smiled wearily. "You used magic. She grows when you use magic."

Wrenley sighed softly, then gently lowered herself into the warm water and moaned. Her entire body ached, and the back of her head throbbed. She felt spent after using so much power. This confirmed that she needed to learn more, train harder, and build endurance.

"We have to leave, don't we?" She whispered, and Bronson nodded, pulling himself off the stool and loosening the buttons on his shirt.

"Yes. Every seer in a hundred miles felt what you did tonight. We must move as far away from here as we can. We'll leave in the morning." He stripped and discarded his clothes absently on the floor.

"I'm so sorry…" Wrenley murmured, breathing in sharply as Bronson climbed into the bathtub and sat behind her. She still was not used to their intimacy as they learned about each other and their relationship. It could still be awkward at times, but she allowed herself to nestle between his legs, her back against his hard chest. He wrapped his arms around her and leaned down to kiss her neck.

"I've seen a lot in this war and others, Wrenley…" Bronson trailed off as if to think again. "But I have never seen anyone do what you did tonight."

"What exactly did I do?" Wrenley tone was soft, and his arms tightened around her.

"You removed a demon that had attached itself to Kage. How did you know?"

Wrenley sighed and shrugged. "It wasn't Kage when I looked into his eyes. It was…death."

"Everything in my body and soul wants to react to this and hide it from you, but I can't do that anymore, Wrenley. It's time you knew the truth."

"The truth about what?"

Bronson leaned back into the tub, resting his head on the back of the tub and looking at the ceiling. "Your father, the portals, everything."

CHAPTER 37

Doors

"We knew there were portals to other dimensions; we just didn't know where or how to access them." Bronson covered Wrenley with a feather-down quilt and pulled her to his chest as they lay in his bed, resting his chin on her shoulder. While she had dried off and readied for bed, Bronson checked in on the twins, Garrick, Gwyneira, and Johnathan. Kage rested comfortably with the help of some pain tonics concocted by Gwyneira.

"Your father had always been curious, but he became obsessed after he married your mother. This book explains things that now make so much sense about what your father was saying. It must have been something we lost in history for thousands of years. Your father must have known about the dimensions and ordered me to help him create portals. We worked tirelessly for years, and I wasn't sure why he wanted this portal so badly. After the queen gave birth to you, we made a breakthrough in our work, and I found a way to cross over into your dimension."

"What about the door? Why not use it?"

Bronson shrugged, "I didn't know about it, or I would have. Whether your father knew about it or not, I'm not sure, but he wanted to break open new pathways. Two months after you were born, the darkness from the sea swept in. Sea monsters, a dark fog, beasts, and animals our lands hadn't seen in centuries, appeared out of nowhere. We had thought they came from across the sea all this time…but maybe we had let them in."

Wrenley turned to look up at him, and Bronson rested his head on her chest now. "To please my king, I had altered the fabrics of time and space, and I think I opened portals from other places. We tried to contain it the best we could, but Earnesh had slipped through somehow…and I think it was my fault."

Wrenley plunged her hands into his hair and gently caressed his scalp. Her heart hurt at the sound of grief in his voice. "It wasn't your fault, Bronson. He could have come from anywhere."

Bronson sighed. "The way we were working, we could have tapped into anything. I had opened just a pocket. What would have happened if I opened an entire damn door?"

"What if Earnesh is looking for a portal big enough for an army?" Wrenley's stomach tightened as dread swelled in her. "Oh, my God…that's exactly what he was looking for..."

Bronson nodded. "And he found one big enough to march an army of those creatures through, right here in Ailios. That must be his endgame."

"How did he know? About anything?"

"It's hard to say exactly because the worlds cross over with each other. Have you seen it, Wrenley, when ghosts appear and strange things happen? It's not the spirits of the dead but others in dimensions parallel to yours. The dimensions find small tears where we cross into each other's worlds, maybe even by accident. For someone who has magic and knows what to look for, they can see where souls bleed through. You may call them 'mediums' in your world. Earnesh must have this gift somehow. He had just waited for a time to strike. When they breached the castle, your father was killed, and your mother handed you to me and ordered me to save you…that is when he made his move. Why does he want to bring an army here? God only knows…"

Wrenley wrapped her arms around Bronson's head, feeling his tears spill onto her chest.

"So, Earnesh found the door? That is why he placed all those troops in the catacombs?"

"Yes, but even though he found the door, he doesn't know how to open it…yet. If he did, this world and the next would be occupied by his forces. I think that's why he needed you. You were the key to unlocking the portals so he could march into other dimensions and conquer them all. He's been working on this for fifteen years, waiting to find you."

"I felt something on the other side," Wrenley whispered, fear forming like a rock in her gut. "When I reached for the door, it was as if they called to me. Why though? Why me?"

Bronson sighed, "I'm not sure, Wrenley…but we have to find out."

CHAPTER 38

Cryptic

The company packed only what they would need: food, clothing, medicines, and weapons. While servants and company members were occupied, Wrenley slipped into the library and tore out the pages containing the information and lore about portals. She knew they would need this knowledge in the coming weeks and only felt slightly guilty for ruining the books. However, she supposed that if the world ended and a demon took over, this would be the least of their worries. She also stole the pages with her mother's beautiful face on them, so maybe someday, if they lived to see it, her daughter would know about her grandmother.

The group was solemn as they descended from the highlands and headed east toward the coast. They intended to stay in the highlands until spring; then, they would venture west towards the capital to meet with Nicolas and any forces he and others could recruit. Unfortunately, her use of power compromised their location. Though her magic was new, and many may not be able to identify who she was through it, it was enough. Though it was warm and safe and the ideal place to hold out for the remainder of the winter, the risk was too significant.

Wrenley sat atop her horse and shivered as the wind whipped around her. She was still chilled, even in her heavy cloak, tunic, and pants, and would probably remain that way for the rest of her life since the Kelpie incident. She wished she could ride with Bronson, but they could move faster on their own mounts. Shivering, she gritted her teeth as she ducked out of the way of a low-hanging branch.

"Your face is blue."

Wrenley turned to the left to greet Johnathan and nodded, "Yes, I imagine it is."

She stiffened as he moved beside her, still not fully trusting the man. Wrenley had tried to like him, but she felt an uneasiness in his energy, and after what had happened with Kage, she did not consider him a part of their company.

"We should reach our destination by nightfall; don't freeze on us now." The older man looked comfortable in his heavy fleece-lined parka, hat, and scarf. He looked different from the rest of them, opting for his clothes from Alaska rather than the current fashion in Ailios. She supposed that compared to the Alaskan tundra, this weather was mild. Not to mention, he had the blood of a beast in his veins to keep him warm.

"You look just like her."

Wrenley gave him a sideways glance and raised an eyebrow.

"Adinnil…You look just like her."

Wrenley felt something in her chest at the mention of the woman she had been researching for all these weeks. Perhaps, now that she knew she carried a daughter in her womb, her mind drifted to her biological mother more frequently.

"What was she like?" she ventured to ask.

Johnathan chuckled, "Hardheaded, stubborn, and a pain in the ass."

Wrenley smiled quietly as she maneuvered her horse through a rocky spot on the path.

He continued, "But she was also beautiful; she was a kind queen and a good friend. She loved to learn, she was brave… she was a paradox. Just like her daughter."

Wrenley snapped her head around now, her eyes wide and her nostrils flaring just a bit.

"I'm not brave," Wrenley finally bit out.

Johnathan looked at her pointedly, "You are braver than you give yourself credit for, my dear."

"I am weak…" Wrenley said softly, her voice almost being carried away by the icy wind that whipped around her face.

"Everyone has weaknesses…" Johnathan shrugged. "But we all have a chance to take a stand. You have proven your courage and strength twice since I've met you."

"Hmmm…" she mused, focusing on the path before her.

"You need to train and hone your abilities," he said coolly. "Remember that your physical and spiritual parts are still adjusting to this world. I feel the strain on my body, but I am also older than you."

Wrenley paused for a moment, weighing her following words carefully.

"How do you turn into Wendigo?" She had been dying to ask, desperate for the secret of Johnathan's transformation. She had seen the beast take out a small army of soldiers; his speed was like lightning, and his strength was otherworldly.

Johnathan wiggled his bushy eyebrows. "You want to know?"

Wrenley nodded earnestly, not only wanting to know the details but wanting a distraction so she would not focus on her frozen arms and legs. Johnathan pursed his lips, his salt-and-pepper goatee making him look older, but his eyes still held a spark of youth.

"Wendigo is a powerful spirit from another realm that I stumbled on while experimenting with my magic. Where you and I come from, he is a cryptic in the northernmost part of the United States. But he isn't just a bedtime story or spooky legend; Wendigo is real, and he shifts back and forth between dimensions. My calculation suggests there are only a handful of them left."

Wrenley felt a chill crawl down her back and arms. "Like Bigfoot?"

Johnathan threw his head back and laughed, and Wrenley could not help but grin at his response.

"Though I have never encountered a 'bigfoot,' I wouldn't be surprised if there were some creatures that resemble him and travel between worlds. During my thirty years in exile, I had some free time to study their commonalities."

Pausing dramatically, he reached into his breast pocket and pulled out his flask. "After researching and investigating these 'cryptic' phenomena like Bigfoot, Wendigo, Mothman...my research suggests that most of these obscure folklore cryptids probably travel back and forth between dimensions through fractures in the veil, and we humans are ignorant of it all."

"Like...through doors?"

He shook his head, "Not that organized. I suspect in certain areas of the earth, there are rifts in the dimensions, and these creatures have found ways to come and go. Like the Loch Ness Monster, for example."

Wrenley's eyes went wide. "How did you find Wendigo?"

Johnathan winced, "I used some spells and magic to trap him in this world; trap him inside me…and he threw a tantrum. Rightly so, I should not have done that to him, but I didn't know better. "

"Which is when you went on the…" Wrenley murmured, pausing awkwardly.

"Killing spree? That's what your Bronson likes to call it…" Johnathan gave Wrenley a skeptical glance.

She shrugged innocently, "…it is what it is."

"Yes. It took me two weeks of being trapped in the beast before I could figure out how to regain control and talk sense into him. The magic had tied us together metaphysically, and I hadn't found a spell to separate us. Honestly, even if I could, I don't think I want to. He has been my companion for thirty years. I've grown attached to him."

Wrenley knew her eyes were wide. She did not try to hide it. "Does he…do you talk to him?"

Johnathan's face seemed to reflect softness. "I hear him in my mind when I am in this form, and he can hear me when his form is dominant. Before you came and retrieved me, I spent most of the time in his form because it was more convenient and warmer. Some nights, I would morph back into this frail human body and sit by the fire, read a good book, and drink some scotch."

"Is he…friendly?"

"Well, friendly is a broad term. He tolerates me as I do him; we have gained mutual respect through the years, and he will listen when I give him an order. He likes you…"

Wrenley drew her brows together, taking it as some compliment.

"I'm sorry…" Wrenley finally confided in a low voice, turning her head to give him an apologetic look. "I'm sorry you were sent away and had to be alone."

"Oh, well, it was complicated. I must give your man some credit; he fought for me until the end…but Dolion wouldn't give in. He was so angry and so bitter…" Johnathan's eyes almost glazed over, and Wrenley felt she was witnessing grief in his stare.

"I lost my friends, queen, life, and work…all in a single

moment." Johnathan took in a breath and exhaled deeply, his breath looking like smoke as it curled from his lips. "But…here I am now, and I like to think I can undo some wrongs."

"Why come back and help us at all?"

Johnathan looked thoughtful, "For your mother, when the time came, she chose to save you. She fought bravely, and she died…" Johnathan's eyes misted over, and he shook his head. "She died saving you, and she died for her people. Knowing the outcome, Adinnil would do it again in a heartbeat because she knew you were just as strong as her and would come back someday. How could I not do the same for her daughter?"

Wrenley felt a sting in her eyes, her hand flying to her stomach, where her daughter nested safely in her womb. The thought of having to make that decision to send this baby away and never see her again, Wrenley could hardly bear the idea of it. She saw Bronson riding ahead, his muscular shoulders stiff as he led the company. Would that be their fate as well? Death? Ruin? Destruction of their family?

Family.

The word hit her like a tidal wave. She felt her daughter flutter in her stomach, and she glanced again just in time to see Bronson peer back at her in concern as if he felt the stirring of their child. She saw the relief in his eyes when he found her among the riders and grinned at her. This was her family now, and she never expected it. She had stumbled into it head-first, a candle in the sea of darkness encircling them. She looked at each of them: Kage, Alcott, Garrick, Gwyneira, all part of her heart now, all part of this baby's life.

CHAPTER 39

Folklore

By nightfall, they entered a small coastal village where Bronson hoped to find lodging. The company was exhausted as they reserved their rooms in the shabby inn on the outskirts of the small town near the ocean's shoreline. Cheap alcohol, fish, and occasionally a waft of piss assaulted Wrenley's sense of smell, and it was everything she could do not to puke. Wrenley felt herself cling to Bronson as they pushed their way through the crowded dining area, praying no one would recognize them or find them suspicious. He kept a protective arm around her and pulled her along, Gwyneira close behind, clinging to the back of his jacket, flanked by Garrick and Alcott. Kage followed from the rear, moving slower than usual due to his injuries from the days before. Wrenley was not surprised to see Johnathan desert the company and belly up to the bar like he owned the place.

Bronson, Garrick, and Alcott agreed that staying in two rooms was the wisest decision: staying close and taking turns watching the entrances overnight. Wrenley and Gwyneira looked at each other wearily as Kage slumped into a chair in the room, his features grey and pale. No one had spoken about what had happened, that there was a demon inside him, as if no one had noticed or cared. More alarming was that Bronson and Johnathan had locked him in a cell below the castle without even a second thought. She was still angry at Bronson for that, but she would deal with him later.

After settling in, Wrenley hunkered in front of the young man, her eyes taking in his defeated posture and hollow eyes. She gauged him, noticing the wound on his arm. The wound looked as if it were healing slowly, but it was still red and inflamed. In hushed tones, she and Gwyneira agreed that Gwyneira would also use magic to speed up the healing, as they both feared an infection. She turned back to him, still crouched before him as she braced her hands on his knees.

"I am so sorry," she said, grasping his hands and holding them to her forehead. "I am so very sorry I didn't step in, Kage."

"You saved me." The words were a whisper, but he looked down at Wrenley with eyes of shame, not anger. "I almost did something unspeakable to you…"

"It wasn't you!" Wrenley hissed, adjusting herself so she knelt between his legs and shook his strong shoulders, careful not to touch the wound. "You had no control, Kage."

"It used me, Wrenley." Kage's face was brimming with humiliation and guilt, tears welling in his young, brown eyes. "It used my attraction to you…"

Wrenley shook her head and gasped as the young man slid off the chair and enveloped her in his arms. His size always took her off guard; his chiseled chest and muscled arms held her tenderly. She realized that he shook with the pain and grief of Astara, of the violation of the demon, of the way the other men looked at him now…it was all too much for him. He held Wrenley tight and wept into her hair, and she let him. She embraced him and stroked his beautiful black hair, murmuring soothing words in his ear.

Wrenley felt as if her heart would break at the sight of this substantial, courageous warrior sag in such dishonor and anguish at no fault of his own. That demon had somehow entered him through a wound, slowly taking over his system and hiding in plain sight. The demon did not know Wrenley, but it had known Bronson. She shifted, his weight almost crushing as she whispered, "You must rise from this, Kage. How will you lead my armies if you cannot return from this?"

Kage jolted back, his face red and tear-stained, and shook his head.

"I could never…"

"You could never deny this to me, Kage. You will be my general. You and your brother will help me reclaim this land. We will hunt down every soldier in those caves and avenge your Mother. And we will make the world a good and beautiful place again. Promise me…for the hope of it all, Kage?"

~ ~ ~ ~ ~

Kage felt her words like a fire, consuming every doubt inside him, and the lingering darkness left by the demon was stifled out. He knew he should insist that she was making a horrible mistake that she would soon regret. However, looking into his queen's eyes, he knew she would never allow him to refuse. And he would do it…for his queen and the friend before him. Kage would lead her armies and kill every single one of those bastards. He felt something heal just a little then; he was unsure whether it was in his heart or soul. The unending blackness and shame were lessening as Wrenley's words landed on his consciousness and soaked into him.

Kage and Wrenley embraced once more from their position on the floor until Kage noticed the silhouette of someone in the doorway, as silent as a shadow. Bronson stepped into the room's light, his sharp gaze cutting through Kage like a knife. Kage knew he deserved it, and even though it was not his fault, Kage would not trust him if he were in Bronson's shoes.

A sense of peace engulfed him then, one he had not felt since before his father and brother left for the war. He knew, without a doubt, that Wrenley would be safe, and Kage could rest in the realization that she was loved and protected fiercely. Unexpectedly, Wrenley was not the beautiful woman he had imagined kissing under the canopy of the foliage of his homeland, amongst the fairies that illuminated the soft darkness around them. She had transformed into his royalty, and he would now treat her as such. She was his sovereign, and he would die to protect her from any evil that tried to touch her or her family.

He looked at Wrenley and then at the man who knelt beside them and grabbed her elbow softly. Yes, he knew Wrenley and her baby were safe in Bronson Aughton's hands, and it was time to surrender her and let her go. At that moment, he felt his heart release as he yielded to the unknown, gave up this woman who had fallen into his life, and changed the course of their futures.

He nodded to her then, "For the hope of it all, Wrenley."

~ ~ ~ ~ ~

The inn was about as drafty as a haybarn. Wrenley wagered a haybarn might be warmer with all the animals lying about. There were several cots in the room where the others slept. Bronson, Gwyneira, and Wrenley took one room while Kage, Alcott, and Garrick took the other. Johnathan had never shown up since he disappeared to the bar, and though she questioned Bronson about it, he shrugged and said, "He can handle himself."

Wrenley sat in the frigid room, tossed the covers off her, and lit a candle. She pulled out the pages she had ripped from the books before leaving. Quietly, she snuck out of the room and sat in the cold hall with her candle, shawl wrapped around her as she pored over the texts. She was silent, not wanting to wake Gwyneira or Bronson as they had been exhausted from traveling the day before. Gwyneira had curled up into a ball beside Bronson on his cot. Wrenley did not mind; she was too tall to share a cot with him, and someone might as well benefit from his warmth.

The origin of the door in the catacombs was unknown; at least, that is what the texts had reported. The lore started at the beginning of existence when a portal was made to be a bridge between worlds. Inhabitants of the different worlds traveled between the dimensions freely. They could easily communicate, work together, and pass through the veil. Wrenley had identified at least three dimensions, but there was a possibility that even more people, races, and species lived amongst one another. They had begun to come together and build an empire.

Then, three dimensions rose up to overthrow the deities, and being threatened by the masses of inhabitants working together, these deities separated the worlds and closed the portals. This led the inhabitants of each dimension into societal spirals, setting them back for hundreds and thousands of years. The deities decided to split the power between them, weaving their plans and powers to control the inhabitants. The portals were closed, and the inhabitants were made to live in different times, languages, and even species. It was as if a reset of the world occurred, and the various deities began to rule their respective realms.

In one of these dimensions, a young lord named Lucifer rebelled against the deities that had closed the portals. His dimension was the most beautiful and powerful of the three kingdoms, their species being the only ones who could figure out how to open the portals back up. When they finally did, they realized the two other worlds had fallen under the darkness of their deities; religions and cultures were created that spread hate and destruction.

Lucifer, a mighty warrior lord of his dimension, led a revolt against the deities to free the inhabitants from oppression and destruction. He went to one dimension after another, slaying the demigods and deities that promoted slavery, hate, and separation. He then came back to the two original dimensions, who had tried to make a structure to reach their deity, a tower; but after centuries of war and fighting, his legions crumbled, and he was defeated. He was then sent back to his dimension, the portals were closed again, and he disappeared from history.

Wrenley sat back and gasped audibly, trying to piece together the information she was taking that sounded so familiar. She paused, thinking back to when she attended church with Ruth and Jim all those years ago. Lucifer was the name of a fallen angel in the religious texts of the church. These stories were not just folklore for this dimension; this could have been the Tower of Babel recorded in the Bible.

Was it possible that it was the same Lucifer? Wrenley then remembered what Bronson had shared about the dimensions rubbing against each other, and when there were 'rifts' in the fabric of time and space, they would overlap. Are there different versions of these events happening in other dimensions? If so, which dimension was this world, and which was the one she came from? Were there multiple Lucifers in various dimensions, or one that had somehow traveled into all of them?

Wrenley continued to study the text, discovering that Lucifer had different names. She did not know whether there were various versions of Lucifer. Historical texts that Wrenley was exposed to described Lucifer as an angel who fell from the heavens and attempted to overthrow Jehovah. So, he must be immortal if he can fight a deity. The Biblical text was supposedly over two thousand years old, and Lucifer weaved in and out of the text. So, if that were the case, he must be immortal and have an army. A magic army? An army that could transcend time and space? An army that had conquered and played with other demigods and deities? That must have meant a powerful army…

In the pages she pored over, she continued to read about Lucifer's military and how he united the legions of disgruntled archangels to rebel against the deity in charge. These legions could be so vast and strong that they could overthrow governments and gods…but why had they not been able to find victory in her world according to the Christian religion?

Wrenley had many questions: Was Earnesh's darkness contained to this world, or was it in others? And what did it want? Did Earnesh wish to march in and destroy all the worlds and pillage them for his reward and gain? Did the dimensions have different versions of Lucifer, or was Lucifer visiting the other dimensions, leaving his mark on history?

"What if…" Wrenley sat back and whispered so quietly that she almost did not hear herself.

~ ~ ~ ~ ~

"What if we went to find help?"

Wrenley kept her voice low as the company sat at the table in the cramped dining area the following morning. Johnathan had sloshed in sometime during the night and was so drunk he collapsed on the floor in their room. Wrenley had to sleep on the cot furthest away from him because of his awful smell. He was still probably sleeping off his stupor, and Wrenley was okay with that. She had decided not to trust him, no matter how valuable his monster could be. The rest looked at Wrenley warily, their eyes imprinted with fatigue.

"How do we even know if Lucifer is real?" Garrick murmured, sipping on a mug of tea and ignoring the breakfast before him. The crew was in rough shape, eyeing her with glazed-over expressions, weary from traveling.

"How can he not be? He is appearing in historical texts in all the dimensions…" Wrenley slapped the torn pages down between them all.

"She's not wrong," Bronson replied warily, massaging his temples.

"I feel like we need to go on more than this…" Garrick said slowly, resting his hand on the papers stack and patting them. "I want to believe you, but this is hard to hear."

"I know…I know it sounds crazy!" Wrenley started in excitement.

"If we could find this Lucifer…if he is even real…" Kage murmured, speaking for the first time in days amongst the group, "What if he could be an ally?"

"He must be real, though…" Wrenley reassured them. "He's not only in this world, but texts mention him in my world back home. There is an entire religion based on the concept of Lucifer."

"Say he is real; how do we know he would be willing to help us? What would motivate him to come here and fight with us to defeat Earnesh? Would we even want him fighting for us if he is known as the 'prince of darkness'?" Alcott asked circumspectly, the only one of them eating the food.

Bronson raised a finger, "I'm going to indulge you for just a moment. Let's say Lucifer is real and out there somewhere…it would be risky to convince him to help us. We would need a way for the fight to benefit him somehow if we could find him. Going to the other dimensions where he is supposedly 'locked' away and trying to convince him to come back to the dimension where he got his ass handed to him the first time, it would be an absolute shit show."

"Such a pessimist…" Wrenley murmured, and Kage grinned at her.

"What do we know about his defeat when he came here?" Garrick narrowed his eyes, curious.

"I don't know…" Wrenley shrugged, "I'm sure there were more books in the library, but I couldn't take everything. But now that I know what I am looking for, I can find out."

"That's if Earnesh hasn't burned the books in the city already. Nicolas is probably one of the only wizards with an extensive library to find this information." Bronson's lips were a thin line, and worry was drawing around his eyes. "And it would not be wise to be anywhere near Nicolas. It's too risky to have all of us seers in the same place."

"I mean, what would it hurt? If we can find Lucifer, why not just ask?"

"If Earnesh's army is as extensive as Moloch showed me, we will need a miracle to survive this." Kage sighed heavily, his eyes still heavy, his continence still downtrodden.

"They called it the Great Wars."

The entire company shifted to look at Gwyneira, the small woman nearly invisible most of the time. She gestured to the pages on the table, sipping her mug of tea nonchalantly, "I remember my grandfather telling us the stories of the old wars, where legions from another world came and tried to overthrow our lands."

"You couldn't have said something before this?" Wrenley said sarcastically, leaning towards her to hear every word. "What exactly did your grandfather say?"

Gwyneira shrugged, "Just that there was a time that an archangel from another world challenged our deity here. They fought, many people died in battle, and eventually, the legions were driven back to their world."

"Does Lucifer sound familiar to you? That name?" Kage's voice was almost desperate.

"Maybe? It's been a while since I heard the stories…"

"So, what do we do next?" Wrenley turned for confirmation from Bronson but raised her eyebrows when she noticed he was gone.

Chapter 40

Blaine Manor

Bronson felt the jab of the knife to his back but did not wince. Slowly, he rose from the table; calm, collected, and on high alert, he allowed the person behind him to steer him away from the table to the outside. He could not tell if the person holding the knife to his ribs was a male or female because of the thick black cloak and hood that concealed their face. Bronson was only mildly alarmed, mostly because he feared someone else might harm Wrenley. Bronson knew this individual would be incinerated within a moment with just an ounce of his magic. So, he allowed himself to be manhandled through the busy streets, passing by shops, bakeries, and other run-down establishments that were probably quite quaint in their prime.

Finally, after minutes of maneuvering through the streets, the stranger stopped in an alley hidden from the road. The stranger shoved Bronson into the dark alleyway, and Bronson allowed himself to thud against the hard rock wall, wincing.

"You don't do a good job hiding," the caped figure glanced behind him, and turned back to Bronson. He pushed his heavy wool hood back to reveal a plain-looking older man.

"Who says we're hiding?" Bronson crossed his arms before him, trying not to show his relief that it was not someone more threatening. Bronson sensed no magic or energy in this man, which meant he was not a seer.

The man's face was taunted, his eyes bulging slightly. "You have a lot of nerve parading her around this countryside with Dragon combing these lands."

"Dragon?" Bronson tensed at the name.

The older man nodded, his face almost turning green. "He rides that lizard beast. He has been pillaging and terrorizing us…" The man shook his head. "You must leave before they find her, please…or we will all pay the price."

"And who exactly do I have?"

The man sighed, rubbing his face with one hand, his thick shoulders drooping faintly. "You probably don't recognize me, but I was at the gathering many weeks ago. I saw you kill those men; I saw our royalty clear an entire table with a snap of her wrist. I am a friend…not a foe."

Bronson took in the man standing in front of him. He was older, probably Johnathan's age, if not more. The man was plump and short; his round face set in a disgruntled frown. Bronson's gaze flickered to the crest sewn onto the man's tunic pocket under the wool cloak, the insignia of the most powerful family east of the capital city.

Bronson allowed a lazy grin to creep over his face and held out his hand. "Perhaps we can help each other."

~ ~ ~ ~ ~

Wrenley hesitantly stepped into the corridor of the quaint but luxurious manor on the outskirts of the village. She thoroughly wiped her muddy boots on the carpet and pulled her leather gloves from her hands, noticing the room's warmth. Gwyneira, Kage, and Alcott flanked her, and she could sense Kage and Alcott's attention to the room around them. Garrick had positioned himself outside the door, standing guard. She noticed the twins rested their hands on the hilts of their swords, their eyes flashing around the room, ready to detect and neutralize any threat. Gwyneira yawned, looking bored, and she rolled her eyes at Wrenley.

"This place smells luxurious," Gwyneira drawled sarcastically.

"Hush!" Wrenley shushed the younger girl as two staff members came to collect their cloaks. Wrenley reluctantly gave over her cloak and gloves, noticing the twins had given up their heavy coats. They wore heavy wool tunics, pants, and brown leather boots like a second skin to their well-defined calves. Wrenley knew they had swords, daggers lined in those boots, weapons on their belts, and even under their tunics. Wrenley felt her magic stir and stuffed her hands in her pockets to hide the sparks, feeling her dagger that was slipped into her left boot.

Bronson had sent a message to the inn asking them to meet him here only thirty minutes ago. The messenger was a young boy who gave them the directions and left without any other explanation. Bronson met them in the hall, and Wrenley could feel herself breathing easier at seeing him. She had tried not to cascade into a frenzy when they had finally all noticed he was missing earlier this morning. Bronson led them into a spacious sitting room area where an older man stood over a map of what looked like the coastline, and several guards were also standing at attention beside him. When the older man noticed them, he snapped up and bowed dramatically.

"My lady!" He straightened and rushed to her, his outstretched arm welcoming her to sit at the table. She glanced behind her and motioned for the twins and Gwyneira to join her. Bronson cleared his throat when they all took a seat.

"Wrenley, this is Lord Blaine Howard. He is the presiding aristocrat over this territory. You may remember him from the gathering."

Bronson eyed her, and she knew enough to nod and smile as if she did. If Wrenley was honest, she did not remember anyone except Bronson. There had been fifty lords and other nobles in the great hall that night, and Wrenley could not pick any of them out of a crowd. Wrenley thanked the older man for his attendance, and she noticed his face was flushed as he motioned for the staff to bring some tea.

"Your majesty, having you in my home is an honor and privilege, but I wish it were under different circumstances."

"I do too, Lord Howard," she said quietly as someone had shoved a cup of tea in her hand and a biscuit in front of her. Gwyneira, with reflexes like a feline, snatched the tea from Wrenley before she could even take a sip, smelling it with narrowed eyes. Gwyneira then stuck her tongue in the scalding liquid and smacked her lips.

The witch shrugged, handed the cup back to Wrenley, and gave a lopsided grin. "It's fine; it's not poisonous."

Wrenley scrunched her nose, set the cup of tea back on the table, and pushed it away from her. Bronson ignored the exchange and continued, "This is Ian Howard, Lord Howard's son, and the presiding authority over this region."

Wrenley and Gwyneira's eyebrows shot up in unison as the captain straightened from his position at the table, his broad shoulders confident as he gripped the hilt of his sword. His chestnut hair was cut short on the sides with a few inches on the top, giving him a military look. Wrenley thought he must be in his twenties, if any older than Alcott and Kage. But those ice-blue eyes were brilliant and full of suspicion. Wrenley also noticed the thick white scar over his left eye and traveling down his cheek to his jaw. The scar was as furious as Ian was beautiful. He was an inch taller than Bronson, and his breadth and width seemed to swallow the room.

Wrenley swallowed as Ian approached her respectfully, took her hand, and gently kissed it. He grinned up at her, "My lady."

"I'm with her." Gwyneira shoved Kage out of the way to stand beside Wrenley and jutted her thumb toward the other female. Ian met her smile and nodded, "At your service as well, lady in waiting?"

Gwyneira looked to Wrenley excitedly, slapping her friend's shoulder with the back of her hand.

"Hah! He called me a lady…"

"She's a witch." Kage snorted from the back.

Ian leaned in to kiss Gwyneira's hand, and Wrenley could have sworn the young woman blushed. For the first time since she had known Gwyneira, she spied a hint of color in her usually pale white cheeks. Ian then turned away from the woman.

"As my father said, my lady, I wish we were meeting in a more peaceful time, but I'm afraid you have wandered into a warzone; it's not safe to be here…for you or us," Ian stated, turning back to study the maps on the table in front of him.

"We know…that is why we are on the run," Bronson turned to the Lord, then Ian snapped to attention when Bronson spoke. "We have been evading the enemy for a while now, but the numbers are growing no matter where we go."

"They are multiplying…" The captain turned to the map but glanced at Wrenley, "Maybe the ladies would like to rest or freshen up before discussing this? It is…unpleasant, to say the least."

Wrenley felt her hackles rising at the insinuation; like hell she would step out. Gwyneira must have noticed it too. The witch's silly smirk was now replaced with that vacant look she gave when she was pissed. Wrenley forced herself to smile as she placed her sparking hands on the table before her, no one missing the surge of her magic.

"With all due respect, Captain, we can handle being uncomfortable."

Something flickered across Ian's gaze as he eyed her, so quickly she almost missed it, but then nodded, "Very well."

Ian cleared his throat, "Dragon's scouting parties moved to this territory a couple of months ago. Before that, we would have an occasional raid, looting, enemy soldiers causing trouble, but nothing like the last few months."

"Dragon…" Wrenley's chest tightened at the recollection, remembering how he had taunted Alcott and Kage. It was the first time Wrenley had used her powers, and she had melted the men from the inside out. She recalled the commander, Dragon, all too well, and her only regret was that she did not impale his head with a sword where he stood when she had the chance. If she had, countless lives may have been spared.

"You have encountered him?" Ian asked in surprise.

Wrenley nodded, "Unfortunately, yes. I don't think he knows who I am, though."

"There are rumors and whispers of a company with a female magic wielder…" Ian again eyed her up and down, perhaps more now than before. His gaze fluttered to her stomach and backed up to her eyes. "I am assuming that is you."

Wrenley nodded silently.

"Dragon has mercilessly terrorized our village for the last two months," the older Lord chimed in, drawing an invisible line across a section of the map. "This is the river that separates us, and he has blockaded the only bridge going in and out from this direction. The only other way in comes from the highlands. The sea traps us on the other side."

"We have lost over half of our defenses, my men…my brothers," Ian said, his voice low with grief. "He sends scouting parties and kidnaps women and children; they kill the men and cut them apart and display them on the bridge." Ian's finger passed over a section of the map, and he shook his head, his ice-blue eyes flickering with fury. "They may look like men, but they are driven by evil; Dragon is not mortal."

"He can be killed..." Wrenley stated, pointing towards the spot on the map where she had first encountered him. "I knocked him over like he was a rag doll. His men will bleed and die like any others," Wrenley tapped her finger on the map.

"If he knows you are here, my lady, I fear a full-fledged invasion...one my men and I cannot stand up against." Ian's voice was almost a whisper, and he looked at Bronson and his father. "We are defenseless if the entirety of their forces hit us. They will overpower us, and your company will be compromised."

The room was quiet then, the silence heavy with the reality of the danger just miles away across the bridge. Bronson turned to the Lord, "We will leave today...We won't compromise your people."

"Or what if we could help?" Wrenley could feel the air being sucked out of the room as Bronson's gaze snapped to hers, his eyes flashing with warning. Gwyneira's eyes widened, and she stepped away from Wrenley awkwardly, expecting Wrenley and Bronson to throw blows at any moment.

Kage stepped up behind her, "I agree...we can't let these people keep fighting alone."

"We are not soldiers, Kage. Though I appreciate your enthusiasm, I'm afraid keeping Wrenley here is not an option." Bronson's voice was grim and level, but Wrenley could tell it was taking all his strength not to explode.

"Bronson, we can help!" Wrenley felt flush, knowing she would get a tongue-lashing from Bronson later for this, but she did not care. "We have a chance to not only help these people but to finally make a stand against this tyrant that tried to kill Kage, Alcott, and me! He almost killed us, Bronson...He killed Astara!"

"He will kill us all if we hang around and wait for him to come calling!"

"Then we don't wait; we take the fight to him. Once and for all, we take this fight to them, and we stop running," Kage countered, sounding every bit like the general Wrenley knew him to be. She felt pride bloom in her chest.

"They outnumber my men three to one, my lady. It's just not possible."

"It's not about the numbers..." Kage splayed his large hands on the map and pointed to the bridge. "We blow it up and cut them off. This time of year, that river is rolling with the water coming from the highlands. They will have to travel twenty miles either way to get around. We cut them off and at least make it harder for the bastards to access the village. After we blow it, we leave and track backward towards the great lake and catacombs."

"We cannot start this war, and if we were to stand with this village and blow up a bridge, the secret is out. Everyone will know you are here…" Alcott's voice was softer, but the concern on his face was undeniable as he looked at Wrenley.

"The war is here already!" Wrenley could feel her chest tightening, her magic flaring as she threw her arms up. "Wake up, all of you! People are dying; our people are suffering! Astara is dead!"

Wrenley stood and slammed her hands flat on the table, her magic rushing out of her, a gust of energy pushing against everyone standing beside her. Wrenley felt the grief, the loss, the anger of time stolen from her, and she wanted to tear something apart. It took everything within her to keep her voice from wobbling at the thought of her beautiful friend, dead.

"My friend, a Mother and an ally, was taken from her home and killed. If that isn't a goddamn act of war, I don't know what is." She eyed each of her people, the company she had pieced together bit by bit over the last few months. This company had given so much…too much for her to ask any more of them, but she would ask, again and again, until the threat was wiped away, and little girls, women, and even men would not have to fear anymore.

"How many more mothers and fathers…friends?" Wrenley turned to Bronson then, pleading in her voice. "We cannot sit back and let this continue. If Astara wasn't enough, what about the rest? Stealing women from their homes, chopping up their sons and husbands, hunting people like they are goddamned animals?" Wrenley was furious now, nostrils flaring, standing square in front of Bronson, the Lord, and the captain. She was sick and tired of being the quiet girl in the corner who took orders from the men around her. She was done feeling helpless and weak; everyone was waiting for her to break apart at the first sign of distress and danger. She would no longer allow people to feel alone, broken, and hopeless…no more…not one more goddamn day.

Astara's broken body lying on the ground in the torchlight flickered through her mind, and the anger roared in her head. She then thought of that girl…that girl on the road, so tiny and helpless with no one who would consider her worthy of saving. She then thought about Kage, tormented by a demon, but no one took the time to see him or to help him. Never again would she allow it to happen; this ambivalence ended with her, and it ended now.

"Wrenley…" Bronson's soft voice snapped her back to the room. She gasped as she shook her head and looked around her, sparks flying as she levitated several feet into the air. The Lord and Ian stared at her wide-eyed as she scanned the room and took a deep breath. Her arms were loosely outstretched, her palms up, and she lowered herself back to the ground.

Wrenley gritted her teeth, energy rumbling as she said, "I don't care what it takes; we will blow up that bridge. And I don't care if it rumbles the very foundations of Ailios, and Earnesh himself in the castle of my ancestors. We will not run away again."

CHAPTER 41

Covenant

Bronson took a deep breath, forcing himself to fill his lungs with air and then release. The alternative was his head exploding, possibly taking the entire building with him. Bronson had been in battles of brute force and magic, transcended between the fabric of time and space to different dimensions, and stood in the company of kings and queens. Even with that undisputed track record, Bronson struggled to keep his cool with this woman before him. The short, fiery, pregnant woman intimidated him as she raked him over with that look he knew so well; she was out of control.

Bronson took another breath and ran one hand through his short, dark hair, pointing at her with the other. "You are so goddamn difficult!"

"I'm difficult?" She spat, a hand flying to her chest in protest. "You do not control me, Bronson Aughton. I am your queen, and I say…"

"Oh, for fucks' sake, Wrenley! You have no idea what you are talking about. You have no experience with war, battles, strategy…"

"That's not fair! Kage knows, and he agrees with me."

"Maybe we should take a breath…" Garrick started to intervene but clamped his mouth shut at Bronson's seething look.

"Oh yeah, Wrenley, that's a great idea…listen to the guy who was possessed by a demon and didn't even know for a week until he tried to attack you in the hallway."

Wrenley's eyes bulged, her lips pulling back in a snarl, "That is enough! How dare you!"

"No, Wrenley, how dare you! You are constantly undermining

my experience and expertise, and doing this in front of the whole company." Bronson roared now, feeling his magic spark as he struggled to control it. "I deserve a little more respect than this."

"Oh, so now I'm embarrassing you? This is about your damn pride?"

"I feel sick..." Gwyneira whimpered, sliding into a chair and covering her ears with her small hands. "I don't like it when they fight."

Bronson squeezed the bridge of his nose with his thumb and forefinger, "Wrenley, no, that's not what I'm saying..."

"I think what he's saying is..."

"Shut up, Garrick!" Wrenley barked, flinging around to Bronson, "So what? I'm not the type of queen you were looking for, exactly?" Wrenley marched over to the bed and ripped her tunic off her shoulders, tossing it aside. "I'm what? Not submissive enough? Quiet enough? I don't let the 'men' do the 'man' things like a good woman should do? I don't need anyone to do this, Bronson, but you keep inserting yourself like you own me!"

Garrick and Gwyneira had quietly disappeared from the room, and any attempts to keep the peace were obliterated. Wrenley fumed, "My mother would never leave these people here to be tormented."

"Wrenley..." Bronson took a step towards her, but she slapped his hand away. "No, don't even touch me. I may have fucked you, but I'm not your compliant wife who is just going to take everything lying down."

Bronson stepped back like he'd been slapped, shaking his head, "Wrenley..."

"No, I don't even want to see you right now. Leave!" She thrust her finger towards the door without even meeting his gaze. Bronson just stood there feeling as if she had reached into his chest and ripped his heart out. He saw the regret in her eyes, but she was so stubborn she would not yield, not this time. Bronson turned abruptly and walked away. Opening the door with so much force that it slapped against the wall, he stepped into the hall and slammed the large wooden door behind him with enough power that he was surprised it did not shatter the windows.

~ ~ ~ ~ ~

She knew she had gone too far.

He did not deserve what she had said to him, and he was right: she did not understand war, battles, strategies…and he did. Bronson had been fighting this war from the beginning. It felt like he was stifling her at that moment, but she knew he was taking care of her and trying to keep her safe. She winced at the sound of him slamming the door. Guilt rushed over her as she hurried to the door and opened it, practically falling into the hall to catch him, but he was not there. She followed the only path she could imagine he would take, down the stairs and to the front door. She noticed Garrick leaning against the foyer wall they had been in when they first arrived, and she slowed her pace as Garrick bowed his head slightly to her. She knew then…

"He left?"

Garrick sighed and pushed off the wall, stuffing his hands in his pockets, "He needs a minute, maybe two. I'm not sure what you said to him, but I haven't seen him this pissed in a long while."

Wrenley covered her face with her hands and rubbed her eyes. "I am a horrible person."

Garrick chuckled, "I don't think horrible is the right word. We are all tired and on edge, and Bronson is just trying to protect you."

"He's always doing that…" Wrenley snapped, throwing herself into an armed chair sitting in the foyer, Garrick meandering behind her.

"Well, what did you expect? If he were to break his covenant …"

"What covenant?" Wrenley's head pivoted towards Garrick.

The man faltered, "Umm, you don't know?"

"Know what?" Wrenley growled, and she could see Garrick reeling, the strong male taking a step back. His handsome face turned a shade of crimson as he fumbled with his words.

"Maybe you should ask Bronson…"

She narrowed her eyes and curled her finger to beckon him closer. "Garrick, get your ass over here. I command you to tell me what you are talking about…now!"

Instead of standing under her scrutiny, Garrick looked like he would rather take on a battalion of demons. He shifted his weight from one foot to the other, a blush staining his face. "Wrenley, the last thing I want to do is be in the middle of this…"

"Oh, you just put yourself right in the middle. Tell me what you know!"

"I can't…I promised him I wouldn't say a word."

"Oh, is that so?"

"He took a blood covenant for you."

Garrick and Wrenley jumped at the deep voice behind them, Johnathan appearing out of nowhere as he always did. Wrenley swore, determined to get him a collar with a damn bell on it. Wrenley sat up in her chair and adjusted her seat. "Blood covenant? I don't understand…"

Johnathan sauntered into the room like a cat, picking a piece of lint from his black jacket. His silver hair was combed back, and his goatee freshly trimmed; he looked as if he had just soaked in the bath for hours and did not have a care in the world.

He took a lazy breath before continuing. "Before Bronson evacuated you, your mother demanded he swear on his blood that he would always be there to protect you. I'm not sure if you…" Johnathan sighed dramatically, "During your extracurricular activities, you noticed a scar under the left collarbone right over his heart."

Wrenley's face heated, but she shook her head, "I guess I never noticed…"

"Well, when you two make up later, I suggest you look."

"Careful, Johnathan…" Garrick snarled lowly, and Johnathan shrugged, holding his hands in defense.

"Sorry, geez, someone is sensitive," Johnathan said, taking the flask from his breast pocket, unscrewing the lid, and taking a long drink.

"Wrenley, Bronson's blood covenant to you trumps his loyalty to his people. He doesn't have the luxury to fuck around and find out. You can order him to do anything, but his first and only purpose will be to protect you. He chose that when he cut his chest for his queen and took you in his arms. It's magic, but also part of his culture, faith, and identity. Where your mother and Bronson came from, a blood covenant is the only thing that matters."

Wrenley had no idea, and a sick feeling flushed her as she

registered Johnathan's words. She had not considered why he acted the way he did sometimes. Maybe it was her own biases against herself clouding her interpretations of his actions.

She groaned and rested her head in her arms, "I'm such a fool."

"Maybe…" Johnathan screwed the lid back on his flask and slipped it back in his pockets, "…but now you know. Bronson isn't notorious for his communication skills, trust me." Johnathan rolled his eyes and began to saunter away.

"What exactly is a blood covenant?" Wrenley whispered, looking up at Garrick.

"It's an oath, a vow, and a pact sealed by blood. Because Bronson made the covenant with his queen, he is bound to it not only by his honor but also by his magic. We guess it's why he feels so connected to you…"

"We? You mean you talk about it with him?"

Garrick shrugged, "Bronson is probably the closest friend I have. We've been through a lot together, and I have been one of the only companions here since the beginning of this war. So yes, we talk about it."

"Tell me about him?" With this new information coming to light, Wrenley wanted to know every detail about Bronson, feeling she barely knew him. She had absolutely no idea he had deep, meaningful conversations with Garrick. Why could he not have those with her?

Garrick tilted his head back and exhaled, "There is so much, most of it is not my story to tell."

"But what about before the war? Where are his parents?"

Garrick's eyes flashed something, but she could not identify what. "Bronson doesn't talk about his father; he's only briefly mentioned him once in all the years we have known one another. Bronson's mother was a very wealthy and noble lady; her name was Chepi Aughton, and she was an influential politician in their lands. Their family was wealthy and powerful…but then war erupted, and everything changed. During the war, they had sent your mother and Bronson to Ailios…but they never returned because your grandmother was killed." Wrenley's heart constricted at the thought of Bronson having to leave his mother at such a young age.

"They both grew up together as brother and sister, and then

your mother's father, your grandfather, our King, died of an illness. That forced Adinnil to marry younger than she preferred and flung Bronson into another role entirely. He became her right-hand man, advisor, and captain of her guard. It was…difficult for him. His heart was with the seer community and learning the magic arts…that's how your mother and father met. Before Bronson's political responsibilities, he was a brilliant student who wanted to learn about magic. Your father and Bronson were friends for a long time."

"What about his homeland now? Does he talk about it?"

Garrick shook his head, "No, he never mentions it. If he wanted to talk about it, he would, so I don't ask."

"He doesn't share a lot…" Wrenley murmured, wrapping her arms around herself as she felt the chill in the air grow heavier.

"Do you want my advice?"

Wrenley chuckled, "I wouldn't trust anyone else for advice about that man."

Garrick grinned, pushing off the wall and stretching his arms above his head. "Bronson has always been one to shoulder the burdens by himself. I have seen the man butcher hundreds of enemy soldiers and make difficult decisions that have cost him his men's lives…I have seen him perform some unspeakable things, take accountability for them, and then mourn his humanity for it. He takes a while to allow people in and tolerate any help, because, in the past, everyone close to him has been taken away." Garrick's voice was low and thoughtful, his mouth peaking in a small, sad smile. "Just…keep trying, and don't give up on him. Promise?"

"I promise," Wrenley meant it with every inch of her. No wonder he shut her out like he did. Everyone who mattered to him had been ripped away from him. Wrenley raised her brow and asked,

"What does he say about me?"

Garrick chuckled and turned to leave, waving a hand. "Absolutely not; I'm not falling for that. Ask him yourself when he comes back."

CHAPTER 42

Swear It

The smell kept returning to him; the smell of blood, of fire…

Adinnil pressed the pennant into his palm and nodded her head. "Give me your blood…bind yourself to my daughter."

Bronson looked at his queen, his friend, his heart constricting and his head pounding as the castle burned down around them. She had never asked for his blood for herself. It was a sacred, ancient custom he had only read about in history books.

"Adinnil…"

She shook her head again, "No. Give me your blood, and give her your heart. I can't do what I need to do until you agree."

Panic flooded him, but he nodded. Adinnil reached out and tore his shirt open, the baby still wailing in his arms. She drew her knife and carved a two-inch slit over his heart. Then, she reached out and covered the sliced flesh with her hand, blood filling up the space between. He felt the magic soak into the wound. He felt Adinnil's love for her child absorb into him so deeply he thought he might buckle. He felt that love take a place inside him, something that was unbreakable and unmovable.

"I hold you to this covenant, Bronson Aughton."

Bronson gritted his teeth as the cold rain pelted against him. He had been so angry that he had not put on a cloak before barging out of the house and pulling himself up on his horse. He had ridden to the coast, finding a stretch of beach that seemed to go on for miles. He allowed the horse to gallop despite the freezing rain. The waves were rough and crashed against the shore, but he wondered if they could compare to all the emotions raging in his soul. His heart ached, the scar of his blood covenant tender as he had turned away from his charge and left her, possibly in harm's way. If he ever purposefully put Wrenley in danger or left her, it would get worse.

And then it dawned on him that Adinnil had known all along; she had somehow known that he and Wrenley would fall in love. She had known that they were meant to be united forever, but how she knew he could not comprehend. She had not forced him into a covenant to bind him. She had asked this of him because she knew their future. Had she seen their baby?

He recalled when he had lost Wrenley by the river, the uncontrollable horror he had felt in that week he had searched for her. The blood covenant jolted him awake and led him towards her. He felt his strength ebb as the days passed without her. It was the same jolt from the blood covenant that alerted him when she had left the house and damn near frozen to death. He noticed that when Wrenley had proposed such a brash, inconceivable plan today, it was not the blood covenant that had snapped him; it was his fear. He knew she was right…he knew that her words and convictions were true to who she was. It would be dishonorable to ask her to go against that conviction.

Bronson was soaking wet and so numb that he could not feel his hands, arms, or face—and he was relieved. He was so tired of feeling everything all the time: war, death, destruction, and living in a constant state of survival. He was exhausted from hiding, hiding Wrenley, hiding himself, hiding what he was…

Everything up until now had been ripped away from him: his homeland, his mother, his friends, and his culture. Then he lost his best friend, Adinnil, and the life he had thought he created for himself in Ailios. How many lifetimes would he have to lose the people that he loved? And now, he had Wrenley, a miracle in herself, and she carried his daughter. He would not lose them, not this time. Never again would he allow those he loved to be ripped away.

Bronson was very aware that Wrenley was under no romantic obligation to him. She did not have to like him, be in the same room with him, or even acknowledge his existence. But she was the center of his universe, not only because of the covenant, but because he loved her. He realized that even if she chose to take the throne with another lover, a husband who was not him, he would still protect her.

Swear it, Bronson.

I swear it.

Bronson knew better than to trap her in a box. She was too much like her mother to be caged like a fancy bird or wild animal. He recognized that for what she lacked in experience, Wrenley had the heart of a queen and the bloodline of ancestors that would guide her on this path. He had an opportunity to keep her safe while doing it, but God…he wanted more than that. Bronson wanted her for himself. He wanted to be her partner, lover, the one she cried with, and adored. He wanted to be her safety and fortress, standing between her and the darkness.

Bronson shook his head, the rain still pouring from the sky, the waves crashing against the rocks on the beach. He groaned and turned the horse around, acknowledging that he would have to accept Wrenley's decision about him and their plan, and that he would do everything in his power to protect her through it.

~ ~ ~ ~ ~

It was late before Bronson made it back to the manor. He could barely feel his body. It was so cold, even though the rain had stopped. His head was pounding, and his body was aching as he slipped into the back door and dragged himself up the stairs, unsure where to go. He would gather his things and most likely sleep in Garrick's room. Bronson found his friend's room, banged on the door with his fist, and waited several minutes before Garrick opened the door a few inches. Bronson was almost faint from the cold but raised his brow at his friend's haphazard appearance: ruffled hair, flushed cheeks, and naked body.

"Now's not a good time…" Garrick leaned his shoulder on the door jam, blocking Bronson's view of the room.

"Seriously? Where am I supposed to go? I'd rather eat glass than go sleep with the twins," Bronson gritted his teeth, pushing into the door. "And Gwyneira would probably turn me into a frog if I showed up in her room."

Garrick chuckled, "Why don't you try talking to Wrenley instead of avoiding her?"

Bronson shot a hand outward, palm against the door before Garrick could slam it in his face.

"Listen, I can't talk to her right now…"

"Yes, you can, and you will."

"She is…"

"…waiting for you in her room. She's been waiting all evening, pacing. I think she made a dent in the carpet in the foyer. Would you talk to her and leave me alone? Unless you want to join…"

Bronson raised an eyebrow as Garrick opened the door ever so slightly so Bronson could see inside. Alcott was lounging equally naked in his bed, grinning at him.

Bronson huffed and pushed off the door, "…you're no help."

"I am, actually, a huge help."

"Goodnight, friend…" Bronson said sarcastically and shook his head as he turned to hide his grin as Garrick slammed the door behind him.

~ ~ ~ ~ ~

Wrenley heard the soft knock on the door and shot out of bed, racing to Bronson as he slipped into the room. She recoiled as he approached, "God, Bronson, you are soaked."

"Yes, I am…" He said deprecatingly, shutting the door behind him.

"You are freezing!" She reached out and grasped his hand, noticing the blue tinge to his skin and lips as he stepped into the light of the fire.

"Yes…I am aware."

"You are going to get sick!" Wrenley pulled him closer to the fire and ripped his sopping-wet shirt off him. She gasped as Bronson then leaned over and threw up, going down to one knee, but thankfully, making it into a bucket they had used to bring hot water for her bath. She stood next to him as he heaved, rubbing soft circles on his back as his body shuddered.

"Sorry …" he said hoarsely into the bucket as he vomited again. Wrenley felt her stomach lurch, but continued to rub his back. He finished, pushed the bucket away, rinsed his mouth with water, and stood to his full height. "We need to talk."

"No, you need dry clothes first…" Wrenley put her hands on her hips, looking at him.

Bronson sighed and squeezed the bridge of his nose with his

fingers. "Why do you have to argue with me about everything…"

"Why did you have to stomp out like a child?"

"You told me to leave!"

It was a checkmate, and they both stared each other down unyieldingly. Wrenley shook her head and walked up to him, unbuckling his pants.

"What the hell are you doing?"

"You are wet and cold. Get these clothes off, eat, and come to bed."

"Do you even want me in bed with you?"

Wrenley paused, shuffling through the pile of clothes, her hazel eyes holding his for a long moment. Finally, she said, "I want you in my bed, Bronson Aughton, tonight, tomorrow night…and every night from this moment forward." Her voice was steady as she pushed her golden curls back from her face and peered at him, slowly handing him the dry clothes.

Bronson complied, pulling his boots off, peeling off his pants and undershorts, and tossing them aside. Wrenley pulled him over to the bed and retrieved a tray with hot tea and some sandwiches, which seemed to suffice since he had just vomited. He did not eat much, but at least it was something. Wrenley tucked him in, leaving for a moment to blow out the candles and, on returning, hearing his soft, even snores.

~ ~ ~ ~ ~

Bronson stirred, feeling the light in the room and movement beside him. He moaned, rolling over, and groaned as his muscles screamed. He must have slept hard and not moved throughout the night. He opened his eyes to notice Wrenley staring down at him, sipping tea out of a mug, and then she smiled at him sweetly. She wore a silky nightgown that dipped in the front, her breasts full and almost falling out of it, thanks to the pregnancy. He groaned in need and turned to lie on his back, avoiding looking at her.

"Are you ok?" Wrenley set down her mug and leaned over him, placing her small hand on his forearm, the touch sending a rush of pleasure through him.

He sighed deeply, covering his eyes with his forearm. "Yes…it's just been a rough couple of days."

It has been a rough fifteen years, he thought to himself. He was tired...so very tired of fighting. They both sat in silence. Bronson tried not to look at Wrenley; her pregnant body was now more evident and attractive than ever. He was still unsure about them or where she wanted him, and he sighed in frustration.

"I owe you an apology for yesterday..." Bronson sat up slowly, propping his head up with his hand, elbow resting on the pillows.

Wrenley nodded, her hand instinctively going to his muscled, tan chest. Her finger traveled above his left pectoral muscle, outlining the scar above it.

She knew. Somehow, she had found out about his covenant to her. Though he could not tell if that was a bad thing or a relief.

"I owe you one as well," Wrenley said finally, placing a hand over the scar, palm flat on his chest, "If we are going to win this war, we will have to work together better than this."

"I know..." Bronson murmured, her touch arousing him almost to the point he could not contain it.

"We need to come to some sort of an agreement about our plan, our marriage, our child..."

Bronson did not let her finish but leaned over to cover her mouth with his, wrapping an arm around her waist and practically pulling her onto his chest. It surprised her, and her arms flailed out to catch herself, both hands pushing against his torso in response.

~ ~ ~ ~ ~

His kiss deepened as he pushed himself into a sitting position and grabbed Wrenley by the hips, lifting her over him and plopping her in his lap, legs on either side of him. She gulped, looking down at her growing stomach, then flushed as she took in his chiseled abdomen.

"I'm like a whale..." she squeaked, pushing away from him with one hand, the other instinctively resting on her belly. She felt her skin flush with embarrassment, but Bronson's grasp on her hips gave her a little more confidence.

"You're a fucking goddess..." He growled, not letting her move an inch and kissing her again so profoundly she felt herself whimper, leaning into him.

"Why didn't you tell me about the blood covenant?" Wrenley

asked softly, stretching her neck to allow him access to the tender spot between her ear and shoulder. He grazed her with his lips, drawing his tongue up her neck towards her ear, and she inhaled sharply. They would never have a conversation if he continued this behavior; the thought made her grin.

"I didn't want…" he started, breathing heavily, pulling her to his chest and inhaling the sweet scent of her hair. "I didn't want you to think that was the only reason I love you."

Wrenley bit her lip, trying to keep it from trembling. She rested her forehead against his and uttered, "I know that…but it is awfully romantic."

Bronson chuckled deeply, the sound reverberating through her. It made her want to moan yet again, and she licked her lips in anticipation. She took in the man in front of her and felt her core heat as she ran her fingers up and down his arms, his neck, into his hair, and back down again. The scar on his chest was at least two inches horizontally across, and she traced it with her fingertips, still in awe at discovering how this man had sacrificed for her. Why had she never noticed it before? She supposed it was because he had countless other scars decorating his body. She loved him, deeper than any darkness, brighter than any light, and more than she could have ever loved another in this world or the next.

"I will follow you forever, Wrenley…" Bronson whispered, hands grasping her hips as she raised her hands to caress either side of his face. "Whether you choose me to be your husband or not…whether you allow me to be a father, or not…whether you choose me to be a part of your court and your inner circle and your advisors…I will forever protect you. I will protect you until my last breath…and even in death, I will still follow you."

Wrenley felt tears sting her eyes, "And I don't want to know a day without you, Bronson Aughton. I choose you to be by my side on the battlefield, in a court, and in my bedroom. I choose you…

Wrenley gasped audibly as Bronson lifted her hips and slid his length inside her, her body convulsing with pleasure as she crumbled into him and moaned. He supported her weight, gently easing her onto him as she inhaled sharply, arching her back.

"Oh God…" she whimpered as Bronson gently thrust upward into her.

"There are many gods, my love, but none of them will love you like I do," Bronson pushed up into her harder. She leaned her head back in pure bliss as he held her steady. She sucked in a breath, adjusting to him as he rubbed her thighs in lazy circles and gently rolled his pelvis under her. She began to climax then, folding onto him in one wave of ecstasy after another.

Would she ever get used to this? Would she ever accept that out of all the souls in all the dimensions, Bronson was the one to belong to her? Her entire life, she had accepted that she was ordinary and unworthy of love, life, and passion. Yet, here was this man, worshiping her. Bronson would die for her, kill for her, and move mountains for her if she asked him to. She felt she could not breathe without him. He was her guardian angel, always watching, always protecting…and she could handle anything if he were by her side.

CHAPTER 43

A Message and a Friend

Wrenley stirred from sleep as she felt Bronson's body hovering over hers. They made love again for hours, taking in every inch of each other. Eventually, they both fell asleep, even though it was mid-morning. She felt her womb tighten as the baby moved, reminding her that she had to get up, relieve herself, and eat something. She opened her eyes to look at Bronson leaning over her, already dressed.

"When you're ready, we must address the company...something has happened." His voice was soft but somber as she noted the worry in his chestnut eyes.

His voice made her snap to attention, and within seconds, she was out of bed, pulling on pants and a tunic. She did not bother with her hair as she burst out of the doors of her room, Bronson next to her. She marched through the hall and noticed Garrick and Alcott exiting from Garrick's chambers behind her. She nodded at them soberly but continued to the sitting room downstairs, where Gwyneira and Ian waited.

~ ~ ~ ~ ~

"It is a message... for us."

Wrenley did not feel the cold wind snap at her cheeks or whip at the strands of hair that cascaded freely over her shoulders, nor did she feel Bronson's hand on her shoulder. She looked at the smoldering pile in front of her, the remnants of the bodies of a family barely recognizable in the ash. A human skull was still visible on the end of one of the taller spikes, the flames having not disintegrated it quite yet. It still smelled like burning flesh in the air, and Wrenley felt the loss deep in her bones.

The blood that froze to the cold ground was evidence that they were not alive when they were burned. The ransacked house and dozens of large, side-by-side tracks were indications enough that this family did not have a chance; they were targeted on purpose. Who knows how long they were tortured before they finally came to the blessed relief of death? Wrenley fell to her knees in the snow, screaming as she took her dagger from her boot and plunged it into the ground, sparks igniting from her. Tears streamed down her face; anger burned in her blood so hot she felt as if she would explode from the pressure of it.

"They know we are here...and this is a message for us," Wrenley said matter-of-factly, and no one disagreed.

Bronson nodded beside her, "The slaughtering was done methodically...they had killed the family, dismembered them, and impaled them on stakes as they burned." Bronson's eyes were heavy, almost as heavy as Wrenley's heart. "This is a common practice for Earnesh, Wrenley, you did not cause this."

"But I didn't help it," she whispered, allowing her tears to pour from her, hands resting on her thighs. She dared not move or even breathe, fearing that her power would detonate and kill them all. It may not be a horrible idea to end her miserable existence here and now, before things get even worse. She knew it was her grief talking and shoved it aside.

"What would you do?" She asked Bronson quietly, meeting his gaze, then scanning the company she had come to know and trust with all her heart these past months. They stood around her; she could not quite comprehend why they did. She had not earned their trust or loyalty...but here they were, ready to fight and die for her, for her people. Wrenley took a shaky breath and turned to them, "I value you and your opinions...and what you have to say. Please speak freely."

The group collectively breathed, looking at each other and then at the dust, ash, and human remains still smoldering. Each of them weighed their words carefully in the following moments, the tension almost palpable.

"Just my opinion, but I want to blast them all to hell," Gwyneira said in her usual nonchalant way, crossing her arms in front of her as she plopped down beside Wrenley in the snow. Her beautiful, porcelain face was not its usual vacant hue but one of grief and agony, puffy and red as if she had been crying in response to the carnage in front of her.

"I second that," Ian murmured, shifting himself to stand by Gwyneira. "This family was a member of my father's circle. They were trusted and faithful to the rebellion. Their son is a guard; he was on patrol at the east end of the territory last night."

"I say we kill the bastards," Kage shrugged, and Alcott and Garrick mirrored the motion. It had been their Mother not so long ago, and vengeance was boiling in their blood. Wrenley turned to Bronson, meeting his gaze as she felt her heart break into a million pieces. She wanted to vomit, but would not allow herself, not here in front of her company.

"What have I done?" She murmured, and she turned back to the pile before her. "Or…what have I not done?" No matter the decision, Wrenley realized she would permanently lose. Every death would be her fault; every life lost would be on her shoulders, and there was no escaping it.

"This is the war we fight, Wrenley…" Johnathan was beside her now, his arms crossed in front of him as he surveyed the carnage. "Sometimes we don't get to pick and choose what evil comes against us, but we choose how we respond…how we fight back."

Bronson nodded, "…and now, Wrenley, it is time for you to choose."

Wrenley straightened and lifted her chin. She felt something kindle in her core, a rage that had been dormant for so many years—the rage of a girl who saw the injustice of the world and had no power to change her course; but by God, she had power now. Wrenley looked down at her hands, which were wrung on her knees, the sparks crackling as if chomping at the bit to be released.

"If Dragon wants a fight, we'll give it to him."

~ ~ ~ ~ ~

Wrenley paced back and forth that evening, waiting for word from the twins and Bronson. Garrick stayed behind and was stationed outside of Wrenley's room. Wrenley watched out her window as Ian rode away into the night with what remained of his guards. Soon after, Gwyneira gently knocked on her door, a large, fat cat in her arms. The cat must have been half Gwyneira's size as it dangled from her arms. The girl entered without invitation and dropped down on Wrenley's bed without a word. The women sat silently for a long while; the only sound was the crackling of the fire and the cat's loud purr.

Wrenley exhaled and nodded, her gaze still locked onto the darkness just beyond the light of the manor outside, "I don't have much, Gwyneira, nothing to offer my people."

Gwyneira shrugged, "I think you being here has to mean something."

Wrenley reached up to cover her face and rubbed her eyes with the heel of her hands.

"I know what it's like, you know…" Gwyneira said quietly, still stroking the cat in her lap, "To lose everybody and everything in a moment."

Wrenley turned from the window and looked softly at the younger woman, "I know you do."

Gwyneira had never talked to her about this before, and Wrenley held her breath as she waited for the younger woman to continue.

"I was hardly a teenager when my parents were killed in the resistance…" Gwyneira's dark green eyes flashed up to Wrenley, but her features remained bare. "I received word of their disappearance, but I didn't want to believe it; I had to see for myself before I would allow my brain or heart to accept it. I traveled for months looking for them, but it was a waste of time. It wouldn't have changed the outcome anyway, I know that…but I think during that time, I went mad."

Gwyneira sighed as the cat finally stirred and sauntered off her lap, "I came home and blockaded myself into my cottage four years ago. People tried to come, but I killed them…every single one of them, even the ones who did not wish me harm." There was no remorse, just fact in her tone as she examined her fingernails in the firelight of the hearth. "Soldiers once tried to come in and rape me, and I set them on fire. A group of rebels came in and tried to confiscate my parents' things for the cause," she lifted her hands in air quotation marks. "They were just some soldiers who had probably turned or deserted their company. Either way, I melted their brains from the inside."

Wrenley sat on a chair across from Gwyneira, not daring to say a word for fear she would interrupt the phenomenon unfolding in front of her.

"My mom was seven months pregnant with my baby brother when she died. I knew it was a boy...I had seen it, like I saw yours."

Wrenley's heart constricted, and she breathed, "Oh, Gwyneira..."

"She was like you, you know? Choosing to fight even with a baby in the womb. She had no choice...just like you have no choice."

Gwyneira sighed and twirled a piece of her ebony hair in her fingers, "After that, I stopped loving anybody. I stopped caring if I lived or died. I stopped caring about the world around me, and I sat in the darkness, praying that death would gently find me...until Bronson showed up at my door that night. Until you showed up that night...and Kage, Alcott, and Garrick."

Wrenley felt her eyes well up, but fought to keep the tears from escaping. Gwyneira looked young and fragile, yet she was as stone-cold as a pillar, powerful and determined. She could not imagine Gwyneira's fear, searching a warzone for her parents and baby brother...and then coming home alone. No wonder she had built up so many walls for herself; she had lost everyone she had ever loved.

"You and your company saved my life that night you showed up at my door. You aren't just a company; you have become my friends, and I figure if I can do something for you and the baby...I will try." Gwyneira shrugged and grinned at Wrenley, "I may have misjudged you just a little bit when we first met."

"Maybe I did you too..." Wrenley offered lowly, and Gwyneira exhaled. "I will do whatever you ask for your baby. I will do it to honor my infant brother, who never had a chance to live. I never had a chance to be a big sister, and I swear your baby will never know what it is to be alone."

Wrenley could no longer fight the tears, nor could she resist the urge to envelop the younger woman in her arms and embrace her tightly. Gwyneira stiffened as Wrenley embraced her, but relaxed awkwardly, waiting for Wrenley to pull away. Wrenley finally did, wiping the tears and snot away from her face with her sleeve and smiling at Gwyneira.

"I am very thankful for you, Gwyneira. Thank you for being my friend."

CHAPTER 44

For Astara

The house fell into an eerie calm after Bronson, Garrick, and the twins returned from their preparations for the next day. Everyone went their separate ways for the final time; the reality of their task tomorrow weighed heavily on them like the calm before the storm. Garrick and Alcott disappeared to Garrick's bedroom, spending every last moment together before the dawn broke. Gwyneira gathered up the cat and trudged up the stairs to her quarters on the third level, muttering something about tea and a book. Kage stationed himself for the first watch and would wait for Bronson to relieve him. Johnathan had slipped away like usual, probably to feed the beast before the task ahead. They all had things to do, words to say, and courage to summon.

Wrenley lay beside Bronson, tucked between his arm and chest, her head on his shoulder just above his scar. The quiet of the night was almost deafening as he gently rubbed her belly, feeling the kicks of the fetus beneath his touch. She did not know what to say to him, realizing she had taken so many moments for granted before this. So many minutes, hours, and days she had wasted being angry at him; years of having him just a breath away, and she had not known. So much wasted time…

"You will have to listen to Kage and Alcott tomorrow…" Bronson murmured, still mesmerized by her protruding stomach. He shifted down as he pulled her nightgown up and kissed her abdomen, and she felt the baby flutter.

"They will make sure no one gets close enough to lay a hand on you, but you have to promise me you will listen to them and obey every command they give you."

"I promise to try." Wrenley grinned, tracing his strong jaw with her finger, and he laid his head against her womb.

"It's a risk, Wrenley, this whole thing is a risk."

"I know," she could hardly breathe, her throat constricting. "This business of saving the world is risky."

"You don't have to be there; I can wield enough magic to make the plan viable. You could stay here…"

"No." Wrenley shook her head. "I need to do this, Bronson."

She thought of Astara and the girl she had seen on the road months ago. She thought of Gwyneira's parents and infant brother, Kage's father and brother… She thought of the ones who would not be named and would never be remembered, but had died anyway. She then saw the family burned to ash just a mile away. No, she would not stay in the shadows, and she would not hide anymore. She had spent her entire life hiding away in a different dimension. It was time to step into the light.

"For Astara…" Wrenley whispered, covering his hand with hers as his palm covered her abdomen. Bronson looked at her and smiled tenderly. Wrenley leaned in to kiss the top of his head, holding his face in her hands, "For our daughter, Astara Adinnil Aughton."

Bronson released a deep breath, his dark eyes searching hers. He opened his mouth to speak, then shut it again. Wrenley raised a brow, "What is it?"

Bronson shook his head, "I am grateful to fight beside you tomorrow, my queen, my love, my life."

CHAPTER 45

The Bridge

The guards at the bridge hovered around their small fire, waiting impatiently for their coffee to perk, warming their hands over the flames. They were tired and cold, weary of spending another night on guard duty. The three guards grumbled to themselves, cursing Dragon for the orders, swearing at the filthy villagers, and profaning the weather. There were many more honorable and high-profile assignments they would have much rather been on, rather than being stuck on the edge of the territory. The only fun they had was terrorizing the villagers. A fog had rolled in from the ocean, making visibility difficult despite the sun now rising in the east.

The oldest guard straightened as he noticed something in the mist. The other two guards also snapped to attention, gawking as the fog unnaturally seemed to part, revealing three cloaked figures walking toward them.

"Halt!" The oldest man yelled, reaching for his sword, "State your business!"

The man was suddenly struck with an unseen force, his body going rigid as it was lifted off the ground. His companions fell back in horror as the man's eyes began to melt in the sockets, blood now pouring from his ears, nose, and mouth. His companions stood in shock as they watched him choke on his fluids and then, released, his lifeless body thumped to the ground in a heap like a husk. The two guards looked towards the three cloaked figures; the one in the front reached for her hood and removed it so that they could see every bit of her face.

"Tell your commander I am here for him…and will gladly accept his surrender."

~ ~ ~ ~ ~

Wrenley would not allow herself to shake, not for one moment, as she stood at the foot of the bridge waiting for the guards to deliver her message. She flexed her gloved hands at her sides, feeling the power welling and raging, ready to detonate from her. She was becoming more attuned to her power, as if it were another sentient being inside her. She looked down at the dead guard and felt her lip curl in a sneer, wishing she could have made his death slower. She realized then that she hated them, hated every last one of them, and she wanted to see them die. She wanted to make them suffer for Astara...

Wrenley closed her eyes and took a deep breath, feeling her energy travel over her skin like a current, her magic knowing what was coming and preparing for it. Wrenley was dressed in a black shirt and pants, her knee-high black boots housing several blades that Kage and Alcott had provided. Her golden hair was braided back, and a short sword was strapped to her hip for easy access. She wore a dark cloak, attempting to conceal her protruding stomach for as long as possible.

Astara's crystal and her mother's pendant were hanging on her neck between her breasts, near her heart. They reminded her of the why: why she fought, why she pushed, and why she risked everything. It solidified the ache of the mother she would never know, and the friend she would never have.

Alcott and Kage flanked her on either side, rage personified, so still it was as if they were granite statues. They were dressed identically in black, with suede brigandines covering their chests and shoulders and draping down to their hips and thighs. The black armor shone in the morning sun, almost matching the thick black braids tied at the base of their necks. Twin blades were strapped to their backs, and Wrenley knew with certainty they had more weapons not visible. Wrenley hardly recognized them; the look of death and destruction stamped on their handsome faces made her pause and almost shudder. She was thankful she was not on the receiving end of their wrath. She knew there was so much more at stake for them in this moment.

They would take revenge for their Mother, yes, but also for their father, and their older brother. She almost pitied the enemy that got in their way: *almost.* It was their duty and instruction to keep everyone away from Wrenley and to defend her from the physical threats so she could perform the magic she needed. She would have chosen no one else for this task. She trusted them completely and felt reassured with them at her back.

Finally, after what seemed like an eternity, Wrenley noticed a familiar figure on the back of his serpent ambling towards them from across the bridge. Dragon was uglier than she had remembered. At least twenty men flanked him, intelligence reporting at least a hundred more behind that. Wrenley patiently waited for Dragon to cross the bridge, his arrogance dripping with every step he took toward her.

"Well, isn't this a surprise!" Dragon drawled, leaning back in his saddle, the beast underneath him shifting and growling under his weight. "The magic wielder whose fame and reputation have been erupting over my territory. I didn't realize I already had the pleasure of meeting you before; needless to say, I'm so happy to see you again."

Wrenley focused on her breathing, steadying her mind and heart before speaking.

"You knew I would come?" Her voice was more potent than she felt, but she eyed him with contempt. He slowly progressed across the bridge onto their side of the river. Every move he made, she counted, calculated, and surveyed every inch for potential surprises and threats.

"And if it isn't the twins," he laughed, shaking his head, "I heard about your Mother. Pity…I would have taken the two of you for her, but we can't always get what we want, right?"

Wrenley could sense the twins tense behind her. There was not a shift or a sound…but she could feel it.

"She wailed, you know, like a fucking whore…when my men took her over and over again. I thought she would last longer…" he spat on the ground between them. "Such a waste. I would have much rather seen my men fuck you than an old woman."

"Fucking bastard…" Kage drew one sword, and Wrenley snapped her head and raised one finger ever so slightly at her side, praying he and his brother would not give in to the trap Dragon was shamelessly setting for them. Kage stood down and sheathed his sword at her movement.

"I still think you're a coward," Wrenley threw at Dragon, trying to gauge how long it would take if he decided to storm the bridge. Not long, she estimated, maybe a minute at most. Wrenley did the approximations in her head, not liking the odds.

"Why don't we just get to the point? Your master is looking for me, and here I am." She held her gloved hands out to the side and shrugged her shoulders.

Dragon's eyes narrowed, and his lips pulled back to reveal ugly, rotting teeth, "You are a catch, my little magician. I must admit, this is a pleasant claim that I shall enjoy very much."

"Yes, well…" Wrenley lifted her hands dramatically and waved them, "A lot of grown men are cowering in fear because of one woman while Earnesh sends his inbred cousin to retrieve me…not very classy."

"You are with child." Dragon's eyes caressed her up and down, and Wrenley felt herself nearly recoil, but she stood firm.

He chuckled then, shaking his head and baring his teeth. "A magician and a whore, what a surprise. What do your friends say about that? You ask them to fight with you, and all you do is spread your legs? Disappointing…" Dragon shook his head and clicked his tongue, the insult rolling over Wrenley as relief and surprise suddenly flooded her.

He didn't know…

Dragon knew her as a magic wielder, but nothing about royalty…he did not think she was the heir. All this time, the efforts to spread the word about the rebellion had hidden her identity. They must have used 'magic wielder' to hide her true identity. To Dragon, she was just another powerful seer and nothing more. Kage snarled behind her, and she shuddered inwardly, schooling her features to appear disinterested as she managed her features into neutrality.

Wrenley forced herself to roll her eyes. "So that's it? Open doors so you can colonize other worlds and kill innocent people? Seems like a waste of time to me." It was a gamble, but she took it. If he knew anything…

"Not a waste, but a reward. The doors will be opened for much bigger purposes, don't you worry."

So, they haven't opened them yet, and they don't know how.

Wrenley made a mental note of it. She would guess they could not cross over like Bronson had done, at least not with that ease. One had made it over when she had fled with Bronson all those months ago, but nothing since. They were buying time until they could make the connection between dimensions, killing innocent people as they went, occupying the territory, and brutalizing citizens for no other reason than for sport.

"So, what's your plan? Open all the doors and march into all the other worlds? For what? What do you have to gain from it?"

"You misunderstand, little magician; we don't want to open all the doors, just one. Humans are fickle, self-obsessed, and lazy. They have been conquering themselves for the last two thousand years. We do not need them…"

Not their world…so which one? Wrenley knew her face was faltering. She knew the confusion showed in her as she processed the words Dragon spat out at her.

"You don't know?" Dragon asked, taking several steps closer to the end of the bridge, a long laugh ringing into the space between them. His men grew restless, looking as if they might charge them at any moment.

"Ahh, I see, your seer hasn't told you the truth yet."

Wrenley blinked once and felt thunder in her chest as her mind reeled. She tried to hold her face unbiased, but she knew it showed. She shifted her weight, her hands almost aching from the energy building. *Told her what?*

"So, what now?" Wrenley crossed her arms before her, feeling the rage of the warriors bubble behind her. She was afraid they would not be able to hold out much longer. She knew to her left, Garrick waited out of sight with his bow to start picking off anyone who would advance on them. She prayed Bronson was in position as she continued, "One of us isn't walking away from this, and I have things to do."

They moved then, with the soldiers rushing off the bridge and surrounding Wrenley, Alcott, and Kage within seconds. They had moved so fast it took Wrenley off guard, and she stiffened as Kage and Alcott drew their weapons. The three were surrounded, their backs together as Wrenley counted the men. They were outnumbered ten to one; at least thirty soldiers crowded around them.

"I'll make you a deal," Dragon's serpent shoved its way through the soldiers. He dismounted, closing the distance between him and Wrenley. "You give up the seer, and I guarantee you will be transported to the kingdom city unharmed. Struggle, and I will cut that bastard from your womb and burn it on the fire," he snarled and pointed to the fire now abandoned by the guards.

"My seer isn't here, obviously…" Wrenley hissed the words, feeling the heat gather in her palms.

"Fine. Then I will take him…" Dragon pointed his large sword at Kage, "I will kill him slowly, and I will make you watch. Then his brother, and then that little witch; I'll find her under whichever rock she slithered under."

Wrenley mustered up one last ounce of courage and said, "I'll make you a deal. I kill you, and I won't have to look at your ugly face again for as long as I live."

~ ~ ~ ~ ~

Bronson used his muscular forearms to lift himself from his hanging position under the bridge. He could tell by the sounds above that most soldiers were across the bridge, probably surrounding Wrenley and the twins at this very moment. Bronson's chest squeezed at the thought, having difficulty trusting the most important person in his life to the two warriors, but he had no choice. Skillfully, he swung himself from one plank to another, double-checking the explosives and fuse placed by the twins and him last night. Only moments now…

Bronson swung off from the beams to the shore, the bridge still above him. He landed gracefully on his feet and reached for Johnathan's lighter, which the older man had lent him under protest. Flipping the lid, he flicked the striker several times, attempting to hold the flame, before hearing a clanking sound behind him. Bronson swung around just as a soldier, probably as tall as Bronson, bulldozed into him, taking Bronson down to the ground, the lighter flying out of his hand.

Bronson grunted at the impact. The soldier had aimed for Bronson's torso and now lay on top of him. The soldier began wailing on Bronson in the face, blow after blow, as Bronson fought to retrieve his dagger from his boot. Head swimming, Bronson contorted his body, trying to reach the hilt of his weapon. He heard a swooshing sound and felt the tremor in the unseen, Bronson realizing there was a power present in addition to Wrenley. He had to get to her, now.

Bronson flexed his power, the pulse knocking the soldier off him long enough for Bronson to grab the dagger. The soldier yelped but jumped up and ran at Bronson again. This time, Bronson was ready and stepped into the force of the impact, bringing his blade down through the back of the soldier's neck. The man slumped instantly, and Bronson pushed the corpse off him. Frantically, he began searching for the lighter that had been thrown when he was hit. He felt the power unleashed above him, and his stomach sank.

~ ~ ~ ~ ~

Wrenley exploded, pushing every ounce of magic out of her towards Dragon. He responded with a curse, and to her surprise, his energy shot from him in response. She pushed back, hands sparking and power flashing around them. Most of the soldiers had descended upon them with an inhuman speed. Kage and Alcott held tightly against her back, slicing and slashing their way through wave after wave of men. Wrenley felt panic when she realized Dragon was also a seer or magic wielder. They had not accounted for his ability to use magic, and his power thrashed down on her with brutal force. She held it, but felt herself buckling under the dark, whitecaps of his magic. Wrenley assessed the situation around her and realized she had extended a force field to Kage and Alcott as planned in reflex. She cursed under her breath, pushing upward on the force field around them to give them room to maneuver.

The magic Dragon was wielding was strong and disciplined, etching at her defenses and trying to break into the barrier she had made to protect them. The plan had been for her to create a force field for Kage and Alcott and to distract the enemy, but she did not know she would also have to fight Dragon lash for lash. She gritted her teeth and growled, throwing the heavy cloak off her shoulders and repositioning herself in a fighting position, just like Kage had taught her. She kept all magic focused on the shields and used any extra to snap at Dragon, like a whip cracking on top of him. He grunted beneath it but did not buckle under its pressure.

"Hurry, Bronson…" She whispered, lifting the force field as high as possible to give her company time.

~ ~ ~ ~ ~

They were outnumbered; Kage knew it from the moment the soldiers descended upon them like waves on the shore. Kage felt the vibration of Wrenley's force field around them, protecting them as the enemy attacked like rabid animals. The shield would not allow them through, but he could step in and out of it, giving him cover when he retreated into the protective buffer. It was like a dance, Kage and his brother weaving in and out as they sliced through the bodies of their enemies. Blood covered his face as he wielded the two swords through the air. He felt it then, a shudder from behind, and he turned to see Wrenley falling to her knees as Dragon inched closer, his hands outstretched, his wicked face grinning as he pushed Wrenley closer to the ground.

He cursed at Dragon, realizing he was using some energy or magic, wielding it like a hammer that crashed repeatedly on her.

Boom, boom, boom, the magic roared as it hit her relentlessly, Kage hearing it thrash against her own. They had not planned for this; they had not known she would have to hold a shield and fight him. Kage's chest heaved as he saw blood begin to trickle from her nose, worry slamming into him. She gritted her teeth and screamed as she pushed her power.

"Let the shield go!" Kage bellowed, slicing through another soldier, blood spattering across his face. If she released the shield, she could take out Dragon easily. She did not acknowledge him, and he knew he was a fool even to consider that she would. She would never allow them to be taken or condemn them to the onslaught of troops slamming into her shield. She would rather die than give in.

Kage felt his grief and rage being replaced with serenity, a calmness that engulfed him like he had never known before. Standing amid the power and gore, Kage solidified that if they were going to die, this would be the most honorable death he could ask for: not only defending his queen, but his friend.

~ ~ ~ ~ ~

Wrenley felt the copper tinge of blood in her mouth and dripping from her nose, but she was persistent. Despite her brutal ass whooping from Dragon, she felt a tendril of strength that traveled up her legs and arms and finally to her ears. *Look to the Earth,* it said.

Astara's words to her. Wrenley had not known what they meant, but then it dawned on her. She felt a tingle below her feet and stomped down into the ground, causing the Earth to buckle and ripple, diverting her magic from the air. She sent a wave of terrain and energy toward Dragon, his men flying as the world rose and fell violently underneath them. She had never suspected she could maneuver the elements...until now. The pendant of Brigid heated at her chest as she began to call to the Earth to respond to her. She was not meant to command it, but to ask it for help, to placate it for a crumb of its mighty power.

Dragon was thrown off guard, pausing momentarily while the Earth warped under him. It was enough time for Wrenley to shift and focus more energy on the force field around them. She heard Dragon growl again and felt his black magic snap at her like a rod. She pulled up more Earth and rocks, catapulting them through the air at Dragon and the soldiers. One hand was holding the force field; the other was struggling to master this newfound power.

She grinned as she pulled up chunks of rock and Earth and made them rain down on her enemy. It was like a song in her blood now, the green crystal between her breasts thrumbling, a whooshing sound in her ears. She pushed and pushed energy outward, all the rage and anger from all the years of her isolated existence channeling into the white light that shot out from her. She had been invisible, she had been only a second thought, she had been left to live out a life of pain and limitations, but not now. Never again...

"They will see me now", she whispered, and then roared.

The battle raged, Dragon sending powerful energy, shadows, and eruptions onto her shields. She wondered where in the hell Bronson was as she looked towards the bridge. Kage and Alcott continued to butcher one soldier after another. More and more seemed to be pouring over the bridge now, more than they had thought. Wrenley gritted her teeth, willing Bronson to blow it up before the whole damn army made it over.

~ ~ ~ ~ ~

Kage once again noticed Wrenley's body being forced down to the ground, and it took both of her hands to hold the shield. He screamed at her to let it go as he blocked the sword of another soldier. Helplessly, he watched her fall to her knees, her hands pushing up as if lifting an invisible weight, as Dragon's blows became harder and harder to deflect. It hit her with such force that her knees dug into the ground. She trembled, blood now seeping from her nose and ears down her neck. Tears streamed down her face as she held off Dragon and the army that was overrunning them. She looked at Kage and Alcott, her eyes ablaze with the courage and bravery they had always known were there.

What could he do? He could not lose her, not after all he had lost already. He would not walk away from this battle without her. He would either walk away with her or die at her side. When he had watched her fall into that river and something told him to jump, he had not known how deep or wide it would take him. He had not realized that the life he was living hoarded in the earth, hiding away from the fight, was a miserable existence. Before Wrenley, it was just about surviving another day. She had taught him that there was more, he was more, and even if there was no promise that things would get better, the hope she had brought into his life had set him free.

Daring to hope after all hope had been snuffed out…

"For the hope of it all…" he whispered to himself, then boomed with a force that made the soldiers turn their heads. A war cry arose, and he moved with his powerful legs to push to Wrenley's side as she held the shield. Without a second thought, he reached back to sheath the swords and stretched for her, wrapping his arms around her waist and hoisting her up. God, it was heavy; he could never have imagined the weight of Dragon's magic or how Wrenley had been holding it up for so long. Blood poured from her, her face growing pale and taut with every moment that passed under the beating. Kage positioned himself behind her, holding her up by the waist as she shrieked under the weight, and he felt it press down on his shoulders like a million worlds. He gritted his teeth and held her, refusing to let her go, refusing to allow her to stand alone.

"You are not alone!" He screamed. "You will never, ever be alone…not while I have breath left within me." Wrenley threw her head back against his shoulder, her eyes wild with bravery, but he knew she was scared.

He brought his mouth down to her ear to whisper, "…you will never live alone, or die alone, Wrenley, daughter of Dolion and Adinnil, heir to the Throne of Ailios. But mostly, you are my friend; friends don't leave each other alone in their darkness."

Wrenley craned her neck to look him in the eyes. Those beautiful hazel irises were replaced with black diamonds, the crazed look subsided just a fraction as she said quietly, "I know."

He heard a murmur in his ear, and he flinched as a soft blue light raced by his head out of the corner of his eyes. He heard it again: *Everything will be okay.*

Before he had a chance to understand it, he heard it: a low rumble, different from Wrenley's power. It grew as the Earth shook under him, and he turned to the horizon to see the bridge explode.

CHAPTER 46

Revelation

The ground shuddered under them. Dragon paused and loosened his assault to look back, realizing the bridge had been obliterated. Fire, wood, and debris flew outward, the shards barraging soldiers as they dove for cover. It dawned on Dragon in that moment that he was separated from the rest of his army, left defenseless in the wake of the smoke and debris, and the only link to his military power.

The smoke lingered thick in the air, and a man's form appeared, walking towards Dragon from the billowing smoke and fire. Bronson shoved the lighter into his pants pocket and tossed his coat off his shoulders, striding with purpose and determination towards the fray. Bronson's eyes glowed with a red fire as he reached back to unsheathe his sword. He was death, anger, and vengeance incarnate…the face of a man who would not stop until he had blood.

"Well, well, well…" Dragon ceased his relentless assault on Wrenley and pivoted towards Bronson, hardly winded. "If it isn't the seer who has been a thorn in my fucking flesh for the last decade and a half."

"You want me? Come and get me," Bronson pointed his sword towards the commander and then twirled it in one hand with ease. "I have been looking forward to this for a long time."

Dragon shrugged and grinned, "It would be my honor to kill you in front of your magician whore."

~ ~ ~ ~ ~

The power of a million stars ignited inside Bronson's chest at

Dragon's crude words. He allowed the power of his people to transform him, finally setting him free from the human mask he had been wearing for so long. Bronson tilted his face up to the sky, allowing his ancient shape to unfold from the chasms of his mortal body. He began to flicker, his body becoming iridescent before it detonated into a million lights and colors. He felt the stretching of his arms and muscles under his skin, the groaning of his shoulders and torso as they strained, the length of his legs raising him to where he could look down at the pathetic commander in front of him. Bronson was pretty sure Dragon had pissed himself as he beheld Bronson in his true form.

~ ~ ~ ~ ~

Wrenley would have been a heap on the Earth if Kage had not held her. She saw Bronson facing Dragon as the black magic that had thrashed her was now preoccupied, and she could catch her breath. They had donned their weapons and were closing the space between each other. Wrenley took in a mouthful of air, waiting for the first blow, the brutal fight to wage between them. She whispered a prayer to the goddess Brigid that Bronson would survive.

Kage collapsed, pulling her down with him, his armor scraping against the Earth and rocks as he enveloped her in his arms.

"You need to leave now!" He panted.

"You have to help him!" Wrenley screamed, twisting to clutch the front of Kage's breastplate. "Please, you need to help…" She stilled as her eyes caught a shimmer from where Bronson stood before Dragon. Wrenley clung to Kage as she blinked her eyes once, then twice, and squinted as Bronson's body turned iridescent, fading in and out. She gasped as his outer form melted away like wax, revealing someone she almost did not recognize. Suddenly, his muscles, flesh, and bones undulated as if the fabric of matter and space were altered, and his form began to distort.

His face was unchanged, but his body had morphed into a figure over seven feet tall; his muscles swelled from under the skin he had seemed to be wearing moments ago. Holding his sword in one hand and a dagger in the other, Bronson's head snapped back, face looking up to the sky, eyes closed as he seemed to crack his neck.

With the 'snap' came a convulsion of power, and light illuminated from every pore. Wrenley gasped as magnificently white, giant feathered wings unfolded behind him, stretching five feet on either side.

She heard Kage gasp in her ear as they both watched Bronson rise above them like a tower. His feathers ruffled as if he had not expanded them for some time. His wings stretched and fluttered so powerfully that Wrenley felt the air from them where she sat in a heap on the ground with Kage. The force from Bronson's flapping wings almost knocked Dragon over as he gawked at the creature who was once Bronson Aughton. She felt the burden of Dragon's magic move from her and focus on the man she loved. She used that opportunity to heave every ounce of her magic to shield Kage and Alcott.

"Go!" She screeched at Kage. He nodded and scooted out from behind her to rush back to his twin to confront the last wave of enemy soldiers. She heard Garrick's arrows swish and hit flesh and bones around her.

Her ears rang as a shriek pierced the air, and she gulped as Wendigo appeared and flung himself into the group of soldiers still overpowering Alcott and Kage. He roared, his long, sharp, claw-like fingers slicing through the flesh of the soldiers surrounding them. His antlers gored enemy troops as he ran forward and thrashed his head from side to side. Wrenley raised her eyes to the river, the smoke from the bridge dissipating enough for her to see Ian and his remaining guards fighting the rest of the forces on the other side. He had slipped off into the night, made the twenty-mile ride to the nearest crossing, and double-backed to slaughter them while they were distracted.

It was chaos around her. For a moment, she stilled on her knees, not knowing what to do or where to go. She felt it from below and from the air around her, the magic sparkling and crackling, almost overwhelming her. She just sat with her hands on her knees, staring off into nothing.

~ ~ ~ ~ ~

"So nice to see you in your true form, archangel." Dragon slipped off his serpent and walked towards the clearing where Bronson now stood. Wrenley snapped her head towards them.

"Forgive me if I don't reciprocate the feelings," Bronson strolled forward, his muscular, long legs taking him twice as fast as the Dragon, his powerful thighs widening on the ground as he took a fighting position.

"I haven't seen one of your kind since the queen..." Dragon spat on the ground and tittered. "Or at least what was left of her."

Bronson's jaw tightened, but he did not respond. He only stood motionless, weapons up, eyes enraged and focused solely on the enemy before him, as if nothing else mattered.

"We took her wings, you know...cut them off while she was still alive." Dragon pulled his sword out, "They are still hanging there for everyone to see. You should join me and see for yourself."

"I will when I lead an army through the gates and kill every last one of you."

Dragon snickered, "What army? You have no idea what you are up against, Bronson Aughton. You are leading these people into slaughter. Give up yourself and the magician whore now, and we will spare your friends and your people; it's just a matter of time before we open the door."

"That's where you are mistaken, Dragon." Bronson smiled, his wings flexing on either side of him, "She is not my whore. She is my queen."

There was a snap and a crunch as the serpent squealed and hissed, writhing in pain. Wrenley had used her sword to cut off its head, which rolled to the side as blood squirted everywhere. Dragon turned momentarily with a roar, and Bronson charged at the distraction. Dragon turned just in time, and the two clashed midair as they brought their swords together.

~ ~ ~ ~ ~

Bronson was not a normal man; she knew that now. His giant, white wings protruded from his back, and his large size, speed, and strength confirmed that he was immortal. Wrenley felt the presence of Kage beside her as she watched the fight, knowing it would be moments before Bronson killed Dragon, who moved with such supernatural ease that it was almost frightening.

"What the hell is happening?" Kage spat, and Wrenley could not respond.

Dragon was a large man, but Bronson was massive. Dragon heaved his heavy sword, and Bronson deflected every single blow. Dragon got lucky and slashed at Bronson's forearm, a small cut appearing, blood pooling down his arm.

"That's the best you got?" Bronson shook his head. "You used up all your black magic on my queen…and now you are a pathetic, weak, disgusting waste of space?"

Dragon attempted to use his magic, conjuring all his strength to push Bronson backward. With one fling of his arm, Bronson deflected the blow. He hit Dragon so hard and square in the chest that Dragon fell backward, crying out as Bronson used his mighty wings to propel himself into the air. He aimed his sword downward and descended upon Dragon with so much force that the ground shook when he made contact. Wrenley winced as the sword did not deliver the death blow she had expected. Instead, the blade went straight through Dragon's sword-bearing arm and into the ground, pinning him. Dragon flailed with a scream, and Bronson stood over him, his lips curled in a sneer.

"Funny thing is, she was able to not only fight you but hold off an entire army of your cronies," Bronson twisted the sword, his magnificent wings splayed wide, "And yet you think it is wise to insult her?"

Dragon whimpered, blood pooling under him from his wounds.

"What is the plan, Dragon?" Bronson was hardly out of breath as he stood over the small man in comparison, in all his supernatural archangel glory. He hoisted his foot onto the Dragon's chest and leaned his forearm on a knee, as if he had all the time in the world.

Dragon sneered from his position on the ground, "You can't win. You never will win, rebellious archangel filth. Your kind will never defeat the great power of the deity. The other universes have already decided. The star has lost, and the great power has staked its claim in this world and soon, the next."

"With what?" Bronson raised his eyebrows, grinning slightly, "With this sorry excuse for an army?"

Dragon's eyes brightened, even though he was bleeding out. "This pathetic excuse of an army is just leftovers. You haven't even seen the real army…" He coughed now, blood trickling from his mouth. "No one can conquer the legions from hell. No one…not even Lucifer himself."

Bronson took a breath and lowered his dagger. Dragon chuckled, "I am too valuable to kill, archangel. Now you are stuck with me. Maybe I will give you the information you need; maybe I won't, but you wouldn't dare end my life now. There is too much at stake."

"I don't give a fuck about your information," Bronson stomped Dragon in the chest with his foot, sheathing his enormous sword as he ripped it free from Dragon's arm. "There is no information you could possibly have to convince me to keep your sorry carcass alive. Unfortunately for you, I won't be the one to take your life."

Bronson raised his eyes to the twin warriors and nodded to Kage and Alcott.

"I almost pity you, Dragon." Bronson's wicked grin split his face, and he spat on him. "Almost…but not really." Bronson then raised his dark gaze to Kage and nodded. "For Astara…and for hope."

~ ~ ~ ~ ~

Kage felt his knees wobble as the archangel looked at him, permitting him to kill the man who had tortured and killed his Mother. He had heard the tales of old, Mother had told him the stories of the demigods who once ruled the galaxies and heavens above them, of the mighty archangels with their immortality, wings, and angelic powers. There had been one in his presence the entire time…Kage knew he had made a fool of himself amid an entirely different type of royalty. Had Mother known all along?

Kage nodded more confidently than he felt, and rallied his strength, forcing himself to move forward from his position next to Wrenley. His body ached from the fight; a large gash drained from his thigh, soaking his armor; other cuts and scratches were nothing compared to the pain he felt at the mention of his Mother's name. He turned to Wrenley as if asking for permission to keep moving forward, and she dipped her head at him, giving him a reassuring smile.

"For Astara…" She whispered as she touched his arm, and

Kage drew his blade.

"For my father…and my brother," he choked out, his mouth now dry, his throat heavy with grief.

Wrenley nodded her head, squeezed his arm gently, and released. "For all those who shall not be named or remembered…"

"For my mother, and my father…and my brother." Gwyneira whispered next to Wrenley, coming up beside her.

"For hope…" Blackness shrouded Kage's vision as he slowly drew his sword, turned to the enemy commander bleeding out on the ground, and moved for him.

"Wait…" Dragon started, watching as Bronson backed away and Kage came forward. The ugly man began to cry, "Wait! I can tell you things…I am valuable!"

"You are worthless," Kage sneered at the soldier. "You took my Mother from us…from all of us."

"I can tell you about Earnesh's army. He has thousands upon thousands not of this world; if you keep me alive, I can tell you where they are and…"

"You know what?" Kage finally stood before him, Alcott closely behind him. "You could give me all the intelligence in the world, and it wouldn't be enough. You will die today, right now, and I will enjoy every goddamn minute of it."

~ ~ ~ ~ ~

Wrenley looked up with wide eyes as Bronson approached her, his towering frame making her feel small and frail. She gaped at him, not knowing what to say, taking in his wings, his angelic form, his brightness.

"Why didn't you tell me?" she finally whispered, stepping back slightly and pausing to take him in.

Bronson sheathed his dagger at his thigh, finally letting out a breath. "I was trying to keep this secret as long as possible, Wrenley. I wanted to tell you…"

"What secret?" Wrenley felt stiff now, the cascading feeling of betrayal hitting her. She ignored the screams of the Dragon in the background as Kage and Alcott filleted him into little pieces, and Bronson shook his head, "Not here."

"Where then?" Wrenley said in frustration, shrugging her

shoulders and trying not to cry. She had stared death in the face today, she had fought beside her company, she had been prepared to die with her child, and she had watched those she loved in harm's way…was this what was going to break her? She stared at him, almost intimidated by his majestic form, his pure gorgeousness shimmering in the sun; even his clothes, gold armor plating his chest, arms, and calves, it was all impossibly regal.

"You are beautiful," she breathed, knowing her mouth was hanging open. She was aware she was staring at him so brazenly that he shifted under her gaze.

"Wrenley…" Bronson stepped closer to her, reaching down to whisper in her ear. He smelled the same; the soft scent of cedar and spices that she had always loved enveloped her, paired with the smell of gore. His deep voice still sent a rumble into her core. His body had changed, but it was only larger now, and she still ached to reach out and touch that sculpted chest peeking out from under his white tunic. She blushed at the feral thoughts that flashed in her head.

"Wait here for me. Let me give my orders, and then we will talk…I promise." He murmured roughly, gently pressing a kiss against her temple, almost causing her to melt. He then sauntered away, speaking to Garrick as the other man swung down from a tree and jogged over to Bronson. The contact made her knees wobbly as she watched him walk away, lingering in confusion at this revelation.

The bridge was destroyed, leaving Ian and the remaining guards on the other side. Wendigo jumped in and swam the river, ordered to take a count of the wounded and dead. Wendigo began to transport wounded men back to their side of the river. Kage was true to his word; he and Alcott cut Dragon into little pieces, so disturbingly so that Wrenley had to turn and walk away, the screams fading out of her consciousness as she blocked them out with her magic.

"So, this is what war looks like?" Wrenley whispered to Garrick as he slipped beside her, hugging herself for warmth and probably more for comfort. His left bicep had been sliced open, and he had tied a cloth around the wound. Shouldering his bow, he favored the arm with a groan.

"Unfortunately, it is my lady, and it only worsens."

Garrick and Wrenley watched as Kage and Alcott approached Bronson after their task had been completed. The brothers were covered in the blood of the enemy. Kage's hair had fallen out of the braid and was saturated with carnage, both of their armors shining in the morning sun as they sheathed their swords as one. They bowed to Bronson, and Wrenley knew her mouth must have fallen open at the show of respect the younger men exhibited. It was as if they had rehearsed it, each taking a knee and offering up a dagger to him, which she could see him decline and reach to pull the two younger men to their feet. They exchanged words, Bronson somber as he grasped both of the younger men on the shoulders; his lips a thin line, but his eyes sincere.

"Did you know?" Wrenley shifted from one foot to the other and watched them interact. "Did you know about Bronson? Know about…whatever the hell this is?"

Garrick shrugged, "I had my suspicions, just as Bronson had his reasons for not revealing it outright. It doesn't change who he is, Wrenley."

Garrick tried to rotate his wounded arm to test it and winced, "He will have one hell of an explanation if you give him time to make it up to you. I can't handle any more fights, though…it's exhausting. Could you all skip to the making-up part, away from me at least?"

"You are a good friend to him, Garrick." Wrenley sighed again, reaching out to squeeze his good arm with one hand; the other hand fluttered to her belly as she felt the baby finally move. During the battle, she had felt her magic diverting, creating a protective barrier around the baby, and finally, it was released; now she sensed it was safe. She felt her muscles aching, her head pounding as she rubbed her temples for even the slightest relief.

"This win…it will change the course of the rebellion," Garrick mused, "You and Bronson standing together…it's going to rally the people like never before."

"We'll see…" she said reluctantly, reaching for Garrick's arm to heal it. Even if that were true, she still did not like any of it. She took in the devastation around her and had to remind herself that this was probably mild as far as war was concerned, as Garrick had indicated. Thankfully, no innocent people were harmed, and no homes were destroyed. Still, the smell of death and smoke filled her nostrils, and she shuddered as she peered beyond the river as Wendigo hauled the wounded over to the other side. She looked down in horror at the pile of bodies stacked around where she and the twins had stood, and though they were soldiers, the loss of life was staggering. Blood ran downhill into the river, the frozen ground from the night before turning into red, gory slush.

She felt something then and pulled her hand away from Garrick; the exhaustion and fatigue pillaging her as her knees buckled, and she crumpled to the ground. She did not cry out, just groaned softly as she felt every ounce of strength disappear from her. Garrick cursed, reacting quickly despite his injury and grabbing her before her full weight hit the earth. Garrick grappled with her body, heaving her into his arms as she lost consciousness.

"Shit, what the hell, Wrenley? Bronson!"

Bronson was beside them in a heartbeat, Garrick moving out of the way as Bronson scooped Wrenley up in his arms, and with one mighty push, he shot into the air.

CHAPTER 47

A Gift

*A*utumn colors. Oranges and reds…
*Wrenley felt herself falling; was it out of the sky?
Or into a hole?*

She thrashed around, trying to find something to hold onto.

She saw red…was it blood?

Things spun again, and she felt like she was moving but going nowhere.

She heard a voice: Wrenley? Can you hear me?

Come find me, Wrenley…come find me…

Wrenley faded in and out of consciousness, fumbling for something to grasp onto as she seemed to tumble through the unending darkness. One moment, she was on the ground, then in the air, and now…now she had no idea where she was. Colors flashed past her, beautiful, bright colors of reds, oranges, and yellows—reminding her of the maple tree outside her office in Missouri. She felt something snap into place around her, and her feet rooted to something solid underneath. The blackness faded then as she found herself upright, breathing and blinking. She stood still and took in the familiar scents and sounds, as she felt a sob rise into her throat. The fireplace, the bed, the familiar chair…she was in room 201.

The sensation of war was like a dream now, though she was very much aware that Bronson was not with her. Where were they? Where was she? She was here in this room, but she felt different, as if it were a vision. She turned slowly and took one step, then another, towards the door. She felt as though her limbs were light, but instead they were weighted down as she tried to move. She reached for the knob, gasping as she noticed her hand was translucent, yet still able to grasp and twist the knob. She slipped out of the room and closed the door, and it was as if she could see the sounds and vibrations as it clicked shut. Her heart raced now, realizing that maybe…just maybe…

"Mom? Dad?" Wrenley yelled and dashed down the stairs to the lower level, only tripping slightly as she had to get used to this translucent form of hers. She ran down and through, passing the front desk where she had first met Bronson. She still remembered the scratch of the old key on the counter. She could still smell the mums that she had dropped to the floor…she still remembered the pain of her hips as she twisted to look at him. She remembered his eyes…God, those eyes that had only been for her. It was like a lifetime ago…

She propelled herself forward without hesitation, noticing important spots shining as if the air were glimmering like gold dust. They seemed to be markers of light and gold in the air, reminding her that these places were special, essential moments in time. She saw the brightest of all the glimmers leading to the library, and almost tripped over herself as she ran. Skidding to a stop, she grabbed the doorframe to keep herself from falling.

"Mom?" She whispered, stepping into the library and peering around, light pulsating from the chair beside the fire. Wrenley's breath hitched as she saw Ruth in that same chair. Nyx the cat curled on Ruth's lap, Wrenley's favorite books perched on the side table as if she had been reading them. Ruth was sleeping, her head gently leaning to one side, and snoring; an elbow propped up on the arm of the chair supported her head. Wrenley slowed, feeling the twinkle of the room caress her, and turned to the sound of the wind rustling the curtains of the open window. It must be spring here…

Wrenley crept forward, approaching Ruth and kneeling before her. Wrenley reached out and gulped as her hand went through the woman, and then the reality hit her: she was not home. The veil between dimensions must have been thin, as if she were peering through a window into her old world, but she was not in a bed and breakfast. She cried, kneeling before the woman whom she had missed so dearly for so long.

"Mom?" She wept, collapsing on the floor at Ruth's feet, covering her face with her hands. "Please, Momma, can you hear me?" The tears were falling freely now as she cried for her mother, her arms aching with the need to hold her one more time, to feel the embrace that had cradled her for her entire life. She was so scared and so alone, and she bowed her head as she curled over her knees and wept deeply, having Ruth so close yet so very far away. With everything she had done…everything she had seen, and everything left to do, she needed just one touch, just one scrap of comfort.

"You aren't alone, my love. Can't you see?"

Wrenley stilled, lifting her head slowly, unalarmed to see another translucent figure sitting on the very chair Bronson had sat with her that first night they had met. Wrenley sat up and inclined her head, realizing she knew this being…

Adinnil was even more beautiful than Wrenley could have imagined. Her long, slender archangel body draped lazily in the seat, one leg propped over the arm of the chair as she grinned at her daughter. Adinnil's hair was like spun gold, cascading over her shoulders. Though translucent, she wore a dress of cobalt blue, and her dainty bare feet swung back and forth playfully. When Wrenley rose to turn to her, Adinnil's face almost split in two with a grin.

Adinnil nodded to Ruth, "I'm afraid she can't hear you, my love, not like you want her to."

Wrenley had no words. She looked to Adinnil and then back to Ruth, tears still tumbling down her face. Adinnil smiled reassuringly and continued speaking softly, "But I have found that if you keep talking to them, they will hear you differently, eventually."

Wrenley sniffed, her lips trembling, knowing if she reached out for Adinnil, she would be unable to touch her, too.

"What's happening?" Wrenley asked, finally finding the words to speak.

"This is your gift, my daughter."

Wrenley shook her head. "I don't understand what that means."

"You have a gift to see between the worlds, as I do. You, my daughter, can see beyond the veil that separates the very fabric of time and space."

"But you are…"

"Dead?" Adinnil chuckled then, a sweet sound that warmed

Wrenley's aching heart. "Death is such a mortal idea, even though mortals and immortals all experience it. Death is only another journey to another place, one we all must take. I took that journey when you were just a baby, but I also have the gift to be able to talk to you now."

"Where are we?" Wrenley reached out to touch the glimmers in the air, and they bobbed as she used her fingertips to push them. "W-where are you?"

"I am where I am, and you are where you are, and Ruth is where she is. We can exist together, but not in the time and space you have come to understand. You and I can see through the layers that divide our worlds. The veil is thin now, my love. Ruth may feel the brush of us as a light wind on her cheek or whispers in the quiet, but she cannot do what we do because she does not have this gift."

"Am I, like, a ghost?" Wrenley whispered, remembering what Bronson had said about travelers passing through worlds. Adinnil nodded, "I guess you could call it that, yes."

"Did you bring me here?"

Adinnil cocked her head to the side. "I have been calling you."

"I-I'm sorry...I didn't know..."

"Shhh..." Adinnil waved her off. "You are exactly as you need to be. Where I am is deep and wide. You had to grow to reach me. You have entertained other travelers...and you have been so kind to them, my daughter. I am so very proud of you."

Wrenley knew then that the ghosts in the house, the spirits of the unseen...had been others. Indeed, she had always been kind and curious, never afraid of what she could not see or understand.

"Mom?" she said to Ruth's sleeping form again and then looked at Adinnil.

Adinnil looked at her with love, "We both are my love; there is space for both of us in this space."

"I'm so scared," Wrenley whispered, crying deeper than any ocean, more expansive than any galaxy, wrapping her arms around her daughter in her womb and rocking to soothe herself. "There is so much bad in the world...and I don't know how to face it. Please tell me...please tell me what to do? You left such important things on my shoulders, but I'm just not strong enough."

She saw their faces: Astara, the girl in the road, the men who had stacked up around her, their lifeblood flowing from them. Gwyneira, Kage, Alcott, Garrick...Bronson. She smelled the death and decay, felt the blows of the dark magic, and at that moment, she could not see the hope she had once had. She felt the pain of the dark magic that had ravaged her; it was almost unbearable. Perhaps she had never had the hope she preached to everyone else; maybe it was all an elaborate dream to make herself feel worthy of the space she occupied in this dimension or the next.

Adinnil breathed as if fighting back the tears that threatened to fall from her hazel eyes, "I cannot tell you what to do, my love, and I cannot tell you how to do it. I can tell you, you have everything you need within you."

"Everyone keeps saying that! But I don't understand how that's enough..."

"You have us..." A whisper brushed her cheek, and she snapped her head to see that familiar blue glowing orb floating past, bobbing up and down as if dancing around Wrenley, reminding her of those little foliage fairies. She paused, the familiar energy encompassing her like a warm blanket: Astara.

Wrenley allowed herself to float back to the times when she felt so very alone. She memorized the moments when no one could understand her, even though she cried out so loudly to be heard. It emerged as anger, rebellion, and resentment, but all along, it was just the fear of being alone. She committed to memory every day that they called her crazy for seeing the worlds that others could not...when they told her she would die from her disease. Without the ability to bring life into the world and with no time to feel love, she would have been lost and forgotten, leaving no impact on the world.

Finally, she recalled the moments when the fear of being unremarkable almost paralyzed her to the point of not even being able to live. The trauma of a love lost as a baby, the result of a girl told she would never be more, and the suffering of a woman who believed every single falsehood they spewed at her. It had been encoded into her, enveloping every piece and part until all she could do was accept that everyone had been right about her all along.

Yet, here she was. Reality made space for her as she began to see the glimmers around her turn into memories: a dark, handsome guardian angel, a witch in the woods, warriors fighting at her side…a girl in the road who took her sweater.

Despite it all…she remained.

Wrenley slowly lowered her eyes to peer at the beautiful miracle growing inside her, and her heart skipped a beat, knowing that when all the lies tried to drown her out, this remained. This consequence of an unfailing love manifesting in her most sacred parts is evidence of love, hope, and destiny growing. Slowly but persistently, love had found a way. She had never truly been alone all those years when she cried in the dark; her whispers had not fallen into the shadows to be forgotten. As she saw his face in her mind's eye, she knew that he had seen every weak and sorrowful part of her, and he loved her anyway.

It was clear to her now that she was not fighting this battle alone. She had something different now that no one could take away from her: a knowledge that she held the spirits of her ancestors, the women of generations, the women who had loved her, and the women who would love her…all coming together in this moment where time and space did not exist. She wiped away her tears with her sleeve, and her hands flew once again to her belly as the baby kicked, and Adinnil gasped.

"I had not seen…" Adinnil's face lit up as she leaned forward in amazement. "Indeed, you have everything already inside of you that you need." Wrenley smiled, too, but noticed that the room around them was morphing and contorting.

"You can't leave!" She said frantically as Adinnil's translucent body faded in and out. "I have so much to ask you!"

"We have run out of time, my love." Adinnil stood from the chair, her body glitching in and out of sight as she looked down at Wrenley, her smile replaced with a somber look.

"There is more to be done; the war is just beginning. You must find Lucifer, Wrenley. Find the Morning Star, and he will help you." Adinnil began to break apart in a beautiful white mist, and, like a phantom wind, she whispered, "Tell Bronson, thank you…for keeping his promise, and that he was my dearest friend. Tell him yes, I had seen…and I had known all along."

"Mother?" Wrenley howled as Adinnil disappeared, the room swirling now. The blue light gently floated to her face, touched it as if to give her one last kiss, and disappeared into the wind.

Wrenley turned to brace her hands on the arms of the chair and cried as Ruth's sleeping form began to wax and wane in and out of the fabric of existence.

"I love you so much..." she choked out. "I love you, Momma! You are going to be a grandma..." She released the words into the atmosphere, and everything went dark again.

~ ~ ~ ~ ~

Wrenley jolted from the bed with a sob, frantically clawing the air around her, weeping for her mothers. Bronson was there, enveloping her in his arms, placing her in his lap as her body trembled with sorrow and power, her magic curling and sparking. She heard and felt a rustling, realizing that his soft white wings had surrounded them on the bed. She did not know how long she had sat there, but she cried everything out and clung to him as if feeding from his unending reservoirs of strength and love.

"Welcome back," he finally murmured against her hair, still stroking her back as she slumped onto him.

"I...I saw...them."

"I know."

Wrenley took in shuddering breaths as she pulled away and looked into his eyes. "We need to find him...we must find Lucifer. You can find him?"

Bronson exhaled slowly and quietly answered, "Yes, I can find him."

"And Adinnil told me..." Wrenley hiccupped, her nose running, eyes puffy and red as she cried. "She told me to thank you for keeping your promise...and that she knew, she had known all along."

Bronson's dark chestnut eyes lingered on her, silver brimming in them as he fought the emotions coming to the surface. Wrenley clung to the front of his shirt, "She was happy, Bronson..." She looked up into the pain-filled eyes of this man and whispered, "She is whole again...you don't have to hurt for her anymore. I don't know where she is, but she has been made new."

They both cried, Bronson's body shuddering with his sobs, and Wrenley now held him in return. Her magic escaped her as it gently entwined them, sheltering them from the outside world, just for a little while. They grieved together. They mourned as one. Wrenley gasped as the baby leaped in her womb, and she laughed. She reached out and pulled Bronson's hand to her belly, and they felt it together. In that moment, healing took place as the spirits of the past and the spirits of the future surrounded them, bringing a glimmer of hope.

~ ~ ~ ~ ~

Ruth gasped and sat up so abruptly that Nyx went flying, knocking her book off the end table with a loud thud. The wind gently rustled the curtains in the open window, bringing the soft scent of spring into the library, with lilacs and honeysuckle filling the air. She smiled as tears fell down her face and looked slowly around her. Jim came rushing in after hearing the cat shriek and the thud of the book to check on her.

"Ruth? Are you okay?" He rushed to her side, and she grabbed his arm firmly. Ruth stared up at him wide-eyed, tears still streaming down her face. "I'm…I'm fine."

Ruth shook her head as if to clear her mind, and she smiled. "Jim, I just had the most beautiful dream…such a glorious, happy dream."

CHAPTER 48

Archangels

"Why didn't you tell me?"

Wrenley asked Bronson hours later, Gwyneira bustling to usher everyone out of the room after seeing Wrenley up and conscious for themselves. When Wrenley collapsed, she went into a deep sleep. Bronson transported her to the manor within minutes and, after assessing her, realized she was not hurt; on the contrary, she was traveling. He had explained to their companions that she had the same gift as her mother, a powerful archangel. Wrenley had the gift because she, too, was half-archangel. Her spirit could travel across dimensions, more powerful and expansive than his ability to cross over.

She had been in this sleep for over two days, even though it felt like only hours for her. Her friends…her family, had encircled her in worry. Even when Bronson tried to explain that she was not in danger, they still refused to leave. Gwyneira had curled up on one side of Wrenley with that ridiculous cat and slept. Bronson slept on the other side and had to swat away Gwyn's arms and legs as she sporadically kicked when she slept. She also had an incredulous habit of shoving everyone to the side, which almost resulted in him physically removing the small witch from the bed. In the end, he did not have the heart to do it and kept readjusting her to her side of the bed.

When Bronson was away for brief periods to address issues related to the resistance, Kage slipped in beside Wrenley to sleep and to watch over her, as if he might miss something by taking his eyes off her. There was no jealousy or resentment between Bronson and Kage as they moved through the motions. Alcott and Garrick slept on the sofas and chairs in the room, everyone eating and sleeping together until she awoke. Now, everyone took a deep breath and wandered to their rooms to rest and restore themselves from the battle.

Once alone, Bronson kneeled before her on the bed and took Wrenley's pale hand. Wrenley tried to sit up against the pillows, still weak from her journey. He had not asked her where she had gone or what she had seen except for what she told him about Adinnil…but she suspected he knew all the same.

"Why didn't you tell me?" She brushed her hand against his cheek, and he leaned into the touch.

Bronson kissed her hand, touching it against his cheek, "I will tell you now."

"You are…not human?"

Bronson shook his head, caressing Wrenley's arm as she rested her head on his chest. She was exhausted, but she refused to go to sleep until he told her everything.

"No…. I am not a mortal man; I am an archangel."

"Like from the Bible?"

He grinned, "That is one perspective concerning our kind. As far as we know, we are a celestial race that is one of the oldest in the cosmos…besides the gods and deities."

"So…are you a demi-god?"

Bronson shifted under her. "Not like you think. Archangels are immortal and have special gifts and powers…most of us have some magic. My gift is the gift of traveling between dimensions…Because I am an archangel, the magic in this realm was easy for me to learn and wield."

"It's why you are so powerful?"

"Yes. Your mother and you share the same gift—you can look between the veils. I can only cross, like stepping from one room to another, but you can create windows to look through. What you both have is rare, and our Astara will probably inherit the gift. Gifts pass down through the bloodlines of the archangels."

"Start from the beginning…"

"To explain that I'll have to go farther back than your mother and me. We must go back to the beginning of everything."

Wrenley shifted next to him, her head propped on his shoulder, her hand traveling to caress his muscled chest. "We have all night, and I need to know; no more secrets."

~ ~ ~ ~ ~

"At the beginning of our recorded history, three dimensions were created and all linked together forming a sacred triad; the Earth realm, where I had hidden you, Ailios, where we are now, and the Welkin...home of the archangels. The Welkin was my home." Bronson sighed then, as if he had been holding his breath, "Our history indicates that these three realms were connected by portals where species from all realms could travel freely back and forth."

"The door in the catacombs?"

Bronson nodded, "That was one of many. The difference between the Welkin and the two other realms was that Earth and Ailios had deities—gods that created and dictated. Jehovah is of the Earth, and the deity of Ailios is an unnamed god; the archangels built their own world without any help from a deity. Because the races of these worlds could travel back and forth through the portals, they grew in strength and numbers. The deities finally noticed how the species between the worlds grew not only in strength but also in intelligence and power, and they got nervous. So, the gods of Earth and Ailios separated the triad, closed all the portals, and put spells around their dimensions so no one could get in or out. These spells separated our world for thousands and thousands of years, and with all the species separated, they were no longer a threat to the gods. The door in the catacombs is probably one of the last of those doors, but it is sealed with a spell, and Earnesh can't figure it out.

"The Earth and Ailios were devastated from the broken connection of the triad. Because they are mortals, it catapulted their realms back millions of years. I suspect that is when the way time elapsed between realms changed. The Welkin was able to withstand the blow of the break, but Earth and Ailios were not immortal like the archangels. We in the Welkin were able to manage the separation better than other species because of our power and autonomy from a deity."

Bronson yawned, and Wrenley popped up an eyebrow, "You were there when this happened?"

"No, but my grandfather was...and was able to tell me firsthand what it was like. It was utter chaos, and it was then that a young archangel named Lucifer began to plan an invasion of the Earth and Ailios, which we call the 'great wars'. He wanted to free other dimensions from the gods who oppressed them. It took thousands of years, but our travelers finally broke some of the codes and spells, allowing them to travel back to Earth and Ailios. My grandfather served Lucifer as a traveler. The great war to free the dimensions took a significant amount of time, blood, and lives…they raged on in the Earth, and then here is Ailios until Lucifer was cast back to the Welkin."

"Were you there for that?"

Bronson nodded, eyes darkening. "Yes, I was there for that. The great wars caused the Welkin to crack within itself, and that is when Adinnil and I came into the picture. Her mother and mine were political figures of the archangels, and we were attempting to reestablish a connection with Ailios after Lucifer's failed attempt to crush the deity. I was able to travel here with Adinnil to try to find another way to reestablish a relationship with humans, and we found a home here while the Welkin struggled to manage the political and social tensions that erupted as a result of the wars. There is so much more, and I will tell you everything as fast as I can without overwhelming you."

"Why hide who you are?"

Bronson shrugged, "Humans hardly remember the relationship between their kind and mine. It was easier to pretend to be like humans to avoid suspicion. But then things got complicated…"

Bronson trialed off, and Wrenley kept herself from asking more questions. Wrenley stilled her hand on her belly, "So what does this all mean?"

Bronson smiled at her, "It means you are a miracle, and this baby is a miracle."

Wrenley shivered at his words. "And now I am asking you to return to your homeland to find Lucifer?"

Bronson turned to grin at her, "I will do it for you. I haven't traveled back there for forty-five years in this time; I'm not sure what the time does in the Welkin. Who knows how long I have been gone in their time."

Wrenley blew a puff of air out of her cheeks. "So, we travel back to the Welkin, hope to find Lucifer…and maybe he can help us beat this deity?"

Bronson chuckled, "That's about right. He is the most powerful archangel in our history, despite his defeat. Lucifer was the only one who had the balls to stand against the gods."

"It's a fucking long shot, but it is what it is."

Bronson took a long breath, "Yeah, it is…but it's one we must take if we are going to win this war. Dragon confirmed Kage's vision: Earnesh is building an army that is not of this world. What we saw at the bridge is nothing compared to what he will unleash on Ailios and maybe even Earth. We need an immortal army."

"Is Earnesh the god?"

Bronson shook his head, "I don't think so…I think Earnesh is a servant or general, but I know now that your father and his experiments awoke something ancient that has been slumbering for thousands of years here in Ailios. Earnesh wants those portals open for a reason, which isn't good for us."

"Did my father know about you and my mother? That you were not mortal?"

Bronson's eyes went dim. "Yes. When Adinnil finally told him the truth, he went mad trying to find the portals, which was right before she found out she was pregnant with you. We don't know what exactly he was looking for, but it eventually got him, and a lot of others were killed."

The two sat in silence, as Wrenley digested all the information Bronson had shared with her, which was overwhelming to hear. Wrenley sat up in bed and stood, stretching her back with a groan from sitting in one spot too long. Bronson hoisted himself up as well, wrapping his arms around her.

"What now?"

Bronson sighed, "I don't think we have any choice. We've got to find help…and Lucifer keeps coming up. If Adinnil told you to find him, we will do it. I'm not sure what she can see from the other side, but we must trust it. She'd never steer us the wrong way."

"So, we go then…" Wrenley mused, "Someone will need to stay and organize the resistance. Thanks to Nicolas and others, we still have troops gathering."

"Yes…" Bronson did not seem to be listening but gazed down at her, and she gave him a look.

"What?"

"Do you still love me? Now that you…know what I am?"

Wrenley looked down at her feet and then back up to Bronson, meeting his gaze with intensity.

"Will you make love to me in your true form?"

Bronson rubbed his temples with his thumb and forefinger, and she could tell his brain was reeling. Something flashed across his handsome face, and Wrenley suspected it was arousal.

"I think we can discuss it," he finally said, grinning as he reached for her. She stepped out of the way, teasing him.

"Can you fly a long way with your wings?"

Bronson frowned when she had escaped his grasp and rumbled, "Yes."

"Do you eat and drink like a human in your true form?"

Bronson rolled his eyes. "We don't need as much, but yes, we eat and drink just like humans. You may eat more than I do because you are half-human."

Wrenley backed away from him, and then a flirtatious grin filled her eyes as she smirked.

"Are you larger? Down there? Because you can hardly fit as a human…"

"That's enough!" Bronson darted to scoop Wrenley up in his arms, and she erupted into a fit of laughs and giggles. She allowed him to carry her to bed and gently toss her onto the pillows, removing his shirt and boots before crawling onto her. He kissed her then, covering her mouth with his as she traced the hard lines of his muscled back and arms with her sparking fingertips. She relished the feel of his solid body on top of hers, careful not to squash her belly.

"There is so much to do," Wrenley mused as Bronson kissed her neck, shoulders, and chest. She closed her eyes and groaned as he moved to her breasts, kissing around her necklaces and then arriving at her stomach.

Bronson paused long enough to whisper, "There is one thing we can accomplish right now."

Wrenley hesitated, opening her eyes abruptly and snapping her head up. "What's that?"

"You can marry me…tonight."

~ ~ ~ ~ ~

They took their vows together under the moon and stars, binding themselves as one, just as they always had been and always would be. Wrenley felt tears rolling down her cheeks as Bronson spoke in his ancient angelic language to her, binding their blood and souls together so that no human, deity, entity, or dimension would or could question it or tear them apart.

Wrenley's thoughts dared to venture to the disabled, anxious girl in Missouri, just waiting for life to end someday. She could not explain it, but she was very thankful for that girl, her courage to hope and believe, and her resilience in never giving up. Many times, it would have been so easy to accept the things that held her back, but she did not. She could dream beyond it, to have enough nerve to follow a stranger into a room, through a dimension, and never look back. She looked down at her swelling belly, her baby moving excitedly as if she knew what was happening in the world beyond.

Wrenley sobbed, trying to commit this moment to memory, knowing it would not last forever. Life was precious, and time was fleeting, she realized. She was determined never to waste it or take it for granted. She looked into the eyes of the man who made up her existence and knew they would somehow face it together, no matter what lay ahead.

Around them stood their company...their family, haphazard and raggamuffin as they were. Alcott and Kage stood at attention as the generals and warriors they had proven to be. Gwyneira swayed back and forth, the moonlight kissing her cheeks as a delicate smile tugged at the corners of her mouth; her green eyes may have shed a few tears. Garrick flanked his best friend, swelling with pride as he witnessed this man who had experienced so much tragedy finally find something pure and sound in a world full of chaos. And, out of the corner of her eye, Wrenley could have sworn she saw the soft glow of fireflies and blue light dancing to the melody of the wind before disappearing into the night.

Wrenley knew they had so far to go; the war was still raging, and Lucifer was out there somewhere. They would have to find him soon. The outcome of the war depended on it. She knew the time ahead would be difficult and clung to the hope they would make it out together. If not, she would cherish every moment with these people for as long as they all had left. As Gwyneira, Kage, Alcott, and Garrick gathered around them, Wrenley almost combusted with joy as they stood together.

"For the hope of it all...." Wrenley whispered as Bronson leaned down to kiss her.

~ ~ ~ ~ ~

Far off in the distance, Johnathan stood watching the ceremony unfold. His chest tightened as he watched Wrenley's young face beam, and Bronson's face cascade in joy as he reached for his new wife, kissing her so passionately that Gwyneira gagged beside them and walked away. Garrick and the twins guffawed and smirked. Garrick slapped Bronson on the back so hard that the seer groaned. They all looked so happy, so right together, and it saddened Johnathan. He had had that once, a long time ago...

He reached for the silver flask in his breast pocket and took a deep gulp, trying to dull the heartache he felt instead of the mirth that should be there. He had no right to feel sadness or pity. It was his duty to put on a smile; he owed it to Wrenley and Adinnil. Images of the love of his life floated around in his brain as he drank long and hard again, hoping the liquor would dull the memories. He knew this union was a celestial phenomenon, and it would change the very fabric of this world and the next in some way or another. He did not know what lay ahead, but he had no doubt Wrenley and Bronson would conquer it together.

...and this was only the beginning.

EPILOGUE

Saraphina had heard the rumors like a song being sung across the mountains. Dragon had been killed; the evidence was in his body parts that had been shoved into baskets and sent across the continent. Bronson had stood at the bridge with another, a magic wielder…whispers from rebel scouts indicated it was their long-lost heir, finally returning to save them. Bronson was a legend in his own right, leading the rebellion ever since she was old enough to remember. She grinned at the memory of her fantasizing about the mysterious, handsome seer who took on the dark, ancient magic that threatened their homeland. She had only been five when the war started, her parents killed in the years since.

Saraphina, or 'Phina' as her friends called her, adjusted her belt laden with knives and a sword so she could lift the four-year-old to her hip. Jamie jabbered on about something irrelevant; his dark, thick head of black curls bounced as he clapped his hands in excitement. His emerald-green eyes contrasted with his pale, pasty skin, unlike hers. She grinned as she noticed him holding out a chubby hand, a shimmer that looked like moonlight dancing on his palm. His magic was growing, and soon he would be more powerful than her.

She was brought back to reality as her friend, Grace, jogged over to them. Though it was dark, the moon and bonfires illuminated her excited features.

"They are gathering the armies. The rebel forces are growing!"

It was the start of a movement. The victory at the bridge breathed new life into the rebel camps that were scattered across the continent to the eastern sea. Phina physically felt it; the energy of the victory swelled through the broken-down, hungry camps, transforming them. People had found hope again, a reason to keep living and fighting. They would follow their queen and the seer to the gates of hell and beyond.

Grace continued, "We ride at dawn to find the Wizard Nicolas…we have a chance, Phina! A chance to win!"

The Wizard Nicolas: Phina had never met him, but the chance to work under him and seek his counsel for her power…and for Jamie…she would do anything for that chance. She looked at the young boy who had fallen into her life four years ago and brushed his thick, ebony curls out of his eyes.

He was not her child by blood. He was the son of a rebel witch commander whom Phina had just happened to stumble upon as she gave birth to him before she died of her wounds. Phina had taken him, and for the last four years, she had raised him as her own child. Every day he grew, and she saw the evidence of great power within him.

She grinned at Grace, and they chatted together until they heard shouts from others in the camp.

"Enemy soldiers are coming! Everyone moves now!"

Grace and Phina looked at each other, dread quenching their optimism as they realized they were about to be overrun by enemy troops. She placed Jamie down on the ground and kissed the top of his head, drawing her sword.

"For a chance, Grace…we fight for hope."

About the Author

A. Ann Sigafus is a mother of four wonderful children and has a house full of animals (who sometimes find their way into the pages of her novels). Living in southern Missouri, she enjoys sitting on her front porch, drinking coffee, and pondering her characters and their stories. A. Ann Sigafus loves exploring her spirituality and weaves her practice into her books. She has a special fordness for traveling to new places, with Scotland being her top destination so far.

When she's not writing, she enjoys playing with the ducks and chickens in her backyard, listening to dark romance and fantasy audiobooks, crafting, drinking wine, and participating in a book club. Her favorite time of year is the fall equinox, when they say the veil between worlds is thinnest. She will definitely light fall candles when it's still too hot outside and start decorating with spooky items way too early... because life is too short not to do whatever the fuck makes life more vibrant and beautiful.

www.ingramcontent.com/pod-product-compliance
Lightning Source LLC
Chambersburg PA
CBHW051437260626
47162CB00001B/135